CRIMEU(

Crank It Up!

A Murderous Ink Press Anthology

****

C000242349

Murderous Ink Press

CRIMEUCOPIA
Crank It Up!

First published by Murderous-Ink Press
Crowland
LINCOLNSHIRE
England
www.murderousinkpress.co.uk
Editorial Copyright © Murderous Ink Press 2023
Base cover artwork © Eaglehaast 2023
Cover treatment and lettering © Willie Chob-Chob 2023
All rights are retained by the respective authors & artists on publication
Paperback Edition ISBN: 9781909498525
eBook Edition ISBN: 9781909498532

The rights of the named individuals to be identified as the authors of these works has been asserted in accordance with section 77 and 78 of the Copyright, Designs and Patents Act, 1988

All rights reserved. No part of this publication may be reproduced, stored in or introduced into a retrieval system, or transmitted in any form, or by any means (electronic, mechanical, photocopying or otherwise) without the prior written permission of both the author(s) and the publisher. Any person who does any unauthorised act in relation to this publication may be liable to criminal prosecution and civil claims for damages.

Every effort has been made to obtain the necessary permissions with reference to copyright material, both illustrative and quoted. We apologise for any omissions in this respect and will be pleased to make the appropriate acknowledgements in further editions.

This book and its contents are works of fiction. Names, characters, places and incidents are either a products of the authors' imagination or are used fictitiously. Any resemblance to actual people living or dead, events, locations and/or their contents, is entirely coincidental.

Acknowledgements

To those writers and artists who helped make this anthology what it is,
I can only say a heartfelt Thank You!

And to Den, as always.

Contents

*First appeared in *The Whitworth Mysteries* (Clarendon House UK 2021)

Just an Eight Banger with Big Baloneys

(An Editorial of Sorts)

In July 1886 the newspapers reported on the first public outing of the three-wheeled Benz Patent Motor Car, model no. 1 — a mere 6 months after filing the patent in January of that year.

Since then the race has been on for the Bigger-Faster-Better-More product that has become a variety of symbols over the decades, with the C3 Corvette Stingray repeatedly stated as being purchased almost exclusively as a middle-age crisis mobile.

So, to honour motor transportation in some of its many roles in the crime fiction genre, we have gathered together a fine collection of short pieces that we hope, in one way or another, will crank up your adrenaline and get your emotions racing without making you blow a gasket or strip a gear.

While every one of these tales is deserving of pole position, first off the grid is *Ed Teja* talking about the **Storefront Assassin**, before we get to drive by the world of *Harry Rhimes* in a short extract from the novel, **So Long Ballentyne**.

From the US we go across to Australia, and new Crimeucopian *Ruth Morgan* shows how **The Result of an Accident** can turn out to be something totally different to what you might expect.

Jesse Aaron returns with a tale about a **Death in the Driveway**, before another new Crimeucopian, *Scotch Rutherford*, takes us back to 1980, with **The Plaster Caster** recounting a time when an automobile's trunk was just the right size for a body, a trench shovel, and a small sack of quicklime.

Billie Livingston makes her Crimeucopia debut by explaining how there's **Always a Price to Pay**, before *Robert Petyo* brings us a piece of sleek fiction in the form of **The Ferrari**.

After Robert comes a veritable BLT style club sandwich consisting of five new authors — starting with *John Elliott*'s **Daggett and the Locked Room**, and continuing with *M.E. Proctor*'s **Borrowed**, which gives us the image of 'a Ford Escort that was held together with bondo and duct tape.'

Blizzard Road, driven by *William Kitcher*, shows you need more than just snow tyres for a successful getaway, which then slides neatly into *R. M. Linning*'s very modern tale despite it being titled **Retrograde**.

Annie Reed explains how to stay cool when the heat is on with her **Hot August Ice**, which puts us onto **The Road to Reconciliation** — the second of *Wil A. Emerson*'s The Driver series.

The Fires at Lake Charlevoix sees the smoky laidback return of *Dan A. Cardoza* before we're presented with **Forks in the Road** from our tenth new Crimeucopian, *Alan J Wahnefried*.

Sam Wiebe steps into the Crimeucopia spotlight with **The Prospect**, proving that nothing is ever guaranteed, regardless of what business you're in, and *Jon Fain* leads us in a merry dance with his **Shoe Shoe Sh'Boogie**.

Closing us out this time around is our last new Crimeucopian, by the name of *Mark James McDonough* and his darkly humorous, off-centre piece, **Like a Brother**.

As with all of these anthologies, we hope you'll find something that you immediately like, as well as something that takes you out of your regular racing line comfort zone — and puts you into a completely new one.

In other words, in the spirit of the Murderous Ink Press motto:
You never know what you like until you read it.

Storefront Assassin

Ed Teja

Billowing black clouds put a lid on the view ahead through the windshield. To the east, the sky was heavy with the threat of rain, and the clouds clamped the sky down, making it look like she was driving into something, heading under a roof maybe instead of from Kingman to Flagstaff.

Behind her, the sky was clear, and bright afternoon sunshine reflected painfully from the rearview mirror. Readjusting the mirror didn't help for long. Every time she got the mirror right, I-40 would twist enough that it shone into her eyes again.

To the north, the clouds were thinner. Tina could see distant streaks of rain teasing the parched ground. Virga, they called that kind of rain, the kind that never quite reached the ground.

Only in the great southwest.

Even if it didn't rain, the storms El Nino tossed around the sky, sucking them up from Mexico, brought the land alive.

The weather seemed to please Hilda. That was the name of the silver Toyota Matrix she'd bought used in Kingman.

Hilda was contentedly and steadily chewing up the miles — not hurtling along like the idiots in the SUVs that flew past her, well over the speed limit, but fast enough.

And without the risk of being pulled over.

Tina liked slow and steady. Nondescript but completely functional, Hilda was turning out to be a good investment.

A business expense.

Tina smiled and pictured herself doing accounts for her new business, writing off travel expenses to a business meeting.

Fat chance she'd keep any records at all. If the IRS had problems with that, they could get in line.

Finding new business, letting the right people know you existed while keeping a low profile was the tough part for a one-woman startup.

She'd only done work for one client, a woman who needed help. Satisfied, she'd told Tina about another woman who needed her help.

Referrals were good, even essential, seeing that advertising would be, well, tricky at best when your job was eliminating bad people without the trappings of a badge.

She used her discretion to solve people's problems with other people.

Despite a rocky start, she had to admit that this work was a lot better than her missions with the Rangers. She'd never liked the idea that someone in a safe, warm, dry office looked at intel and maps and came up with solutions to the problem at hand.

Then they'd hand it down the plan. Go do it.

No discussion even when the restrictions they inevitably put on the team made the mission more difficult than it needed to be. More dangerous.

She didn't think the hip she'd injured when the IED went off was that bad. It only slowed her a little and didn't hurt that much except in the extreme cold.

But Army doctors, a whole bunch of white-coated snobs, wouldn't listen. They didn't agree. So she found herself on the outside, with a medical discharge.

That left her standing in the cold, asking the question many asked: What does someone trained to kill do when you dump them into a world where killing is frowned upon?

Potential employers praised her service to her country, gave her resume what they referred to as "serious consideration" and then quickly added that they didn't have any current openings for someone who could infiltrate enemy positions or blow up a bridge.

Quickly, very quickly, she found she didn't like selling. Not real estate, cars, or burgers. Burgers figured on the list because her last job before launching her own business was working in a diner in Bullhead City.

Launching a business was tricky, but she found it suited her.

Applying her skills out from under the watchful disapproving eye of bureaucrats, she put herself back in the action. She would just do the part she liked.

Combat, when you weren't getting blown up, was exciting.

And she had her first client to thank for it. And she got her client because she served her a crappy meal but smiled when she did it.

Business was slow in the diner, and that smile, gratefully received, invited conversation.

When her shift ended, they went out for a drink and she and Martha — that was the woman — wound up swapping stories of woe.

Martha's problem was a man. A man she had divorced but who still made her life hell, making sure she knew he was lurking nearby.

"I worked with one of those storefront lawyers," she said. "He got me a restraining order, but he goes after any guy I date, threatened my boss... I'm scared shitless."

"A creep like that needs to die," Tina said.

The light flickering in her eyes told Tina that she couldn't agree more.

"Too bad people like me can't afford a hit man. You know, the world could use storefront assassins... killers that regular folks could afford."

Martha made it a joke, but the idea struck Tina as hard as the IED had, only this blow felt good.

The idea that there might be a market for her services in this world after all, using her otherwise useless skills to solve Martha's seemingly intractable problem had great appeal.

"Just as a way of imagining things," she said, "what if there was such a person?"

Intrigued, swept up in it, they imagined it together. As they do, one thing, one idea, led to another.

And they came to an arrangement.

The next day, some junkies found the body of a certain man in an alley with his throat slit. The police called it a robbery gone bad. Martha called it a happy outcome.

"I'm free," she said.

"Me too," Tina said. She quit her job in the diner.

"Come into some money?" the boss asked.

"I did."

Not much, but how much did she really need?

Tina had a minimalist lifestyle and liked it that way. And that launched her new career.

Only in America, right?

And now she had a business appointment down the road.

Outside of Flagstaff, she pulled off the freeway, taking surface streets to Route 66 and turning east again.

Driving slowly, she checked out the area, passing the diner she was looking for. There wasn't much around it and the diner had seen better days.

She rolled on. Less than a mile further on she found a motel.

Nondescript, not part of a chain.

The Indian woman (from India, not a Navajo or something) working behind the counter barely looked at her.

Tina booked a room toward the back for three nights.

It was threadbare but clean.

She opened her only bag on the bed. That leather bag held the sum total of her worldly possessions: a couple changes of clothing (one set dirty), a pair of black leather gloves, a bottle of whisky, the medications for pain the military provided free of charge, a Colt 1911 automatic, two extra loaded magazines, a trashy romance novel, some toiletries, and a notebook with a pen attached by a cord.

She was always losing pens.

She'd seen a coin-operated washer and dryer next to the ice machine, so she undressed, showered, put on clean jeans and tee shirt, then took the dirty things down to wash them.

4

Walking to the laundry, she found that sitting so long in the car had aggravated her hip. A small twinge of pain hit her with every step, making her limp.

Fortunately, she had time to do some stretching.

The prospective client worked the breakfast through lunch shift. Their meeting wasn't until just before dinner.

With the clothes in the dryer, she returned to her room, stripped down, and went through the exercise routine that Jake, the Army's rehab guy, had developed for her.

She hadn't been doing it regularly. Her bad.

Truth was, she'd paid more attention to the exercises they'd done together in her bed in the evenings than anything he'd shown her in the rehab center.

He'd been good at that, and the nighttime treatments had helped her disposition, if not her recovery.

But your mental attitude is important, right? And now, doing the exercises worked out the stiffness.

Not all the pain, though.

She got out her whisky bottle and grabbed one of the paper-covered glasses the motel provided to pour herself a tall, family-sized shot and drank it.

Dressing again, she retrieved clothes from the dryer. Then she tucked her gun in the back of her waistband, put on the really cool Western-style suede jacket (with fringed sleeves) she'd found at Goodwill, and started walking to the diner.

Walking let her check out the position and number of CCTV cameras. She spotted enough that she had to assume one or two might actually work.

She walked to the back of the diner, around the dumpster, past the employees' cars, and checked out the back door.

A screen door was closed, but the inner door was open, letting out the smell of grease.

Just inside the door was a rack of lockers where employees could leave wallets and purses during their shifts.

Ordinary.

She completed her walk around the building and went in the front door.

Going in the front, the food smelled more like food. Greasy food, but good enough to stir the juices in her stomach.

She sat at a booth near the front that gave her a great view of the parking lot, if you could consider any view of a parking lot great.

The waitress came over, looking tired.

Tina knew that feeling.

"Long day?"

That earned her a tired smile.

"Only an hour to go, so hanging in there."

The tag on her breast said her name was Hilda.

Same as her car.

Was the universe whispering something good or bad?

"Is there a special today, Hilda?"

"What would be special is eating somewhere else," she said.

Tina chuckled. "Anything especially safe? I'm too hungry to travel another step."

Hilda tapped her order book with a pen.

"The club sandwich won't kill you, and it comes with fries."

"Sounds like it might require a couple of beers to keep it down."

"We only have domestic."

"That'll do the trick," Tina said.

Sitting back to wait, Tina took in the place.

The meal turned out to be halfway decent. Filling, anyway.

She dawdled over it, and then, when Hilda took the plate away, sipped the second beer slowly, just letting it trickle down her throat.

The diner did a fairly steady business.

It would either ramp up at dinnertime or die down completely. Depended on the surrounding businesses. The one she'd worked in filled up at lunch, but most of the customers worked in the surrounding tech campuses. When they went home, the place died.

Hilda came up. "I need to settle your tab, honey. I'm going off shift."

She overpaid in cash, telling her to keep the change, then watched Hilda go behind the counter.

Hilda wiped her face with a cloth as she glanced around the diner, looking around. She was looking for the woman she expected to meet.

Finally, she shrugged, yanked off her apron, and went into the back.

Sliding out of the booth, Tina grabbed a toothpick from the counter, and went out the front door, heading around to the back to meet Hilda when she came out.

"I think you are expecting me," Tina said. "Martha said she'd called you."

"You?" Hilda asked.

"I was scouting around before I identified myself," she said.

"Oh."

Tina winked. "I have a room at the motel up the street. We can talk there."

Hilda scowled, then turned and looked down the street as if she could see it from behind the diner.

"There?"

She heard the hesitation in the woman's voice. "You need help… we have to talk it through. We can't talk business here."

"My car?"

"Leave it here."

They walked in silence and then, inside, Hilda sat on a bed and Tina poured them each a drink, putting in the last of the ice from the ice bucket.

"Tell me about your problem."

"Martha said you could help."

Tina refilled their glasses. "Tell me what it is, and we will see."

Hilda sighed, took a long, thirsty drink, and then told her a pretty standard story.

She'd been working for a bank as a teller. She fell for the manager. Fell right into his bed.

"The guy turned out to be mean and vicious. I wasn't going to put up with that."

"But?" Tina figured she knew what was coming.

When she went to break it off, he wasn't thrilled.

"He fired me for some made-up thing."

"So you went from bank teller to waitress?"

"Banks are secretive. You get fired from a bank, they don't tell the other banks why, but it scares them off from hiring you."

"So he had his revenge."

"I can deal with that. The thing is, Jerry embezzled some money. He's some kind of a whiz with computers. He called me and said that if I didn't come back on his terms, then during the next audit, it would appear that I'd taken some money before I left."

"Did you report his assaults to the police?"

She scowled. "I tried. They weren't interested. No marks. I think I would need for him to put me in the hospital to get a restraining order from those clowns."

"Justice and fair play and all that," Tina said. "So, your concern is that the guy won't take no for an answer."

She nodded. "He's blackmailing me, and I didn't do anything."

"Where did you leave it with him?"

"Yesterday, he said I had until Friday to agree. He wants me to go with him this weekend. I'm afraid of him."

Tina considered it. "Okay, we have options. We could try to intimidate him."

"With what?"

Tina smiled. "Have him beaten up and give him the message that, if he bothers you in any way, there is more coming. Or perhaps we make him think we have proof he took the money himself."

"You could do those things?"

"Yes, but they are uncertain. Using muscle can make them more determined. The second is tricky. We'd need to find out some details of the money that disappeared. That would mean you talking to old coworkers."

She shook her head. "They are afraid to talk to me about the weather now."

"Okay. That leaves the ultimate solution."

"Which is?"

"Kill him before he points the finger at you. Before Monday morning."

She laughed. "Right."

Tina shrugged. "It's simple and clean and eliminates the possibility he takes you on his weekend of pain and then frames you, anyway."

Hilda put her hand to her mouth. "I hadn't thought of that."

"Guys like that…"

She didn't mention the possibility that the entire embezzling story was bullshit and that Jerry was bluffing. There was no way to know.

"I have no idea how to get in touch with a professional killer, and I couldn't afford one if I did meet him."

"I guess Martha wasn't clear," Tina said. "You've already done the first part."

Hilda's eyes grew wide. "You?"

"I make hiring an assassin affordable. It's my thing."

"Why?"

"You know about storefront lawyers, right?"

"Sure. Ambulance chasers."

"Some are. Others are good people who went into law to make a difference. They keep the overhead down and that makes their service affordable for people who need their help. That's me. I'm your storefront assassin!"

"You don't look like a killer."

"Nope. The pros, the ones who don't get caught, look like accountants and waitresses."

She wasn't sure that was true, but it sounded good.

"You work cheap and still earn a living?"

"Not a great one. You try to make it up in volume."

"Not that I like the idea of paying to have someone killed…" she sighed. "But… if I did, how much would it cost?"

"I'd charge you a grand. Can you do that?"

Hilda stared at Tina, her face frozen. "For a thousand dollars, you will kill him?"

"That's the deal."

The price got her past her reluctance to order the murder of a fellow human rather quickly.

"What do you need from me?"

"His full name and address and a recent picture of him."

Hilda shifted into eager mode.

"I have that on my phone."

Tina gave her the number of the burner phone she'd bought when she started her business (another business deduction, right?).

While Hilda's thumbs went to work, Tina played the operation out in her head.

"He gave you until Friday... what's the arrangement?"

"I'm supposed to be ready to go at the end of my shift. He'll pick me up behind the diner." She looked at Tina, sizing her up. "He is mean and strong."

"Good. I hate being a bully."

"How will you—"

"Don't ask."

She let out a breath. "What do I do?"

"Not much. I thought I'd need for you to arrange to meet in a relatively deserted place, but he took care of that for us. It's Wednesday. I've got plenty of time to prepare. Do you have a good friend you could arrange to be with when you get off work on Friday?"

Hilda grinned. "My alibi? Lucy works the same shift, and she was asking about getting together for drinks after work."

"Set it up. At the end of your shift, drag your feet getting out the door. I'll need a few minutes to do my work."

She nodded. "Friday... how will I know it's happening for sure?"

"I'll come in for lunch. When you see my smiling face, you'll know things are on schedule. You go for that drink. When it's safe, I'll text you something about club sandwiches and you bring the money to my room."

"Club sandwiches. Funny."

"It wasn't half bad. You can't say that about some diners."

"Can you make it look like suicide, so they don't think I am involved?"

"I planned on it. It's neat that way. His remorse will be overwhelming."

"Sweet," she said.

*****

After she walked Hilda to her car, this time wearing a hoodie with the hood up, Tina got in her Hilda and drove around, getting a feel for the part of town.

At a liquor store, she bought a bottle of Jack Daniels.

At a local hardware store, she bought a can of black spray paint.

Then she went into the worst-looking pawn shop she could find that was reasonably close to the motel.

She checked out a sweet older Stratocaster guitar and amplifier, negotiating with the owner over the price a bit, but all the time checking out a .38 revolver.

A police special with a short barrel. Nice gun.

Back at the motel, she showered, put an overpriced porn video on the television, and watched it before setting the alarm clock and going to sleep.

At midnight, she dressed in jeans, a black tee shirt, and black hoodie. She grabbed a small tool bag that she hung around her neck (tucked inside the hoodie), the spray paint, and her gloves, and went out on foot.

Her first stop was a women's clothing store, one of those mid-priced chain places with decent copies of more expensive clothing.

She didn't see any cameras and the back door was easy to pop. She stuffed a few things in a shopping bag, getting them in a couple of sizes because you couldn't be certain.

She carefully locked the door as she left.

The pawn shop had the usual pretentious, but minimal security.

She sprayed the lenses of the CCTV camera black in case they weren't dummies. The heavy, barred door at the back had two shitty locks that took her less than thirty seconds to crack.

Inside, she cracked the gun safe in the office and found the revolver and a couple of boxes of bullets.

She took the other guns and tossed them in the dumpster in the back. The odds were near zero that they would still be there in the morning.

Then she trashed the place and took a few things that looked valuable and a cleaning kit for the gun.

Job done, she left, relocking the door.

Back in her room, she cleaned and loaded the revolver and went back to sleep.

*****

One important aspect of Tina's business model that she hadn't mentioned to Hilda was that the plan she'd laid out for the client wasn't what she intended to do.

A client could get a sudden attack of conscience and call the cops or warn the target.

Besides that, a kill, like any hunt, wasn't a certain thing. You had to expect to try and fail. But it was important to make sure the attempts didn't tip anyone off or you would scare off the game.

And she had a couple of ideas to try. Today.

If things went well, by the time Jerry was supposed to pick her up behind the diner, it would be over.

So, Thursday morning would be show-and-tell day.

She put on the new clothes.

A white blouse and black skirt, stockings, and a pair of heels. Things a woman who wasn't Tina would wear to an office.

Feeling awkward in her new garb, she drove a few miles to a Denny's and used her phone to find the location of the local bank Jerry worked in while she ate the breakfast special.

It wasn't far and opened in an hour.

Right after opening, she found herself swept eagerly into the manager's office.

Jerry looked like a regular guy. Not excitingly handsome, but good-looking and fit.

"I'm Tina. I'm in town for a job interview," she told him. "I think they will make me an offer, and I'm looking at what that will entail."

He seemed pleased. "How can I help?"

"Well, I'd be transferring my banking here and need information on the accounts and terms."

"Good thinking."

"I thought a local businessman might be able to point me to good people, such as a real estate agent, to begin with, and then an accountant... all those things."

Painting herself as mid-level management.

"I'd love to help." He shoved some brochures at her about the bank, along with forms. "I know the best people in town."

She gave him a slightly more than friendly smile and held up the brochures. "Rather than take up your time here... I'm sure you must have important banking work to take care of... maybe we could meet for a drink this evening?"

Looking like a cross between a man who'd won the lottery and one of those little dogs with its head on a spring you see in the back windows of low riders, he nodded. "Sure."

"I'll give you my number. Text me with when and where."

And then she left.

He'd taken the bait. Executing the plan would be simple.

They met for drinks, and he played city insider, giving her names she immediately forgot. Then he invited her to dinner.

Then he invited her to his place for a nightcap, where she nudged the gentle seduction forward.

Hours later, lying in his bed, Tina got an uneasy feeling.

Jerry wasn't what she imagined.

He was a considerate, if not exciting, lover. Nothing like the person Hilda described.

Granted, this was their first time together, but you could tell these things.

Something stunk.

Before dawn on Friday morning, Jerry's phone rang.

He scowled and answered.

A woman tore into him.

Lying with her head on his chest, Tina knew the woman was Hilda. Her tone alternated between scolding and threatening.

"I've got the file that will cover your ass," she said. "Unless you want to go to jail, you transfer the money to me. Then I'll give it to you, and you can run it."

"Run it?"

"Transfer the money today, before you leave the bank. Then park behind the diner at the end of my shift. I'll give you the file. Otherwise, good luck with the auditors."

Tina sighed.

Jerry looked stressed. "Shit," he said.

"Are you being blackmailed for something?" she asked.

He looked sheepish. "You heard that much. I might as well tell you all of it."

"Yeah, you should."

"Stupidly, I had an affair with one of the IT people at the bank. She stole my username and password and embezzled some money. Then she quit."

"Framing you."

He nodded. "Now she is demanding three grand for a program that will cover up the transactions."

"I see."

It was a slick plan. Jerry gives her money for nothing, or for a bogus program. Then he is found dead — a remorseful suicide.

Anger made her tremble. Tina didn't like being played. That had to have consequences.

A big-deal assassin, she knew, would be to go on as planned. Fake Jerry's suicide with the police special and then wait to collect her payment.

But she was different. Tina was a storefront assassin who liked Jerry and had a client trying to use her.

"I think I can take care of this for you."

"You?" he asked.

She nodded. "Jerry, I'm going to solve your problem, but you can't ask questions. You can't know my plan."

"I don't understand."

She nodded. "And you won't. You can't."

"What do I do?"

"It's what you don't do. Don't transfer any money to Hilda's accounts."

"How did you know her name?"

She waved a hand. "Watch the news. Over the next few days, you'll learn everything it's safe for you to know. Just don't mention the blackmail to the authorities, and this will work out well for you."

"I don't understand."

Her brain raced, fleshing out the new plan, incorporating her existing arrangements.

She held up a finger. "Hilda is going to have an attack of remorse for her actions."

"I doubt it," he said. "The bitch planned this carefully."

"When you get to the bank today, leave your car unlocked. Put the keys in the glove compartment," she said.

"But…"

"I'll need to steal it," she said, and then she laughed at his expression. She kissed him. "Do it my way and stay out of jail."

"When will I see you again?" he asked.

She sighed and shook her head. "You can't let anyone know you ever met me, beyond my appearance in the bank."

When a sad and confused Jerry went to work, she drove her car to the motel, showered, and changed. Then she walked to the diner.

"All set?" Hilda asked, her eyes bright.

"I need a club sandwich, fries, and a beer."

"You are a pretty predictable person for an assassin," Hilda said.

"No sense of adventure," she said.

Back at the motel, she called a cab to take her to the bank.

Jerry had done as she asked, and she drove his car back to the motel. Then she set the alarm and took a nap. Jerry had kept her awake much of the night.

Waking refreshed, she drove the car behind the diner and parked it.

Hilda poked her head out briefly. Checking.

Leaving the car, she walked back to the motel and packed. She put her things in her car, jammed a wad of paper in the door lock, and checked out.

She drove to a mall parking lot and parked. After texting client Hilda, she left Hilda the car to wait and walked back to the motel, and slipped into the room.

Hilda arrived, looking excited. "Is it done?"

Tina nodded and handed her a drink. "I did my part."

Hilda pulled out an envelope and handed it over.

One thousand dollars.

"This doesn't make a dent in the money you stole, does it?" Tina asked.

"Stole?"

"The money you embezzled from the bank using Jerry's login information."

Hilda sat back. "How did you know?"

"Then you told him you'd sell him a program that would cover it up? Clever."

Hilda smiled. "With him dead, no one will know but us girls."

A sly, knowing smile crossed her face. "I get it. Now you expect me to pay you extra to keep quiet, right? Well, the money should be in my offshore account by now. How much do you want?"

"Nothing," Tina said. "I'm an assassin, not a blackmailer."

"You should expand your business model," Hilda said. "You are limiting your horizons. Think bigger."

"I'm a specialist," she said, bringing out the police special and enjoying the fear that showed on Hilda's face. "I'm good with my current operation."

If anyone heard the shot when Tina fired a round into Hilda's temple at close range, you wouldn't know it from the response.

That was the great thing about these low-end motels, if you could find a clean one.

She put the stolen gun in Hilda's hand, then took Hilda's phone from her pocket and typed a confession into the notepad. Snuggling the phone in the woman's other hand, she left her in the motel room.

Driving her Hilda toward Safford in a dark, drizzling rain, she considered changing the car's name.

The poor car was nothing like the only other Hilda she'd known.

She texted the audio file she recorded of her chat with Hilda to Jerry and also to a number at the FBI.

It turned out they had an entire division that focused on cybercrime related to banks. And their number was right there on their website.

It made her wonder what kind of crazy world she lived in?

"Zelda," she said.

She felt the car surge forward. Yes, Zelda was a much better name for a car. For her car.

Extract from So Long Ballentyne

(Harry Rhimes book 2)

John A. Connor

I pulled open the door and headed towards the bar, the smell of hot salt beef and sauerkraut vied against the equally tempting aroma of corned beef and cabbage. The background clatter and chatter of the diners was augmented by the low volume sound system pushing out a steady stream of rhythmic, twangy, bluegrass which, for a change, seemed to have surprisingly life-affirming lyrics.

> *"So I'm riding down this highway,*
> *With my foot hard on the gas,*
> *While her brother's eighteen wheeler,*
> *Is riding close up to my ass.*
> *An' when he catches up with me,*
> *I know things won't be the same.*
> *'Cos I believed everything she said,*
> *So I've only myself to blame…"*

Mindful of the waitresses working tables as fast as they could before the lunchtime crowds departed, I glanced around and caught sight of Pearl. She was holding court and keeping a watch on everything from the safety of her observation post by the cash register. She's a petite woman of indeterminable middle age, who's made no secret of her desires to slip disgracefully into retirement once she's made enough money to do so. Diminutive in stature – though apparently perfectly proportioned throughout, if you believed the gossip around the tables of more than one private poker school — Pearl is four foot seven inches tall in her six inch spike-heeled shoes.

"Well, hello stranger!"

I smiled good naturedly at her. "Stranger than what, Pearl?"

"Honey, you're no stranger than half of what I get to see walk through that door on a daily basis. The other half? They're just dull, boring and normal — not worth spit, or the time of day, believe me!"

That's what I liked about Pearl. She could backhand a complement faster than any tennis pro. I smiled wryly. "All heart, Pearl."

"Got no heart today, Harry. Only salt beef, pork belly, jellied knuckles..." She let her voice trail off into a grin. "Twelve Rabbits is over in booth 15 with one of the oddest looking things I ever seen come in from the canyon. He said they were waiting for you to join them."

Pearl describing someone as 'odd' made me wonder for a moment or two. Mentally I shrugged my shoulders. What the hell, it wouldn't hurt to find out what the deal was, and get a free lunch out of it as well.

Still mindful of the waitresses criss-crossing between the tables and the bar, I headed on further back to the booths, and found the one that had a big "15" on it in bright egg-yellow numerals.

Inside the booth, close to the far wall, on one side sat Twelve Rabbits in what looked like a hand-tailored, ash-grey, casual cotton two-piece suit, white shirt and pastel sage green tie. He still had the slim elegance of a true Latin American – clean shaven, dark black hair brushed back and cut just above the collar, carefully manicured hands.

In contrast the wizen old man sitting opposite him, nursing a glass of beer, appeared to've been transported from some kind of alternative universe, where time had ceased to move on since the early 1950s. I'd seen classic zoot suits in style magazine pictures, and sometimes on stage when the local travelling repertory company had performed some of Damon Runyon's Broadway stories. But I'd never seen an original this close up. It was a navy blue base overlaid with a lighter shade of sky blue chalk-stripe, running vertically. It had hand finished lapels wide enough to launch aircraft from, and shoulders padded to the point where they wouldn't have looked out of place on a football team. With the jacket unbuttoned, the large, wide tie of acid yellow, vermilion and lime green geometric designs was something I suspected would leave an after-image burned onto my retina if I stared at it for too long.

Poking turtle-like from the white shirt collar was the head of an old man. Deeply tanned, his hairline had receded into what some called a Widow's Peak, with the bone-white hair oiled and slicked back — as if someone had greased down the white head crest of one of those Chinese Hairless dogs. Yet, despite all this, his amber brown gaze seemed to take in and evaluate everything around him in a slightly emotionless, reptilian manner.

Twelve Rabbits stood, shook my hand warmly, and indicated I should sit beside him, across from the stranger. No sooner had I sat down than Pearl saw her chance and sent across a waitress. She was suitably armed with a large Bunn flask of coffee in one hand and a pitcher of beer in the other. She refilled Twelve Rabbits' half empty cup, poured me a fresh one, then carefully poured another beer for the stranger. Setting the jug and the pot down on the table, she smiled, took our order, collected the pot and jug back up, then headed off to the kitchen. Efficiency with warmth. Y'all come back, y'hear.

When she was gone, Twelve Rabbits cleared his throat.

"Mr. Rhimes, allow me to introduce you to one of my company's investors, Mr. Francis Nixx." The guy silently nodded his head in a short and sweet 'hello' as Twelve Rabbits continued, "Mr. Nixx has been telling me about a problem which two of his friends are experiencing at present." He turned to look across the table at Nixx, gesturing with his head for Nixx to pick up and carry on with the explanation.

I'm not sure what I was expecting. I'd seen the scars on and around his throat, and I'd been waiting for him to take out an electrolarynx from a jacket pocket. Instead he seemed to fluently bark, belch and croak his words out, adeptly using an array of oesophageal voice speech techniques.

"Call me Frankie," he said, then rapidly took a gulp of air. "Friends of mine would," — another rapid gulp of air — "like to discuss hiring you." He paused for a moment to swallow more air, then, "To investigate someone." He lifted his beer glass up and swallowed a mouthful of foam off the top. Putting the glass back down again, he said, "Find out why he committed suicide."

I was starting to get used to his speech pattern, ignoring the fractional breaks, but held off for a moment before saying, "I take it the reason for his suicide isn't obvious?"

Nixx cocked his head and sounded cranky. "If it was, then we wouldn't — be looking to blow — a pile of money on you."

I smiled sheepishly. "Point taken, but sometimes people are blinded by denial. They don't accept the obvious, even when it's presented to them."

For some reason my comment seemed to hit a raw nerve and Nixx said sharply, "Look, we may be old — but we're not stupid. The Woodstocks — just want to know what pushed him — over the edge." He paused for a moment to lift his beer glass up, and this time he took a proper drink. Wiping his top lip with a napkin, he added, "An apt expression, considering he," gas from the beer now gone, he was back to swallowing air, "tossed himself under a subway train."

Letting that fillip of information slide for the time being, I asked, "Who are the Woodstocks?"

Nixx gestured to Twelve Rabbits, "Can you take it from here — I need to rest a moment."

Twelve Rabbits nodded, turned to me a little, and said, "They are the clients who wish to hire you. They would have been here in person, but they're a little adverse to travelling long distances, which is why Mr. Nixx is here to represent them, so to speak."

He fell silent as the waitress returned with our orders, refilled my coffee, then disappeared back into the lunchtime chaos again.

Twelve Rabbits picked up where he'd left off. "The person who has apparently discarded his life — Mr. Anthony Wolfe — was an important friend to Mr. And Mrs. Woodstock."

"And they want me to find out why he committed suicide?"

Frankie Nixx looked up at me. "Why," he shrugged his shoulders as he swallowed a short gasp of air. "If," — a longer gasp — "it's all the same thing." Having stated his point he went back to his lunch.

I knew from personal experience that in reality it wasn't the same, but I didn't feel like arguing the point. All in all, it sounded like a simple case — just go out, ask around, find out what had gotten to this guy Wolfe, and then report back to the Woodstocks. It wasn't unusual for someone people thought of as an 'important friend' to slip into depression, become withdrawn, and quietly lose contact before hitting the bottom of the deep black spiral. Provided that was all the Woodstocks wanted me to do then I was game for the work.

Looking over to Nixx, I said, "Okay, when do I get to meet up with the clients?"

Frankie picked up the napkin from his knees and wiped his mouth, tossing the crumpled paper square onto his plate. Taking a large mouthful of beer, he said, "We're all living in a retirement community — called Ballentyne — out near Petrolia." He paused for a moment, working more air down. "I can get you there and back — by nine this evening." He looked at me expectantly from under his slightly hooded white eyebrows.

With some of the Orion and Nadler money still behind me to take care of the bills, I was in a position where I could actually pick and choose, and the prospect of a little easy private work had its appeal.

Frankie finished off his glass of beer. "Of course," he belched, "Mike and Bette may want to — hire someone else."

I smiled at him. "True, there is that. But then why go for pot-roast when you can have Grade A prime steak such as myself?"

Without smiling back, Frankie just stared at me silently. I glanced at the doll-like figure and wondered how he'd managed to survive not only the savage cruelty that any cancer brings with it, but also the changing world around him. He seemed almost impervious to change, going about his own sweet way as if cocooned in a time-frozen bubble.

His voice broke in on my thoughts. "You good to go?" His facial expression was still as flat as when I'd first sat down in front of him, and I had the turtle image back in my mind for a moment. With an assertive nod I said, "Ready as I'll ever be," before standing and moving out of the booth, careful of the foot traffic as I waited for Nixx.

Frankie looked over at Twelve Rabbits. "Thanks for your time, Bunny. We'll be in touch soon." Then leaving Twelve Rabbits to finish his lunch in peace, he picked up his wide brimmed felt hat, moved out of the booth, and we headed over to the cash register.

Offering no resistance, I let Frankie pay the bill — thus proving there is, sometimes, such a thing as a free lunch. He told Pearl she should keep the change, which generated a very heartfelt "Please, come dine again!" and as we walked past the bar, Frankie indicated he wanted to go to the restroom.

"Be back in a couple of shakes. You wanna take a whiz before we go?"

I shook my head. I figured even with the coffee over lunch I could still manage the distance to Ballentyne without the need for a restroom break.

While Frankie was gone I strolled across to Pearl. "You don't mind if I leave my car parked around the back for a day or so?"

She eyed me with suspicion. "You still driving that old clunker of a Ford? I mean, it's gonna start when you come back and collect it, ain't it?" Then, after a moment's thought, she said, "Yeah, why the hell not." At least she was smiling as she said it.

Back outside in the sunshine Frankie's Golden Hawk had sent out vibrations into the ether, attracting the attentions of the local hotrod, rev and petrol-head tribes. Several obviously modified road machines had pulled up alongside it, their owners and others already reverently circling the Hawk, humming and hawing over what, to them, must have seemed like a truly mythical beast.

Alongside me Frankie just smiled. "Gets 'em every time." He took out a set of keys attached to a fob which wouldn't have looked out of place in a ZZ Top video. He paused for a moment, then made a show unlocking the car. Opening the drivers' door, he took off his hat and carefully dropped it on the back seat. Then with almost stripper-like exaggeration he unbuttoned his jacket and took it off, careful to fold it several times length-wise, before putting it alongside his hat. He stood and looked across at the gathered crowd, his shirt bleach-white against his two-tone blue suspenders, the tail of his large toxic-coloured tie pointing almost lewdly at his crotch. Then, like the Cheshire Cat, he seemed to disappear into the vehicle until only the memory of his smug grin was left.

Not to be outdone, I took off my jacket, revealing my lemon yellow open neck polo shirt with the roadkill green thing on the left breast pocket. Opening the passenger door, I tossed the jacket casually into the back somewhere, before finally sliding into the passenger seat.

The afternoon sun had warmed the interior, releasing a heady, nostalgic combination of odours: hot leather, plastic and dashboard polish mixed with a touch of grease — all of which enfolded us, glove-like, as we settled ourselves on the old-style coil-sprung seats. Automatically I fumbled around for the seatbelt before remembering they'd not been compulsory back in 1957. No doubt Frankie wanted to keep the vehicle in perfect, concourse condition, but it made me feel distinctively odd not having the comforting pressure across my chest.

We both seemed to sit there for a moment, and I found myself watching Frankie as he watched his audience watching him, waiting for him to turn the key and spark the beast into life. Again the reptilian impression — reminding me of a lizard on a rock, carefully eyeing up its prey.

Putting on a pair of round, wire-framed prescription sunglasses, Frankie made a noise in the back of his scarred throat, which I took to be a chuckle. Then he fired up the engine.

It caught first time — a deep, throaty sound coming from the exhaust, coaxed from the engine. Frankie teased them — pushing his foot down hard on the accelerator before almost immediately released the pressure. The petrol-heads let loose a collective sigh of pleasure, moving closer around the vehicle. For a moment it felt like they were about to start swaying rhythmically, chanting an ancient and mysterious ritual known only to those initiated into some kind of secret petrochemical slave-lust cult. Well, this is California after all.

With theatrical flamboyance, Frankie slipped the car into reverse. Backing out in a steady arc onto the main street, I heard the distinctive noise in the back of his throat again, as he straightened the car and we headed off in the direction of the 299 at an impressive twenty-five miles an hour.

* * * * *

We slowly cruised along the back road out of town before finally joining up with the 299. Frankie put a touch more pressure on the accelerator, letting the motor have a little more gas, and before long we were up around the speed limit, with the engine barely working itself into a sweat.

There was an old, manual, AM radio set in the dashboard, with two black and chrome coloured knobs — one for tuning, the other for the volume — but I resisted the temptation to turn it on. Frankie seemed to me to be one of those people who preferred to do their driving in silence, as opposed to anything else. Just the sound of the engine, and the tyres on the blacktop.

I let the mechanical background noise play for another couple of minutes before I tried to ask Frankie some questions.

"Is there any chance you can tell me some more about the Woodstocks? Or the guy they want me to check out?"

But Frankie kept silent, his head moving regularly to look in the rear-view mirror until, moments later, he croaked, "Ah. Here they come."

I dropped the sun visor down and used the vanity mirror to see out the back without turning my head awkwardly. Behind us was Eddie Delanys' Chevy pick-up truck, closely followed by a half dozen of the other hot-rodded vehicles from town, gradually gaining on us. Frankie grinned. Downing some more air, he said, "I knew the sucker couldn't resist."

"Couldn't resist what?" I was pretty sure Eddie and Frankie hadn't said a word to each other the whole time we'd been having lunch. Part of that was down to Eddie already being barred from Madam Pearl's establishment several years before. Also I knew Eddie. He didn't go looking for trouble in bright public places, though he was almost always the centre of it within his social group.

Frankie looked over at me as he gently applied the brakes and slowed the Studebaker down to a crawl. He reminded me all the more of an old snapping turtle. Silently slipping under the water, about to take down a duckling from below. He grinned wide, though didn't show any teeth, and although I couldn't see his eyes behind the black corrective lenses, I suspected there would be a bright, predatory sparkle to them.

Several of the entourage sped up, drove passed, then started parking up on either side of the highway ahead of us. Still slowing, Frankie gently turned the steering wheel and moved the car over into the left hand lane, settling in the middle of it as Eddie's over-modified Chevy pick-up came up alongside us, matching our slowly decreasing speed. As Eddie Delany wound down his window, Frankie pressed a button on the centre console and my window rolled down, filling the car with a blast of hot early afternoon air. Without saying a word, both vehicles eased their speed down until they finally stopped, side by side, their bumpers even with each other. Ahead of us the road was straight as far as the eye could see — though going by the thickness of Frankie's glasses I was beginning to have doubts as to just how far that might be.

But Frankie kept looking unwaveringly at the highway ahead of him, his lips slightly parted, the tip of his tongue flicking over them to keep them moist in the dry atmosphere. In his bullfrog voice he shouted. "You think you can do it?"

Eddie Delany kept looking straight down the highway at some distant point where the blacktop met the horizon, and adjusted his Ray-Bans so they sat a little easier on his nose. Without even smiling he shouted back, "I'm going to clear the first half mile before you even put that piece of junk into gear."

One of the petrol nerds from town got out of the pick-up then jogged a little way down the roadside, slightly ahead of the two vehicles. From out of his pocket he pulled an old, oil-stained rag, and held it up above his head as if it were a starter flag.

I muttered something indistinct under my breath and shook my head in disbelief. It felt like I'd stumbled into the alternative reality of a B-grade sophomore teen movie, where the underlying pecker contest was forever going to be settled by having a road race. I was going to suggest they do it after we'd come back from Ballentyne, but Frankie was already revving the engine, and Delany was following suit — matching him engine rev for engine rev. Still keeping his gaze out front, Frankie took a large swallow of air. "Don't worry, Harry, I've never — had one of these — blow up on me yet."

27

I was about to say something along the lines of there always being a first time when the guy by the roadside dropped the rag. From that point on, all I can remember is seeing Frankie's knee go down as he floored the accelerator and we rocketed forward in a cloud of tyre smoke — all possible hope of conversation drowned out by the deafening roar of the two powerful engines being given free reign.

The mass of dials on the dashboard meant nothing to me, except for the rapidly climbing tacho and speedometer, which I didn't want to look at on the grounds that if we were going fast enough then we mercifully wouldn't feel the impact when it happened. Instead I looked away from Frankie's intensely rigid form and out through the open window frame at the Chevy pick-ups' nose. From where I was sitting it seemed to be slowly edging ahead us. Looking back up at Eddie, I could tell he was just as focused as Frankie seemed to be, though he was smiling with obvious satisfaction as the Chevy started to pull away.

Then the Golden Hawks' supercharger came alive and the world around me suddenly jerked as the new-found acceleration pushed me firmly back into my seat. In rapid succession we went beyond eighty, then ninety, and broke the one hundred mile an hour barrier. Not satisfied, Frankie kept his foot down hard, pushing the Studebaker out beyond one-ten, then one-twenty.

As we finally tore past the pick-up and veered smoothly back into the right-hand lane, Frankie rested his left elbow on his open window frame. Leaning out a little, he slowly raised his forearm straight up, his hand clenched in a fist except for the upraised middle finger. At around one hundred and thirty-five miles an hour, Frankie Nixx was flipping Eddie Delany the bird.

It took us several miles and a curve in the highway before we were back down to a semi-respectable speed again. Frankie just sat there with a satisfied grin on his face, while I tried to relaxed and let the adrenaline filter out of my system. Another dozen or so miles along the highway I asked him again if he could give me some background on Mike and Bette Woodstock.

The Result of an Accident
Ruth Morgan

Lightning tore jagged rents across the clouds.

Thunder shook the earth followed by a deluge of heavy drops that made small plumes of dust as they pounded the dry soil.

Another thunderclap.

The figure tried to move faster, stumbling over his feet.

Twin beams of light pierced the darkness.

An engine revved.

He sensed danger, confused by alcohol he hesitated.

The engine revved again.

As the lights began to move towards him, he tried to run.

A whoosh as air was driven from his lungs.

A thud as his body bounced over the roof, sliding to the ground.

Grating gears as the driver engaged reverse, putting a booted foot on the accelerator.

Tyres spun, pushing against the obstacle before it gave way.

Headlights revealed a motionless shape lying face down in a puddle.

First gear, and this time the wheels moved easily.

Red taillights disappeared into the distance.

The storm moved away.

Silence returned.

*****

Senior Constable Alex Williams was in charge of Colbrook Police Station. In fact, he was the only police officer for the small community located on the banks of the Murray River. A southerly wind whistled through the trees, tugging his hat and rustling his oilskins. On the rough gravel road, Douglas Harrison lay face down in a puddle. Muddy water was tinged with blood seeping from the distorted skull.

The call had been made by the driver of the dawn milk truck collecting from Rafferty's Dairy. He'd stopped when he saw the body, identified it, and called the police before continuing on his rounds. Collecting milk from the local dairies and taking it to be processed looked after the living, while the devil would look after dead Douglas Harrison as one of his own.

Gunbower Island was a teardrop shaped land mass surrounded by the Murray River. The island and Colbrook were connected by a single lane wooden bridge. Williams stood, pondering his next move. Harrison was a drunk, a wife beater and a notorious womaniser. Williams had been called to Harrison's house last week by neighbours who heard a violent argument. It wasn't the first time Lizzie had chased her husband with a tomahawk when he came home drunk, his shirt covered in some tarts lipstick.

Puddles dotted the road and on the wet ground it was easy to trace the tyre tracks of other vehicles as they wove avoiding the deepest potholes. As Williams crouched lower, his bushman's eyes were just able to pick out one set of ruler straight tracks broken in the middle by the body.

On the town side of the bridge, he heard the sound of a throbbing V8 engine, and burying his hands deeper in his coat pockets, waited.

'Bloody cold morning to haul a man out of a warm bed,' the dulcet tones of Dr James Churchill, local GP and occasional pathologist rang out.

'Especially when it's not his own,' muttered Williams. 'I've been up longer than you have. How did you get that heap of US junk started on a cold Colbrook morning. What's it called again?' The pattern of banter was well established.

'It's a Ford Mustang. And a prime example of a muscle car,' the usual protest emerged.

It was obvious from Williams' body language that he wasn't in the mood this morning for humour. 'So, who do we have here?' Churchill's tone became crisp, business like.

'Douglas Harrison. I need you to certify he's dead. Then I've gotta tell Lizzie. Can you give me a rough time of death?' Williams had his police notebook in one hand and was making notes.

Churchill snapped on a pair of rubber gloves and bending down lifted the outstretched arm. Harrison's nails were well shaped, clean, the hands pampered and soft. 'Rigor is starting to wear off. His clothes are soaked, so I'd say he's been out all night. Rain started about 11pm. Hit by a car?'

'It looks that way.'

'Accidental you think?' Churchill queried.

'No sign that the vehicle swerved.' Williams pointed to the tracks on the road. 'Even without street lights, the driver would have had headlights.'

'You'll be spoiled for choice with suspects.'

'Trust you're not going to say that to Lizzie?'

'I'm surprised he lasted this long,' commented Churchill.

The dead man was almost universally loathed, and in a tight knit town, mouths were likely to be shut even tighter. He'd be battling to find a killer in a community who believed Harrison got what was coming to him. Williams had no doubt it was murder. Everyone knew Harrison drank at the River Arms pub well after the doors were shut. He was often seen staggering home across the bridge to walk the two kilometres to his bed. Someone bided their time before striking. He'd been involved in numerous drunken brawls and his vicious temper saw him regularly thrown out of the pub. Despite most of the town giving him a wide berth, he always managed to pick a fight among his drinking mates.

He wondered what his Maggie would say to the news Harrison was dead. She'd been outspoken last week when she returned from the shopping.

'Alex,' Maggie had said. 'You have to do something. Lizzie has a cut above her eye, and there are black marks on her arm.'

'I can't do anything Love, if she doesn't make an official complaint.'

'That's nonsense. She didn't get that shiner last week when she fell over in the garden. Or those broken ribs from lifting something too heavy. He's a philandering wife beating bastard and someone ought to put a bullet though him.'

'I trust my Love you're not planning to do just that? Make my job difficult if I have to arrest my wife.'

Harrison had been run over, not shot. He could take Maggie off his potential list of suspects.

'Car or truck?' Churchill looked closely at the imprints on the waxy white skin.

'It would take something heavy to do that sort of damage.'

Most locals owned a truck. They were more practical for carting stock, or fodder and the varied necessities of a farming community. There'd be damage to the vehicle, especially the front around the radiator and bonnet. Recent heavy rains had brought out the big red kangaroos to graze the tender new green shoots along the roadside verges, resulting in increased collisions. If the truck was still roadworthy, the dents were ignored. Testing all the vehicles that looked worse for wear for anything that looked like blood was impossible without help. And strong evidence.

Around the body farmers gathered, everyone voicing their own opinion. Williams listened with one ear but his focus was on recording the scene before billowing rain clouds delivered another deluge. The small group fell silent, and parted. When he looked up, there was Lizzie, standing tall and straight, her steel gray hair lank. And alongside her, Joe, her oldest son.

'Is it Douglas?' she asked, her eyes fixed on Williams' face. The black bruise around her eye had faded to a sickly green and yellow. Her blue eyes missed little.

'I'm sorry for your loss Lizzie. I was coming to tell you. The crime scene…' his words faded away.

Her attention was focussed on the battered corpse of her late husband.

'Lizzie,' James Churchill moved towards her. 'Let me drive you home.'

She shook her head. 'I expect you'll have questions Constable Williams?'

'Yes. Will you be at the farm?'

She nodded. 'Nowhere else to be. He was gentle once. I loved him. Her eyes were glistening. Work roughened hands reached up to wipe away a single tear. 'He wasn't much of a human being but he was mine.' The words were a whisper, just audible over the whistling wind. Joe stood close by his mother, the strong silent archetype of a bushman. He put his arm around her waist, and she grabbed it tight.

She turned and walked away, a solitary figure in patched trousers and torn coat. Her posture was upright, dignified, her shoulders back, her step lighter as though a weight had been lifted from her shoulders. And perhaps with Douglas's death, it had been. Her son, tall and wiry kept her pace, his tattered felt hat pulled low over his ears.

Williams' phone rang and he turned from the watchers to answer it.

'A problem?' asked Churchill accurately reading the look of frustration.

'Whitworth can't do the autopsy until tomorrow afternoon. And they're having problems with their cooler. We've been asked to store him overnight. Arthur Parsons has a commercial chiller. Well-wrapped Harrison could spend the night there.'

'Artie won't be happy about that,' muttered Churchill, 'and neither will the town be when they find out. Most get their meat from Parson's Butcher.'

'He doesn't use that chiller now since the cool room was built on the back of the shop.'

'We'll still have to make sure he's wrapped well.'

Williams made careful measurements around the body and took photos from every possible angle before he pronounced himself satisfied. The two men rolled Harrison into a body bag, enclosing it in another to be sure. Before Williams pulled the zippers, he took one last look at the man who'd given him so much aggravation.

In death Douglas Harrison looked shrunken, almost vulnerable. The anger and malice so habitual to his expression was extinguished. His face was covered in mud, its handsome contours distorted by the wheel. Blood trickled from both nostrils, and ears, soaking his white shirt red.

Between the two men, they loaded the body into the back of the police 4WD just as the hovering storms delivered another heavy shower.

'Who needs refrigeration,' muttered Churchill. 'He'd stay fresh enough left out in this damn wind.'

Gusty southerly winds roared through the tall river red gums, the ancient trees swaying.

It was a ten-minute drive to the collection of small shops at the end of town. Puddles lay on the road from the heavy rain. In a matter of days the surrounding vegetation would spring back into life covering the dusty red soil with fresh green life.

In comparison the diesel engine in the William's police 4WD was silent. The V8's burble in Churchill's cherry red Mustang was no longer noticed by the locals, only visitors speculated about the car's owner. In William's experience, most men in their mid 40's who went out and bought a Mustang were suffering from an increased paunch and waning virility. Churchill fitted neither of those categories. Happily single he played the field with discretion and charm, arguing that a man had to spend his money on something.

Constable Williams parked in the vacant block behind the butcher shop knowing that town gossip would have already circulated the relevant information about his cargo. In any small community, the bigger the secret, the faster it spread. Speculation about the killer's identity was already the prime subject of gossip. No doubt tonight when he called into the pub for a beer, the town would already have weighed up the most likely suspects. It may even help narrow down the list that was currently as long as the bridge linking Colbrook to Gunbower Island.

The butcher shops burly owner opened the screen door and walked towards them.

'Good thing I rarely use the chiller.' He gestured towards the long black shape. 'Hate to contaminate a good load of meat with trash like that.'

'Dr Churchill and I will drive him to Whitworth tomorrow.'

'Never liked the prick much, dead or alive. He treated Lizzie real bad, and you did nothing to stop it.' His green eyes fixed firmly on Constable Williams face.

'Artie, my hands were tied. Lizzie wouldn't make it official.'

Artie snorted. 'Well someone's made it official now. He won't leak?' asked the butcher taking the other end.

'No, used two body bags.'

The chiller was a big silver painted box, the size of a small shipping container. At one end a door, at the other end a motor connected to overhead power lines powering the freezer unit. Artie closed the door, and reaching into a pocket attached two padlocks, pushing them shut.

'The slippery bastards wriggled out of lots of things over his miserable life. He won't get out of that,' said Artie, and patting the closed door, walked away.

'Do you want me to come with you to see Lizzie?' asked Churchill.

'No. Can you get the paperwork ready for the autopsy tomorrow?'

Churchill nodded and in minutes, the red Mustang was heading south towards his small surgery.

Both Alex and Lizzie had been born and bred in Whitworth. They'd gone through school together. Then Lizzie met Harrison, got pregnant at 16 and moved down to Colbrook, disowned by her parents. She lost the first baby, but by then she was married, and there was no divorce available for Catholics. The next baby came along ten months later. There were five kids. Joe and Johnny were the two oldest boys. Together they ran a timber cutting business. Katie, the youngest child was sixteen and away at a school camp. The two middle girls lived in Perth.

Williams crossed the bridge, the timbers rattling beneath the vehicle. Grass in the small park alongside the river was brown from the long drought. This year the seasons had been kind and the much-awaited winter rains had arrived. Farmers now had something to look forward to when spring arrived.

The gravel road was easy driving in dry weather, apart from the potholes. Rain turned the clay into a treacherous glassy surface and accidents were common. Despite protests and petitions to the council, the road remained unsealed. Distracted, he was driving faster than was wise in the conditions. As he turned the corner, the vehicle began to lose traction and he took his foot off the throttle letting it slow. He wondered whether the driver had deliberately chosen a rainy night to wash any blood from the vehicle and make his tyre tracks unreadable. His, Williams corrected himself. Lizzie was a competent bush driver. Whoever had been behind the wheel had remained in control. There'd been no wavering in the ruler straight marks. That suggested a high level of skill or an intimate familiarity with the island.

As Williams pulled up outside, the screen door opened, and Lizzie Harrison came out to meet him. She was wearing a grey dress, a clean checked apron tied around her waist. There was a touch of flour on one cheek and the smell of fresh scones in the air.

'Please come in,' she said ushering her guest inside.

Williams glanced around the small house. As usual, it was spotless.

On the crisply ironed tablecloth, clean cups, milk and sugar stood alongside the waiting teapot. In the background the kettle bubbled on the wood stove. All was prepared in the tradition of the best country hospitality.

Here, all the houses were built cheaply of tin, and wood that contracted and expanded in the heat making a characteristic 'bing bong' sound. Lizzie rented three hectares of land. Half adjoined the river, and was rich in alluvial silt that was washed over the heavy clay with each flood. The fields were productive. Any excess vegetables were sold to those in town who were less industrious or who didn't have the space or inclination to grow their own.

'The kettle has boiled. Pour the tea please Joe,'

He did as instructed and brought the tea tray with him into the front room. His face had the same structure as his father's, though the crinkles around his eyes were caused by laughter and squinting in the bright sunlight. There were deeper lines than Williams remembered. The freshly shaven cheeks were sunken, and the trousers loose.

His mother poured the tea. 'Do you have milk Constable?' she asked.

'No. Just black, thank you.' And accepted a buttered scone from the plate.

'Was it an accident?' Joe asked, his deep brown eyes looking carefully at Williams.

'It seems unlikely. I'll need to know where you both were last night.' He dabbed his fingers on the serviette, and reached into his pocket for his notebook.

'Lizzie?'

'I read for a while, and was in bed early. I woke up when it began to rain.'

'When was the last time you saw Douglas?'

'Wednesday afternoon. He'd taken a load of veggies into Kennedy's

Restaurant. He came back for a shower before he went out again. Wednesday night. There was always a poker game in town.'

'Joe?'

'I went out earlier, about 6 I guess. I'm not sure what time I got home, the clock in the truck is broken. The roads were wet, there'd been an inch or so by then, road was slippery.'

'And you saw no sign of your father?'

'No. There were still lights on in the pub so I guess he was having a few for the road.'

The conversation was stilted, and Williams caught an occasional glimpse of another emotion as they talked, but was unable to name it.

As he stood to take his leave, Lizzie had a question. 'When can I … we have the funeral?' she asked. He could see the shine of grief in her eyes and knew she would never cry in public. Tears were a private matter, to be shed behind a closed bedroom door.

'Depending on the autopsy results, I'd expect the body to be released by the weekend. Thursday next week? There may be some more questions later. Thank you for the tea, and the scones.'

As he got into the 4WD, he could hear an argument break out inside. He wound down the window, hearing Joe's angry words. 'The bastard doesn't deserve a decent send off. His body should be thrown out into the saltbush for the foxes and feral cats to eat.'

'No,' Lizzie's calm voice rang out clearly. 'Regardless, he was still your father.'

'Yeah, and I have to live with that.'

Williams turned on the ignition, wound up the window and headed home. Joe drove an old Bedford truck. He was an experienced bush driver and his hatred for his father was well known. His movements were unaccounted for around the time Harrison had died. His number rose up the list of suspects. A pensive Williams had his usual beer at the pub after dinner. As he walked into the pub, the chatter that had filled the room stilled. He drank his single beer feeling excluded, an intruder in a town and community he loved. Draining the glass, he left with relief, and behind the closing door the noise resumed. It was obvious that Harrison wasn't mourned, and if the identity of the driver was known, the information wouldn't be shared with the police.

*****

There was more rain overnight, and when Williams parked behind the butcher shop, there were puddles everywhere. Artie helped load the body and make sure it was secure.

'Glad to get rid of him. I wouldn't have been surprised to find the padlocks open and Dougie boy gone. Now to get this chiller clean before the Health Department close me down. I'll send you the bill,' he muttered and got to work.

In the distance the sound of a burbling V8 and a red Mustang pulled into the car park.

'You're almost too late James. Douglas and I are rearing to go.' Alex's wry comment.

'Ready when you are gentlemen,' Churchill muttered as he climbed into the passenger seat closing the door loudly and pulling on his seat belt.

The trip north was wet, with regular heavy showers. Puddles lay alongside the verge, wherever there was a shallow depression in the soil. A faint tinge of green was beginning to show on the sandy soil.

In the passenger seat sat an unusually quiet Dr Churchill.

Alex loved driving over this country. Seeing the road stretched out before him, with long sweeping curves. It was flat country, covered in blue grey saltbush, food for kangaroos and grazing sheep. Clumps of dwarf eucalypts were spread out so that each group got the moisture they needed and didn't compete with its neighbours. They'd been struggling for survival in the long drought, and were soaking up the welcome rainfall. With the arrival of spring, they'd send forth fragrant flowers to fill the air with the scent of honey and the buzz of bees. Despite the body in the back, and the silence of his friend, Alex found himself for the moment anyway, a largely contented man.

It was obvious that James had something on his mind, and Alex knew if he wanted to talk, he would.

They pulled into the hospital grounds and followed the road to the rear.

'Unconventional delivery,' commented the hospital orderly as Alex delivered his cargo.

'With your dodgy storage and the closure of Parker Brothers, we don't have many choices.' Parker Brothers had been the only funeral parlour servicing Colbrook and surrounds and was a surprising casualty of the long running drought.

The body bag was loaded onto a gurney and both men went to pull on disposable scrubs.

'Nice to see you James,' said a nurse her face lighting up when she saw the handsome doctor, 'The body bag, it's not that lovely young…'

'No,' his voice was sharper than a scalpel. A startled look crossed her face, and putting her head back, she stalked away down the long corridor.

'Before you jump to conclusions,' James tone was blunt 'It's a medical matter, and confidential.'

'Not if it relates to the murder investigation.'

'It doesn't. The pathologist is waiting,' said Churchill, leading the way followed by a thoughtful Alex.

The body lay on the stainless steel table, waiting. The tyre tracks formed a clear pattern over the waxy skin.

Soon the white tiled room echoed to the sounds of Def Leppard, making conversation difficult. As the CD finished, Alex spoke.

'Cause of death?' he asked.

'Take your choice. The initial impact appears to have been from the rear and had sufficient force to break ribs. The broken ends penetrated his heart and lungs causing massive internal bleeding. His skull and ribcage are both fractured in numerous places. Once would have been enough, but your killer wanted to be sure.'

Again Alex wondered who'd been behind the wheel.

In silence, the two men walked back to the vehicle.

It wasn't until they were halfway back to Colbrook that Alex spoke. 'Do you want to talk about it?'

'There's nothing to discuss. I've already told you that. And it's nothing to do with your investigation.' Churchill turned away to look out of the window, keeping his eyes focussed on the passing scenery.

*****

A week later the recent rains had vanished into the porous red soil. Winter was suddenly replaced by an unusually hot day and temperatures soared. Canny locals knew the respite would be brief but hoped the dramatic weather change would result in more rain. And a bumper crop. The bright sun bleached the sky blue, and the graveside mourners squinted in the glare.

Death notices in the local paper read:

Douglas Harrison; the result of an accident.

Close family and friends gathered around the open grave. John stood opposite his mother, looking uncomfortable in his Sunday suit. Lizzie had chosen to wear grey. A full circle skirt, nipped in by a thin black belt. Katie, her pale face impassive, leant for support on Joe's arm. There were flowers from the girls in Perth on the coffin. Joe stood motionless alongside his mother. Dr James Churchill joined the family at the graveside.

Under the dappled shade of a pink peppercorn tree, a watchful Alex Williams kept his distance. The heat was dry, but already his white uniform shirt was soaked with perspiration.

In the bright light of noon, the first shovels of earth thudded on the coffin, a wisp of dust rising from the grave. Lizzie waited until her daughter joined her. Joe and the two women walked away side by side, never looking back.

A dry wind blew around the gravestones, stirring the fine red loam. The grass verge was bleached white, dotted now with green weeds - always the first things to spring back to life. The city of the dead was surrounded by a picket fence dividing the living from the dead. Blue saltbush grew through the gaps, the only thing capable of surviving in the salt affected soil.

Colbrook was a tight knit community; the drought had increased the already high poverty levels. There was too much booze and violence, especially against the women. Maybe Lizzie had reached her limits, and fought back. He'd known Lizzie for decades. And wasn't convinced she'd have killed Douglas in such a calculating fashion. She'd chased Douglas around the island in anger to frighten rather than kill.

Alex watched as mourners got into vehicles to follow Bill back to the house. A puff of black smoke from the exhaust as the ancient motor started and the vehicle headed for the bridge. The procession took the roads at slow speed. The surface had dried into a series of deep corrugations. The truck groaned as it crossed the bridge as much from protest at hard usage as from age. It made no difference whether its cargo was human or a ton of timber cut by cross saw, and brought out from the nearby scrub.

Williams hadn't yet ruled out anyone. He'd made extensive inquiries and got nowhere. He knew one thing for sure - someone he knew was responsible for murder. But no one was talking. He could predict the Coroner's report: Walking home at night, under the influence of alcohol, Douglas Harrison had been accidentally hit by a truck and killed. The vehicle and driver were unknown.

Alex could speculate, but suspicions wouldn't stand up in court and he was too experienced to act without solid evidence. Increasingly, in a town where he'd felt at home, he felt more and more isolated. And now, he'd been asked not to attend the afternoon tea. James was taking Maggie. She'd baked a plate of jam drops, and a tuna casserole for the family later.

Maggie heard the Mustang pull up outside. She delivered a fleeting kiss on Alex's cheek and left with her large shopping basket in one hand.

James was a regular guest at Sunday night dinner's, but had excused himself citing mountains of paperwork to complete.

Alex didn't want to talk. Instead, he'd buried himself further into work trying to drown the voice that kept asking if his best friend was responsible for murder. It didn't matter what he did, the question kept circulating through his mind.

It was totally out of character for James to be rude to a woman - especially one so attractive. Alex's instincts had been stirred by the nurse's assumption that the body bag contained the remains of a lovely young woman. James was the best driver that Alex knew, he could drive anything with ease and the driver of the truck had been skilled. It was all circumstantial, but the deep feeling of unease remained. The loud silence in response to his questions about Harrison's death could only be the result of a collective decision to protect someone. So far, no one had cracked.

Churchill was an outsider, born in the city, and a resident in Colbrook for five years. It had been long enough for him to become well established, and regarded with a combination of affection and respect.

Yesterday, Alex received the file he'd been waiting for. It was on his desk, amidst a pile of other papers. He'd had no opportunity to open it, and had chosen to wait until the funeral. He'd known he'd be asked not to attend the funeral. Colbrook was on Lizzie's side, they didn't want Harrison's killer caught.

Making himself a mug of instant coffee, he walked into his office, and closed the door. The chair squeaked as he sat down. A sip of the scalding liquid and he opened the file. An hour later the coffee was cold, and his mind was racing.

He leant back, put his feet on the desk, and closed his eyes, letting the pieces come together.

A southerly gust of wind carried with it the burble of a V8 engine, and as it drew closer he put the file into the safe and walked from the office to the kitchen. He sat down to wait. The Mustang stopped in the street. He half expected it to drive off without James coming in for a cuppa. He heard both car doors open, then close, and the key in his own front door.

'Excuse me for a moment gentlemen, while I change my shoes. My feet are killing me.'

James hesitated at the kitchen door.

'Come in, the fire is warm,' Alex suggested.

James nodded and sat opposite.

'Tea or coffee?' Alex busied himself in the kitchen. The small space crowded with the conversation neither of them wanted to start.

Maggie returned, her formal footwear swapped for more comfortable ugg boots. 'I'd forgotten how uncomfortable those shoes are. A cup of tea please Love,' taking the chair in the middle.

For a long moment there was a silence, outside the wind grew stronger, and in the distance the rumble of thunder.

'More storms,' said Maggie. 'The grass is greening up beautifully on the Island, this will help.'

'How was the afternoon tea?' Alex asked, taking another mouthful of tea, the words in the file turning over in his mind. Unusually, he wasn't sure how to begin.

'It was a good turnout,' Maggie remarked.

'And a lot of support for Lizzie,' James added.

'And none for the copper who wants to arrest a killer. Regardless of Harrison being a bastard of the first order. He still had rights as a human being. Tell me what happened?'

Maggie drained her cup, and rested it on the table. Raising her green eyes to meet his, she looked steadily at him. 'And if I know something?'

'Murder is a crime,' his voice matter of fact.

'And the man I love would still be a policeman?'

He nodded. 'There is no clear evidence, no eye witnesses, nothing to make a case. I have a suspect list that includes most of Colbrook and Gunbower Island.'

Maggie reached out laying her hand on his arm. 'Then, let it go.'

'I can't Maggie Love. James, tell me?'

James Churchill put his shoulders back and began to speak. 'Do you remember when you went away for training earlier this year?'

Alex nodded.

'I was woken in the early hours of morning by someone banging on the door. I put the lights on and went to check. Sitting on the step was Katie, Lizzie's youngest, there was blood everywhere. I rang the ambulance and they raced her to hospital in Whitworth. The nurse remembered and recognised me.'

Alex could feel the story in the room, the building tension as the storm outside continued to grow.

'James?'

Churchill shook his head. 'It's confidential. I'd be breaching patient privacy if I gave you specifics. I can't. And won't.'

'Then tell me why you moved to Colbrook.'

White-faced, James stood. 'Thank you for the tea Maggie,' and began to walk towards the front door.

Maggie went after him. 'James, please,'

The two men stood at each end of the corridor, Maggie in between them.

'You've read the file?' Churchill asked.

Alex nodded.

'My father raped my sister. She panicked when she found out she was pregnant and tried to abort the baby. Instead she perforated her uterus, and when I found her she was dead in a pool of blood. He was arrested, charged, and died in jail. Everyone I worked with knew what had happened, everywhere I went there were memories of her. So I moved to Colbrook and met Douglas Harrison, a man just like my father.'

Alex looked steadily into Churchill's eyes. 'Did you kill Douglas Harrison?'

'No. But I'm not sorry he's dead.'

'Do you know who killed him?'

James was silent. His hand reached out for the doorknob.

'No. I don't know who killed him. You have no conclusive forensic evidence, no eyewitnesses, and an extensive suspect list. Alex, let this case be the one that got away.'

He opened the door, pulled it shut and walked outside into the storm.

*****

The island was dark, no streetlights, and no moon tonight. The stars were hidden beneath the clouds of the approaching storm. A bitumen road led to the bridge crossing the river and beyond that a single dirt road wrapped around the Island. Katie Harrison glanced in her rear vision mirror.

Her father knew the way home, drunk or sober. Time and repetition had trained his feet and he followed the path like a bloodhound.

Katie sat in the driver's seat of the old Bedford truck, waiting. Once, long ago, the truck had been a deep red colour. Time and rough driving had covered the vehicle with dents, and patches of rust.

It was ten thirty.

Overhead the storm came closer, the lightning flashes brighter and more frequent. She was motionless, her hand resting on the column gear change, foot resting near the throttle. Her ears listened to the sounds of the night while her deep-set brown eyes kept flickering to the rear vision mirror.

She'd made the decision. It was the only possible decision. Now she waited without anxiety or alarm, focussed on the task ahead.

Her focus was so intense that she didn't see the shadow moving towards her through the darkness. She heard nothing until the driver's door was hauled open.

'Shove over,' said Joe Harrison, standing on the road. 'Move.' The crack of command in his voice.

'Why?'

'Because you'll run the bloody truck off the road and get killed.'

'I don't care!' a spray of anger.

'Well I do. This heap of junk helps me earn a living.' A long pause, 'And if he survives?'

'He won't.' Her hands gripped the steering wheel tightly. 'Go home Joe.'

'No. Come on sis; move over into the passenger seat. We're running out of time. Please,' there was a pain-filled note of pleading she hadn't heard before. 'I know about Whitworth...' his eyes shone as he looked at her face. 'Move over.'

Reluctantly she released the wheel and slid into the passenger seat.

*****

Joe knew what Katie had planned. And he knew why. He'd made a decision. It was the only one possible. He'd sworn to look after those he loved.

A flash of lightning showed a weathered, lined face without movement, or emotion.

His sister's hand reached out to take his.

Behind them, another flash showed an unsteady figure crossing the bridge.

Death in the Driveway

Jesse Aaron

The black paint job and the polished chrome shot the rays of the sun back into my face the way a flashlight beam sticks you in the eyeballs in a dark room. The light left imprints on the inside of my eyelids, so that every time I blinked I would see the outline of the front grille over and over. Then the image gradually faded into oblivion.

It reminded me of my memories of all the cases I had worked. They started out as solid film reels of light, sound, and random facts. Then, as the years rolled on, they dissipated. First into vague blurry images, and then finally evaporating into wisps of forgotten dreams and interactions.

I was here because my current client had an odd request, and odd requests were my business. He was selling his car, and he wanted me to represent him with a possible buyer. He told me over the phone his name was Lester Bowles and explained that he was afraid to meet the buyer himself. He told me some crazy story about a friend of his who had tried to sell his car online and ended up without his head in a ditch.

Lester sounded genuinely scared on the phone, so I agreed to come and look at the car and to learn more about the request before I turned him down. It sounded like a straight muscle job, but there was something odd in his voice. I could not explain it, except to tell you that the little man that lives in my stomach called "instinct" kicked me in the ribs to remind me something smelled funny. But I needed the work and the money, and his offer was more than generous for a simple job like this.

Lester lived in a very nice suburb located about thirty miles from the city. The neighborhood had started out as a reasonable alternative to city life for working middle class commuters. The layout followed a simple formula. Every third house was the same style, and all the houses were situated on the same sized plot of land. Each house was just far enough away from the next one to give the appearance of affluent privacy without actually offering it.

As property values soared this area changed. It was now a haven for Tech. mavens and hedge fund managers from the city. Most of the houses had been altered to add more rooms or levels. Now most of these houses bulged out to the edges of their property lines as far as they could go. Many of them had the appearance of an overheated popcorn bag about to burst.

Lester's residence was no exception. It was a two-story box Colonial that was an even square all the way around, except for the right side, which had a two-room edition jutting out from the back. The house looked like it had a tumor growing out of the rear of the otherwise symmetrical design.

Lester must still be inside the house, but I didn't wait for him to begin my examination of the car. I realized right away she was a beauty. Nothing like the plastic garbage they churn out of every corner of the world today.

She had a square and long hood with round headlights buried in the front grill, and she looked mean from every angle. The front of the car looked hungry for the road, ready to chew up and swallow every mile while asking for more. She was the epitome of muscle car bulk and power.

I glanced inside and saw leather and chrome. The bucket seats were blood red, and they had the car's emblem on the top by the headrest. As I admired the car, I realized it was the same model my father had owned when I was a kid.

She was a different color, and had different seats, but I immediately recognized the same assertive rectangular aggressive shape. I shook my head slowly and whistled. The case was worth taking just for the possibility of driving this car.

She was polished so vigorously that I could see my wavy reflection in the front quarter panel. My dark slicked back hair and slightly hooked nose seemed to droop over my square chin. I straightened up unconsciously at the sight of my sagging reflection and my client appeared in front of me. He had moved so quickly and soundlessly that I jumped back when he greeted me. He seemed to appear out of thin air, as if he had been transported there by a magical beam of light.

"Hello, Mr. Burden, so glad to see you, you sure got here fast!"

Lester stuck out a thin and bony hand. His long fingers wrapped around my meaty palm, and it felt like I was shaking hands with a living skeleton. His handshake sent a silent shiver through me, and once again the little man named "instinct" kicked me in the guts.

There was also something vaguely familiar about him, but I as I quickly flipped through the yellowing rolodex cards that were my memory, I could not find a match. I ignored all this due to the infatuation and curiosity I felt flow through me for the car.

His bright blue eyes stabbed into me like two fire pokers. His hair was curly and neatly trimmed, falling just below the ears. He was thin and tall, wearing tightly pressed grey slacks with an immaculate bright blue short-sleeved polo shirt. To top off the look he had on brown loafers with matching socks. He wore thick brown rimmed glasses, and he exuded rich Tech. nerd.

"You can call me Sam. I know you told me over the phone, but can you go over it again? This is not the type of work I would normally take on, but you sounded pretty honest, and this car is a beauty so here I am. What is she, a sixty-seven?"

Lester smiled as he released my hand.

"You know your cars Sam. She is a sixty-seven alright. Now let me explain a little more about my request. You see, I need to sell this car. I'm relocating soon, and I love the car, but I am moving across country, and I can't rely on this car to get me there. It's not a very reliable daily driver. Also, these old cars don't have the features of the newer cars — you know, the heated seats, the trunk space, that kind of thing."

Lester leaned on the hood, and I could see the muscles in his arm stand out like metal wires as he flexed his hand.

"Long story short Sam, I don't want to deal with the buyer, and I don't completely trust him. He answered an ad online, and he could be anyone. Unfortunately, other than an auction, which I don't have time for — this is the only way to sell a classic car like this these days. For my peace of mind, and since I don't have the time, you would be doing me a big favor by taking this job and meeting with this guy. I can text you all the info."

Lester smiled, and his bright white teeth filled up his face. I stroked my chin slowly in contemplation.

"Well Lester, I might take this job. It sounds simple enough. First, I need to run your tag. Standard procedure in any case involving a car. I will also need to do a full examination of the vehicle. If I'm going to represent you on this, I need to know exactly what I'm dealing with."

Lester's plastic smile turned down slightly at the corners, and I could see a small tick lift the side of his lip.

"Slight problem there Sam. You see these old cars had a separate key for the ignition and the trunk and I seem to have lost the trunk key. I aim to have a locksmith replace the trunk key cylinder, but for today he will have to agree to the purchase without seeing inside the trunk. You can let him know we can put that in the contract if it makes him more comfortable. I'm flexible on the asking price."

I leaned back and looked at the rear profile of the car. The squared off triple taillights screamed power, and the dual exhausts poked out the back as a reminder of the speed she carried. She was built to move and there was nothing subtle about the form.

From front to back she projected a silent growl and a hunger for speed. It was almost as if the car was drooling for the open road. I was overwhelmed with the sheer beauty of the car. The lack of access to the trunk spooked me a little and sent off an alarm bell in my brain. I was about to say no when Lester leaned in a little closer and hooked me in with a throaty whisper...

"Take a look under the hood Sam. You've got to see this engine. It looks like it just came out of the factory."

Lester led me around to the front of the car. He popped the hood and when I saw what was underneath, my jaw practically fell off of my face. Lester wasn't kidding. The V-8 was immaculate. The engine was polished clean and shined in the sun, and she looked like she had just left the line in Detroit. As I unconsciously caressed the engine with my fingertips Lester's broad smile returned. He knew I was hooked. Damn the trunk not opening. Damn any doubts I had. I had to take a ride in this car.

"Alright Lester, I think I can work with you on this. Let me take some pics and run the tags."

I pulled out my phone and snapped some pictures of the license plate and the VIN number listed on the front window. For a moment I could see a slight twitch in Lester's face that made me feel uneasy, but then it was gone, and the mile wide smile was back.

"Sure Sam. Whatever you need."

Lester remained leaning on the hood while I tried to call my connection at the DMV. I quickly realized I had no service.

"Lester, do you mind if I go inside to use the landline? No service here…"

Lester stepped to the back of the car to let me pass.

"Sorry Sam, no landline. Service is really bad here. You should be able to make the call once you are on the road. This buyer is anxious to see the car. As soon as I email him from my laptop he can meet you there — he only lives ten minutes from the meetup spot. He is waiting for my call to meet you with the car at the address on this paper."

Lester handed me the paper and the keys. I recognized the address as a strip mall about ten miles from Lester's house. There was an old motel located across the street I worked a case on a couple of years ago.

"Alright Lester, I will take the car over there. We already negotiated my fee on the phone. You can pay me when I get back. I'm not going to lie, I can't wait to get behind the wheel."

Lester nodded at me and stood there smiling as I slowly and carefully backed the beast out of the driveway. As soon as I started her up, I knew I was in love. The exhaust had a deep and throaty rumble, and I felt the vibration run through my guts like the slow and steady shake of an earthquake.

As I drove in the direction of the meetup spot, I was in a trance.

Something in the back of my brain was still scratching at my memory and trying to wake me up about Lester and my recognition of his face.

I was mesmerized by the polished chrome, the ornate plastic, the overt ornamentation, and a severe wave of nostalgia. Driving with the windows down the smell of the spring air and the leather lulled me into a joyous trance. I could see my old man sitting right next to me, smiling and tapping his hand on the dashboard. I was so lost in the euphoria of this beautiful machine that I almost rear-ended another car at the next traffic light.

I jammed on the breaks and slid within inches of the rear bumper of the car in front of me. The driver flipped me the bird and I felt a bead of sweat roll down my forehead and into my eyes. Before I got to the next traffic light, I heard the whelp of a siren and saw the blue and red lights in my rear-view mirror.

I immediately pulled over and assumed the safest position possible, which was to place both of my hands on the top of the wheel in plain sight. I was on a case so of course I was carrying, but the gun was a small automatic tucked safely away under my sport coat on my left hip. Still, you never knew. The county cops were notorious for being jumpy. They liked to shoot first and then let the D.A. clean it up later. I knew some of them personally, but there were no guarantees, especially during a car stop.

I peeked out my side view mirror and immediately felt the nervous tension slowly bleed out of me. I recognized the hulking form of Officer Tom Polhouse before he was even up to my window. He spilled out of his uniform like a lion trapped in a cloth sack. He was still built like a linebacker, but the only thing he tackled now were donuts and six-packs.

We had worked together on many of my cases. Tom used to be in the Detective squad, but he pissed on the wrong politician and was bounced back to uniform. He was probably the only guy in the county police more cynical than I was, and this quality bonded us instantly when we first met seven years ago.

As soon as he saw I was the driver he seemed to lose some of the tension in his shoulders.

"Huh. Surprised it's you Burden. What are you doing in this fine automobile? I know you can't afford this kind of car on your meager gumshoe salary."

As he said this Tom leaned down and put his elbow on the edge of the driver's side door to get a better look at the interior.

"Yeah, sadly I have to agree with you on that. I'm going to meet a buyer for this baby for a client. He's some Tech. nerd that is too afraid to meet the person himself. He needed a little muscle to represent him."

As I said this, I flexed my bicep, and Tom let out a slow and steady laugh.

"You? Muscle? Has this guy actually seen you in person? Anyway, how much is he asking?"

"Actually, he hasn't texted me that part of the deal yet. All I've got is an address at some strip mall and the first name of his client, Joe. I don't normally walk this blindly into a deal for a client, but once I saw this car I had to drive it. I'm in love Tom. I might just stop at the jewelers to get her a ring."

Tom continued to smile. I could see the coffee stains on his large teeth and smell the cigarettes on his breath. He rubbed a hand through his salt and pepper crew cut and let it rest on his large square head for a few seconds as if he was thinking something over.

"You know what Sam, if this buyer does not come through, I might want to make an offer. My ex-wife can't collect alimony twice, and what the Hell, I always wanted one of these. What's another fifty points off my credit score?"

"Sure Tom. Let me text you the address."

Tom stood up and put his hand out.

"Don't need it, ran the tag when I started the car stop. You know why I stopped you? Dispatcher said we got some anonymous 911 call that a drunk was weaving in and out of traffic in a car fitting this description."

I scratched my head and squirmed in my seat. It didn't make any sense. I had not been on the road long enough for that type of call to be made. It could it have been the other driver that I almost rear-ended, but it seemed unlikely. It all seemed strange, but I was very glad it had been Tom who had handled the call.

Tom waved me off and I pulled out into traffic. I almost hit another car on my way to the strip mall as I was lost in thought. None of it made sense and every alarm bell was ringing in my brain, but for some reason I just could not put all the puzzle pieces together. They were still scattered in a big pile in the middle of the table, and the distraction of the car was not helping.

I pulled into the lot and waited for twenty minutes. No one showed. While I was waiting, I sent a text to Tom with the owner's address. My phone had lousy service, so the text showed it had failed to go through. I would have to try again when I was in a better service area. That is, if I remembered.

Something was not right. I didn't have enough to take it any farther, but I decided I had waited long enough for "Joe" to show.

Ten minutes later I was stopped at a light five minutes from Lester's house. My phone buzzed that I had a voicemail, but it was from a blocked number, so I decided to save it for later. It reminded to resend the text to Tom with Lester's address and this time it went through.

Minutes later I arrived at Lester's driveway. Before I got out of the car, I pulled up my pants and made sure my automatic was still in the holster. It was a nervous habit I developed when I was still a cop on patrol in the city. He was waiting by the front door to the house and waved me over.

I approached Lester slowly. His hands were at his sides, and he didn't look armed. The only thing I could see in his pocket was the outline of his cell phone and what looked like a billfold. Despite this, my mind was screaming at me to walk away. Something was kicking me in the back of my Swiss-cheese brain that this was not right.

I had to keep going to see what it was. I had the instinct to always keep pressing, to keep moving forward until I could solve the puzzle. It was probably what kept me going as a P.I., but it was also this same drive that got me into so many jams. I was on the scent of something, and I could not stop. The obsession would drive me to a solution or to my death. Either way, there was no other option for me.

Just as I got within arms-length of Lester it hit me like a right cross from a prize fighter. I remembered Lester's face. Then everything went black.

*****

The deafening sound of a screaming guitar woke me up. I realized I was wearing over the ear headphones and that was the source of the music. I had a foul taste in my mouth which was stuffed with a rag that tasted like an old moldy blanket. I was blindfolded and could only see a dim light at the edges of the cloth covering my eyes.

I thought I was going to vomit which might choke me, so I held it down. I tried to move my arms and legs, but I was tied down to something hard and strong. I was in a sitting position, so I guessed it was some kind of chair.

I tried to struggle, but the bindings were plastic and were secured tightly. I could feel the plastic digging into my wrists and ankles. I could also sense that my gun had been removed from the holster. The weight didn't feel right on that side of my body.

Suddenly, there was a blast of light that drove a splinter of pain into my skull. The headphones were removed and thankfully the screaming music stopped. The rag was pulled out of my mouth, and I felt like I could finally take a full breath. Everything was blurry but slowly I was able to focus.

I was in a basement of some kind. It was bare except for a boiler on the opposite corner and a small lamp a couple of feet to my right. For a few moments I felt the pure terror of being completely disoriented grip me by the spine, but slowly it came back to me who and where I was. I realized that I was probably still at Lester's house. As bad as the situation was, at least I had that much.

As my eyes adjusted and as everything came into focus, I could see Lester standing a few feet away from me, smiling at me with the same plastic grin he exhibited when he first showed me the car.

"Ahh, finally awake Sam. Good. You are going to enjoy this next part. Somehow you avoided my original plan which was to humiliate you and have you arrested for the girl in the trunk, but you managed to slither your way out of that one. Now I go to plan B.

I'm going to kill you Sam. I thought about just burying you alive, but I decided I wanted to chat with you first. You don't remember me, but I could not forget you and what you took from me. It's your own fault. You set this whole thing into motion. It's kind of funny when you think about it, no?"

He let out a long and slow giggle as he said this. I had to think for a minute but then I remembered the last thought I had before Lester knocked me out. I didn't feel any pain on my head so he must have sprayed me with something or stuck me with a needle to take me out.

After I got past that part, I remembered who he was. About eight years ago I served him with divorce papers. His wife had found some weird porn on his computer, and that, plus a lot of other things, had ended their marriage.

I racked my brain, and it came back to me that the Detective working the case had shared the order of protection with me before I served Lester. I now remembered that I had enjoyed serving him with the divorce papers. Most divorce cases are basically "he said, she said" affairs, but that case had been a little more.

Lester had been into some sick things. The wife found violent porn on his computer, and while there had been no proof he physically harmed her, all the evidence had suggested that Lester had been mentally and physically abusing her for several years.

I cursed myself for being so gullible. All the signs were there, but I had ignored them. I had been blinded by my lust for the car. I had committed the private Detective's carnal sin. I had let greed and my own infatuation with the past overrun my common sense and my gut instinct that the entire case was wrong from the start.

For some reason at that moment, I saw my dead father's face clearly, and he was shaking his head back and forth. He was disappointed in me. My father was a cop and detective for twenty-five years. He didn't say anything, and he didn't have to.

I knew that I screwed up. My father always told me that other people can make mistakes. Cops can't, because a mistake as a cop can cost you your life, or worse, the life of another person you are tasked with protecting. Lester had made a patsy out of me, and he knew it. I let the rage flow through me and spill out of my body. The only thing that could save me now would be the determination of pure fury.

I took a while to answer, first looking around and trying to measure everything around me as best I could. I had to take advantage of every small detail. I slowed my thoughts down and tried to focus. Whatever Lester drugged me with still left a thin veil of fog over me. I shook my head and tried to spit to the side to clear my brain, but my mouth was bone dry.

All I had was the dimension of the room and the placement of the lamp and the chair in relation to the wall and the stairs. There was a roll of tape on the floor behind Lester, and that was it. There was nothing in the room to help me, and I think Lester was enjoying watching me realize I had no way out of this.

"Yeah, I remember you, you were a twisted scumbag who I served for a divorce. Know what the sad part is? You were so insignificant that it took me all day to even remember who you were."

Lester smiled and giggled again. It made me shiver even though I was tied tightly to the chair.

"Oh, trying mind games Sam? Very nice try. But no worries, we have all night. I don't need to leave until tomorrow. Until then we can play. Do you know how many pain receptors there are on the human body Sam? I do. So does that dead bitch in the trunk of my car. I'm not going to tell you. I want it to be a surprise and you will probably lose count or pass out before you find out, but it's worth a try. I have faith in you, you can do it my friend!"

I glanced at the stairs again. They were only about fifteen feet, no, make that about twelve feet away, but it felt like miles. My freedom, my life, everything I was and could ever hope to be led up those stairs. I buried this despair and tried to remember one thing. Lester had made a sucker out of me, and no one makes a sucker out of Sam Burden.

"Now that I think about it, you were really pathetic. You had all of these fantasies and you couldn't even do anything about them except to your poor little wife. What was she, five feet tall? Look at you. My guess is you are six feet tall and at least two hundred pounds of muscle. You are the classic abuser. Always picking on the weak. Too afraid to go out in the real world and live your twisted fantasies so you take it all out on your poor little wife."

I could see Lester's lip begin to twitch. I had to keep pouring it on. It would either drive Lester to kill me quickly or create a series of events that might give me an opening to those stairs.

"Oh wait, now I remember. I looked at the drive on your computer. Really sick stuff Lester. You like the really perverted stuff too, don't you…"

Lester pulled his hand back and slapped me so hard the chair almost fell over. It hurt and I could taste the copper flavor of blood, but it told me I was making progress.

"You don't know anything about me. And you deserve this. If you hadn't served me those papers it all could have been fixed. We could have…eh, enough of this, time to be gagged again."

"Yeah, I could tell you were into that weird stuff the minute I…"

I could not finish as Lester jammed the rag back in my mouth. He reached behind him and pulled the tape from the floor and wrapped it around the gag.

"You know what Sam, I just changed my mind. I'm not going to take my time with you. Oh, you will still suffer, but I'm going to focus on more pain and less time. What the Hell, so I leave a couple hours earlier. One more thing before we get started. I want to you to know that for every kill I make it is your fault. I want you to die with the guilt of knowing that you could have stopped me but instead you took a ride in a car. You threw away your life and the lives of all the other women I will kill for a ten-minute joy ride. I hope it was worth it."

Suddenly I heard knocking at a door upstairs. I prayed it was the front door. Before the next knock Lester slapped the headphones back on my head and placed the blindfold back on my eyes, and I was back in the dark cave of terror that is complete sensory deprivation.

I counted to eight and then tried to remember the exact distance to the lamp and the wall behind me. During my brief view of the room, I had counted the steps to the lamp and the wall behind me.

The first thing I did was inch the chair back to the wall. Thankfully, the chair was not bolted to the floor. It was a cheap plastic chair, so it was light and easy to move. I was able to scoot it backwards enough until I felt it hit the wall.

Then I turned the chair slowly to the side so that I was now parallel to the wall. My next move was going to hurt but I had no choice. I smashed my head into the wall as hard as I could until the headphone began to come loose. First, I thought I could just smash it until the sound went out, but then I realized there was another way. I swiped my head against the wall just enough to get the headphones off one ear.

I let out a large grunt. Now at least I had one sense back. I could hear footsteps upstairs and voices. I tried to scream but the gag blocked all the sound, and it came out as a dull grunt. I inched the chair back the way I had come from. My only hope was to knock over the lamp and pray that whoever was upstairs would hear it. Of course, it could just be the Amazon driver or the mailman, in which case I was dead.

But I had to try. I slowly inched the chair back in what I thought was the direction of the lamp, but after what seemed like an eternity, I realized I was going the wrong way and had moved farther away from it, not closer. I realized this miscalculation might cost me everything. I took a deep breath and worked my way back the other way, one little skid at a time.

Sweat enveloped my body but I also realized that this was helping the blindfold to slide down. I moved my head up and down as I kept moving the chair across the room. Slowly, one centimeter at a time, the blindfold was coming down, and I was getting closer to what I hoped was the location of the lamp. Finally, the blindfold slipped down, and I could see I was right next to the lamp.

The voices had temporarily stopped. Was the visitor gone? I had to hope with everything I had that the person was still here. I pushed as hard as I could. The lamp swayed, first one way, then back towards me but it would not fall. I could feel silent tears streaming down my face. I was so close.

The voices resumed, a little louder now, more challenging. This gave me hope and one last surge of energy. I pushed out with every ounce of my being and the lamp finally tipped over and smashed. In a brief flash I saw my father's face. This time he was smiling with a nod of approval. It might be the last lucid thought I would ever have, but it made me feel that at least I had done everything I possibly could to try and redeem myself.

I heard a pause, then some yelling. Then I heard a struggle and several large thumps. Then silence. It seemed like hours, but seconds later the door opened and I heard the sound of feet coming down the stairs. I saw the black boots first, and then heard the squawk of the police radio. Just as Tom's square head came into view, I passed out again.

*****

Tom told me that five minutes later the first sector car showed up, and twenty minutes after that the first detective arrived on the scene. I waited in the back of an ambulance while they sorted it all out. A short while later I saw them wheel Lester's body to another ambulance and take him away. I watched as a uniform cuffed Lester's limp wrist to the gurney and got into the ambulance with him before they drove away.

A few minutes later Tom approached me with a metal flask in his hand.

He cocked his large crew cut at me with a look of deep concern.

"Hey Sam. Here, take a sip of this."

Tom placed the flask in my hand, and I drank down the burning liquid and felt it slowly seep into me and warm my body. I handed him back the flask and he stuck it in his back pocket.

I quickly explained how Lester had knocked me out and what had transpired in the basement prior to his arrival, and he nodded as if he already knew everything I was going to say.

"It makes sense. We found a body in the trunk of the muscle car. Young girl, fresh D.O.A. Body is not deceased more than about fifteen hours — multiple stab wounds. We think this guy is the highway hacker, serial killer, working the East coast. The girl in the trunk was at least victim number five, but there may be more that we never find. We knew this scumbag was out there for the last few months, but so far we kept it out of the papers.

We needed more on him. He kept switching cars and was changing his appearance for every kill. It's not your fault Sam. Even if you had his M.O. you never would have made him as the killer.

He was hacking into the social media accounts of the victims and using that information to lure them in. Inside the house we found some high-tech. stuff. Apparently, he was blocking the cell and wi-fi signals inside and around the house. Didn't want to take the chance any of his victims could make a call. We also found a high-end police scanner. Lucky for you I did not put my location out over the radio until after I knocked on the door. I wasn't sure what I had until I saw his face. Then I knew it was trouble.

Best guess is that he was going to try and frame you for the body in the car. We have not traced the call yet, but most likely the anonymous 911 DWI call was from him trying to frame you through a car stop. I ran his name, and it looks like he was served with some divorce papers and an order of protection by his ex-wife.

Based on what you told me he said to you in the basement he blames you for everything. The D.A. probably could have looked deeper into it back then and maybe collared Lester for assault, but you know how they work, churn um and burn em. Just close out as many cases as they can and too bad for the victims. If anyone is at fault here, it's the D.A., not you Sam. You were a good cop and everyone knows as a P.I. you can be trusted.

It also looks like he was ready to leave town in a hurry. We found another car parked inside the garage packed and ready to go. He was getting ready to make another move and change the hunting ground again to another city. We'll know more once we get crime scene down here and we interview him — if he wakes up that is. He made the mistake of trying to take out a former All-State high school linebacker."

Tom smiled at me as he said this and flexed his large arms.

"Thank God you texted me the address. After our car stop, I decided I wanted that car. I drove over to the address in the DMV computer. I figured I would wait for you to come back and make an offer. I quickly realized when I knocked on the door it was a phony. Then I got your text and flew right over here. Giving me that address and the noise you made saved your life Sam. I saw your car in the street and his car in the driveway. I knew something wasn't right, but the crash of the lamp gave me all that I needed to save you. Well, that and all those years I practiced with the tackling dummy."

I smiled and let out a small laugh which made my head hurt. Tom looked down at me and rested his hand very gently on my shoulder.

"I'll be down to the Hospital to check on you and take a statement later. Have a nice trip."

As Tom walked away, I shook my head. I still felt like an idiot. The sad part was I knew it would probably happen again. Maybe not with a car, but next time it could be a girl, or a friend, or something else that puts me into a trance and lets me forget who and what I was.

I felt like I had crossed a line and now I could never go back. I was on a one-way street to nowhere. I did not know if there was any way back. I looked to my father's image again for answers, but he had none. At least he was smiling at me. I smiled back. His image and my memory of his honesty and integrity had saved me. I nodded and whispered "Thanks dad" as a few tears slid down my chin.

I had narrowly avoided the end of my life, but it didn't feel that way. The sun was out, and I suddenly realized it was a beautiful day. I looked down at the bucolic setting of the suburban street and tried to pretend I was just relaxing on a nice spring day, with nothing to worry about except crab grass and the price of a gallon of gas. It didn't work.

The Plaster Caster
Scotch Rutherford
June 8, 1980

Angelo Maranzano stared down a sea of sprawling concrete. It was at least a couple thousand feet to the edge. Uneven and faded from the relentless L.A. sun, it ran parallel to a gnarled set of railroad tracks outside of a high stakewall topped with rolling razor wire. The sun was red-eyed and vengeful as it hung low in the sky, winking as speeding cars collided with it. Glowing fiberglass and sheet metal flashing up and down Normandie Ave.

They were inside Tony Capra's mirror-black '79 Seville on the edge of a deserted parking lot about the size of the one outside of Dodger Stadium. He was behind the bluish lens of a quasi-limo tint. The AC was stifling, and the calming rumble of a stand-up base, and the gentle rain of piano keys flowed through Hi-fi Sony speakers, as Tony Bennett sang one of Sinatra's songs. The music was low and couldn't compete with the baritone voices engaged in antagonistic discourse, which drowned out the sound of his gut crying out like a bullfrog being suffocated. His stomach clenched like a fist, relentless like a Charley Horse.

"Hey, you mind if I smoke?" Angelo said, stopping them in mid-conversation.

Dom Russo started to turn in his seat. They called him "Opti" — short for *The Optician* — because he'd given a guy a detached retina back in his Golden Gloves days. And they said it like he was some neighborhood savior. Like he was Marciano or some shit. When everybody with any sense knew Dom Russo wrapped his hands in plaster. That was how he won the gloves back in '61. Word is, the kid he sand-bagged hit like Duran. Plaster. To Angelo, Dom Russo would always be known as *The Plaster Caster*. Still a soldier and pushing 40.

The Plaster Caster was twisted all the way around in his seat. He had a foul look. And foul teeth. Not all his teeth, just the bottom ones. But still, when a guy makes it to the folding money, he should always get his teeth fixed. The way he sneered; the guy acted like Angelo was half a queer 'cause he'd never gotten his button. Like it was his fault they never opened up the books. "I just quit," he said.

Angelo met his glare with some intensity. "Then it won't be a shock to your system. An early meeting like this? With no breakfast? It's fuckin' with my stomach."

The Plaster Caster flashed a look at his cousin — the one that says 'can you believe this fuckin' guy?' His cousin, Giovanni had said about three words the entire drive. Overdressed in a raw silk suit. Satin shirt with an open collar, with a gold cross drowning in chest hair. Like he was playing a wise-guy on a film set. The guy talked a good game about being an actor and knowing Jimmy Caan and Bob DeNiro. Said he was in "The Godfather". Angelo never saw it. Too exploitive. But for Angelo's money, the guy never made it past Featured Extra. Did he think he looked tough in his gangster suit, chewing on a kitchen match in his mirrored aviators?

The Plaster Caster said, "Sure Ange. Crack the window."

Angelo tried the window. Finger-fucked the switch again. And again. Nothing.

Tony hit the switch up front and gave him six inches of open air.

"Where are we, anyway?" Angelo said.

"Torrance. It's a chemical plant." The Plaster Caster said.

"Saw a sign that said *Montrose*." Angelo took a drag.

"Yeah."

Angelo blew smoke. "They've been dumping DDT in the bay for over a decade."

"Yeah. Your cigarette smoke ain't gonna make this air any more toxic."

"Jesus Christ, Tony," Angelo said. "This guy brought us to Cancer Row, for fuck's sake."

"Relax, Ange." The Plaster Caster said. "If the smog don't kill ya, something else will. Trust me. I'm an authority."

Angelo watched as Tony handed The Plaster Caster a fat envelope. He'd told him not to. His brother-in-law might've had skills, but the guy was a savant. No common sense. Couldn't read a room. The feds flew him out here after he turned state's evidence back in Boston. One year later, he walks away from The Program. Starts earning again, but now he doesn't have to kick anything up. Starts making money hand over fist—all the while claiming he's keeping a low profile. Enter The Plaster Caster. He catches Tony in the act—living and breathing. But instead of putting him on ice, he squeezes out a vig. Then the bastard asks Tony for a favor. The Plaster Caster asks Tony for help feeding someone to the feds, of all things. So Tony delivers, and with a little help from me, Tony gets himself out of giving this parasite 5Gs a week. Then Tony up and calls him again. By now this bastard's got to figure whacking Tony is worth more to the old greaseballs than Tony's action.

"What's this?" The Plaster Caster said.

"Five Gs," Tony said.

The Plaster Caster cocked an eyebrow. "For what? Toldja we were square."

"For listening to my proposal," Tony said. "Remember?"

"The book thing?"

"Yeah," Tony said, pulling an immaculate manila file folder from a leather document holder wedged between the two front seats. "Here. Have a look. It's the synopsis. And the logline. There are some photos of me in there, too."

"I took those," Angelo said. But it fell on deaf ears.

"Fixer: The Tony Capra Story. The life and times of the greatest horse racing handicapper in history," The Plaster Caster quoted. "Very modest."

"I understand you know Neil Olsen," Tony said.

"You want Mario fuckin' Puzo to write your biography?"

"Hey," Tony said. "I had Sports Illustrated contact me. Listen, I'm gonna get some big writer to do the book and then I'm gonna be a star. Then they're gonna make it into a movie."

The Plaster Caster turned around and gave Giovanni a look. "Listen to this guy."

Angelo sucked in his last healthy drag. He never liked smoking a cigarette all the way down to the filter.

"Hey," Tony said. "You know movie producers, don't you?"

"Yeah," The Plaster Caster said. "I got a meeting with one this evening."

"No shit," Tony said. "Who with?"

"Jackson Steel," The Plaster Caster said.

Giovanni belted out a hearty laugh.

"The porno guy?" Tony said.

"Hey—beggars can't be choosers. You lookin' for somethin' for nothin'?"

Angelo didn't like where this was going. "Hey, do they make Sulphuric acid here?" He tossed his cigarette butt onto the pavement. "Tony, you can kill this window now."

The Plaster Caster shot Tony a look. Then he turned to Angelo, who really didn't like where this was going.

"I believe they do," The Plaster Caster said. "Acetone too. That's what you use to develop pictures, right?"

"That's right," Angelo said.

"You know, you're quite the photographer," The Plaster Caster said. "You know how to shoot."

He knew how to shoot pictures the pictures that saved Tony's ass. "I've got years of training," Angelo said. "Hey, stugots! I'm breathing in the fumes."

Finally, Tony flipped the switch and powered up the window. The guy was stuck in his own head, and never knew how close he came to dying.

"Sorry I couldn't give you a discount," Angelo said. "But you know. A guy's gotta earn."

"Right," The Plaster Caster said. "Money's like the sea to me—it ebbs and it flows. I get it back one way or another."

"As requested," Angelo said, handing The Plaster Caster an envelope. "The negatives."

"These all of them?"

"God as my witness," Angelo said.

There was a loud crack. Then everything went black.

Angelo couldn't feel anything. Couldn't move. But he could still hear. Everything was garbled. Faint and muffled. Like he was underwater. He couldn't understand why he wasn't gone.

*****

Angelo's brains looked like a side of meat loaf shot out of a leaf blower. All over the rear driver's side door. The window demolished. Crystalized shards of glass on the leather.

"Jesus Christ, Opti," Tony said. "I just had the interior cleaned."

Dominic "Opti" Russo gave his cousin a look. Giovanni's 9mm had twice the barrel length with the silencer. Smoke wafted from the ejection port. Giovanni pulled the cash envelope from Angelo's grip, and handed it to Opti.

"I tried to get your attention. But you had to roll the window back up. Maybe you'd rather you didn't have to worry about it," Opti said.

"That it?" Tony said. "You gonna whack me too?"

The word had come down from the boss on high. Tony had stood up in front of a grand jury and named names. He was supposed to be clipped on sight. They'd put the fat bastard in the program, but he'd walked away from the feds. Now he was back fixing races, making money hand over fist. Paying zero tribute. Fucker was swollen like a tick. Opti had been squeezing him. The fat fuck bled money. Then Ange comes along with his hand out, threatening to send pictures of him and Tony together to the underboss, back home.

Opti reached into his blazer.

"Oh Jesus," Tony said. The fat man trembled.

Opti's hand came out with a business card. He handed it to Tony. "Neil Olsen's number and address. Write to him. Drop my name. He knows better than to tear it up. Maybe we'll make a million bucks with this thing. Me as your agent."

"Hey thanks, Opti."

"Hey look," Opti said. "The old man is old. And you know, Howie Winter is probably going to die in the can. And the guy out front for Winter

Hill's a bigger rat than you are. And we both know it."

Opti nodded towards Tony, then turned around and nodded at Giovanni. Then he said to Tony, "I suggest using acetone. As an astringent. On that." Then he pushed open the door.

"So...Fifteen percent?" Tony said.

"More like fifty," Opti said. "A guy's gotta earn."

"Looks like you're doing okay," Tony said, chinning towards the pearl white Cadillac Eldorado parked next to them.

"I needed a new set of wheels. Recently acquired. Guy wrote me into his will at the last minute." Opti said. "Pull forward."

"What?"

"Pull forward," Opti said, gesturing towards the loading dock. Leaning into the passenger side door, he said "You didn't think I was going to leave you to clean up my mess, didja?" Opti pushed the door shut, and pointed at the deserted loading dock, about 500 feet ahead.

Tony pulled forward.

They were out of their cars outside the loading dock, when Opti told Tony "Grab his legs". The fat fuck had the nerve to look at him like it was a request.

"Opti, my sciatica..."

Tony was a real-life idiot savant. Six-four, and about four bills. Built like he could've been a linebacker for the Patriots when he was younger. But no athleticism. No fundamental knowledge of anything outside of fixing races. But it turns out he could take a hint. One shrewd look from Opti fixed his wagon.

Opti and Giovanni each took an arm, and the three of them carried Ange's dead weight up the ramp, through the yellowed plastic strip curtains and through the loading dock. No one else was there. Place was quiet, save the fall of their feet and the ruffling of their clothes. The soul-sucking yellow lights that buzzed like they were in a high school gym beat down on them like the sun. When they reached the open vat of acid, Tony stopped short, like a dog outside a veterinary clinic.

"Let's go Bluto," Opti said. "Just a few more paces."

"My back." Tony was shiny with sweat. Rings around his neck and arm pits, like he'd just sprinted five blocks.

"Okay, put him down," Opti said. Angelo only weighed a buck eighty-five at best, but that's a hell of a lot when it's dead weight.

The white bubbles danced in the coffin-shaped 500 gallon open faced Polyethylene tank, like Alka seltzer.

"You're in for a real treat," Opti said, chinning Giovanni. "Here," he said tossing him a pair of elbow-high chemical-resistant butyl gloves, and an apron.

"Ho," Giovanni said, sliding on the gloves. "All you can eat. Long John Silvers."

Opti turned to see Tony hoovering over the body. "Hey. Don't do that. Don't look a dead guy in the eyes. Bad luck."

"His eyes are still moving," Tony said.

"Involuntary reflexes," Opti said.

"Trust me," Giovanni said. "He took a 9MM slug to the head. He's gone."

"Now if it had been a twenty-two…" Giovanni said.

"Bounces around the skull," Opti said. "This one time…"

"JESUS." Tony said.

Opti and Giovanni spun around like their heads were on a swivel.

"I saw him move," Tony said.

"Oh Jesus fuckin' Christ," Giovanni said. "Want me to take his vitals?"

"Okay, enough. It's nerves. Left over. C'mon, let's get him up." Opti threw a pair of chemical-resistant gloves at Tony. "Put those on, fatso."

Tony slid his right hand into the inside pocket of Angelo's safari jacket, and fished out his wallet.

"Hey," Opti said. "That goes too."

"Just taking the cash," Tony said, pulling out the bills. "He's got a couple hundred here…" Tony slid the bills into the pocket of his Members Only jacket, then fell back on his ass.

Giovanni belted out a laugh.

"I saw him move!" Tony said.

"You're fuckin' robbin' the guy," Opti said. "What do you expect?"

"He fuckin' moved," Tony said, leaning over the body. "He…"

And sure as shit, Angelo's arms shot up, and wrapped both hands around Tony's fat neck. The fat man's face went from bright red to purple. His eyes rolled back to white like two spinning lottery balls.

"Holy shit," Opti said.

Angelo tried to speak, but his mouth and lips just wobbled, while his body shook.

Giovanni blasted him three more times in the head. Blood splattered Tony's face and neck, and all over the deck. Angelo's body went limp, but his hands never let go.

"Motherfucker," Giovanni said. "Fuckin' Night of the Living Dead."

"Now look at him," Opti said.

"I think I'm havin' a heart attack...You said it was bad luck..."

"Fuck that. Look at him," Opti said. "Take a good look."

The fat man took in the dead man's gaze.

"You owe me two Gs. Every week," Opti said.

"But you said free and clear..."

"Fuck that," Opti said. "Free and clear is what you're lookin' at. So take one more look at your brother-in-law. 'Cause he's about to disappear." Opti pried the cold dead hands from the fat man's neck. "Eventually your wife will stop asking. It'll be like he was never even here."

*****

For the rest of it, they moved silently as a funeral procession. They held the body up about nine inches above the acid. Opti nodded, and they all let go. The acid splashed up over the side of the polyethylene tank, seething a smoking ring into the deck's concrete. The acid backlash missed them all by an inch. Then Giovanni tossed in the 9mm, and the photo negatives. From several feet back, they watched the acid go to work. The boiling white fizz swelled. It had a maniacal crackle, bubbling higher, as its reaction swelled with violence. Piranha solution: Sulphuric acid mixed with hydrogen peroxide. Watching it go to work on a body was like watching a high-speed terminal car crash at 12 frames per second. When the piranha solution finally calmed, there was nothing left.

Always a Price to Pay

Billie Livingston

Every time she lays eyes on him, Mavis Garner gets an itch in the balls of her feet — an urge to drive the point of her high heel into his windpipe. Look at him. Strolling through the restaurant lounge, past the jazz quintet, grinning his bon mots to scribbling food and travel journalists, winking for cameras as he fingers the silver tastevin dangling from a chain on his neck. Ronan Peltier: *Master Sommelier,* pretentious son-of-a-bitch.

Standing next to Mavis is Gummy. She watches him take an hors d'oeuvre plate from a passing tray of lobster frittata. Gummy likes any kind of opening night — far as he's concerned, everything tastes better when it's on the house. He pops half the frittata into his mouth, head bobbing offbeat to the band's hipster rendition of *Fly Me to the Moon.*

Eyes back on the sommelier, Mavis says, "Like to punt that jackass to the moon."

Gummy says, "Peltier? Why's he get under your skin so bad?"

He's got to ask? This place is just the first — The Santa Monica location is set to open in a month. Santa Barbara, a few weeks later. They're talking hotels from Seattle to San Diego. It's the hottest ticket on the west coast hospitality scene. A monster score for Mavis if she can keep Mariposa on as wine supplier — move to the Spanish Riviera and Never Look Back kind of money. For now, she'd just be glad to keep her leaking ship afloat. Now they've gone and put a self-important prick like Peltier in charge, calling the shots.

Mavis says, "He's a spoiled little prince."

"You're describing half the city." Gummy turns his hound dog eyes back to the crowd. His gaze snags on a girl in a pair of faded boy-jeans. Fashionably shredded, half her derriere is showing. "Why would you go out Saturday night looking like a derelict? Think she did that to them herself?"

"They come that way," Mavis says. "Distressed."

"Distressed? They're in freakin' agony." He looks away. "Anyways, you didn't used to get so aggravated. Not from a guy like him."

Gummy is Frank Gumm, Mavis's business associate. Employee, strictly speaking. He's got a point. Ronan Peltier is a vainglorious, power-hungry bastard, but what's new. This is Hollywood. Bullshit is the price of admission.

Gummy mutters something she can't hear over the music. Mavis leans to him.

"I said, maybe you got a yen for him."

Mavis gives Gummy a groin-shriveling glance and turns back to the room just as Ronan Peltier stops a pretty young server. He plucks the shoulders of her tuxedo shirt and straightens the girl's bowtie. Gold cufflinks glitter on his bespoke black shirt. Whispering into her ear, he slides his thumbs up her slender neck.

"Heard his wife finally left him," Gummy says. "Hired some shark from Wasser and Abel."

"Can't imagine why."

Gummy signals the nearest waiter with a serving tray. "Let me get a little more of that lobster pie." He swaps his empty plate for a full one. "You need to make nice, darlin'"

"Don't worry your pretty head, Gummy."

Gummy's been Mavis's right hand going on 20 years now. Ever since she packed her bags and her son and came out to Los Angeles. Ever since Peter took off on her. No note, no phone call, no nothing. Gummy and Peter used to be pals in New York, back when they were just a couple of young punks looking for an edge. Some people take sides when there's a break-up. Gummy took hers.

She lifts one Manolo Blahnik off the bright Moroccan tile and rolls her ankle. Feeling the tingle of a stranger's gaze, she catches sight of a red-bearded guy running his eyes up the length of her. Striped t-shirt under a formal blazer — looks like a hairier version of the kid from the Harry Potter movies. Could be him for all she knows. The guy cocks an eyebrow and gives her a sly grin.

Too many ogling idiots this evening. Go play in the traffic.

She looks away, sizes up the crowd: An exclusive blend of fat cats from Brentwood and Rolling Hills, mingling with actors and models, a few pro athletes, and a dozen or so food journalists. And, of course, those God-forsaken *influencers*. 22-year-olds climbing on chairs, angling their phones to capture the perfect light on the perfect glass of wine.

The clink of spoon on crystal pierces the smooth stylings of the jazz band. The musicians quit and a man in a sherbet-colored silk suit steps up center stage, wireless mic in hand. With that white shirt of his, he looks like a big shiny Creamsicle.

"Good evening!" he says. "I'm Charlie Madison from the Madison-Chang Hospitality Group. Welcome to the Evolution!"

Opening his arms politician wide, he starts into his spiel. He talks comfort-of-kings. He talks voice-based and digital, it's all about you, and how about a personal valet? Then he looks up suddenly, as if calling to God. "Evolve?"

The convex dome in the ceiling shimmers with color, aims a sphere of light at the floor and then a ghostly 3D image appears. A man in what looks like a butler's uniform stands before Charlie Madison. The butler nods his head and says, "Yes, Mr. Madison."

"Evolve, would you close those curtains for me?"

The apparition turns and looks over the heads of the audience to the windows facing Wilshire Boulevard. He raises his diaphanous arms. As he brings them together the drapes are drawn.

"Evolve," Charlie Madison says. "Order me a glass of wine from room service."

"Of course, Mr. Madison. What kind of wine would you prefer?" The butler transforms to a 4-foot wine list suspended in the air.

"Can I see that list in Japanese?" The hologram letters become Japanese characters.

Charlie requests a female butler instead. "*Buona sera,*" he says and she answers in sultry Italian. "*Guten Abend*" Charlie says, and the butler switches to German.

The crowd gawps, awed and giddy with the spectacle.

Mavis stares. Sweet Jesus. She says, "I don't know if that's the coolest thing I've seen or the creepiest."

"Don't knock it," Gummy says. "Generation ADHD. They love this shit."

He's right, they're eating it up. And isn't it perfect, an illusion inside of an illusion: The very definition of L.A.

The spokesman changes gear now and says it's the people who make The Evolution truly special. He introduces the restaurant's celebrity chef with his Michelin Stars, his *James Beard Award* this and *Bon Appétit* that.

Gummy takes out his phone, thumbs through messages.

Mavis looks over. "Anything important?"

"Nah. Just Nikita Kozlov from Café Gotika. He wants to try out the new Burgundy. Says the foie gras is going to land in a couple days." He stuffs the phone back in his pocket. "By the way, you know about any underground poker games in town — Celeb stuff? Kozlov keeps asking me. Said I'd keep an ear out."

Mavis opens her purse. Kill for a cigarette right now. She glances toward the back doors that open onto a terrace decked with outdoor sofas and potted palms. Hell, you can't smoke *any*where anymore. Snaps the purse shut. "What does Kozlov want with poker?"

Gummy shrugs. "I told him your boy works in the movie business. Maybe knows some guys."

Her boy maybe knows some guys. Gummy doesn't know the half of it. At least he better not. Mavis's son screwing around in the underground poker scene — and she had to hear it from her damn lawyer. That's the thing with this city and its incestuous monoculture. Everybody knows someone who knows someone. But Greg's gambling is sure as hell not something a guy like Kozlov should know. That's all she needs.

Mavis says, "Niki Kozlov at a poker table with a bunch of preening actors. Quite a picture. Like a bulldog on skates."

Gummy licks his front teeth, wipes his mouth with a napkin. "You know, you've been back in town what, three months? Four? Mariposa went a little wobbly all that time you were swanning around in Europe. If you want to take this thing to the next level you gotta start showin' up, grease these connections."

Next level? Grease? Christ, if you'd told her a year ago that she'd be back at it — in L.A., trying to massage schmucks like Mr. Master Sommelier — she'd have said, fat fucking chance. And she'd have said it with a smile.

Ronan Peltier is up there now, mic in hand. He's talking wine — the dynamic list, energetic purveyors who will be his eyes and ears, prying out special wines, unusual bottles. He spots Mavis, raises his glass of red.

"Tonight's luxury offering is a Burgundy Grand Cru. *Michelle Chanton, Clos des Chanton 2015* comes to us from Mariposa Fine Foods." Swirling the wine, he takes an indulgent whiff. Sips, blinks. Frowning a moment, he holds the glass up to the light, brings it back to his nose and then sniffs again.

A few heads turn to Mavis, offer nervous smiles. She keeps her lips upturned. Insouciant.

"Shit." Gummy shifts his weight, mutters, "The hell's he doing?"

Ronan Peltier finds Mavis in the crowd again as he takes another swallow. He says, "This tastes like the beginning of a beautiful friendship."

Appreciative chuckles. Smattering of applause. Guests raise their glasses. Mavis smiles. Didn't realize she'd been holding her breath until she let it go.

Peltier grins to his audience. "Cheers, everyone — Enjoy!" He tosses his mic, pumps a fist at the bass player and the band strums into Steely Dan's *Show Biz Kids*.

Mavis watches Peltier swagger toward her. God almighty, that smug kisser of his. It's enough to make you buy a gun.

"Play nice," Gummy says. "But keep your elbows up."

"Mavis!" Ronan Peltier calls.

Gummy drifts off toward a tray of Kobe beef.

Peltier moves in close. They exchange an obligatory peck on either cheek. "Mavis Garner, my oh my." He takes her hands and makes a show of giving her the once-over before he pivots and stands shoulder to shoulder with her. He surveys the room as he continues. "Classy lady. Not like some of these girls who need to show every inch."

"Thank you, Ronan. High praise from you." Mavis nods to a familiar face from the LA Times.

Peltier smiles. "I've got a suite here at the hotel, you know. Jacuzzi. Bubble Bath. I'll bet you look good in bubbles."

Mavis regards him. At 38, he's nearly a decade younger than she. Nice head of hair. Trim. Truth be told, Ronan Peltier is a good-looking man. All that bravado, it's tempting to see what he's got under the hood. Of course, a guy like him is all about the chase. She looks at her watch. "Delightful as that sounds...."

He chuckles, keeps his eyes on the room. "The thing about people in glass houses, they kinda *have* to answer the door."

"Is that a fact, Ronan?" She glances at his glass. "How many of those have you had?"

He turns his head, gives her a sober look. "Do you know the hardest part about earning the title of Master Sommelier?"

This ought to be rich. She says nothing.

"Knowing what's in the bottle." He taps the side of his nose. "Most people fail that part of the exam, have to take it over and over. Not me. I'm what they call a supertaster. And this wine of yours...?" Without moving his eyes from hers, he sips. Smacks his lips. "It's not a bad fake. In fact, it's a damn good one. Probably 99% of people would believe this is a Grand Cru."

Her eyes are still. Reading, deciphering. Is this a threat? Some kind of power play? "What's on the label is what's in the bottle." She gives him a sympathetic smile. "Perhaps you've got a cold coming on."

"Mavis, Mavis...What are we going to do with you?" He gives his head a slow deliberate shake and peers into her eyes. "Come on upstairs. We'll talk."

Come on upstairs? Really. And if you tell him to get stuffed? What's he going to do? Expose you? Threaten to have one of your bottles analyzed? He could. You know he could.

Mavis brings a hand to Peltier's chest, gently lifts the tastevin hanging from his neck. "If I didn't know better, Ronan, I'd think you were trying to extort a little sugar."

He looks down, watches her hold the shallow tasting cup in her palm and trace a finger over the bright dimpled surface.

"Not that I don't find you attractive..." She lets the tastevin go and looks at him. "It's just that this town is full of gossips. A woman in business — I've got to maintain a level of decorum."

Maintain decorum. Maintain decorum. *Son-of-a-bitch.*

Peltier smiles. "I'm nothing if not discreet." Then, as if bidding her goodnight, he shakes her hand. She feels the hard edge of a key card against her palm. He lingers at her ear and murmurs, "Room 1401. I'd love to see things work out for both of us."

*****

Five minutes later, Mavis stands outside the door of Suite 1401, looking from the key card in her left hand to her car keys in the right.

Her heart is detonating small angry bombs against her breast plate. Her brain is pulling taffy: *You have to do this. You don't have to do this. Get in there. Get out of here.* And if she doesn't make this go away? Then what? This self-serving dirtbag is the only thing standing between her and living the sweet life again. Maybe it won't be like it was, but at least she could get herself out of this city.

Gummy's voice scrapes the inside of her skull: *You need to make nice, darlin'.* Glancing down the hall, she takes a breath, exhales slowly. Let's get this over with. She slides the key card into the lock, hears the snick of release, and opens the door.

He's already here. In the center of the room, the silhouette of Ronan Peltier stands facing the last rays of the evening sun. Mavis can hear birdsong and one of the city's ubiquitous police helicopters in the distance. The sound of the outdoors is disorienting — as if they're on a rooftop. Then she realizes that the far side of the room is almost completely gone. Its massive sliding glass doors currently tucked inside the walls, the suite yawns onto a terrace with a private pool.

Cell phone to his ear, Pelletier glances over his shoulder. He raises a finger to signal Mavis's silence. "I know," he says into the phone. "This is something I'm keenly aware of." He smiles at her and points to the chrome and black lacquered bar festooned with wine and spirits, glassware and snacks. Peltier gestures that he'll be one minute. He steps out onto the terrace, moves beyond the sun beds to the balcony railing.

Mavis runs her eyes around the open-concept suite. The walls are pale grey slate, the floor black granite. The room itself is D-shaped, everything orbiting that open wall. Mavis walks deeper into the room and the sound of her heels reverberates. In the kitchen area, the granite-top island sports a bottle of the *Michelle Chanton, Clos des Chanton 2015* that Mariposa supplied. He's making a spectacle of it. She sucks her teeth.

A short stroll from the kitchen is a king size bed, its creamy goose down duvet dappled with light from the pool. She looks into her hand at her keys again, the little black fob calling to her. She takes a breath and exhales. Setting the keys on the nightstand she takes her phone from her purse.

*****

A few minutes later, Ronan Peltier comes in from the terrace and sees the violin shape of a woman perched on a stool at the kitchen island. Mavis Garner. Jesus, look at her…Legs like a showgirl and a mind like a steel trap. "Apologies. My lawyer. He's got terrible timing."

"Don't they all." She eyes him over her shoulder.

"Honestly," he says, "I'm a little surprised that you came."

"Somehow I doubt that."

"You're right. I'm not really." He grins and heads for the kitchen. "Glass of wine?"

She eyes the Burgundy in front of her. "Why not?"

Peltier reaches into his pocket as he walks, pulls out a black, waiters corkscrew. He picks up the bottle. Pausing to study the label, he chuckles softly, then puts corkscrew to bottle and in a single fluid motion, pops the cork. He reaches down to a lower shelf, brings up two big-bowled goblets, and sets them on the counter. "*Clos des Chanton*," he says. With smirking skepticism, he adds, "2015?"

Mavis undoes her jacket and sets a hand on her hip. "That's right."

Pouring a half inch into one glass, Peltier picks it up and swirls. The red liquid rises and falls. He eyes the rivulets as they slide down the inside of the glass. "Nice legs," he says. "Not unlike yourself." He pushes his nose deep into the glass, inhales, and then lowers it. "Ripe cherries, ripe strawberries, some blueberry, and some strong spiciness." Eyeing her over the rim, he says, "A little too strong for *Clos des Chanton*." He sips. "The cherries give a mildly sour impression, medium tannin, minty mineral impression, but again, there's that spice." With a *tsk*, he picks up the bottle again, fills Mavis's glass and then his own. Moving in close, he puts the second glass in her hand.

Ronan Peltier drops his voice to a conspiratorial murmur. "Someone once said that drinking wine is like using magic: there's always a price to pay." He touches his glass to hers and then takes a sip. A moment passes. "I would love to work with you, Mavis. But…this is a huge contract. It's a lot of team work. A lot of hustle. I don't know if you're a team player."

She can smell the wine on his breath, his *Sauvage* cologne.

His eyes drift over her face, her hair. "You know that I'm renowned for my palate. My taste. That's why I'm here. Directing the show. A word from me can make or break someone."

Mavis gives him a long silent look. Finally, she says, "Are you finished?" She sets her glass down. "You don't have to threaten me, Ronan. I'm not a girl, I'm a woman. I came up here because I was intrigued." Her tone is amiable, but disappointed as she continues. "I thought you were a little brash, sure. But smart and *very* attractive. A man who wasn't afraid to say what he wanted. And here you are playing kids' games." Plucking her phone from inside her blazer, she checks the time. She sighs, looks around for her keys, spots them and heads for the night stand.

Behind her Ronan blinks hard. His jaw clenches in tandem with his groin. He sets his glass down too fast and it tips, smashes against the stone counter. Lurching after Mavis, he grabs hold of her elbow. She pivots and shoots him a hard look.

For a split second he thinks she's about to throw a punch. He grips her face between his hands and opens his mouth on hers in a hungry kiss. Mavis takes his lower lip between her teeth, a light bite, and then gives him a gentle shove toward the bed. She sets her phone on the nightstand with the keys. Reaching for her ankle, she eases off one high heel.

"Leave them on," he says. "I love your legs."

"You do, do you?" She slides her hand slowly back up her calf.

"Christ," he says. "Do you know how sexy you are? You do, don't you. Say it."

Standing in front of him, her lip curls into a smile. She raises one foot and sets the toe of her black pump on his crotch. "*You* say it."

"You are so damn hot."

She leans, plants her shoe. "What else?"

He gasps, wraps both hands around her calf. "I want to lick every part of you. Spread those long legs of yours and pound you till you scream."

"Good boy." She lifts her shoe. "Lie down."

Peltier licks his lips, kicks off his shoes and drops into the pillows.

Kneeling on the bed, she tugs her skirt up enough to straddle him. She undoes the first button of her shirt. Then another. "You like that?"

"I love it." He slowly bucks his hips. "You feel how much?"

"I do. You're not a good boy at all. You're a bad boy." She undoes another button.

"Yes. I am. Bad. Just like you." Looking into her open shirt, her lacy blue bra, his eyes spark like an arsonist with a match. "You and me, if we teamed up, we could own this town."

"We could." She traces a fingertip across the bow of his lip. "But you've got a lot on your plate right now."

"What? My bitch wife? Ex-wife. She thinks she's going to bleed me. Two words: shell company."

A throaty laugh from Mavis. "I knew you were smart."

"Damn right. I've got a little surprise for her." His breath coming fast now, he puts both hands on the cups of her bra and kneads her breasts.

He pulls the fabric aside, sits up and latches onto her nipple.

Skirt riding up her hips now, Mavis looks down at Ronan Peltier's mouth, suckling, like a big famished baby. "Okay, that'll do." Palm to his forehead, she pulls back and her nipple pops from his mouth like a cork from a bottle.

Ronan falls back on the pillow and pants expectantly. As if she's going to be strict again. Make him beg for it. Mavis climbs off him, grabs her phone and keys as she goes. Tugging her skirt down, she starts buttoning her shirt.

"What're you doing?" he blurts. "Where you—"

"That's enough," she says and waggles her keychain at him. The fob in particular. "Nanny cam. Make 'em small, don't they? Your wife's going to love this."

Ronan launches off the bed as if he means to break the camera first and then her neck.

"Sit!" Mavis commands, firm as a dog-trainer. "It's *gone*. Straight to the cloud. Try to squeeze me and I'll send our little movie to her lawyer."

"Try it." He sinks onto the bed, eyes red and panicked. "I will wreck you."

"*Don't* threaten me, Ronan. You have no idea who you're dealing with. If I tell certain people about this threat of yours? It won't be just a video that goes to your wife. It'll be your balls in a doggie bag."

Her face is hard, eyes like straight-razors. He believes her.

Mavis smiles. "You really do have a little surprise for her." She turns and strides to the door.

*****

Gummy scans the lounge. He looks at his watch. Crowd's thinned a little since the speeches finished, but he can't see Mavis. Just a bunch of barely legal females mooching free booze, and trolling for movie stars. That prick Peltier has disappeared too. Guy had a cocky look in his eye when he was making for Mavis. Like a cop who'd found an ounce in the glove compartment.

That's all she needs right now. Peltier shaking her down. Mavis has no patience these days. She's not the same since she came back to Los

78

Angeles.

Gummy checks his phone. Nothing. He heads for the door to the hotel lobby, looks up and down the hall. An elevator dings. The doors open: Mavis with her compact out, putting on her lipstick. She snaps her purse shut, smooths her hair and steps out to the cool marble floor.

"Hey," Gummy walks toward her, checking for some kind of tell, like she's been in Peltier's room. Not like it's his business, but the thought of it doesn't feel so good. "All right?"

"Fine." She heads for the doors, shoes tapping the floor like sticks on a hi-hat.

"Where were you?"

She hands him her keys. "You mind driving?"

"Sure." Gummy takes them, peers at the black and silver fob. "What's this thing?"

"A good luck charm." Eyes forward, Mavis strolls through the parting glass doors and walks into the night.

*****

Pulling onto Wilshire Boulevard, Gummy glances over at her. In this light, Mavis still looks the same to him. Like when she first came out from New York. He had a thing for her back then. Not a lot of guys would take on a woman with a kid. He thought she might go for it, him as her white knight. Nope. Not interested. Kinda hurt actually. Forget it. He got over it.

He keeps his tone light, says, "So, where'd you disappear to? You never said."

She doesn't answer. Mind elsewhere.

Gummy watches the road, the hard red of brake lights. "Seemed like you and Peltier had words there. Like maybe he was grilling you about the product. You go up to his room?"

Mavis sighs. "Gummy, if you're finished with the interrogation, I'd like to rest my eyes."

He looks over. Her eyes closed, a tiny smile on her lips. Head back, those cheekbones of hers high as a queen, neon lights through the windshield painting her red and blue and gold.

The Ferrari

Robert Petyo

The fiery red Ferrari blared its horn as it passed me on Highway 315.

I had always wanted one but considered them too expensive. Olivia used to tease me about that. "Live your life," she said.

She was driving a red Ferrari the last time I saw her, racing with the top down, her hair blowing in the wind. She just bought it and clearly wanted to let me know how she was thriving after our breakup, living an active exciting life. That was five years ago, before she died, ending all my hopes of a reconciliation and starting my dismal downward spiral.

As I recalled our happy times together, my boxy sedan drifted into the passing lane. Another horn snagged my attention and I focused on the road.

Live in the present. Olivia was gone, dead in her Ferrari halfway down the side of Back Mountain. Our relationship was even longer dead. Our last year together before the split had been agony.

But I never stopped hoping that we would get back together. I loved her. And the hope of remaking our future together kept me going, fighting the booze and the drugs.

Then she died.

Sighing, I took the Drinker Street exit and looped around to a red stoplight. Just as the light changed, a red Ferrari shot past me in the left turning lane. Frozen, I watched it speed up Drinker Street, until the car behind me tooted to urge me through the intersection.

Get yourself together, I thought.

But it had to be the same car.

How many red Ferraris did you see in this backward town?

And if I kept seeing a red Ferrari, kept reviving the sad memories of lost love and lost opportunities, I was going to flip out.

I tried to focus on the road. Maybe I should stop at Harvey's for a drink. That always soothed me. I was almost to the entrance to the mall parking lot when I saw the Ferrari coming up in my mirror.

What was going on? Why had it looped around behind me?

This time, as the Ferrari passed me, I got a good look. The top was down and the woman behind the wheel wore sunglasses. Her dark red hair flowed in the breeze. She screeched in front of me and turned left, heading back to 315. I followed. There was no one else in the car with her, and she seemed to suddenly slow down to allow me to follow.

She was playing with me, trying to get my attention, flirting with me. Was it someone who knew the special affect a red Ferrari would have on me?

And the red hair.

Olivia had long red hair.

I wished I had gotten a good look at the driver's face, but the large glasses were like a mask.

I held a breath.

Olivia loved wearing sunglasses. She thought they added mystery to her appearance.

She started pulling away again on 315 and I sped up. Still, she was far ahead of me when she swerved into the industrial park entrance. When I got there, I went down the ramp and drove onto the main street that sliced through the rows of factories and warehouses. I caught a glimpse of the Ferrari swinging into one of the lots. I pulled into that lot, Hartman Printing where I used to work. The last I knew, Olivia's father ran the place, but that was years ago. I didn't kept track of her family after the breakup, and certainly not after the crash.

Again, I held a breath. The red Ferrari had pulled into the lot owned by Olivia's father. The sad coincidences began to overwhelm me.

I needed a drink.

There was no sign of her car, but I knew she had pulled in here. She must have driven straight through to the back exit.

I pulled closer to the Hartman building. It was second shift, past six o'clock, the quieter shift that I had worked, and the lot was only half full. I parked near a black Mazda and took a few deep breaths. I had enjoyed working here, but as my relationship with Olivia Hartman soured, the bosses here started making things tough for me. Then, Hartman fired me. Just like that. No explanation.

But none was needed.

As I sat in my car, the back door of the plant opened. I waited, the car rumbling softly, until I could see that it was a thin man wearing a hooded vinyl jacket. I rolled down my window as the man suddenly veered left across the lot. "Bobby," I called.

He stopped and looked around, uncertain where the voice had come from.

I called him again.

Holding the small backpack in front of him like a shield, he took a few reluctant steps toward my car.

"It's me. Joe."

His pace quickened. "Joe? What the heck are you doing here?" He reached the car and bent toward the open window.

"Just passing through, my man. How's it hanging?"

"I'm doing okay."

"You just getting out?"

"A little OT." Suddenly, he straightened and looked around the lot as if checking for security cameras.

"What's wrong?" I asked.

"Let's go somewhere else to talk."

"Hartman still run this place?"

"Yeah."

"Meet me at Harvey's Sports Bar," I shouted as Bobby jogged toward another car. I shifted into gear and left the parking lot.

When Olivia's father fired me, he made it clear that I wasn't welcome on the premises. He had no legal reason to bar me, but it was his company, his plant, and his world to do whatever he wanted.

And Olivia was his precious daughter.

But I had never harmed her. Our breakup was mutual. Money, and that one drunken mistake I had made.

That had been years ago.

When I parked in the large lot for Harvey's Sports Bar, I saw the red Ferrari, its top up, parked just off the road, far from any other cars as if unwilling to mix with the common people. I got out and took a few steps toward it until I could confirm there was no one inside. I looked toward the bar. Had the redhead stopped for a drink? A coincidence? Or did she know this was my favorite place? Had she seen me here before?

She had to be flirting.

For five years I had been bemoaning lost opportunities with Olivia. Her death had dashed my hopes. There was no one in my life. Just booze and drugs. There never would be another Olivia.

But that woman was flirting with me.

With a fantasy that, perhaps, my life might be about to improve, I strode into Harvey's.

It was a large place, but the enormous screens and the overpowering noise made it seemed cramped. The square bar, each side topped with two overhead screens, was in the center, and a single row of tables lined the exterior walls. A quick check of the place didn't show a redheaded woman so I moved to the bar, seeking a spot that would allow me to see the main entrance and watch for Bobby. I climbed up on a stool near one of the corners and ordered a beer when Zack, one of the young bar tenders, waved.

I told Zack I would be running a tab and watched the front entrance.

Bobby grinned as he strode toward me. "I haven't been here in ages," he said.

I pointed at him and gestured toward Zack, before setting a twenty on the counter to indicate that whatever he ordered was on me.

"Thanks." Bobby squeezed onto the stool next to me. "So, what were you doing at Hartman's?"

The urgency in his tone surprised me. "Just passing by."

He stared up at the screen. "You know, I really shouldn't be talking to you." He accepted the beer from Zack and raised it in a slight toast before gulping down half the glass.

"Oh, come on, Bobby. I'm not contagious. It's been years since I was fired. Besides, you can talk to whoever you want to. Hartman doesn't control your life."

"That's where you're wrong. It's Hartman's world. He can do whatever he wants. Fire whoever he wants. He blames you for what happened to Olivia."

"That's crazy." That one hurt. I had never been able to banish the thought that if we had stayed together, Olivia might still be alive. Without me, she started living a wilder life, buying an expensive car, taking chances. Crazy, but I couldn't shake the guilt. And hearing that Hartman felt the same way didn't help. "Do you really think he would fire you for talking to me?"

He ran a finger along the rim of his glass before lifting it. "Let's just say I don't want to find out."

To prevent snapping at him, I looked away. "I had nothing to do with the accident that killed Olivia."

"Some people think it wasn't an accident."

"What?" I had heard those rumors but had quashed them. I didn't want to rehash old torturous memories. Bobby should know that. Bobby had been close to Olivia, too. They even dated a few times after we broke up.

"I still see her," Bobby said softly as he gazed over the bar.

"What?"

"She haunts me. I see her everywhere. At the plant. In the parking lot. At my house." He snapped his head toward me. "It's like her ghost is haunting me. Blaming me."

"Blaming you for what?"

Bobby's eyes widened as he looked past my shoulder.

I turned and saw the redhead standing near a table about ten feet away. She wore a tight sweater and white slacks that ended about a foot above her spiked heels revealing bronze skin on her shins. I slid off my stool, and so did Bobby.

The redhead staring at Bobby. Her sunglasses were in one hand. I fixated on those wide spaced eyes.

Impossible.

But it was Olivia.

I was seeing things. Olivia's Ferrari missed a turn and went through a barrier on Back Mountain Road, bursting into flames as it tumbled down the side of the cliff. Yet, here she was. Could this woman be a twin?

No. Olivia had no siblings.

A cousin perhaps?

At the sound of a shout behind me, I turned to see Bobby running from the bar. As I watched, the redhead rushed past me, chasing him out the door.

What was going on? I followed the procession and got outside in time to see Bobby getting into his car. The redhead stood with her hands on her hips as she watched him start the engine, but she didn't approach him, didn't call him.

"Excuse me," I said.

She didn't react as she watched Bobby screech out of the parking lot.

I moved up behind her. "Miss?"

She whirled and her hair flopped around, almost striking me in the face. She had pencil thin eyebrows and thick red lips.

Again, I felt a sledge hammer in my chest. Just like Olivia. But it couldn't be Olivia. "My name is Joe," I whispered.

She seemed to be debating her response before finally saying, "I know."

"You do?"

"I know your name. Don't you recognize me? I'm Olivia." She paused. "Your one true love."

"Huh?"

"At least, that's what you used to tell me. Before we learned the truth about each other."

The truth? I made one mistake. That's all. For several seconds my mouth hung open. It was Olivia's sexy voice. Slightly husky. "Olivia." I couldn't say anything else.

She turned away. "I have to go."

"I don't know who you are, lady, but why are you doing this? Why are you following me?"

That brought her back around and her moist lips parted in a half smile, half sneer. "I'm not following you." She accented the last word.

"So, all those times I saw your car? That was just a coincidence?"

"Yes." Her eyes came alive. "I mean, no." She pointed in the direction Bobby had gone. "I wasn't following you. I was trying to get you to hook up with Bobby. He's the guy you have to deal with."

"Why Bobby?"

"Because he killed me."

It was a punch to the heart. I reached for her arm, but somehow, she eluded my grasp. I stumbled forward but kept on my feet. "What did you say?" My words were weak, barely audible. I wanted to repeat them. I wanted to ask more questions. But I couldn't speak.

"He killed me," Olivia said. "And he has to pay for that. It's been a long time. I need your help."

"No." It was a loud chirp.

She ran toward the Ferrari. "I have to see Bobby."

"Don't go." I jerked a few steps toward her, still struggling to keep my balance, before stopping and changing direction, heading toward my car. But I was too late. She was out of the lot by the time I got my car started. I'd never be able to catch her.

But she said she was looking for Bobby. I knew where he lived, at least where he had lived years ago when we worked together. I'd find Olivia there.

No.

I slammed on the brakes and rammed my hand repeatedly against the steering wheel. That wasn't Olivia. Olivia was dead.

But.

Bobby had said something about Olivia haunting him.

A ghost?

She said Bobby killed her.

Impossible. It had been an accident.

"Stop it," I shouted. Olivia was dead. I was rekindling my dreams of lost opportunities. I could never love Olivia again. Olivia was dead. That woman was an imposter. I didn't know what her game was, but I had to find out.

Bobby lived in the Green Lands not far from the factory. I turned onto Glendale Street halfway up the hill that led to a small park. There were multi-unit dwellings on both sides of the street and I stopped at 127. There were spots for four cars at the side of the building and I saw Bobby's Ford parked there. No sign of a red Ferrari.

I stepped into a small alcove and saw names and unit numbers on a warped sheet of paper pasted next to the door. Bobby was upstairs to the right. I knocked on the wooden door.

"Go away."

"It's me. Joe."

"Go away."

"What happened with you and Olivia?"

Silence.

"You said you've been seeing her ghost. You said she's haunting you." I rapped on the door again.

It swung open and Bobby appeared pale and weak like he could barely stand. "I'm so sorry," he whimpered as he backed away from the door.

"Why is she haunting you, Bobby? What happened? Tell me what happened."

"It was an accident. I swear it," He kept backing away, finally stopping at the wall.

I stepped into the dark room. "Olivia died in that car crash. I cried that night. There was never a chance for us to get back together."

"I cried, too." Bobby staggered over to a narrow chair, his hands clasped between his knees as he sat, leaning forward, staring at the paneled floor. There were no lights on in the room. Only a distant kitchen light gave minimal illumination. "We hooked up after you guys split up," he said. "You knew that. But it never went far. She always treated me like I was leftovers, you know?"

That warmed me for a moment. Perhaps she, too, dreamt of a reconciliation.

Again, the realization of what could never happen tore at me. "What happened?"

"I was driving," he said.

"What?"

"We were arguing. About you. When I started to lose control, I dove out of the car."

"But Olivia?"

He shook his head.

"The car caught fire."

He shook his head again.

"Did you do anything? Did you call the police? Call for help?"

No response.

"You never told the truth?"

His shoulder started to quake.

I clamped my hands on each of his upper arms and started to shake him like he was a doll. "What the hell's the matter with you?" I half dragged him from the chair.

He started blubbering like a child, his teary eyes squeezed shut.

"You killed her, you bastard!" And I shoved him deeper into the chair. My vision began to blur as images of Olivia screaming in agony as the car burst into flames swamped me. All the pain of lost opportunities I had been bearing since her death took total control.

Suddenly, Bobby was on the floor and my right hand throbbed and swelled like a siren. I didn't remember him falling. Had I hit him? I kept gasping, trying to control my breathing as I stepped forward, my talons spread as I stared at the crumpled man. "Get up."

But Bobby didn't move.

I bent and grabbed his lapels, yanking him a foot off the floor, and I threw him down again, listening to the satisfying hollow echo of his skull striking the wood floor.

My heart bounced like a basketball, pounding against my ribs as I stepped back.

There was a noise behind me and I spun.

Olivia stood in the doorway, dressed as she was earlier at the bar.

Lustrous red hair. Tight slacks. "Thank you," she said. "Revenge is sweet."

"Revenge?"

"We can't act directly. We can only influence people." She looked toward Bobby's body. "I didn't want to use you, but I had to." She looked at me. "Thank you."

"We can never be together," I whispered. "Can we?"

"Not for many years. But maybe now you can live your life and forget about me." And she winked out as if she had never been there.

When I turned back to Bobby, who lay with his head twisted awkwardly, I noticed the streaks of dark blood on the wall and on the floor.

Daggett and the Locked Room

John Elliott

It was a ninety-minute drive to where the deceased employee was found.

Before the call came in to the St. Louis Postal Inspection Service, Inspector Dick Daggett had been speaking to his fellow inspector, Allan Rochwal, beginning one of those spiraling monologues which usually landed him on the opposite shore of the river from where he started.

"Everyone's in bondage, Rochwal, it's human nature, whether it's the rites of religion, family obligation, gaming, gambling, race car driving, or working out the mathematics of the universe, everyone has an obsession, a compulsion, something they can't do without."

To say Daggett was overweight would be an understatement. His apple-shaped physique bursting beneath his clothes, an unlit cigarillo in his mouth and his always scrutinizing eyes were trademark characteristics and a contrast to Rochwal's lean body and relaxed manner.

"The ones I like especially," Daggett continued, "are those people who think they are free of any ritual or obsession. I like to prick them and show where they are wrong. If you're human, you're obsessed with something, and it's easy with guys because they're always obsessed with..."

At that point his phone rang. He looked at it with annoyance, for he knew it was work related, and though he enjoyed solving crimes, the physical effort was anathema. The intrusive phone was also interrupting his discourse, and he let it ring a long time before he answered. For the next few minutes he listened intently, occasionally wrote something on a notepad next to his doodles, asked a few questions, and then with a sigh, hung up. He looked at Rochwal as if perplexed, though he wasn't: "Postal employee dead in the boonies."

Rochwal got up, but Daggett said: "No rush. The dead man isn't going anywhere. You could say he's tied up. I want to finish what I was saying."

Which he did, ending with: "That's why the need for freedom—to counter the ever-present bondage." He smiled and looked for Rochwal's approving agreement, which was sparse. In a few seconds, Daggett added: "Why don't you bring a car to the street entrance where I'll join you?"

He waited a minute after Rochwal left, made a phone call, then sat awhile contemplating the situation before leaving his office. Joining Rochwal out front, he got into the car as a passenger and asked that they take certain roundabout streets to the freeway. At a certain point in their progress, he commanded: "Stop here at Pasqual's Liquor."

"Is there any way out of St. Louis that doesn't have a liquor store that you know about?"

"Only if it opened this morning."

When he returned from his foray into the liquor store, Daggett had a bag of pocket snacks: peanuts, pork rinds, chips, and, of course, five packs of cigarillos. For the first time that morning he smiled pleasantly, swung his mass with ease into the car and looked at his companion. "Well, let's move, Rochwal. Can't sit here all day!"

While they drove, Daggett said little at first, but as they entered the countryside, he began remarking on the lack of farming and the need to reforest areas not in use "which would counter climate change, Rochwal. Something positive must be done about that. Five acres of forest eliminates the carbon from eight hundred cars."

When they arrived at the deceased employee's house, curiosity seekers were still about as was the sheriff, who filled them in: "Robret Lee Sharp, 37, is the victim. A neighbor hadn't seen him around even though his truck was in the drive, and when he didn't show at work, the local postmaster came out to his house. Not being able to rouse anyone, he walked around the house and through a small break in one of the curtains, made the discovery."

"Robret?" Rochwal asked.

91

"Yeah. Someone misspelled Robert on the birth certificate and the family decided they liked it." The sheriff gave a chuckle, then added in a serious tone: "I called in the state forensic team. I thought the scene needed their expertise."

The house was like many in the area — wood sided, small covered porch, minimal garden of shrubs and lawn, graveled drive and the roof pockmarked from hail storms. They took the two worn steps up to the porch and entered the house where the forensic team was at work. Down a hallway was an entrance to a bedroom which had been modified for a special purpose. The door to that room was badly damaged.

The sheriff explained: "When we got inside the house, this door was secured by a case-hardened lock. We virtually had to destroy it to get it off, but the door still wouldn't open, so we used an axe on the door. Why we couldn't open the door was apparent when we got in. There was another case-hardened lock on the inside."

The room was exceptionally cared for, filled with Amish-crafted oak cabinets, work benches, display cases and gun racks. More than two dozen guns of all types were in view: pistols, semi-automatic handguns, revolvers, shotguns, semi- and fully automatic rifles — a virtual armory. The exception to this orderly display was the condition of the deceased Robret who was sitting in a chair, bound tightly with ropes, his head slumped to the side. He looked older than his stated age of thirty-seven, had light brown hair and the extra pounds of a truck driver who spent his working hours sitting. Gagged and strangled, he faced a bed not more than four feet away, the bedding in disarray as if recently occupied.

"It looks like someone tormented him," Rochwal remarked.

"In more ways than one," Daggett replied.

"Without a list of his guns, there's no way of knowing if any have been stolen."

"Or if they got the information they wanted."

Iron bars were bolted into the sills of the windows, there was no opening to an attic and the flooring was solid, the forensic team having moved the bed to exam the floor, which was tiled in twelve-by-twelve-inch parquet.

After perusing the victim, the firearms, benches and cabinets, Daggett went outside and walked around the house. There were vents at the base of the house near the locked room as well as on the other sides, all of them five by fourteen inches. In contrast to the locked room, the outside had little care: the eaves were peeling, the paint on the siding needed to be refreshed, the front porch had loose boards and the lattice work skirting it was broken in places. The meager flower bed was crushed in one place. As he watched, a deputy stepped off the porch into the bed rather than take the stairs in an obvious shortcut to the driveway.

Rochwal called an ATF friend and though it wasn't yet an AFT case, he came to look over the weapons and assist where he could. Then Rochwal went to the sheriff's station and was given a desk where he could work. Daggett remained on site and spent his time sitting on the steps of the porch. The woods were close in and often separated the houses in view. He watched with amusement as a jay and a mockingbird vied for a place on a preferred limb of an oak—first one, then the other in possession. The time passed pleasantly enough for him and he was enjoying his day, his delight in the world only briefly interrupted by a phone call and the few minutes that he took to slip into the locked room now that most of the guns had been removed. With the help of a deputy, he pulled cabinets and work benches away from the walls and assured himself there were no hidden doors.

Fifty minutes later Rochwal came back from the sheriff's office. "I have some surprising news for you, Daggett."

"Yes, I know: Three withdrawals of $20,000 were recently made by Abby Sharp from the Sharp's bank and/or credit union accounts."

"How did you know that?"

"I wish you'd accept that I'm psychic, Rochwal," he replied with a chuckle.

"I don't. Your usual banking connections?"

"And no charges on any of their credit cards since the murder."

"Abby Sharp is using the cash to keep us from knowing her whereabouts."

"No." Daggett shook his head. "She doesn't have the cash. Her lover does."

"She's with him, though."

"No. No. That's the sad part. Well, I suppose we had better interview a few people. Let's start with the postmaster."

From the interview with Russ Kopperud, postmaster:

"Yes, I got along well with Robret. He was a good employee. Drove the day's dispatch to Springfield and delivered in the rural areas. His wife delivered the mail here in town."

"So Abigail Sharp worked for you, too?"

"Yes, and before... Well, you'll hear things anyway. I want to make this statement. I only had a professional relationship with Abby—any rumors to the contrary are untrue. This town is full of gossip, always has been. The person you should really be looking at is Forrest Givens. Robret owed him $50,000 from way back and has never paid him."

From the interview with Gloria Swetlic, Abby's best friend:

"I admit I'm put out with Abby. She told me that she planned to run away with someone, but she refused to tell me who—and I'm her best friend! Now she's done it, gone off without a word after all these years that I listened to her and cared about her troubles. She said that if she told me, she'd likely also say it to someone else and then everyone would know. Self-protection, she said, but not against you, Gloria, she said, against myself, she said."

"You think it was Russ Kopperud, her boss?"

"Maybe she's hiding in his house right now, I don't know. She had an affair with him, that's certain. It was fairly recent, and she told me they only did it once, but you know, what people say and what they do, the moon and sun, you know. Said she felt ashamed and didn't want Robret to find out."

"Anything else?"

"Yeah, she promised me that when the dust settled, she'd write me a letter and let me know where she was."

From the interview with Forrest B. Givens, Robret's best friend:

"What bullshit! I've known Robret twenty-five years. And it was only $500, not $50,000. It became a joke between us. Pay me, I'd say. Next month, he'd say, when I get my paycheck. Besides, he's given me guns and rifles that are probably worth more, so he doesn't really owe me. He's got quite an arsenal, or had, since he's dead now. As far as Abby goes, maybe she did, maybe she didn't do it with Russ. Ask him."

"$500 or $5,000," Rochwal asked, to which Forrest replied: "More like $50."

From the interview with Marcella Than, hairdresser:

"Of course Abby was having an affair with Kopperud. Everybody knew it, at least all the women who have sat in my chair. The real rumor is that she's sweet on Forrest. People have seen them eating lunch together. Ask Anna Garcia, she works at the bank. She saw them. And check out Scary Mary."

"Scary Mary? Why her?"

"I don't know, but she talks a lot about Abby whenever she's getting her hair done. Bad mouths Robret a lot, too. I think she and Robret hate each other."

From the interview with Scary Mary, motorcycle enthusiast, farm hand and hay baler:

"Nothing, Rochwal. The Neighbor on the left doesn't associate with her."

"The neighbor on the right does. He told me she took off a day or so ago. Packed up a lot of her things and put her cycle in her pickup."

From the interview with Anna Garcia, Abby's second-best friend:

"I don't think Abby is having an affair with Forrest. They're close friends, of course, since Forrest and Robret are buddies. And no, I never saw them at lunch together. One time last week Forrest was in the bank when Abby came in, so he waited until she was finished to say hello to her. Of course, everyone knows she's having an affair with the postmaster. She told me it was only four or five times, but people aren't dumb. The rumor is that Russ Kopperud nearly shits in his pants every time he sees Robret, which is often since Robret works for him. He always thinks that's the day Robret will kill him. After all, Robret has all those guns and automatic rifles, and he can be pretty possessive."

"Did Robret know about the affair since, as you say, everyone knows?"

Anna shrugged.

From the interview with the local notary, Floyd Willus Sharp:
"Yeah, we used to joke about it and say we were cousins, but I've done my genealogy and Robret and I only share our last name, not blood. You want to know about the will? I've notarized most of the wills of those that live here in town or nearby, and I'll tell you what I told the sheriff just two hours ago. Robret's will left everything to a cousin who lives in Perryville, Arkansas. Abby can protest that, but since the house is separate property in Robret's name, she won't get anywhere. I'm not sure the cousin even knows about the will, but he's into guns just like Robret, at least that's what Robret said to me. Said his cousin's one of those Proud Boy types, though he doesn't really belong to the organization."

As they left the notary, Rochwal said: "Enough gossip in this town to keep a gaggle of geese busy on a gloomy-wet day."

"Yes, and unfortunately, it's all probably true. You've always enjoyed having multiple suspects, Rochwal, so feast on it. I'm going to take a break and smoke a cigarillo."

"And have a bag of chips or pork rinds?"

"If there are any left."

Daggett again sat on Robret's porch as Rochwal went off to speak with the sheriff. The mockingbird was nowhere to be seen, nor was the jay. Had they been fighting for a place on that oak limb in earnest or for sport, testing out what it was like to switch places? He ate a bag of chips and smoked as he waited for Rochwal to return. Not impatiently, for he was enjoying the serenity of the town. Besides, he knew who the murderer was, and that would entail some energetic action.

When Rochwal came back he was accompanied by the sheriff, who informed Daggett that he had contacted the sheriff in Perryville, who in turn let Robret's cousin know about Robret's death and his will. The will was news to the cousin, as Robret hadn't informed him. He was told he would have to make the funeral arrangements if Abby couldn't be located.

Daggett listened pleasantly to the report, then made an appeal. "Sheriff, I was wondering if one of your deputies could do me a favor. Could you have him crawl under the porch, through that broken lattice would be easiest, and work his way under the house to beneath the locked room? I think he'll find it enlightening. I'd do it myself, but as you can see, my uh, breadth of, I mean width, might be a hindrance, to say the least."

The sheriff scratched his neck as he thought. "I'll have Teresa do it. She's the smallest deputy I have."

While they waited for Teresa, Daggett said cryptically: "She's here, Rochwal."

"Teresa?" He looked around.

"No, not her. Abby. She's here in town."

"With Kopperud? The Postmaster?"

"Is that your guess?"

Rochwal shrugged. "Possible."

Sheriff Teresa Wilmot arrived. A petit woman, she had dark red hair cut in a short bob and an enthusiastic face. She shed all of her equipment that might be a hindrance, including her firearm which she handed to the sheriff, and knelt down by the broken lattice work. She wasn't enthusiastic about crawling through dirt and cobwebs, but she did want to show she was full-on and capable at doing any duty assigned. She glanced at the house and the area of the locked room. "Toward there," she pointed.

"Yes," Daggett replied, "as best you can."

She spent twenty minutes under the house, crawling carefully while avoiding shards, building debris and jagged rocks. When she returned, she had a smile of satisfaction on her face.

"It's very interesting, Sheriff. Under the locked room was a series of clamps joining foot-long 2x6 boards to the floor joists. I thought that might be the answer to the locked room, so I took them off. Two of them were tighter than a rat's ass, and once they were unclamped, I could see these short boards were permanently attached to the subfloor. But the big discovery was when I checked some black construction plastic. We have another body."

"Shit! I don't like the sound of that. I'll get a crew."

"No, sheriff," Daggett suggested. "No one needs to crawl underneath. Let's go into the locked room. And bring a screw driver and pliers."

In the locked room Deputy Wilmot pointed out where she estimated the clamped boards had been.

"I noticed this earlier when I doubled-checked the locked room. There are two screws, both the same color of the parquet, one near a wall and one where Deputy Wilmot indicated she found the clamps. They're driven into the parquet as if to fasten down a loose tile rather than pulling the tile out and resetting it." He loosened the one near where Deputy Wilmot pointed so it could be grasped with pliers but not be pulled out, and with a little grunt work managed to lift a section of floor, exposing a hole underneath large enough to slip through. The forensics team entered the passageway, took photographs and brought the body up. It was Abby Sharp.

"Now all we have to do is arrest the murderer," Daggett said with resignation. "Let's go. We'll take him to the sheriff's station."

"I'm with you," the sheriff said forcefully, leaving no doubt about his anger at the murderer. He drove to the suspect's house, handcuffed him and took him to the station. He was a thin-faced, dark brunette with a shadow of a beard. At the station, the handcuffs were removed. Rochwal agreed to Daggett's request to let him do the interview with Rochwal only observing.

Interview with Forrest B. Givens by Inspector Daggett:

"Your middle name, the initial B, does that stand for Braxton or Bragg or Beauregard?"

Givens scoffed: "What the fuck does that have to do with anything? Why am I here?"

"We told you when we arrested you. You're here because you murdered Robret and Abigail Sharp."

"No, I didn't!"

"What I said was a statement, not a question." Daggett chewed on his cigarillo a few seconds, took it out of his mouth and said: "Beaureguard was a famous Confederate General and far better than Braxton Bragg. He commanded the Confederate troops at Sumter, first Bull Run and Shiloh." Daggett continued with a long narration of the exploits of Beauregard during the Civil War, listing battles lost and won, made a comparison to Bragg's generalship, and when he had finished, took only a single, deep breath and began a long polemic on the Lost Cause, explaining why it only appeared to be correct when in fact it wasn't. He gave the history of when the idea was first proposed and how it was modified over the years.

At last, Forrest Givens slammed his fists on the table and yelled: "What does this have to do with anything! I didn't murder Robret or his wife!"

"Of course you did. I figured it out when I realized what was going on between you, Abby and Robret. Since you were his best friend, it's logical that you participated in Robret's fantasy of seeing his wife with someone else. Robret's bank account was emptied by Abby, and my guess is she wanted to run away with you. You saw your chance to get your money back and do away with any connection to either Abby or Robret, and you took it.

"As far as the murders go, you strangled her first. We'll find your DNA on her neck. Simple. Your fingerprints will be all over the locked room and as a friend you can explain that, but not that they are on the construction plastic and bits and pieces underneath the house, and, of course, the clamps. It was also a mistake to strangle Robret with your bare hands, though I can imagine why you did it that way, your anger at him. It's a personal touch you couldn't pass up. Your DNA will be on his neck also. There will be more than enough forensics to put you in jail, maybe the death penalty, so I'm not worried."

Givens was stubbornly silent awhile, then said with a sneer: "Isn't it about time you start the bad cop/good cop routine?"

"No, that only happens on TV. And why would we? You're cooked. I don't need a confession out of you." Daggett chewed on his cigarillo as he looked at Givens with intensity, then said: "I love these. Ever smoke a cigarillo?"

"Nasty habit," Givens said contemptuously.

"Ah, yes, but so is murder. I will say I admire your ingenuity about the locked room, attaching the subfloor and parquet tile cutout to 2x6 which you clamped to the joists. Interesting, though elaborate."

Daggett continued to talk casually to Givens, using both flattery and indifference, until he loosened Givens's tongue. In passing he mentioned they were getting a warrant for his house and bank accounts and would find the money.

"When did you get the idea to build the porthole into the room?"

After hesitation, Givens replied: "When he first decided he was going to build the locked room, that's when."

"Before he actually built it? OK. You were planning to murder him at that time?"

"Hell, no! I wasn't planning anything, but the reason for the locked room was all those guns he was going to buy. I wanted a way in should I want one."

"A lot of work, wasn't it?"

"Actually, it was easy. I had time when they went off together on vacation. Robret had given me a key to keep an eye on their place. The only sweat was when I secured the false floor with the clamps and had to crawl out, and more recently when I went back under the house to release them. I didn't want to be seen and I had to wait awhile each way to make sure no one was around."

"Did you ever take any of his weapons? Even after you murdered him?"

"That would be stupid. If someone found out I had one of Robret's guns, that would point to me. I was going to wait and buy them at auction."

"With their money, of course."

Givens smiled.

"You loosened the clamps before the murders, didn't you? Making the floor unstable."

"Not much, it was pretty tight, but Robret made it easy for me by placing the bed over my escape hatch. I found the right time a few days before to remove the clamps."

"When did your affair with Abby start?"

"About a year ago, but Robret brought it on himself. He wanted to act out this fantasy of seeing Abby fucked by someone else, and since I was a close friend and he could trust me, he asked me to do it."

"Just once?"

"Hah! As if.... The imbecile became obsessed with it. Then he wanted to add bondage to make it seem like he couldn't stop me while I either raped his wife or had an affair with her. By this time he had finished his locked room, even putting the padlock on the inside to give him this feeling of, I don't know, security that no one could walk in, or maybe some weird fantasy that he was a prisoner and helpless—the complete opposite of the way he acted in real life. He even wanted to be gagged so he couldn't protest, just muffled screams."

"By this time Abby was in love with you?"

"Yeah," he smiled at the thought of his conquest. "She was the one who wanted us to run away together. I went along with her and made plans, and she got the money and gave it to me. She thought we'd leave that night after making love in front of Robret, leaving him there a day or so before calling someone to untie him. I imagine what I did was quite a surprise to both of them. I enjoyed making love to her that last time knowing what I was going to do, then I strangled her right in front of him. You should have seen the panic in his eyes. I pulled back the bed, opened the hatch, retrieved the construction plastic I had hidden and wrapped her up, even letting him watch as I slipped her under the house and positioned her where I wanted. Then I came up, chided him a bit, and strangled him."

Daggett studied Forrest Givens for a long minute, then said: "Well, that's it, Rochwal. All we have to do is transport him back to St. Louis." He turned back to Forrest. "Wouldn't it have been simpler just to run away with Abby?"

"I'm not an idiot! Why would I want a woman who would cheat on her husband? And steal from him? Some people just don't have morals."

Borrowed

M.E. Proctor

Andy was the wealthiest of the four of us. His dad gave him a Corvette for his seventeenth birthday. That left us all open-mouthed and drooling. Ray was in a different income bracket. He drove a Ford Escort that was held together with bondo and duct tape. We seldom used Ray's car. It was a mess outside and inside, where the field of debris looked like a plane crash site. Joe didn't have a car. He went everywhere on a blue bicycle. My ride was my mother's beige Camry. She'd switched to a Rav4 and I inherited the thing. The Camry was our workhorse. Roomy and reliable. I could have written the ad copy. Andy's Vette only came out of the garage for special occasions. *His* special occasions. Hot dates that he bragged about before and after the fact, generating even more drooling from the rest of us sad sacks. Despite all that, Andy was my closest friend. We shared everything, except the Corvette, of course.

It was my Camry that ferried the bunch of us to Friday football games, Saturday parties and Sunday movies at the mall.

We nicknamed it *The Getaway Car*. It was so neutral, so bland that I often forgot where I parked it. One rainy evening I even walked by it and didn't see it. It was close to invisible.

"We should rob a bank, Mike," Andy said. "We'd make a clean break. The cops couldn't get the witnesses to agree on the color. What *is* that color anyway?"

"Mom calls it *taupe*." I shrugged. "Gray, beige, light brown, whatever. It's the shittiest color ever. I always put the car in the driveway. If I parked on the street, day or night, people wouldn't know it was there. They'd bang into it. Road hazard."

"Could you let me have it tomorrow?" Andy said. "Dad asked me to pick up tools he ordered. I'm not sure they'd fit in the Vette."

I knew he was concerned about his leather seats and pristine trunk. And being spotted at the hardware store didn't match his sophisticated persona.

And so it began. Soon, my car was communal property, a modern variation on the medieval mill. I still owned the Camry and I was its main user, but my three friends borrowed it regularly. I set up rules. Always fill the tank after use. Leave a sawbuck in the glove box. I was on the hock for the insurance, and my buddies didn't mind contributing. In the beginning, they came over to pick up the keys, but that turned into a hassle, and we started to use a dead drop, spy-movie-style. They just gave me a call ahead of time to ask if I needed the car. My parents weren't aware of the arrangement, they would have blown a gasket.

It was a small miracle that nobody ever got in an accident or collected a ticket.

That year, we were all seniors contemplating college. I secured scholarships and had my pick of a few nice places, Ray was on a budget and would go to school in town, Joe was going west, and Andy was shipping out to the same Ivy League elite joint his forebears had patronized. We would soon be separated and swore friendship forever, no matter what.

Little did we know.

*****

My parents were news junkies. They watched a succession of news bulletins every night. National to begin with, then a click to local, mostly for weather and traffic, then a little bit of political commentary. After that, it was sports or a movie. My sister Julie and I joined them sometimes, but usually we were either on our devices or buried in a book.

The news flash wouldn't have caught my attention if Mom hadn't let out a loud *Oh, my God* that cut through my texting. I was trying to arrange a concert date with Liana, my latest romantic obsession, and I was absorbed.

"That happened right here," Mom said. "The golf course at the back of the neighborhood. Can you believe it?"

"I didn't see anything driving in," Dad said.

"Well, you wouldn't. You don't come in that way."

I looked up. "Something going on at the golf course?"

I caddied there occasionally and I knew the people. I leaned on the back of Dad's recliner. The TV screen was an explosion of police lights. The front of the club house was barely visible through the pouring rain and the cluster of cars and ambulances. A reporter in a red raincoat stood left of center, dwarfed by the scene of mayhem behind her. The story was simple and horrific. The body of kid, a boy, had been found by a groundskeeper in a bunker on hole 17. I knew that bunker well. It was wickedly deep.

"They don't know who it is," Mom said. "Poor kid."

The reporter said the police would hold a press conference later. An ad for a lubes place obliterated the drama at the golf course. It reminded me the Camry was due for an oil change. I should swing by the garage after school tomorrow.

Over the next couple of days, the gruesome murder made headlines in the paper and on the local news channels. It even got traction nationally. Details were added little by little. The boy's name was Robbie Garner. He was nine years old and lived in one of the new developments on the west side. He was killed somewhere else and dumped at the golf course. The articles didn't dwell on the graphic nature of the crime, but it was clear he had been assaulted and tortured. The inevitable memorial with teddy bears, candles, and flowers that had sprouted from the ground as soon as the cop cars were gone grew so much the golf course manager decided to donate the flowers to the local hospital. For an entire week, our neighborhood was traffic-jammed. It took forever to get in and out. My father dubbed the visitors *crime tourists*. I called them ghouls.

Then the frenzy abated. Other tragedies hogged the front pages. Life went on. I thought I was in love with Liana. Four colleges had accepted my application and I had trouble choosing.

*****

"Mike?" Mom stood in my bedroom door. "There's people downstairs to see you."

My first thought was that a football coach from a hifalutin school wanted to recruit me, which didn't make a lick of sense because I didn't play football. Then I saw my mother's face. She was pale, eyes too big, with that pinch at the corner of her mouth that I knew well from the days and nights she watched my sister battle chicken pox.

"Mom?"

She closed her eyes. "They're in the sitting room."

Two men, jeans and sport jackets, sensible shoes. Faces like blank walls. Cops. I don't know how I knew, my only interaction with the police was an occasional wave at the amiable constable who patrolled our streets.

"Michael Garrison," the taller of the two said.

It wasn't a question. I nodded.

"You drive the Toyota Camry parked in the driveway."

That seemed to require a real answer. "Yes," I said.

"We have a few questions." He pointed at the sofa. "Please, take a seat."

Mom was right next to me. Her elbow brushed my arm. "What is it about?" she said, a slight tremor behind the words. "They're police detectives, Mike."

It shook me out of my immobility. "I don't know, Mom." I sat down, aware that I perched on the edge of the couch, a sign of diffidence, to be avoided in interviews. I straightened up. "I don't know your names."

That caused the smaller of the two to emit a grunt.

The taller one spoke. He was in charge. "I'm Sergeant Cotton, this is Sergeant Rivey. HPD Homicide."

I turned to Mom. She put a hand on my shoulder. "I'm calling your dad," she said.

"I would like to speak to your son alone, ma'am," Cotton said.

"I'm staying right here." She pulled out her phone and speed-dialed Dad. She didn't take her eyes off the two cops the whole time she talked to Dad. I knew my mother could be tough. These men had no idea how tough. "You need to come home right away, Henry," she said into the phone. "There are two homicide detectives in our sitting room. They want to ask questions to Mike." Dad must have had questions of his own. She listened, shaking her head. "I don't know. We'll wait for you." She hung up. "He'll be here in twenty minutes."

"Where were you the night of February 21, Michael?" Cotton said. "A Monday night," he added helpfully.

I didn't have to think. I never went out on school nights. "I was here," I said.

"Mike, shut up," Mom said.

I sighed. She watched all these crime shows. Next, she was going to ask for a lawyer. Cotton's question sounded innocuous to me. I was home that night. I remembered it rained non-stop. Then it hit me. That was the night the boy found at the golf course was killed. What the hell did it have to do with me?

Cotton was staring at me. Glacial, intimidating. Rivey smirked. I could picture him hitting me over the head with a phone book, old-style. Maybe they had a cupboard full of phone books at police headquarters just for that purpose.

Dad got home in record time. He must have blown past every traffic light.

"What's going on here? Why are you questioning my son?"

Rivey puffed up in outrage but kept his mouth shut. Dad towered a full head over him. The tension in the room made my stomach hurt.

"We are investigating the murder of a child, sir," Cotton said.

"It's a tragedy. I cannot imagine what the parents are going through. Why are you in my house?"

"Michael drives the Toyota Camry parked outside. That makes him a person of interest. Your son said he was home the night of February 21. We have reasons to doubt that is the truth."

I couldn't hold it in. "It is the truth!"

"What?" Rivey barked. "No little job, no shift at the burger joint? You some rich kid that don't need to hustle?"

His fake regular-joe-speak got on my nerves. "I have a job. I tutor kids remote. Check my computer." Why I bothered to tell him, I don't know. This guy had it in for me, for some reason.

Dad kept his calm. "We were all here, Detective. It wasn't a night for going out. The back yard flooded, and the front wasn't much better. Mike didn't drive anywhere."

"Fucking liars," Rivey spat. "We have the video."

Cotton shot him the kind of look that makes your balls shrink.

"Video?" Dad said. He turned to me. "You know something about this?"

I shook my head. I felt like I'd been punched. The words had trouble coming out. "I was here, Dad. I swear."

"I believe you," he said. "What is this? You're trying to frame my kid?"

Cotton took a deep breath, exhaled. "We have footage from a security camera that shows the Camry near the club house, at the golf course, the night of February 21. Do you want to amend your answer, Michael?"

Amend? I could feel anger building. "I wasn't there. You can't have a video of me. It's impossible."

"The car, kid. Somebody drove that car." Cotton was looking at Mom and Dad now. "What about your daughter, sir?"

"Julie?" Mom shrieked. "Are you out of your mind? She's fourteen."

"Enough of that nonsense. I'm calling a lawyer," Dad said.

Their voices, shrill as they increasingly were, started receding, pushed back by the thought Cotton's words put in my head. *Somebody drove that car.* I pictured the keys in the dead drop. My friends borrowing the Camry. None of them had asked for the keys recently and I hadn't checked if they were still in the hiding place. Did Andy, Ray, or Joe take the car that hellish night? I grabbed the seat of the sofa, nauseated.

"Michael? Something you want to share?"

I shivered. Sergeant Cotton. The man must be a mind reader. Or were my thoughts plain for everyone to see? My friends ... One of them a murderer? It couldn't be. It had to be a mistake.

"Okay, we continue this at HQ," Rivey said.

I thought Cotton was going to rip his partner's head off. For the second time, Rivey had stepped into it. I welcomed the interruption. I didn't know where this was going. I needed to think.

*****

The following days were a thick broth of confusion. Occasional flashes of anger and violence pierced the murkiness. Media vans camped in front of the house, reporters harassed the neighbors, we stopped answering the phone, Julie went to stay with the grandparents in Florida, social media erupted in hatred. The house, our family were like a ship buffeted in a storm.

The cops put pressure on all of us, but I was their prime target. I understood the strategy. Wouldn't a guilty parent confess to spare their innocent child? It was a fool's game. None of us had anything to do with the murder. A friend of Dad's had put us in touch with a lawyer, Aaron Collier. I don't know if he believed our protestations of innocence, at least initially, but it didn't matter, he was a feisty little guy. He got me out on bail after I spent a terrifying night in jail, alone in a cell for safety reasons. It was bone-chilling freaky.

Then Aaron ripped the so-called video evidence to shreds. It was a lousy recording from a security camera across the street from the club house. The car looked like the Camry, its color indistinct through the sheets of rain, as it usually was. There were no identifying marks or decals, and no clear reading of the license plate. "Worse than circumstantial," thundered Aaron.

It turned out the only reason the police came to the house was my stint as a caddy at the golf course. Put that together with living in the neighborhood and the similarity of the vehicles, and I was the handy fall guy.

When the forensics on the car came back from the lab, the tide turned. There was nothing incriminating in the Camry. The trunk, where the boy's body was supposed to have been stashed, was clean. From a criminal perspective that is. No blood, no body fluids, no hairs, or fibers. Only what one would expect in a car used to haul groceries. The passenger area was a CSI nightmare. Half the high school must have sat in there, smoked, got drunk, and done other dubious things. The

110

analysts threw up their hands in frustration.

The media people vanished from our street and the internet calmed down. Maybe I wasn't the monster after all. Even Aaron dropped his lawyerly neutral countenance. He sat down with me in his office one afternoon.

"It's been a rough couple of weeks, Mike. I'm sorry you had to go through this."

"It isn't over," I said. "They don't have the killer."

"There are rarely clean endings in cases like this. My gut feeling is that the freak will do it again. It reeks of compulsion." He looked at me over his bifocals. "The DNA results should come in soon."

Against his advice, I had agreed to be tested when the cops hauled me in. I didn't rape and kill the kid. I had no reason to refuse giving a sample. Aaron had warned me that it could be iffy. The body had been left exposed to the rain for hours, some degradation of the biological material was to be expected. He made it sound like I was rolling a dice. That was when he was still unsure about me. We had made significant strides in trust since then. Now, Aaron was convinced I had nothing to do with the murder. Yet, I never told him about the car keys. When the pressure on me was at its worst, I was tempted to offload and transfer part of the weight to Andy, Ray, and Joe. Anxiety made me sick. But bringing my friends into this mess wouldn't prove I wasn't guilty, it would just inflict misery on more people. When I saw the blurry video from the security camera, I was comforted in my decision to keep mum. It was impossible to prove what I saw on screen was my Camry. Maybe it was. Maybe it wasn't.

The doubts burned there, in the back of my mind, hot like a low-grade ache. I had not seen my friends since the cops showed up at our house. I hadn't heard from Liana either. I lived in a bubble. From time to time, Sergeant Cotton visited. My parents avoided him. I didn't mind. He was a patient man and I had a lot of questions. I couldn't tell him anything that helped his case. I knew he sensed that I hid something from him but he had no way of figuring what it was. I had stayed away from the dead drop. As far as I knew, the car keys were still there.

"I had no idea DNA tests took so long," I said.

"The lab is clogged," Aaron said. "Lots of crime out there." He gave me a probing glance. "It's faster, for a price, if you use a private lab."

"It isn't worth it, Aaron. I'll wait. The damage's been done. My sister's been kicked out of the swim team. I've been told to graduate early, so I don't have to show my face at school. Dad does the grocery shopping because Mom is insulted everywhere she goes. If we had a dog, he'd be kicked out of the park."

"How's your college sitch?"

"On hold. I might try the merchant marine instead. The circus is no longer a commercially viable option."

He chuckled. "Were you that cynical three weeks ago, Mike?"

"Probably. I just had no opportunity to practice. We're joking, Aaron, but little Robbie is dead and there's a sick fuck running loose."

Those were the conversations I had with my lawyer while we waited. It didn't look like there would ever be a trial but we didn't hang our hopes on it. And doubts about Andy, Ray, and Joe still gnawed at me.

*****

I was in the kitchen when the bell rang. Mom went to open the door. We'd learned that people were less likely to be aggressive when they saw her.

It was Cotton. He preempted her slamming the door shut. "I have news," he said.

"I'll handle it, Mom," I said.

She stepped back and leaned on the wall, one hand on her heart. She'd gone very pale.

"It's good news." Cotton made a face. "For you."

That was more emotion than he had expressed so far. "The DNA results? Aaron told me they were due any day now."

"You're off the hook, Mike," Cotton said. "Everybody in this house is cleared, actually, the way DNA works."

"Cup of coffee?" I said.

He twitched, switched his weight from one foot to the other, and crossed the threshold.

Mom leaned forward. "So it's over?" She sounded out of breath.

"Yes, ma'am." He seemed to brace himself. "I'm sorry."

"Sorry?" She jumped away from the wall. It must be what a taser or a cattle prod did to people. "Sorry? You're sorry? Fuck you!"

"Mom!" I'd never seen her that spitting mad, and she never cursed. I grabbed her by the shoulders and turned her around. I realized in a flash how much smaller than me she was. "It's my thing, Mom. Please, let me handle it." I could feel her trembling. It made me want to cry. She nodded and patted my arm.

I led Cotton to the sitting room. He didn't need to be led. He'd been there a lot. I got us two coffee mugs, took the time to put sugar in a pot and milk in a pitcher. We were civilized at the Garrison house, even if the world around us had shown it wasn't.

We both took a sip of coffee.

"What does the DNA say?"

"No match. At all. There is no case against you, Mike. The test excludes your parents too." He did that thing with the deep breath and the exhale that I was familiar with. "We should never have brought you in, it's as simple as that."

"I told you I was home that night."

"It was expected you'd say that."

"Will you issue an apology?" I said.

"We don't do that."

"No, of course you don't. Smash the crockery, blame the cat. My sister gave up swimming. She was up for regionals." I shrugged. "Do you care?" It was silly to lash at him. Cotton was doing his job. He was kind enough to come in person. The news could have come through my lawyer. He put himself on the line. "I apologize."

He shook his head. "No. We were hasty. Unprofessional." He leaned forward. "You can tell me now."

God, he was persistent! "I was home all night. I never saw that kid in my life."

"Where was the Camry?"

"In the driveway, as far as I know." I hoped my doubts were buried deep enough.

"What if he kills again, Mike?"

I could not, I would not think about that. "Maybe he's killed before," I said, and Cotton flinched.

*****

I was walking out of the bookstore when I found myself face to face with Andy. I looked over his shoulder, as a reflex. The blue Corvette wasn't there.

"I sold it," Andy said. "It was a stupid gift. I couldn't even get a blow job in these bucket seats."

"I never thought about the mechanics of the thing. How you doing?"

"Leaving in a week. What about you?"

"End of the month." I'd decided to go to Columbia. It was the farthest away I could get from my home town.

"You have a minute?" Andy said.

We sat at a small table in the bookstore coffee shop.

"I expected a knock on my door, anytime" he said. "Why didn't you tell them about the car keys?"

"I thought about it. Either the car was used that night or it wasn't. If it wasn't, why would I drag you into it? And if it was, I guess I didn't want to know. Does it make sense?"

Andy smiled. He looked sad. "Your parents stuck with you. Mine would have run all the way to the other side of the world. It's a sobering thought."

"You're not your parents."

"I hope not, but the odds are not good. For all it's worth, I didn't take the car that night."

I wanted to believe him, but to quote Sergeant Cotton: *it is expected he would say that.*

*****

I was in my second semester at Columbia and feeling like a longtime New Yorker—doesn't everybody after six months?—when Mom called with a piece of unwelcome news.

"They brought the Camry back," she said. "What do you want to do

114

with it?"

I pictured a patchwork of powder-dusted seats and side panels, torn carpets and eviscerated storage compartments. "Is it still running?"

"It's an indestructible piece of machinery."

That was scary. "Sell it," I said.

"We were thinking Julie could use it. You know, as a learner car?"

"No." The thought of my little sister driving that car filled me with dread. "I'll be home soon. Keep it for me, okay?"

At first, I pictured a Viking funeral, a bonfire, a sacrificial offering. In the end, I settled for a slow crush at the junkyard. The sound of crunched metal and popping windows was deeply satisfying. I'd invited Sergeant Cotton to witness the execution.

He lit a cigarette. I didn't know he smoked. He offered me one and I accepted. I didn't smoke either. It just felt appropriate. A communion.

"We need symbols," Cotton said. "Must be our lizard brain."

"Are you still looking?"

"There's no statute of limitation for murder, Mike." He tapped the side of his head. "These cases stick in here." He blew a little smoke away from me. "But you know that, right?"

Blizzard Road
William Kitcher

The plan was for Pete to drive his car with Vinnie, Joe, and the hockey bag full of money, fifteen minutes down County Road 14 to an empty stretch, and pretend that the car had broken down. Shaughnessy would come along, shoot Vinnie and Joe, and then he and Pete would split the money and disappear separately into the night. Pete wasn't sure that Shaughnessy would actually leave him with his share of the money, so Kathy would follow Shaughnessy to the murder site. Pete wasn't sure he could trust Kathy either, but he at least knew where she lived. That was the plan.

Despite the biting cold and the mounting snowstorm, Pete set out with Vinnie, Joe, and the money in tow.

As the car came down the hill, the wind whipped up, and Pete put the wipers on high. He let up on the accelerator. "Ah crap," he said, deliberately loudly.

"What?" said Vinnie.

"The car's dying, got no gas."

"Jeez, Pete, I told you to get rid of this piece of crap a long time ago. Never buy domestic."

Pete pretended to lose a little control of the car, and pulled over to the side of the road, not more than twenty yards from the massive oak tree rising above the strip of spruce that was the reference point.

"What the hell, man," said Joe.

Pete took his phone out. "Can't get a signal."

Vinnie and Joe checked their phones. Nothing.

Pete got out of the car, and looked back up the hill, seeing nothing but blizzard.

Vinnie and Joe got out of the car. Joe repeated, "What the hell, man." None of them were dressed for a January blizzard. Jackets instead of parkas. Running shoes instead of boots. They didn't even think to wear work boots. At least Joe had a toque, one he wore all year round.

They checked their phones repeatedly. Nothing.

Pete looked up the road. No sign of Shaughnessy.

"What the hell, man."

"Shut up," said Vinnie.

"I'm not staying here," said Joe, attempting to pull his collar up over his neck and not succeeding.

Vinnie turned his back to the wind blasting down the hill. "We just passed a house on the other side. I'm going there."

"Way too cold here," said Joe. "I'm going with you."

Pete saw the whole thing unravelling and had nothing to say except, "I'll stay here with the car." Where was Shaughnessy? Where was Kathy? Crap.

Vinnie and Joe peered into the snow, saw nothing, and just went for it. They lowered their heads and began to walk back up the hill.

Pete watched them go, had no idea what to do, and moved away from the car down the road several steps. He looked at his phone again. Nothing. What to do. He could take off with the car but that wouldn't solve the problem of Vinnie and Joe. They'd find him.

Vinnie and Joe made little headway against the blizzard, and the ice was slamming their faces. They turned around and began to back up the hill. The snow was so heavy and piling up they couldn't tell if they were still on the road or on the shoulder.

Vinnie heard something and turned around. A car was barreling down the road toward them. He lunged at Joe, slammed into him, and pushed them both off the road.

The car's driver saw them at the last moment and swerved. Off to the right. Toward Pete.

Vinnie looked up. "Isn't that Shaughnessy's car?"

Joe wiped the snow from his face. "What the... What's going on?"

Shaughnessy lost control of his car and rolled right over Pete. The car continued on and smashed into the oak tree.

Vinnie and Joe got up and slid down the hill to the wreck. Vinnie held his hand up against the driver's window and looked in. Shaughnessy was slumped over the steering wheel, blood oozing out of his forehead and gushing out of his nose. A gun lay on the other seat. Vinnie pulled on the door but it was locked. He called to Joe, "Where the hell's Pete?"

Joe looked under the car. Pete was sprawled out, his legs at weird angles. "He's under here. He's done."

"We gotta get out of here," said Vinnie. "Get his keys."

Joe crawled under the car, went through Pete's pockets, found nothing. "They're not here. Did he leave them in the car?"

They headed back up the hill, falling several times. They made it to the car, and Vinnie pulled the door open. He looked in the ignition. There was nothing there.

"Damn, man, they must be in the snow somewhere."

Joe had gone around to the back of the car and was hammering on the trunk. Finally he gave up. He came back to the front of the car and squatted in front of it, shielding himself from the icy blasts. "We gotta get outta here."

Vinnie squatted beside him and looked at him with an expression that said how stupid that comment was. "How?"

They stayed in that position for a while, looking at each other, saying nothing. Joe wrapped his arms around himself and slapped his biceps to get some warmth back into them.

Vinnie heard something and turned to the sound. A car was coming down the hill. The car slowed and pulled up in front of Pete's car. The high beams went on, illuminating the wreck by the tree.

There was a pause, then the driver's door opened. Kathy got out and pulled her parka's hood over her head. She looked at the wreck for a moment, then turned to look at Pete's car. She saw Vinnie and Joe.

They stood up and took a couple of steps toward her. "What the hell are you doing here?" said Vinnie, knowing exactly what the hell she was doing there.

Kathy stammered. She couldn't explain. She looked back at the wreck. "Where's Pete?"

"He got run over. By Shaughnessy. Shaughnessy's not doing so well himself."

"What the hell?"

"What the hell is right, Kathy. What's going on?"

"Nothing. I swear," she said. "I was just following Pete to make sure everything was OK."

"How did you know he was here?"

"I... I... He told me where he was going."

"And you just happened to stop here."

"Hey, you see a car at the side of the road in a blizzard, you stop to see if you can help, right?"

"Especially if it's Pete's car, right?"

"Look, Vinnie, I don't know what you think is going on here but nothing is going on here. We have to do something."

"Gonna call the police?"

"I... I... What?"

"No, you're not going to do that, obviously. Do you have another set of keys to Pete's car?"

"No, of course not."

"Well, we have to get into the trunk."

"Yeah, I guess so," she said.

"Because we all know what's in there, right?"

"Look, we'll split it. Fair?"

"If we can get in there. And if you don't have a weapon on you."

"Why would I—"

"We're not stupid, Kathy."

The wind whipped up even faster and the snow hit Kathy directly in the face. She turned away and squatted down. Vinnie and Joe squatted again in front of Pete's car.

There was a rumbling sound they all heard but forgot about instantly as they individually tried to figure out what to do.

"We gotta get a crowbar or something," said Kathy. She turned to Vinnie and Joe and saw headlights through the windshield of Pete's car.

A snow plow was lumbering through the blizzard down the shoulder of the road, the driver unable to see where the road ended and the shoulder began. He saw Pete's car at the last minute and tried to brake but it was too late. The plow piled into Pete's car, pushing it forward through Kathy, Vinnie, and Joe into Kathy's car. Kathy's car and Pete's car slid into the ditch, leaving the three bodies lying in pools of blood slowly being covered by snow.

The snow plow operator got out of his cab. "Ohmigod. Ohmigod. Ohmigod." He went over to the bodies he could see and nudged them with his foot. "Ohmigod."

He slid down the hill to Shaughnessy's car and looked inside. "Ohmigod."

He worked his way back up the hill along the ditch. He looked in Kathy's car. There was no one else in there. He looked in Pete's car. He went around it to the trunk, which had popped open, probably due to the collision when he'd rammed into it.

There was a hockey bag in the trunk. He could tell it was a hockey bag from the Canadiens' logo on the side of it, and the smell of dried sweat, which hit him as hard as the wind. He unzipped the bag.

It was full of money, neatly stacked and banded bills of all denominations. He picked up a stack and riffled through it, not because he knew how to count bills like that, but because he'd seen people do that in movies for some reason.

He turned around, expecting to see someone coming up behind him, but there was no one there, only the snow lashing his face. He zipped the bag up, then crawled back up the shoulder to his snow plow.

He climbed into his truck, threw the bag on the seat beside him, took a deep breath, then put the plow into gear. He disappeared into the night.

The blizzard continued. By the time the police came across the wreckage, no tire tracks could be seen.

Retrograde

R. M. Linning

I've made the drive to Burlington virtually every weekday for almost a decade now. All my best ideas come while driving or in the shower. At first I would shout them into a recorder app on my phone but then feel ridiculous when I replayed them later. Your recorded voice never sounds like it's your own. Now if I have a good idea I pull over and scribble it into one of the little notebooks that I'm always carrying. I juggle the also-rans in my head hoping I will remember them when I get to my "hole in the wall".

That's what my wife calls where I do the bulk of my writing. At first I think she was a little suspicious - she probably thought it was where I brought all my romantic conquests. That was until she saw it. I rent a tiny attic room in a bed and breakfast in the Old North End of Burlington. It's close to the lake and the Nepali Dumpling House.

When I arrived the day my troubles began the proprietor of the bed and breakfast informed me that her new guest, an elderly woman from Ohio, had made a special trip up to Vermont just to meet me. It would appear that my "lurid and impossibly labyrinthine" mystery novels had made inroads into the spinster demographic. Groaning inwardly, I agreed to spend some time with her after lunch and then pounded up the stairs.

My sanctuary consists of an eight-by-ten foot space, its vertical dimensions shortened on two sides by the slant of the roof. Against the short vertical walls below the inclines is a patchwork of shelf units I picked up at the second hand stores in town. They're filled with books and piles of clippings. Amidst that chaos and across from the door a small desk sits below a small oval window. In front of the desk is the one thing I spent good money on - a comfortable, ergonomic swivel-chair.

Once inside with the door locked behind me I threw my jacket onto one of the shelves and sank into the chair. Looking out the window I can see Lake Champlain in the distance and below lie sleepy streets lined with unremarkable Rockwellian houses. To this day I've never quite figured out why this arrangement works for me - maybe it's the total remove from the rest of my life.

*****

I get free internet and that's where my problems began. My daily routine starts and ends with a quick check of my emails. Whenever I can I try to reply to people who take the time to write to me about my stories. Occasionally I get some crank mail. And then there are the wrong addresses or mistaken identities. I got one of the latter that day:

> Hey, Sam. I never knew you wrote books.
> We need to talk right away about that
> night back in college. Get back to me.
> Jack.

I didn't recognize the name, number or address of the sender and so deleted it. Then I got on with my day. I worked on my latest novel for a couple of hours, half of which was spent researching how the Venetians built the foundations of their city by driving massive wooden piles into the lagoon. After a lunch of dumplings I went, with some trepidation, to meet my latest fan. To my surprise she was a spry old bird with a classily salacious sense of humor. As soon as we parted I raced upstairs and scribbled down my impressions of her for use as a potential future character. Back to work for a couple of hours and off for home ... but then another oddball email:

> Sam. Please we really need to talk. I'm
> getting really worried. They're going to
> start excavating by the old pool soon. We
> have to talk. J.

The guy sounded pretty desperate so instead of deleting his message I sent a short *you've got the wrong person* reply. I opted for some Mozart for the drive home, I needed to think my way around a particularly knotty plot twist.

*****

I was greeted the next morning by another email:

> Come on, Sam, don't bullshit me. They're going to dig up around the old pool! We have to do something. I know you're there. I'm not going to deal with this alone. Call me NOW!

I was starting to get annoyed and a little uneasy. There was no way I was going to call him and so sent off another email telling him in no uncertain terms to leave me alone.

My day was a productive one. I had another lunch with the woman from Ohio and she was thrilled when I told her I might base a character on her. I also managed to work around the hitch that was holding up progress on my current project.

But then in the afternoon another email:

> I don't know what you're playing at, Sam. I KNOW it's you. I saw your picture on the back of one of your books. You're really starting to piss me off! CALL ME!!!!

I deleted his email. I was a little rattled by its vehemence but half way home had forgotten all about it. I had a big weekend planned with Val and the kids.

*****

The weekend was a roaring success. The birthday party for my twin ten-year old daughters went off without a hitch and I even had time on Sunday to drive out to the cabin. My wife is a city girl from New York and while not averse to raising a family in Vermont insisted that our primary residence be in some sort of population center. When we drove through Montpelier we both fell in love with the place. The summers are sleepy but there is enough of an influx into the small nearby colleges to inject a tiny spark of excitement into the rest of the year.

Before the girls came along we bought a large lot on Mirror Lake about fifteen minutes out of town. The sale of my first novel had made the purchase possible. It's a heavily wooded area, very private and has great fishing. We are having a small cabin built there and I was returning from checking on some foundation work when my cell went off. I pulled over to the side of the road.

"Sam?" a voice asked when I answered.

"Sorry, you have the wrong number," I said.

"Okay, then, Dan?" the voice asked. "Daniel Wright, the author?"

My heart sank.

"Are you the guy that keeps emailing me?" I asked.

"Damn right I am. It's me, Jack. Look, man, we gotta talk. I'm going nuts here. They're going to start tearing up the concrete around the pool next week. We gotta do something, quick."

The man seemed to be teetering on the edge of hysteria.

"Look," I said, trying to keep the edge out of my voice. "I don't know what you're talking about. You've got the wrong person. Please don't call me again."

He started to shout something as I hung up. I threw my phone down on the seat next to me and was preparing to pull back onto the road when it went off again. It ran through the ringtone three more times before I decided to answer it.

"Hello."

"Don't you hang up on me, you bastard," he shouted.

"Listen, I don't know who you are or what you want. Do I have to call the police?"

"Call the police? Are you out of your mind?" he asked, more with disbelief than anger.

"Do not call me again," I said as calmly as I could. The phone rang over and over again as I continued home. I finally turned it off. I was very angry and more than just a little rattled.

*****

I had almost forgotten about the phone calls when I arrived in Burlington the next morning. I was tempted not to do my usual morning email check but when I did:

> I'm flying into Burlington tomorrow morning, Tuesday, at 10. You can't avoid me forever. We're going to sort things out whether you want to or not. I'll phone you when I'm off the plane, Jack.

I've dealt with disturbing emails and phone calls before. The persons involved had desisted as soon as I put up a firm but polite front. I always remind my wife that moderately successful mystery writers don't rate the real crazies and as far as I knew my sales hadn't spiked recently. I didn't know what to make of this Jack. He was forceful, yes, but not threatening and his reaction to my threat to call the police was odd to say the least.

I decided that rather than have the cops meet him at the airport I would try to sort this misunderstanding out myself. I dug up one of his emails that I had deleted the previous week and replied telling him I would meet him at one of the busier bars in town. I added some platitudes about crossed signals and the like.

I got very little writing done during the day and spent a very restive night back at home. A litany of possible scenarios kept running through my head as I tried to sleep.

*****

I arrived at the bar a full hour early and nursed a Green State Lager while I waited. I had taken a table in the center of the room with a clear view of the entrance. The comforting hubbub of the lunch crowd surrounded me. As the hour crept by I began to doubt the wisdom of my plan. I knew nothing about this guy. Did I really know what I was doing?

Noon came and went and I began to hope that he wasn't going to show when a man entered the bar, took a quick look around and then immediately strode directly towards me. He was familiar in a generic sort of way. He was of average height with sandy blonde unkempt hair that needed cutting. His face was long with an oversized hooked nose beneath large red-rimmed green eyes. He was wearing sneakers, jeans and a billowing army surplus jacket. I rose to the balls of my feet as he neared ready for anything. He just stopped at the table, gave a tired little smile and extended his hand.

"It's good to see you again, Sam. You've hardly changed," he said.

I had no idea what to do. I began to stammer out something and reaching out shook his hand. He looked at me angrily and closing his eyes shook his head. With a sigh he pulled out the chair opposite from me and sat down. A waitress came over and he looked up at her.

"I'll have whatever he's having," he said. The waitress looked over at me.

"Green State?" she confirmed.

I nodded and slowly sat down. With the waitress gone Jack leaned forward. He rested his hands on the table. They were visibly shaking.

"Look, Sam. You've moved on," he said in a plaintive tone. "I get that and I don't blame you. I've tried to, too but we have a serious problem and ..."

"I don't know who you think I am or what you're talking about," I finally managed.

He slammed both fists hard down onto the table. All heads in the bar swiveled in our direction.

"What's wrong with you?" he almost shouted and then visibly drew himself together. He forced his hands back out flat onto the table and then said very quietly through gritted teeth. "Sam, they're gonna fucking dig her up ..."

I pushed myself back in my chair. This had been a mistake. He was looking at me, tears welling up in his eyes. I wanted nothing more than to bolt for the door. The waitress was at the bar looking at me with a questioning look. I shook my head very slightly. Jack saw.

"I'm not here to hurt anyone, Sam," he said. His hands were still plastered to the table. "You have to believe me. We just need to figure out what we're going to do."

I sat there paralyzed for several moments, my heart racing. I could feel a cold sweat forming over my brow and the back of my neck. I tried to focus on his face but I couldn't stop from checking his hands. If they moved I would throw up the table and jump him. He saw that too. His hands flexed over the table's surface and then he slowly brought them together, interlocking his fingers as if praying.

"I've never left Rock Hill," he began. "I've walked by there every day for the last twenty fucking years. I needed to know everything was OK but when I heard they were planning some kind of development by the complex I started to fall apart. And you weren't around. You just disappeared … after what you, we did … and you just up and vanished."

Tears were streaming down his face now and he was wringing his hands. He took a quick look around and saw the shocked looks of the people closest to us. He took a massive shuddering breath and forced himself to calm down. His hands went back flat onto the table.

I've never seen such a look of desperation before. I was paralyzed with fear and uncertainty. I've never been to Rock Hill or even South Carolina. I had, however, spent one wasted year at Duke up in Durham. We sat there in silence for several minutes looking at each other and then he started again.

"I thought we would be OK, I mean, all that concrete around the pool. I thought about leaving but I never did and especially not after you took off when your parents were killed. You never once came back, never called. After what you did, the way you roughed her up after she wanted to stop. We were so drunk. We could have just walked away but you wouldn't … I can't stop thinking about it. I'm just so tired and now they're going to find her."

I sat there listening, waiting for him to run down and then I came to a decision.

"How did you find out about me?" I asked. His face broke into a hopeful look. "I mean what makes you think you know me?"

He descended back into gloom and clenched his teeth so hard that the muscles of his jaw stood out like cords. He looked around furtively and took a few more deep breaths to calm himself.

"I saw your picture on the back cover of one of your books, Sam," he said. "I traced your new name to here. I couldn't believe you wrote a story about her. What were you thinking? But we're wasting time."

That caught me off guard. I had written a story about a murderer who hid the body of his victim under concrete. The story had come to me in a dream. Despite my uneasiness I was starting to get annoyed. What was next? Was he going to accuse me of killing Jimmy Hoffa?

"I must look like someone you knew," I suggested as calmly as I could.

"No! God damn it!" The hands pounded down on the table again and he half-crouched above his seat towards me. I rocked back in my chair. A couple of men at other tables turned and were getting to their feet. He put up his hands placatingly. I raised my hands mirroring him and shook my head at my would-be saviors.

"Look," I said. "I'm not who you think I am. I'm going to leave. If I ever see you or hear from you again I'm going to call the police."

Now it was his turn to be confused and it showed on his face. I threw down a few bills, got up and walked quickly past the waitress bringing our beers and out of the bar not looking back. Once out the door I darted around a corner and then another. When I finally looked around I found that I was alone. I backed up against a wall and took a few deep uneasy breaths. The back of my neck was oily with sweat. I hotfooted it to my truck and drove home without going back to my office.

*****

That night Val knew something was bothering me but didn't push it. She was busy getting the girls ready. We were taking them out of school for the rest of the week. She was driving them down to New York to celebrate their birthday with her parents who had made a big production about the Big Ten celebration ever since they had been born. I wasn't making the trip to New York, there was long-planned work to be done at the cabin that I didn't want to reschedule. The next morning, after another poor sleep, I saw them off.

I had turned my cell phone off since my meeting with Jack and saw no reason to turn it back on. If there was a problem Val could get hold of me using the landline we still kept at the house. On the drive to our cabin I replayed the previous day's meeting over in my head. I would be lying if I said it hadn't rattled me but I was still convinced I wasn't in any real danger. Clearly Jack was a disturbed individual but there was no indication that he was of a violent nature.

One thing, however, had struck me - he had said that I had disappeared after the death of my parents. There was some truth to that, my parents had indeed died but shortly after I was born. I was an orphan and had been raised by my mother's parents. They in turn had died in a car accident about twenty years ago. I hadn't dealt with that well at the time. In fact, I went through some very dark times - drugs, booze, and some pretty heavy counseling. It wasn't the proudest time in my life but I didn't hide it from my wife or my readership. I never laid out all the details - they were for me alone. Maybe this is what Jack had read in some bio online and that coupled with some kind of physical resemblance and the story I'd written fostered his misguided need to hunt me down.

I encountered a problem once I got to the cabin. It had been quite windy the night before and a tree uphill of the building site had been uprooted. This caused a small landslide which had knocked over a stretch of the forms shaping a cement platform I was having poured the next day. I would need some replacement rebar and lumber as well as a pry bar to set it straight. Before heading back to town I did manage to dig out the incline of rubble that had caused the damage.

I was in the hardware store when one of the clerks pulled me aside, a man had been asking after me. He wasn't a local and the clerk sent him on his way none the wiser. I thanked the clerk and after loading up my truck headed back to the cabin. It was getting dark by the time I finished the repairs. I stopped off at one of the roadside diners for dinner and when I got home all that was left of the sun was a hazy red band over the horizon.

I decided it was time to get a little writing in and took my laptop down into the den, dimmed the lights and sank back into my recliner. Soon I was lost in the intricacies of my latest locked-room mystery. A couple of hours later I was contentedly reviewing what I had accomplished when I heard the front doorbell go off. It was pushing eleven and I had no intention of answering it. A few minutes later it sounded again but I was too engrossed in my story to care.

The next thing I remember was waking up with a stiff neck and a laptop with a dead battery. I scrambled around for the power cord and after plugging it in restarted the laptop. The autosave had worked properly and I breathed a sigh of relief. That's when I heard a sharp shattering of broken glass upstairs. I slid the laptop on to the table next to me and reached for my phone which of course wasn't there. I had turned it off and left it upstairs on my bedside table. Swearing silently under my breath I reached up, turned off the light and sat in the darkness listening.

I could hear the usual creaks and groans of the house each of which now took on an ominous aspect. Maybe a bird had crashed hard into a window? But then several minutes later I heard the slipping of the back door bolt followed by the creak of the door opening. I sprang to my feet. I needed to get to the landline phone receiver at the top of the stairs. I padded along as quietly as I could on the balls of my feet to the foot of the stairs and then slowly, cursing every tiny crack and pop the wooden steps made, started up.

I was two or three steps from the top and poised to snatch at the receiver when I heard a couple of tentative steps down the hall to my right. I froze. Another stepfall. I lunged for the phone but my stockinged foot slipped out beneath and I fell, my knee connecting hard with the lip of a step.

"Sam?"

I reached up, grabbed the receiver and twisted to look up at the source of the voice. It was Jack swaying slightly in the darkness. He had a gun in his hand. It wasn't pointed at me, he was waving it in the air. With his other hand he was feeling for a light switch and when he found it we were both momentarily blinded. I scrabbled away crab-like down the hall.

"No, Sam, wait," he called out. I rounded the corner and managed to get to my feet. Jack was blocking the route to the front door so the back was my only avenue of escape. Just before reaching the door I felt a large shard of glass slice up into the sole of my foot. I froze not knowing where to take my next step and Jack stepped up behind me. The kitchen lights came on and I turned towards him. I looked down at my foot and saw more than half an inch of glass protruding. I reached down and with a howl wrenched it out and threw it at him. He jumped back in surprise but then shakily leveled the gun at me.

"You stay there, Sam," he said. His face was covered in sweat. He had clearly been drinking.

"Fuck you," I half-growled but didn't move. There was a steady drip drip of blood from my foot hitting the floor. There was a small minefield of glass pieces around where I stood.

"I didn't want this to happen, Sam. I just wanted to talk, you know, figure out what we're going to do," he said, the gun bobbing with every word. He looked more afraid than I felt. I held up my hands and then slowly moved away from the door and glass to the kitchen table. I sat down and taking a paper napkin tried to stanch the flow of blood. Jack watched me solicitously the whole way. The gun also followed me, tracing a sinuous pattern in the air between us.

"Okay, you've got me you prick. Now talk," I said. My foot was throbbing and I went through two more napkins before the bleeding seemed to stop. I threw that last one at him and he jerked back away. He shifted from foot to foot watching me.

"I'm sorry about your foot, Sam," he said. I stared at him.

"You're sorry about my foot?" I asked incredulously. I could feel something growing in me that I hadn't felt for years. This guy had broken into my house, pointed a gun at me and now was apologizing for my foot? I watched the gun waver in his shaking hand. "You gonna shoot me? How can I help you if you shoot me?"

"No, I don't want to shoot you," Jack almost howled. The gun lowered slightly and then whipped back up. "I just need you to listen."

"Well, I don't have much choice. I'm listening," I said. I waved at the chair across from me, he pulled it out and sat down. I was ready for the slightest slip.

"We have to go back to Rock Hill and stop the digging. If they find her we're done," he was almost blubbering.

"So I have to go and clean up your mess?" I asked. He seemed less threatening by the minute and I was becoming very angry.

"No, not mine. She wanted to stop but you wouldn't," he said. The gun straightened and I leaned back and put up my hands. "She wanted to stop but *you* wouldn't. When she screamed *you* hit her and when she wouldn't stop you just kept hitting her. Why didn't you stop?"

"But you were there," I goaded him, looking directly into his eyes. "Why didn't you stop me?"

"I wanted to but you were so wild. I was so scared. I've never seen anyone like that before," he said. The waterworks started up again. "Why didn't you stop?"

"And then what?"

"You know what. She was dead. We waited until late and then we dug the hole at the work site, at the complex, and we put her in it and covered her up. The next day they poured the cement."

"But now they're going to dig her up?" I asked, my eyes never leaving his.

"Yes! Yes! I told you that, Sam. What are we going to do?" he whined. He was blubbering now. I put my injured foot flat on the floor. It hurt like hell but I forced it to stay flat.

"But you never went to the police?"

"No! I couldn't do that! You're my friend!" he wailed. The gun was shaking in the air.

"You know what I think?" I said. A tiny glimmer of hope came to his face and I forged on. "I think you've got a screw loose. Or maybe you killed her. How about that? Because I haven't got a fucking clue what you're talking about."

"No! No!" he was screaming now. The gun was loose in his hand, oscillating wildly.

I pushed down now with both feet. The pain was excruciating. I flipped the table up at him and the gun flew up into the air. It clattered to the floor but didn't go off. I was on the top of the overturned table, on top of him. He had twisted onto his side and was frantically trying to reach the gun. I pulled back his arm and drove my fist as hard as I could into the side of his face. I could feel his cheekbone give with the impact.

"No! Stop, Sam," he managed. I lunged for the gun. My battered foot scraped against one of the table's legs and I shrieked with pain. I shifted the gun to my right hand and started pounding at his face with it. He flailed at me but could get no real purchase trapped under the table. After a while, I don't know how long, he eventually went silent and limp. I rolled off and slid to a sitting position next to a cabinet. Another small piece of glass had cut into my arm but I was beyond caring.

I sat there panting, staring at the floor. Finally, I summoned the resolve to look over at him. He was on his back half-covered by the table. His arms were splayed out and his face was a mottled red-blue pulp. I dragged myself to my feet and limped to the door careful to avoid the broken glass strewn between streaks of already drying blood, my blood. A small pool of blood was forming under Jack's head. I wrapped my wounded foot with a hand towel and then jammed my feet into a pair of slippers. I turned off the lights and sat down on a chair to think. Then I went on autopilot.

I wrapped two garbage bags over Jack's head and chest and taped his wrists and ankles together. After a horrendous effort and more burning pain I managed to drag him into the back of my truck. Back in the house I cleaned up the blood and broken glass. It was two in the morning when I started out for the cabin. The roads were absolutely empty.

I didn't stop until I reached Forest Lake where at a secluded stretch of the road I limped out and threw the gun as far out into the water as I could. Doubling back to our site I dragged Jack's body down to the forms I had repaired earlier in the day. It was a slow go. I used my flashlight only when I had to. There was just one light visible across the lake but I wasn't taking any chances.

Then for the next three hours I dug Jack's grave in the center of the area cordoned off by the forms. I sawed away a couple of thick roots and pulled out several large rocks which I later laid atop his body before throwing the soil back over him. By the time I was done the lake was shimmering under the morning sun. I climbed back up to my car and waited.

The rumble of the cement truck woke me from a fitful sleep. I was hot and sweaty and my foot throbbed heavily inside its boot despite its loosened laces. I must have looked like hell but my story about the fallen tree passed muster and after a cursory inspection of my repairs the pouring of the concrete began. I stayed another hour after they finished looking out over the lake with my foot propped up on a rock.

*****

There was no way to make what happened look good - at least that's what I keep telling myself. I could have called the police but how would I have justified what I did? I would have had to explain why I hadn't called them earlier. But the more I think about it I wonder why I didn't call them immediately. As it is now all I can remember is the pain and the rage.

I patched up the window and eliminated all traces of what happened that night. My family returned from a very successful celebration and I was ready to get on with my life but it's not easy to bounce back from an experience like that. My foot took several weeks to heal after two trips to the doctor to treat a nasty infection. I told my wife I had broken a glass and then stepped on it.

I still drive to Burlington every weekday but once there I just sit in front of my laptop and stare out the window towards the lake. Sometimes it's almost like I black out - I'll shake myself out of my reverie and find that the whole morning or even the day has passed by. It's been a couple of months now and I haven't written anything of value. I can't help thinking about Jack, his story and what happened. It hasn't been lost on me that I buried him in exactly the same way that he said we interred the girl.

I want nothing to do with the cabin now but I know that I can never sell it. How I'll explain that away to my wife I don't know.

I don't sleep well anymore and it's starting to wear me down. My temper is fraying and I've even gone off a few times on Val and the girls. I've always been a frequent dreamer but now dream only of things that I can never write about. Jack has started appearing in my dreams and with each one he becomes more familiar. I also have recurring dreams about someone trapped under the ice of a frozen lake. But it's not a lake and there is no water or ice. The person, a woman, is trapped under a slab of concrete. She's slowly, so very slowly, clawing away at the cement as if she knows that someday she'll scrape her way through. Initially she was just a dark shape but with each dream she becomes more distinct. I dread sleep now, terrified that I might know her.

Hot August Ice
Annie Reed

Heat waves shimmered off the asphalt of the casino's outdoor parking lot. Bright, unrelenting sunshine glinted off row after row of classic cars, all buffed and polished to within an inch of their lives. The sky overhead was a washed-out blue without a single cloud in sight. Not even a hint of an afternoon thunderstorm building over the mountains to the west to alleviate the heat.

No breeze to cool the sweat trickling down Rey's spine beneath her plain white cotton shirt.

No respite for the wicked.

Ten thousand feet tall, those mountains were. Lake Tahoe nestled on the other side of the highest peaks. Clear sapphire blue water, ice cold even at the height of summer. She imagined taking a dip in that water, lazing on a public beach with about a million other people all trying to escape the oven that was Reno in early August.

Next week, she promised herself. She'd have enough cash to book a nice little room on the north shore. Let the tourists flock to the casinos at south lake. Casino gambling was for losers. She never gambled. She was a pro.

Lift a wallet here, nab some cash there, never let the mark feel a thing. All those ballet lessons she'd taken as a child had built on her natural grace and dexterity. The magician she'd dated after she'd graduated high school, a lecherous old coot who'd gotten his jollies from dating an eighteen-year-old, had taught her sleight of hand. The pickpocket she'd caught with his hand in her shoulder bag had agreed to teach her the tricks of the trade in exchange for not turning him in.

She'd been earning a more-than-respectable living for years working tourist events in Northern Nevada. Summers were her busy season. People got careless when their brains fried in the desert heat.

Men quit wearing sports coats that covered the back pockets of their pants, choosing instead to wear light-weight linen shirts that were silky smooth and easy to reach beneath. If they felt the slight brush of her hand, they'd think it was a hoped-for breeze, not the thin, pretty girl in the loose, low-cut peasant blouse with the billowy sleeves and the multi-colored peasant skirt whose folds concealed a variety of pockets.

She'd smile at them with an open, honest expression that said, "I'm out to have a good time, just another tourist like you trying to beat the heat," and they'd nod and keep on doing whatever they'd been doing. Later, when they noticed that their wallet or their fold of cash was gone, they'd never suspect her. After all, she didn't even carry a purse, and the sleeves of her blouse were gauzy enough to show that she didn't have anything hidden next to her tanned and slender arms.

So much easier than the clumsy bump-and-lift the pickpocket had taught her at first.

Today she carried a tote bag, but it was mostly empty. She was blending in. This part of the classic car show, the area's annual ode to all things at least fifty years old—music, fashion, and most of all automobiles—featured cars entered into the show by women. The show's attempt, no doubt, to make the event appear less testosterone heavy.

The predominant fashion among the women who stood by their cars, proudly showing off refurbished leather interiors and gleaming engines beneath their cars' propped up hoods, were poodle skirts and ankle socks and high-heeled patent leather shoes.

Rey didn't go quite that far. Poodle skirts couldn't conceal the large pockets she needed for her work. Instead she wore a ridiculously full black skirt splattered with large white polka dots. A stiff, full, frilly underskirt made of red lace made her feel like a float in the Thanksgiving Day parade, but the volume of material and the polka-dotted print served to hide the deep pockets she'd sewn into both sides almost as well as her peasant skirt.

A wide black belt cinched in her plain white blouse. She wore white boat shoes instead of patent leather heels, and she'd tied a red scarf around her neck, the ends resting in the V of her blouse. The red tote bag merely served to complete her outfit.

All very much black and white and red all over. Just like the old riddle, as much a classic as the cars she was pretending to enjoy.

The one thing that put her in the category of tourist rather than car owner was her lack of ostentatious jewelry. Cars weren't the only things these women spent their money on. The tennis bracelets alone were worth a fortune, much less the rings and earrings and necklaces. The men who accompanied the women wore gold watches that would have brought a pretty penny if Rey had decided to steal them.

But Rey didn't lift jewelry. Her slight of hand was more than good, but she'd never mastered the skill necessary to unlatch a watch and slide it off a man's wrist without him noticing. And she certainly wasn't about to break into a hotel room to steal jewelry that had been left behind.

She lifted wallets and cash, but she never simply slipped them inside her bag. Some of the venues she worked required security to open and inspect bags and backpacks, looking for weapons. Rey never took the chance that extra wallets might be noticed during an inspection, and she never worked a venue that would require her to empty her pockets and walk through a metal detector.

The classic car show was the perfect type of venue for her. She could walk through the crowd, *ooing* and *ahing* at all the bright, shiny cars, and look like just another tourist drawn in by the lure of the era. For all intents and purposes, she was just a young, thin, pretty brunette searching for an *American Bandstand* rocker of her own to take her to the car show's sock hop that night.

She pretended to admire the old cars, most painted candy apple red, and all of which were huge and heavy compared to modern automobiles. Now and then when the opportunity presented itself, she lifted a wallet from a back pocket and stashed them in her own pockets to rifle through later.

Alcohol flowed freely at this event, mostly beer in clear plastic cups. Men who'd had a few too many beers leered at her. A few even tried to chat her up. She'd smiled and chatted back—blending in was important—but she never let the conversations rise to the level of a flirt. She was on the job.

Twice she almost ended up wearing someone's beer when an obviously intoxicated man bumped into her. At least they apologized. She'd nodded and moved on, satisfied that the contact had been unintentional, not the act of another thief working the crowd. She wasn't naïve enough to think she was the only professional working the show. Ostentatious shows of wealth tended to attract people like her.

It was the third bump that got her in trouble.

This time the man was her age, good looking in a stubbly beard kind of way. He wasn't holding a beer and he wasn't dressed in sock hop clothes straight out of the '50s. He wore a Hawaiian print shirt, open in the front over a plain white t-shirt, and his dark hair wasn't jelled into a D.A. His one concession to the theme of the show were the sunglasses he wore. Thick metallic Elvis frames and dark lenses that hid his eyes.

He bumped into her from the side, a hard enough shove against her shoulder to knock her off balance. She stumbled sideways, glad that she hadn't worn heels. A twisted ankle would have put an early end to her workday.

"Excuse me," he said immediately.

He gave her a sheepish grin and offered his hand to help her steady herself. She ignored his hand. She didn't like being touched by strangers.

"No harm," she said.

She flashed him a quick smile of her own before she let the flow of the crowd move her to the next car in line. A long, sleek convertible, it was painted robin's egg blue and had wide fins in the back. A young woman not that much older than she was sat in the driver's seat, her head tilted up to look at an overly tanned and slick-looking man in his fifties dressed in a white summer-weight suit standing next to her. The suit only served to accentuate his gray hair and the air of affluence he projected like a spotlight.

The young woman's left hand rested on the steering wheel. She wore a wedding ring that sported a diamond that dwarfed her slender finger. If Rey had been a jewel thief, a diamond that size might have been nearly irresistible.

It wasn't the largest jewel she'd seen that afternoon, but it was one of the prettiest. She might not wear jewelry—or steal it, for that matter—but that didn't mean she couldn't appreciate pretty things.

Later, when she was alone in a bathroom stall in the casino, her skirt billowed out around her as she sat emptying the cash from the first of the wallets she'd stored in her pockets, she realized the man in the Elvis shades hadn't bumped into her by accident.

Her breath caught as she realized he'd left her a gift.

It lay in the bottom of her tote bag, glittering in the light from the overhead fluorescents like distant stars, a new constellation in the dark night sky of her nearly empty bag.

A diamond-encrusted tennis bracelet worth a small fortune.

*****

Rey hadn't always been a thief. A wild child? Yes, she'd been that.

Hard to handle, her father said, but she secretly thought he'd been pleased that she liked to run and play with the neighborhood ruffians, as her mother called them. Kids a year or two older than she was, the majority of them boys with skateboards and perpetual scabs on their knees and elbows.

The ballet lessons her mother signed her up for were supposed to instill discipline into her life. Lessons and the long hours of practice at home were supposed to leave her no time to get into trouble. Her mother even had a ballet barre installed in their garage for Rey to use, and she made sure Rey practiced every day. A fit body produced a fit mind, according to her mother, and Rey had become the most fit person in her fourth-grade class.

Every now and then, Rey's father would wink at her behind her mother's back, like they were co-conspirators in their secret opposition to the woman who ruled their house with her unwavering opinions and incomprehensible rules.

Rey's mother had been a hard woman, structured within an inch of her life. No alcohol in the house. No cigarettes. No swearing. Dinner on the table by six, homework done by eight, followed by the one television show a night that Rey was allowed to watch. Lights out at ten, even for her parents.

That structure had been blown to hell one week before Rey's thirteenth birthday. The day her father left them.

She'd come home from her ballet lesson only to find that he'd packed all his clothes and left while she'd been at school.

No note. No tearful farewells. No promises to stay in touch. Just a present wrapped in tissue paper that he'd left on Rey's bed.

A jewelry box with the figure of a ballerina inside. The ballerina was supposed to twirl and dance to a music box tune if Rey wound the key.

She only played that tune once. The twinkly, happy music made her angry, as angry as she'd ever been in her life.

The next day she threw the jewelry box in the trash.

Her father had been the one thing that made living with her mother's rules and structures bearable. Rey wanted her father, not the stupid present that was supposed to make her feel... what? Not abandoned? Not left behind so he could make a new life for himself?

She stopped going to ballet the next day.

Not that she told her mother that. Rey simply found other things to do while her mother was at work. When her mother was home, Rey would still go out in the garage in her workout clothes, but she didn't practice ballet. She read magazines she wasn't supposed to have, and the pictures and articles taught her how other people lived. She read books she wasn't supposed to read. Books with swear words and bad people who did bad things.

Her mother was too distracted to notice. Her world had fallen apart too. Her heart had been broken, but at thirteen, Rey was too self-involved to notice.

Rey had no allowance to buy the books and magazines she read. If she couldn't borrow them from her school friends, she lifted them from stores. She became the wild child again, only now she did all the things teenagers weren't supposed to do. She tried cigarettes and found she hated them. She tried alcohol and decided some of it wasn't so bad. She dabbled with pot, but it never gave her the same kind of high as getting away with stealing something from a store.

Her life might have turned out differently if she'd been caught back at the start. Scared straight, as the saying went. But ballet had given her the kind of grace and dexterity that made lifting things easy.

Her mother quit taking notice of the things that Rey did, and eventually Rey realized that her mother had quit caring. While Rey had only tried alcohol, her mother had taken refuge in it. She fell asleep on the couch most nights long before ten, the television on to fill the silence in the house.

Rey had been eighteen and working at a fast-food restaurant when her mother didn't wake up one day. She'd passed away in the hospital three days later.

Rey had been on her own ever since.

She did yoga now instead of ballet as a way to keep herself limber and fit. She practiced slight-of-hand magic tricks for hours in front of a mirror. A few years ago she'd taken an adult education class on dressmaking and bought herself a secondhand sewing machine. Now she either made or altered her clothes to incorporate the extra-deep hidden pockets that were so necessary to her trade. She surfed websites at the library and picked up flyers for the local events that were her bread and butter, and then she studied the culture behind those events to make sure she fit in.

Over the years, she'd developed two hard and fast rules. The first was to never work a casino floor.

In a casino, someone was always watching. Security cameras. Security guards who weren't tired old men just putting in the hours. Pit bosses who were paid to pay attention.

The very best venues for her particular work were the summertime outdoor events, like the classic car show or cooking competitions, like the annual rib cookoff or the Greek festival.

She had a series of day jobs, as she thought of the stints when she worked as a cashier or a waitress. The jobs provided her with a visible means of support and easy enough to come by in a tourist area, and were easy to walk away from when it was time to move on.

Her second rule was something far more personal: she never stole from women.

After her mother died, Rey had to figure out how to go from being a teenager with a part-time job to a woman on her own who needed to do adult things like pay rent and buy food. She'd gone through her mother's desk, found her bank records and a stack of bills that needed to be paid. It had been an eye-opening experience.

She'd been appalled at how little money her mother actually had. As difficult as her mom had been to live with, she'd managed to stretch that money and support the two of them for years without any help at all from Rey's dad.

Women were easy targets for pickpockets. They left purses in shopping carts while they reached for something on a bottom shelf. They carried open-topped tote bags along with diaper bags and shopping bags, and many kept their gaze on the pavement—or on their children—while they walked. Young children distracted them.

But even if the women appeared wealthy and able to afford to lose whatever money they carried with them, Rey never stole from them.

The woman who'd worn the diamond tennis bracelet certainly must have been well off. Rey didn't even want to hazard a guess at the value of the diamonds in that single piece of jewelry.

If she was caught with something like this, she'd be looking at mandatory prison time. Rey had always been careful to keep a day's take in the misdemeanor range, so that even if she was caught, she wouldn't be doing time.

She had to get rid of this thing. The thief had picked her out of the crowd so that *he* wouldn't get caught. She could throw it in the trash, but what would he do when, not if, he came back for his prize?

She wasn't naïve enough to believe he'd just walk away.

She wasn't a violent person, she never had been. She had pepper spray in her bag, but that was the extent of her means of self-defense.

Women had been beaten and killed over less. Just because he'd been easy on the eyes didn't mean he was a nice guy.

She sat in the stall, her hands shaking.

She had to do something. She couldn't hide out in here all day. Someone would eventually notice and call security. They'd find her, find the bracelet, and call the police. Whoever had owned this bracelet must have reported it missing by now. Otherwise, why would the thief have dropped it in her purse?

The police wouldn't believe that she hadn't stolen it. Not when they found all the wallets in the pockets of her skirt.

First things first.

She rifled through the wallets, removing just enough cash that might seem reasonable a woman like her would carry in her bag, then dumped the wallets in the stall's trash receptacle. She didn't worry about leaving fingerprints on the leather. She'd never been fingerprinted in her life, and she hoped to continue that trend.

She actually flinched when someone banged into the stall next to hers. She could smell the reek of alcohol followed closely by the stinking sounds of someone purging their stomach.

That decided her.

She needed to leave now. She tossed the last wallet into the trash without even looking at the money inside. The receptacle was full now, but casino bathrooms didn't have security cameras. They wouldn't know she was the one who'd dumped the wallets.

She needed to leave the casino. Leave the classic car show behind, but she had something important to do first.

The handsome jewel thief had involved her in this mess, but she could put an end to it. She'd just have to do something she'd never done before.

Put something back.

*****

Rey had never worked with a partner. The closest she ever came was during what she thought of as her apprenticeship with the pickpocket.

He'd been good, she had to give him that. Good with his hands. Good at picking the perfect marks.

Good in bed.

She hadn't fallen in love with him. Sometimes she doubted she'd ever be able to fall in love, and for that she blamed her dad. Here with their family one minute—putting up with his wife and buying his daughter presents—and gone the next, never to be heard from again. Her dad had been a real peach.

Rey wasn't about to put herself through that kind of heartbreak. She'd seen what it had done to her mom, and her mom had the strongest will of any person Rey had ever known.

The pickpocket had been easy on the eyes, she'd give him that. Slender with fine-boned features and gentle hazel eyes, and with just the slightest nasal quality to his voice. He'd reminded her of a movie star. Not the leading man, and certainly not the villain, but more like the leading man's best friend. Someone you could rely on, those hazel eyes insisted.

He hadn't deserted her. That alone had earned her undying gratitude, and she'd stayed with him far longer than she probably should have.

They'd wound up in Vegas, the two of them. Three glorious weeks at a top-notch hotel—one not attached to a casino—and they went to shows and museums and outdoor concerts. A working-man's vacation, he'd joked, because of course he was on the job whenever they went to outdoor events.

That vacation was their last hurrah, although neither of them had known it at the time. He'd plied his trade and she'd watched, learning all the moves he knew, practicing on him and then doing it for real on easy marks he'd pointed out to her.

And it had been easy.

Right up until the time he'd tried to lift a wallet from an undercover cop.

Nobody could have tagged the man as a cop. He'd worn his disguise well—a tourist with a wife and two kids, one still in a stroller. Rey had never known why the cop had been undercover or what type of sting she and the pickpocket had stumbled into.

The pickpocket had been whisked away by two uniform cops before he could say a word to her, but he'd saved her just the same. He didn't even look for her in the crowd. A slight shake of his head had been the only clue she got that this was goodbye.

Heart hammering in her chest, she had faded away through the throng of tourists without a single look back.

It had been the closest she'd ever come to being caught.

She could use a partner now. Hundreds of people, men and women alike, were crowded in the parking lot among all the classic cars. She was skilled at picking out easy marks in crowds like this, but she had no experience trying to pick out someone who had been another thief's mark, much less the right someone.

The skin on the back of her neck, hot and sweaty just a short time ago beneath her red scarf, crept up in gooseflesh as she worked her way through the crowd. The jewel thief was out here somewhere. He might be watching her now, waiting to make his move to get the bracelet back.

She didn't have much time to return it to the woman he'd stolen it from. Whoever that woman might be.

Speakers suspended on metal poles blared out rock 'n roll tunes from the '50s and '60s. A slight breeze picked up the smell of exhaust and hot metal and greasy French fries from a food truck parked at the other end of the sea of cherry red and sky blue and mint green cars and trucks. A loudspeaker crackled to life with a canned announcement about the night's sock hop dance at an outside stage behind the casino.

Everything looked normal. No overt police presence. If the police had been here, they'd taken a report and left. The few security guards wandering through the crowd were in their sixties themselves, hot and tired looking in their black uniforms, shuffling along beneath the cloudless desert sky as if their feet were killing them.

She'd just started down another row of cars when a hand landed on her shoulder from behind.

She stiffened.

"Act natural," he said.

The jewel thief had ditched the Elvis sunglasses. He'd also ditched the Hawaiian shirt he'd been wearing over the plain white t-shirt. He'd slicked back his dark hair and shaved off his stubble. Now he looked the part of someone going to a sock hop.

"We're going to take a little walk," he said. "Look at a few cars. Peer under the hoods."

She shrugged her shoulder. Her heart was thumping wildly in her chest, but nobody touched her without her consent. Ever.

"I don't think so," she said.

He took his hand away. He tilted his head and gave her a sheepish grin that didn't reach his cold blue eyes. "You have something of mine. As soon as I retrieve it—without anyone noticing, of course—you'll never have to see me again." He glanced at the crowd around them. "And I don't think either of us want anyone to notice, do we."

It wasn't a question. He knew exactly what she was. Could he prove it? Everyone had a cell phone with a camera app. He could have taken her picture at just the right time.

And she did still have the bracelet.

This time when he put his hand on her elbow, right above where she held the straps of her bag in the crook of her arm, she didn't shake him off. Instead she let him steer her through the crowd. It seemed like he knew exactly where he wanted to go.

"I do have to admit that you're good," he said.

She sniffed. "I'm better than good," she said.

He acknowledged that with a slight tilt of his head. "We would make a good team."

She almost told him to dream on, but then he added, "Too bad I don't work with partners."

The heat from the asphalt was leeching through the soles of her shoes. She thought of the cold, ice blue water of Lake Tahoe. The last time she'd been there, she'd rented a little two-seater pedal boat—just her—and pedaled out on that clear blue water. Then she sat there, just floating, letting the shallow waves rock her. Not thinking about anything but the feel of the sun on her skin.

She'd get there again after this day—after this job—was over.

He directed her through the rows of cars until they came to a beautifully restored, pale blue '57 Chevy. The chrome gleamed, the interior seats were pristine leather. The hood was raised to display an engine that was nearly as clean as the car.

The woman who clearly owned the car must have been nearing seventy. Her fluff of silver hair looked like a halo around her tanned face. She wasn't wearing a poodle skirt. Instead she was dressed in sage green linen slacks and an ivory silk blouse. A floral printed silk scarf was wrapped around her neck, the ends tucked into the V of the blouse. The lenses of her prescription glasses had turned dark in the bright sunshine. Heavy gold bracelets circled her thin wrists. She stood off to the driver's side of the car.

"Let's take a closer look at this one," the thief said.

Rey stopped alongside him on the passenger side of the car, her red bag in between them. She crossed her arms below her breasts and pretended an interest in the car she didn't feel.

She didn't like plying her trade around people who wore dark glasses. She never could be quite sure where they were looking.

The owner of the car smiled at her across the raised hood of the car, and Rey smiled back.

"Are you interested in cars, my dear?" the woman asked.

Rey shrugged.

"She's more interested in the fashions," the thief said.

The old woman raised one hand as if to shoo that comment away, but stopped with her hand in midair. Her smile faltered, and she let her hand drop with a sigh.

Rey glanced at the thief. His blue eyes had taken on a malevolent glint, although his friendly grin remained in place.

"Fashions come and go," the woman said. "Memories made in cars like this, they last a lifetime."

Rey took a closer look at the woman's jewelry. The gold bands on her wrists weren't costume jewelry. A diamond glinted here and there among the gold, and the ring on one arthritic finger bore a cool sapphire and a deep red ruby. Birthstones, maybe?

"Of course, you're too young to realize that," the old woman said to Rey.

"Did you make memories in this car?" she asked.

"A great many." The woman's expression took on a dreamy look. "Of course, it didn't look like this at the time. My husband and I, when we found this car, we didn't have much money to live on. It was in as sad a shape as we were, but it didn't matter. It was what we could afford. We'd sit out under the stars and talk about the future. Sometimes we'd play the radio and dance."

She shook her head and seemed to come back to herself.

"Oh, my," she said. "I usually don't go on like that, but it's been a trying day. My son says I shouldn't come to things like this anymore, but I'm not ready to sit by myself in an old folks' home." She sighed. "I suppose he might be right."

The thief squeezed Rey's elbow. She realized she'd missed the perfect opportunity to slip the bracelet from her bag into his pocket. Her skirt was full enough to hide the movement from anyone behind them, and the car was between them and the old woman.

But Rey had been distracted not only by the old woman's story, but by the suspicion that this woman had been the jewel thief's mark. That the diamond bracelet in her bag belonged to this woman, and its theft had been the source of the woman's trying day.

The jewel thief had steered her to this particular car for a reason. He was reliving the moment when he'd stolen the bracelet from the Chevy's owner. Rey could see it in his eyes—the same exhilaration she'd felt the first time she'd stolen a magazine from the store and gotten away with it, only this was a thousand times worse.

He hadn't just stolen jewels from someone. He'd stolen her joy in this moment, a time when she could revel in the memories she'd made in this car and share them with a random stranger who'd stopped to admire her car's beauty.

"You've done right by this car," Rey said. "It's clear that you love it." She leaned forward, pretending to get a closer look at the engine.

The old woman swiped at her cheek with one hand, and Rey realized her eyes had gone moist behind her dark glasses.

"We do tend to fall in love with our possessions," the old woman said. "They last much longer than the people in our lives do, provided we're not careless with them."

That sealed it. Rey knew what she had to do.

She shifted her tote bag on her arm until she held it in front of herself. Besides the bracelet and the money she'd stolen, the bag held the usual items a person might find in a woman's purse. Lipstick the color of her scarf. A brush for her hair. A compact mirror and a cell phone (a burner she'd picked up at a convenience store).

And a travel size pack of tissues.

The thief clamped down hard on Rey's elbow. A warning, but Rey pretended not to notice. She took the pack of tissues out of her bag and reached across the open engine compartment to offer them to the woman.

One tissue poked out of the top of the pack. Rey had palmed the bracelet in her hand beneath the pack. It was a risk, but she was willing to bet that the woman would take just the one tissue, not the entire pack.

She was right.

"Thank you, my dear," the woman said. She dabbed at her eyes with the tissue, and while she had her eyes closed, Rey let the diamond bracelet slip from her hand. It landed on a shiny bit of the engine next to a clamp that held a hose in place. Not obvious, but not buried deep inside the workings of the car either.

The drop had been perfect.

The thief had seen the whole thing, of course. His grin thinned into a tight-lipped line. He was holding her elbow tight enough now that Rey knew she'd have bruises, but she continued to ignore him.

The old woman balled the used tissue in one hand and nodded at Rey. "That was very nice of you. My husband used to say I was too trusting, but I believe in random acts of kindness. Is there anything I can do for you?"

Rey shook her head and cast her eyes downward, pretending a shyness she didn't feel. "That's all ri…"

She trailed off and widened her eyes, as if she'd just caught sight of a glint of sunlight shining off the diamonds inside the engine compartment.

"Oh, my!" she said. "Is that… did you lose a bracelet or something?"

She used her free hand to point at the bracelet. "Is that yours?"

The old woman's gaze followed Rey's pointing finger. She gasped, one hand to her chest. Then she reached inside her car, arthritic fingers shaking, and pulled out the bracelet.

"I am such a foolish old woman," she said. She held the bracelet to her chest, her eyes leaking again. "I thought this had been stolen, and here I'd just lost it inside my car. It must have caught on something when I was showing it off." She gave Rey a watery grin. "Thank you!"

Rey shrugged, although it was one-sided since the jewel thief still held her elbow tight. "I just noticed it," she said. "That's all."

"My husband gave this to me on our fiftieth wedding anniversary. He passed away three months later. I don't know what I would have done if I'd lost it."

The old woman was still holding the bracelet to her chest.

"It must be very valuable," Rey said.

"I suppose it is," the old woman said. "But it's the memories that matter, that make a thing valuable."

"Like this car," Rey said.

"Like this car," the old woman agreed.

*****

The jewel thief disappeared into the crowd without another word. Rey understood. The tennis bracelet hadn't been the only thing he'd stolen that day. He'd only dumped the bracelet into Rey's bag because the old woman had made a fuss as soon as she realized the bracelet was gone. Now that he'd lost the bracelet, he didn't waste time hanging around a place where he might get caught.

The old woman had made a fuss again after Rey "found" the bracelet. She'd insisted on buying Rey dinner that night. "Before you go to the sock hop, dear," she'd said. "It's the least I can do."

So they'd eaten at one of the restaurants in the casino, the bracelet once again encircling the woman's thin wrist. Rey had listened while she talked about her life with her husband. About her children. And about her love for the old '57 Chevy she'd so lovingly restored.

Right before desert, the woman's son had joined them. He was tall and handsome and sported a plain gold band on his ring finger. He thanked Rey for helping his mother, which made her feel uncomfortable enough that she excused herself without waiting for the slice of cheesecake the old woman had insisted she order.

"Have to freshen up for the dance," she'd said.

But of course, she didn't go. Instead she took a twenty-dollar bill from her purse and stuffed it in the tip jar on her way out of the restaurant. The wait staff had been exclusively female.

As she walked to her car, she caught the sounds of old time rock 'n roll from the outdoor stage behind the casino. The night had cooled only marginally. Rey unknotted the scarf from around her neck and stuffed it in her bag. A breeze from the west felt good against her skin. August days in Reno were an oven, but August nights were tolerable.

She had no possessions that brought her the kind of joy the car and the tennis bracelet brought the old woman. Maybe someday she would, but not now.

Then she thought about the pedal boat. About floating on the clear blue water of Lake Tahoe, all alone, just her and the water, the sunshine and the gentle waves. Her mother had never taken the time to relax and enjoy life like that, and not for the first time, Rey felt bad for her mom.

But was that true? Had her mother always been so structured, even before she'd met Rey's father? Or had she been a wild child like Rey? Someone who actually had fun?

Rey would never know. When she'd been a teenager, she hadn't thought to ask.

Thinking about the pedal boat brought back memories. The boat hadn't belonged to her, it was just a rental, but the thought of it was doing the same thing for Rey that the car and the tennis bracelet must do for the old woman.

Maybe she'd buy a pedal boat of her own someday. It didn't have to be fancy. Her car was nothing special, certainly not a classic, but it was big enough that she could put a rack on the roof to carry the boat.

Who knew. Someday she might even find someone to share the ride with.

The Road to Reconciliation

(The Driver's New Assignment)

Wil A. Emerson

Five-thirty on a rainy Friday evening and I'd just poured a short glass of bourbon on the rocks to sip while I pondered what I'd do with the free night ahead. Nothing scheduled, I'd let two rookie drivers take the less lucrative passengers who had clients or friends in D.C. for the weekend. With three straight weeks of very successful runs, I needed a break. A night alone didn't seem like a bad choice after the bourbon eased me into a comfortable state of mind. Netflix or HBO Max might be the answer.

However, the doorbell rang at the exact moment I was easing back in my comfortable black leather lounger. At the exact moment I'd clicked the little red button to put my big screen in the streaming mode.

The chime on my doorbell wasn't a preset buzz from the manufacturer. Mine was a simple tinny tone; one I'd rigged by adjusting the little spikes on the microchip that prompted the digital recordings. A melody of sorts took over, one of either a prelude to a sonata or blissful waltz. I'd chosen the tunes on purpose so I wouldn't be jarred out of that blank mental state, when the sole focus was whatever thought, picture or book had control of my mind.

Of course, getting in that kind of meditative state was a necessity for sleep, too. A sudden, harsh noise could send me over the cusp, into another PSTD calamity. I wasn't even close to needing sleep.

The rigged doorbell, it's doe, re, me, re, me sound kept me from being reported to apartment management. There were rules against *individual announcement apparatus*. A means of keeping the halls quiet and tenants not disturbed by pranksters or solicitors. I agreed with the concept, but I also had a dire need to be forewarned if someone was looking specifically for me. Prudent people, even those with a desire to do damage such as steal your electronics, can and do press a button just to see if the resident isn't home. Yes, the usual buzzer at the entrance didn't prevent strangers from entering uninvited. In fact, all one had to do was wait for another person on the street level who asked permission to enter Alexander Gardens Apartments, and just tag along. Even residents seldom questioned who walked through the doors with them.

Surprise sounds and strangers are a trigger for me. I won't belabor the PTSD problem but it does put me in a fetal position for hours at times.

I looked through the door's peephole, saw no one and took a step back. A couple of women friends were short enough to not be picked up by the angle of the small lens. Or someone could easily press the button and step aside. That's exactly what I would do. Who likes being spied upon while they wait?

Curiosity got the best of me. With caution, I eased the door open. A moderately sized woman with disheveled gray hair and a dowdy sweater came into view. Slim and carelessly dressed, one might suspect a street person had strayed inside Alexander Garden Apartments to request monetary assistance. I pass homeless people every day on the corner of Mt. Vernon Avenue. Food or shelter is never on the list of needs, it seems.

"Sorry," I said, "Not…" And then I leaned closer. "How did you find where I live?" I paused for all of three seconds. "Of course, why couldn't you find my address when you have all the resources in the world at your disposal? The real question, why are you here?" I pulled the door wide. With a certainty, she wouldn't want to remain in the hall for any length of time.

"Michael Lafferty, you could say welcome, how about a drink?" She smiled but just as quickly came back to her natural state. Lips tight and a flat affect.

"Do you really want a drink or are you just suggesting I *should have* immediately offered you one?" I paused long enough to let her answer, which I didn't really care if she did or not, then continued, "Sorry, maybe it's bad manners on my part, but I generally offer a drink to a friend I've invited to my apartment. Ma'am, I know we are not on each other's *friend* list."

"Then offer me water," she said dryly. As she spoke, she pulled off the gray wig and quickly released the reddish/brown hair held tight to her scalp by several long hair pins.

"You didn't answer your cell phone," she said as she pocketed the pins.

I handed her a half-filled glass of water I'd got from the kitchen faucet.

Then she took another jab, "No bottled water?"

"Not in stock, Ma'am. Only when I have invited guests." I watched her eyes, hoping I could catch a hint of amusement or fright or caring, some connection, something that would give me a clue as to why she'd shown up at my door. While puzzled by her sudden appearance, I wasn't surprised by the neglected woman's attire she wore, though. She'd worn various costumes each and every time I'd driven her unofficially on one of her clandestine road trips. On official trips, those in the record book, she wore top-of-the line business suits, pants or skirts. Generally, the skirts stopped short at the top of the knee. Because she has fabulous legs and knows it. On occasion, she's been in a dress, tailored grays, blues or black, yet of highest quality and a touch of pure, viral feminism.

This unexpected visitor, a middle age, high ranking congresswoman, continues to be the head of a committee that pretty much controls the whole congressional organization. She can make men and women beg, and often she does. As the Czar of Ways and Means, nothing is taken for granted when this red/brown haired nuclear warhead sits at the table with her gavel. She can bring a president to his knees, as she so chooses, and not always in a flattering way.

I never stated her name in public and, to this date, I've never mentioned it in private, either. My rule has been to stick to 'Ma'am' but I am tempted often to put her in her place and call her a name that is fitting for her personality.

Instead, I said, "Would you like ice in your water, Ma'am? Ice maker's in the fridge drawer." And added a smile and pointed to the couch as I sat down in my comfortable leather recliner and let the foot extension rise to elevate my feet.

"Bottled sparkling water over rocks, is what I prefer."

"Good for you. Perhaps at the next meeting."

She eyed me, assessing if I was being coy or just mean.

"There's a situation I'd like to talk about with you. Not exactly dire, but something that needs correcting in the next few weeks."

"Should I point out that I'm a limo driver and have a very nice Lincoln Continental that feels like a second home. Fully licensed and with a squeaky-clean record."

"That you are, Michael. This is a confidential matter. And because you have an impeccable service record, as a driver, and a military veteran, I think you are perfect for the job I have in mind."

"Have you heard the term 'barking up the wrong tree'?" I sighed and flicked the channel.

"Do you really need to be rude? I'm in dire need of a favor."

"With all due respect, Ma'am, how did you get here?"

"Let's just say I didn't walk."

"Then I suggest you 'just say you didn't walk' and turn around in the same manner to wherever you came from. I won't get up to show you the way. The door is self-locking."

"Fifty thousand dollars. Half if you say yes now."

*****

I buckled my seat belt, placed my cap on the passenger seat and adjusted the rear-view mirror. As a matter of habit, I eyed the passenger on the right side of the back seat. A broad-shouldered guy, bald pate, sideburn with shadows of mousey brown hair and a full size, three-inch dark brown beard. His eyes on a cell phone, not sure if they were steely brown or midnight blue. A newbie to the private service. All I knew about the passenger was he'd paid in advance with a platinum American Express. Daniel Levin.

"Sir, if you need a return ride, here's my private number. Text me and I'll reply."

"Thanks, but I'm covered."

He did take my card, though, and placed it in his jacket pocket.

The tactic was used with all new customers. A means of obtaining private service by someone who didn't like to use the contracted drivers for a variety of reasons. Success rate for me about thirty percent.

The drive was going to take a good forty-five minutes. Due to traffic, rush hour, and road conditions beyond the metro area, I eased back on the pedal to study taillights and judge how smooth the ride would go. Usually on this kind of haul, the passenger worked, played video games on his cell or started a chat. I took bets on having the nervous kind, type A, working on a heart attack, and staying silent. But if the passenger had anxiety issues, could not sit silently, he or she would start a conversation before I got to the first red light.

I was about seven cars behind the first light, yellow glowing, when he opened up.

"It's going to be a long evening. Looking forward to it, though." Then he pulled out a cigarette pack.

"Sorry, Sir. No smoking allowed."

"What the hell. I'm paying for the drive. Isn't it the same as if I were driving and smoking in my own car?"

"It's a company rule. Protective measure for passengers who are allergic to cigarette smoke. Sorry, Sir."

"So, it's not your rule. Okay, what difference does it make? Be the good guy and don't tell the boss."

He pulled out a gold lighter and flicked it on.

I turned on my blinker and eased over to the right lane. "Sir, Mr. Levin, I'll have to let you out here. If you want to smoke outside the car, I'll wait. My pleasure, Sir."

"Hell, what's the big deal?" He paused, then pocketed the lighter but held on to the cigarette. Between his fingers, close to his mouth, the long Marlboro from the white and gold box dangled like a dare.

"If you stop a couple of times, I'll be late. Shit."

I got a good view of his eyes, steely gray, crow's feet, brow a little heavy. Someone who stewed over problems. To ease his concern, I could have asked if he had a preference for music but decided to let him carry his weight. My gut said he'd want heavy metal or rap. And there weren't any rules to prevent it except for my utter dislike.

I'd won round one with the 'company no smoking rule' and didn't have to use 'I own this car' which I reserved for the most persistent smokers. As far as musical enjoyment being a conflict, I managed to skirt the issue with other riders by interrupting the play if I hated the choice. A faulty system couldn't be repaired until the next day. The tactic worked ninety-nine per cent of the time. I had a feeling, it wouldn't with the smoker in my back seat.

"How'd you get into this business? No college, not thinking about the future?" He cracked his knuckles with each question.

"Long story." His brashness offensive but then I had made assumptions about him, also.

"Well, probably not as long as mine. But if you missed out on college, there's time to go. Hell, it's the connections you make. Never mind what the colleges push down your throat. The new lefties control what's dished out. Rehash modern history, make up another version. Most of what you need to know about the new world is better learned on the street. Get behind someone who's running an import business or maybe a major sports team. Those are the connections you need, only way to move up, live the high life."

I decided I didn't like this guy at all. But, then again, he wasn't the first person with political connections who had metaphorically soiled the backseat of my limo.

As a diversion, I put my cap back on, pulled the brim low. A cover of sorts. Out of sight, out of mind. The passenger settled down in the back seat. As I sped down highway 66, my thoughts went back to the how and why I drove a limo instead of building on my dreams. My skin bore all the ear-markings of war wounds but I'd had never stepped on foreign ground. Not the heroic route for an early honorable discharge with full benefits from the Army. Not my fault a zealous enlistee-kid played macho with a truck full of explosives and hit a brick wall while I stood in formation during a training session.

Was it an intentional hit? Domestic terrorist? Never proven. But my zippered, glued, screwed together, aching bones reminded me of the event each and every day.

This wasn't the first time I thought about that eventful day while driving, but it was the first time a passenger had questioned why I had a 'lowly' job. I thought I'd gotten over the disappointment; pay my dues as an officer after college, then police department, work my way up the ranks. Maybe run a big force. I hadn't acknowledged the hole in my gut for a long time. Now, though, it felt as if the wound had reopened. Pain that lulled on the back burner kicked in, my legs shook and the race to torture had begun.

I swallowed hard; thought about the emergency aid I kept locked in the glove compartment. I hadn't needed those white pills in six months. If the thunderous ache got out of control, I'd have to suck it up. An hour from my apartment meant I'd be driving under the influence if I popped the two necessary pills. Not a risk I could take. I'd have to wait until I dropped off the jerk who now nodded in the back seat.

I pushed the radio button, a set station on Sirus; low volume always and sound from the front speakers so passengers wouldn't complain. A sap for soft classicals, Mozart's music usually soothed the tension, distorted my senses enough to avoid a calamity of pain. Mind over matter, PTSD symptoms under control, the beast within tamed. It worked seventy-five percent of the time. If not, and if in the city, I drove home, changed clothes and went on a vigorous run. Natural endorphins, push through the pain. Sometimes a steamy shower settled its pace, not a roar just a gentler howl.

Summer or winter, exercise and adjusting my body temperature served as the best elixir. The shrink, a guy name Luther MacKenzie, only ten years older, taught me to maintain control over every situation. No different than driving a car, he said. Fitting, I replied, since the only thing I was capable of doing at that point in life, shortly after I woke up from a coma, was walk at a slow pace.

Months later I cruised by the restricted driving limitations the injuries caused due to another unexpected incident. Desperate to return to the real world after a year of aimlessness, my first job interview was with a shady trucking company manager who only glanced at my license. I'd applied for logistics manager; he needed a driver. Next came a random favor for a legitimate limo driver friend of mine. One thing led to another, I got a commercial license by not filling in all the boxes and before long, I earned a decent living instead of living off the dole. Oh, I still banked my government pension. Rainy day theory, never knew when my body would rebel and PTSD would wipe out reason and logic.

I still reminded my friends to not say 'boom' too loudly. Explosive sounds. Heavy metal music. The trigger effect, I told them. I might roll into a tight ball, cry like a baby again.

"Eine Kleine Nachtmusik," my passenger said.

"It is indeed," I replied. "Do you mind?"

"It's my ringtone. On my private cell, that is."

I was tempted to ask the difference between his private cell phone and the public one, but thought better of it. Sometimes less information is healthier, safer. I disliked the guy as it was. No need to add fuel to the fire.

"People expect certain characteristics, traits, preferences. Put you in a mold. You can turn the volume up if you want. Don't need it loud."

I adjusted the volume and sighed. He closed his eyes again.

*****

Two days later, mid-morning, my private cell rang. Ding, dong. Simple.

"Mr. Lafferty, I need a favor." The caller said.

The voice sounded vaguely familiar. "I'm driving. Leave a name and number, I'll call back within the hour."

"Thanks, that has to work," he said.

Cell back on the seat, focused again. Near the Capitol Building, I didn't need any distraction. I had a VIP in the back seat.

I caught her eyes as I glanced into the rearview mirror. Business attire. No wig, no baggy sweater, just the telling red-brown hair and the grimace or smirk on her peachy, laser treated face. How did I know laser? I'd had a series of treatments to help with the fragmented skin on

163

my own cheeks after the accident at Fort Briggs.

"I have a private engagement next Friday evening," she said. The contract service had arranged for this particular ride.

My first thought was to say 'booked' but then again, her special requests were generally very lucrative. I intended to keep this relationship all business no matter my past experiences with her. Her late-night intrusion to my apartment had not been considered in the two weeks that had passed. Tonight, all I had to do was pick up and deliver. Tight lipped, not even smile. Job done with satisfaction.

"This appointment will be an extended one and requires wait time. You can adjust the rate accordingly."

"I'll need a range of time. To block it out."

"Four hours, max. To Fairfax and back. Can I text you for pickup? It, of course, will be around four. Friday, shorter day."

I expected it would be a trip to Bethesda or Baltimore. More her usual haunts. Coincidence, though, she asked to go to Fairfax. The new passenger, the politico I didn't like, had requested that route only without a return. I brushed it off as coincidence.

"Sure, Ma'am, I trust your adjusted rate. Just send me the details on Friday."

I dropped her off at the Willard Hotel, just blocks from the White House, then watched her strut up the walkway as if she owned the place.

Before I eased back into traffic, I looked at my cell, the recent caller and pushed redial.

The not-so-familiar voice answered, "Thanks for getting back with me. I'm in a bind and need a ride."

"Sir, I'd like to help but I've got a schedule to follow."

"I'll make it worthwhile. Really, I need a pickup."

It would have been so easy to say no, hang up. But something struck me about the plea. Not from the cocky guy I'd driven two days before to the suburbs. This guy was frightened, more so, anxious. Hung over? I paused long enough to raise concern I'd not help him out.

"Five hundred. Cash. I'm desperate. Burger King in Manassas Park. I think it's on 28th Street." He clicked off.

I didn't know the area well, but I knew there weren't a lot of Burger Kings in the small township. A place you pass through, unlikely to linger unless a local. Why Manassas Park instead of Fairfax where I'd dropped him off was none of my business. The cash was my business.

One more call and I had the appointed rides juggled. All too soon Falls Church was in the rearview and Fairfax loomed ahead. If the Burger King in Manassas Park didn't have a line, I'd pick up a Whopper and reheat it when I got home. Fast food, a rare indulgence.

He was easy to spot. Suited up, standing in a crowd of high school kids and a few walk-ins dressed in construction gear. As I pulled in the drive, I could tell he wasn't in the best of shape. Suit wrinkled, knees dusty, collar open, dark markings on the front of what should have been a fresh white cotton dress shirt. Before I fully braked, he jumped in the front passenger seat.

"Thank god," he said. And then crumpled forward, his head on his knees.

"Want to lay down in the back seat," I asked.

"No. Do you mind pulling through the order line? Cheeseburger, anything." His voice was shaky. "Something to drink, anything."

While I had my eye on a Whopper, I decided small might work better. Wouldn't tempt him. If this guy was hungry, one bite of the elephant at a time. It might prevent him from throwing up in the limo. I ordered four regular cheeseburgers and two sixteen-ounce diet cokes.

"Want me to park?"

"Hell no. I want out of here as quick as possible." He raised his head, looked behind us and then glanced out the side windows. "Looks safe. Go, go."

Once we were back on 66, he seemed to relax, sat upright and reached for the burger bag.

"Hungry, nothing for two days."

"Enough liquids?" I asked, thinking he'd been on a bad bender. Alcohol, no real food.

"One bottle of water. Small size."

"Generous guests, huh?"

Within a few minutes his eyes were closed and a soft snore followed. Half the burger still in his hand. The large coke consumed.

We had about thirty miles before I needed to know where to drop him off. No need to hassle the guy now. I couldn't help think there was more to his story. More than I needed to know. This didn't seem like the usual boy's night out, drunk as a skunk, situation.

As if on cue, he woke at the Falls Church exit. The proverbial fork in the road as far as entering D.C. traffic. North, South or to the heart of history and deception.

"Need a destination, Sir."

It took so long for him to answer, I thought he didn't hear me.

"An address, Sir."

"Not sure that will play in my favor." He paused. "You don't know me from a hole in the wall, but, I promise, I'm not out to scam you or anyone. I need a place to sleep until I straighten this whole thing out. I've got nearly a grand in my wallet. It's yours if you take me to a safe place."

There are times in everyone's life when instincts tell you to run. Red flag, red flag. Conditioned as I was to follow those gut feelings, I did a complete mental somersault, face in the wind kind of spin.

"I've got a spare room. I control the liquor cabinet. Rule is no loud noise. Lights out at ten."

It was the tone of his voice that got to me. As if a lamb had come to rest at my feet. The cocky guy, macho man, had reversed to the boy he must have been. No bull shit in his request. My imagination? Somehow, I understood he'd reached the edge of a cliff. Turn back or jump.

I'd been on the same 'hang ten', ready to go over the edge, a few months after being released from the VA hospital. The world seemed to be nothing but a cold, relentless shit storm. Little hope left.

The mirror reflected a scarred, broken man.

Not willing to leave a stranger in my apartment upon arrival, I called my supervisor and opted out on calls till noon the next day. I promptly reheated the three remaining burgers, tore open a bag of chips and pulled out two bottles of water.

"I don't like sharing. Spare bedroom has a small bath."

"Works for me." He laughed. "Mind if I eat first. Then I'll take a shower. By the way, call me Dan."

"Michael. You'll need some clothes, Dan. Boxers, sweats, that's about it."

"Beggars and all that. Grateful."

He sat at the table, slowly munching on the burgers and dipping into the chips and going through two sixteen-ounce bottles of water. His silence didn't bother me.

Hunger under control, Dan headed for the shower. I changed into my sweat gear, then decided I'd forego my run and plopped into my leather lounger after I poured a shot of bourbon into my favorite Clayton and Crume leather wrapped cocktail glass. If he asked for the same, I'd consider my options. Risk or relaxer?

The shower ran for longer than I expected but then I hadn't taken one in a long time looking like I'd lost a bar fight. I heard him shuffle around in the bedroom, sit on the bed, walk a little and then sit again.

When the door opened, an hour had passed.

"Anything special you're watching?"

"Netflix. Harry Bosch movie. Old stuff."

"Oh, Michael Connelly. I like his work. Mind if I watch with you."

"Be my guest," and I laughed.

And that was how the evening went. Two strangers, watching an old detective movie, with a broken protagonist making an attempt to find purpose again by solving a cold case.

I turned off the TV at ten, drifted into my room and closed the door. I'd put in an hour of reading and fall into a deep sleep. That was always my intention. Some nights took me back to the explosion, some nights I woke up in a cold sweat and screaming. I could only guess what this unusual night would bring.

After a few turns, left, right, back again, I pushed the LED spot on my watch and glanced at the time. Broke another rule in doing so. It made me more anxious when I knew how little sleep I'd gotten. To my surprise, I'd slept until seven. Solid, with a stranger in my home. Hell, he could have walked away with everything and my armoire, too. I'd track him down if that happened.

The armoire meant more than any human being in my life. A polished, black walnut, antique piece I'd taken from my mother's apartment when she died. It contained a lot of her history and mine. Pictures of my brother and I. My music collection. Every CD I'd purchased and the only music I listened to when I was a teenager. Two guns in a leather box, locked but any thief could figure out how to get it open. I sat up, pissed, then cursed myself for being such a fool.

I thrust my foot into my sweat pants so hard, I ripped away the band at the bottom. Shit. Got them on and pulled open the door. My eyes went to the wall, the treasured armoire. Door closed on it. Nothing in the room looked out of order. Then I heard a hum in the kitchen.

He stood facing the sink and the small window facing out the back of the apartment. A small courtyard and a gravel walkway to the street. The only nice view I had. I smelled coffee. And then he turned.

"Late sleeper, huh? Good for you. I'm too nervous to sleep beyond five."

"Too bad. Habits? Okay, none of my business. But I do want some of my coffee."

"Thought maybe you wouldn't mind. Second pot. I can replace the coffee."

I had to laugh. "No problem. Nice to not have to wait for it."

"Are you suggesting we make this permanent," he said with a harty laugh.

Then his cell rang and fear shot through his eyes. The kind that makes you want to duck for cover or hide in the bathroom. His hand trembled as he put the coffee mug on the counter.

It buzzed about seven times. When it stopped, he took a deep breath.

"You've gotta set that thing so it goes to voicemail after three rings. Easier on your nerves." It was obvious this guy had problems. But I didn't want to become part of his problem or the solution.

I went right to the core of the matter. "I'll take you wherever you want to go. Or the bus line is right out the front."

"No subway?"

"Down at Dupont Circle. Short walk."

"If I leave, they'll find me and kill me."

"Shit." I refilled my coffee cup. "I'm taking a shower. I should be the only one in this apartment when I'm dry."

After a long shower, I dressed in my standard black uniform. Ready to get on with my routine. I liked driving a limo for the most part. My own boss, few complications. If not for the red-brown haired beastly woman who'd set me up with her vile plan of eradicating someone who threatened her political life and put me at risk for going to prison for the rest of mine, I pretty much enjoyed my existence. If I could have rigged votes to guarantee she'd never be in Washington, D.C. again, I would have done so. But a limo driver, a contented one at that, is powerless. And I had no earthly interest in anything political or remotely tied to politics to try and jockey in position for revenge. That was one aspect of my well-being I would fight to retain.

I'd not heard any sounds from the kitchen after my shower, or while I dressed so I presumed my overnight guest had left. I took a step back when I saw him stretched out on my couch.

"Sorry, I don't have the guts to go out there and get slaughtered. Can't do it. Call the cops if you want. That might be better than what I'd face with the characters looking for me." He pointed out the window. Imaginary 'them' or did he have real enemies?

He sat upright, "I've been asked to do something that is totally against my grain. I'd say against my ethical standards. But at this point, I can't say that. I've done some shady deeds. Illegal, all for the job. Shit, I thought being a lobbyist was simple. Connections, good life. One thing led to another and now they've got me between a rock and a six-foot-deep shit hole."

"Metaphor's a little off but I got the message. So, you can't say no. It's a lose-lose situation."

"It's him dead or me. Is that lose-lose enough?"

I swear I thought the guy was going to cry.

"Leave town? Hide out?"

"Thought about it but she's got every means of finding me. With one simple phone call. The whole god-damn U.S. government eating out of her frigging hand."

I knew instantly who he was talking about. Pure evil. The worst woman I'd ever encountered. The one who had me in a vise, too.

The memory of her twisted tale about a secret son she'd given up for adoptions years ago but out to ruin her precious reputation came back with a vengeance. I'd driven her to a secluded spot where she plotted to end his life. I witnessed the whole sorry event and then let her place the murder weapon in my hand. Fingerprints could confirm who pulled the trigger. The whole story so uncanny, unreal that every time I thought about it, played out each scene, I could hardly believe how naïve I had been. I served myself up to her on a silver platter. And to this date, I hadn't found a way to get out from under her thumb.

Daniel Levin unraveled the scheme she'd plotted for him. The plot was to cajole a junior representative to vote on a particular bill the dragon lady wanted passed. Land grants, big money, control of oil deposits for those who fell in step. Because it was his constituent's territory it was imperative in her view that this low-level representative vote as she dictated. From the get-go the junior rep knew it was all about a few people prospering. Levin's role? He'd been paid a large sum to use all his guile and wit to nail the guy into signing on. But the rep wouldn't budge.

Then they, her strong arms, cornered Levin with the deadly proposition. The trip out to Fairfax; the threats against him, tone changed from bribery to removing the obstacle by deadly force. They expected Daniel to strike the hapless representative a killing blow. Had evidence of a money exchange, bribery. He hung in there, wouldn't cave. Refused to go along and finally, a stroke of luck, climbed out a bathroom window and broke away. If it hadn't been for the card in his pocket, they would have tracked him down. Easy to spot a beaten man walking the highway back to D.C.

We sat huddled for another hour. Finally, I knew what had to be done. I grabbed my keys and went back to work. A full afternoon, probably well into the evening, I'd drive and contemplate.

Daniel Levin? I had little fear he'd rob me blind. My apartment was his only sanctuary.

*****

I'd learned years before, football maybe, that sometimes the best defense is going along with an opponent's plan. Let them play it out. And then snap, make a quick adjustment and counterattack. Won't say the number of times it worked or didn't but presently it seemed like the best way to beat the beast at her game.

Two days passed, Levin still in residence but busy with a new plan, before I received another call from my highest paying customer. I wasn't happy to answer when I saw her number but then again, if I didn't, the current problem wouldn't be resolved.

"Are you ready to accept the offer?" Salutations not a strong suit of hers.

"Considerable thought has been given to it."

"I need a drive beyond Fairfax. Will require you to wait."

We arranged the pick-up time and then I sweated out if there'd be an opportunity to set a trap. She had a lot more experience than I had on how to work a con, frame someone or bribe an innocent person into doing a nefarious act. On my side, though, was Levin who assured me he knew enough about electronics to capture any conversation in my car and had a skill set for discreet cameras, too. His part-time, low paying job at Staples during college could pay off. And with luck, I might get enough evidence on the red-haired witch who ruled over Ways and Means to set me free of the bind she held over me. I wasn't a criminal, had not killed the man she said was blackmailing her but, damn, I was thinking about a means to an end. I never wanted to be in her grip again.

I decided the first criminal act I was about to commit had to be in a secluded area of metro D.C. A place where her security detail wouldn't have immediate access and yet, somewhere she felt she still had the upper hand.

When I picked her up, she was dressed as if she had recently been released from a nursing home. Flat wide shoes, gray wig, bulky sweater, a paper sack and a large battered cotton tote over her shoulder. I had to give her credit for sneaking out of her luxury townhouse and not being nabbed as a vagrant. Once we hit Highway 66, she asked me to pull into a gas station where she discretely removed her disguise and revised her hair. All shine and sheen, back to being the dominating back seat passenger.

When I opened the back seat to remove her tote bag to the trunk, I inadvertently pulled out the wrong bag.

"Hey, not that one." A quick tug, it fell to the ground. But I'd made the exchange Dan Levin had cleverly planned.

"So sorry, Ma'am" I picked up the shabby garments off the ground, tucked them in the bag and placed them in the trunk. I had ample time to deposit an arsenal of 'contraband' in an unexpecting pocket of her sweater and in the bottom of the bag. I turned on the recording devise Levin had installed in the limo and then got back to our mission.

On the drive to Manassa, she sat quietly in the back seat, glasses on, reviewing a few pages of printed notes. I wanted to ask about the contract, the payment, get it on record but knew not to push the envelope for fear she'd become suspicious.

Finally, I said, "Address, Ma'am."

"Oh, yes." She rattled off the street number, name and the subdivision. I wasn't surprised that the address was the same as where I'd taken Levin. Two black sedans were parked in the driveway of a stately two-story house, upper income, far enough away from the maddening crowd. Far enough for sinister acts and shady deals. A tall man in dark pants and a baseball-type sports jacket stood at the front door. Another man was posted by the garage. I adjusted the rear-view mirror as I pulled into the drive. Mrs. Ways and Means had her eye on the front door.

"Park down at the bottom of the drive. Lights out. Best to not communicate while you wait. The contract agreement, half, under your seat. One of the gentlemen will signal you for action. Tomorrow, the settlement." She handed me a type written note taken from the sheets she'd been reviewing. "Read, follow to a tea, burn at curb side right away." She eyed the men again and nodded.

So, I surmised they stood guard to insure I'd do as she bid. She flicked a book of matches over the seat perhaps as a safety measure. "No one smokes in your car so I know you'll need these."

I didn't pick them up. No need to leave fingerprints for her to use against me. Besides I had my own plan. When I parked at the bottom of the drive, less than a quarter mile from the house, I opened my glove box, took a tissue and placed the Willard Hotel matchbook she'd thrown on the seat inside a plastic bag. I had a replacement to put on the seat in case the plan fell through and she returned to the car.

The outside light was still strong enough to read her note without using the interior lights. Clear and concise. At exactly 8:15 I would start the car and advance to the bottom of the long drive but not enter the drive. At a lighted signal, one, two, three, I would accelerate.

An unfortunate accident for the junior representative?

However, I knew the dinner party would end long before 8:15.

Mr. Junior Representative had been forewarned that his death would be imminent if he didn't take a risk and accept the dinner invitation. He couldn't arouse her suspicion. But he had removed himself from the table before the last course was served. A matter of a few convincing phone calls from lobbyist Levin who initially tried to persuade him to concede to the illegal wishes of Mrs. Ways and Means. Risky on both their parts. We couldn't be sure the calls weren't recorded.

Convoluted as it all seems, it's been my experience, that politicos are exceedingly convinced they can make history at a whim, can control the destiny of mortal humans and have the right to call all the shots. It's not unheard of to discover that some will kill just to gain more power. A common person out-wit them? Never.

When Junior Representative staggered out the front door of the stately home, it wasn't because he'd consumed too much alcohol as was to be their claim, fell on the cement, brain injury, dead. Instead, he'd stealthily self-administered Ipecac so he'd vomit at will. A dash to the door, bushes as a receptacle. Manners aside, no one likes to watch a grown man barf two courses of undigested food.

While the hidden camera on the windshield side of my rearview mirror didn't capture the entire event, it did get the full entourage as they stood at the open door. Looks of distress on the faces of Mrs. Ways and Means and two highly recognizable individuals who would profit the most from the land grant, shady deal.

I saw her hand go to her suit pocket and watched her pull out her cell. Fingers tapped, my cell rang.

"Mission aborted."

Mr. Junior Representative was flat out on the porch. Hard to run over someone at that point.

Mercy, compassion, afraid of the abrupt illness leaving traces of a vile substance, the motive wasn't clear, but someone called 911 and within ten minutes an ambulance arrived to promptly take the suffering man to the hospital. Levin would have been pleased to witness the whole event but he was safely tucked in the trunk of my limo, awaiting his role in the overall scheme to end the career of Mrs. Ways and Means.

I drove to the pick-up area in the driveway, barely had the door open before she scurried in the back. Anger was evident on her face.

"Take me back immediately."

"Apartment or the other stop?"

"What the hell difference does it make?"

Rhetorical, but I knew it made a big difference. At any rate, she wouldn't be going to either place until she'd had the comeuppance meeting with Daniel Levin and myself.

"Do you want your tote from the trunk in the back with you, Ma'am?"

"Not here. Drive a few miles. Let me have quiet, please."

I guessed it would take at least thirty minutes before she realized I'd gone off course. Headed up Rock Creek Parkway before she started eyeing the darkened landscape.

"Where are you going? This isn't the route."

"Tonight it is. The route to reconciliation."

"How dare you? I'll have security on you in a flash if you don't turn around right this minute."

"No fear, I'll turn around, take you back to your apartment. But first we're going to revisit that trip we took last year. You know, your son might appreciate a visit to his burial place."

"Don't be foolish, Michael. I have all the evidence I need to send you to jail for a long, long time. You're mistaken if you think you can pull a nefarious stunt."

She hit the call button on her cell that she pulled from her tote bag. Daniel had removed the Sim card and the phone she held wasn't her original.

"Wired, Ma'am, and blocked. A techy friend has been very helpful."

I pulled off into the side road, just as we did on the fateful night when she killed the son she'd given up for adoption many years before. When I found the hideaway, near the burial site she'd forced me to dig while she held a nine-millimeter to my head, I tooted the horn. Levin would soon be free from the cramped spaced he volunteered to stay in so we could set our trap.

A smile greeted me when I opened the truck.

"Got it all," he whispered.

No doubt relieved, he'd waited almost three hours for fresh air.

We imagined, as we plotted, that if her scheme for me to hit the Junior Representative with the limo went awry, her brute of a guard would finish him off, and then kill me, too. A reasonable story for the police. It would read like this: 'I'd hit the man and ran from the accident. They found me with a gun in my hand and when I fired on them, they had no recourse but to defend themselves'.

It would have made Post headlines and gotten the red-haired monster sympathy, too.

I pulled a shovel from the trunk, went to the passenger side and pulled Mrs. Ways and Means out of the car.

"Start digging. Time for you to make amends."

She took the shovel in her hands but didn't move, "You're crazy if you think you can get away with this. You actually think I'll dig a hole so you can bury me with his body? That's disgusting and impossible. He's dead. I don't care. Shoot me if you will but I won't dig my own grave." She thrust the point of the shovel in the ground.

Daniel came into view at the same time and snapped a photo. "Got'cha."

Luckily, the cards had fallen in our favor. The pictures sealed the deal as she stood over the makeshift grave site. We then placed a gun in her hand that we would soon bury after more photos were taken. Then we snapped the exchange of money from her tote bag that I'd taken from under my seat and placed in her bag. No mistaken identity about the red-haired lady.

She'd let anger get in the way of claiming innocence. But she still had to protect her image and hastily changed back into the gray-haired, fragile matron garb. Big mistake but worthwhile for getting two fairly respectable men out from under her thumb.

With recordings, photos and fingerprinted evidence all intact, the three of us rode back into D.C. A quiet ride. I thought I heard a sniffle at one point. But if it was a drippy nose, it was more likely caused by the pollen in the air than remorse.

I said goodnight to Mrs. Ways and Means and left her with strict instructions not to call me again for private rendezvouses. My private service would never include her again. Bank account might suffer but then how much money did I really need after all was said and done.

Daniel slept in my spare room again that night. Safety still a little shaky. Good reason for two guys to share a fine glass of bourbon, another Bosch movie. By the end of the week, he'd moved all his belongings out of his apartment and made arrangements to head back to his hometown. The dream of being a lobbyist in D.C. had been fulfilled and duly busted.

"Might get my old job back at Staples until I know what to do when I grow up."

"Start your own limo service. Not a bad way to earn a buck."

I laughed, shook his hand, said goodbye to my new friend.

Two weeks later, much to the surprise of the nation, Mrs. Ways and Means announced her retirement. More than a shock to her countless supporters, she stated she would close her office immediately. Health issues offered as the reason. Ah, that runny nose?

Nerves, I figured. She'd never know when one of those pictures, the evidence, would be leaked. Better to go out on a high note than behind a veil of suspicion.

Sure, I had several pictures but in the whole scheme of things, they weren't very damaging. Anyone can rig a photo these days. Or tell a big story. And, not being a politician, I'd never blackmail her or anyone else. For the present time, though, the satisfaction, the power I had over her was a tremendous relief.

Sometimes, especially on Friday evenings when I didn't have a favored customer in the back seat, I'd take my trusted, sleek, highly polished Continental and drive Rockwell Creek Parkway, circle about the Tidal Pool, ease by the Capitol building. A limo driver? Not a bad life. I had my PTSD under control. Totally in charge of my life once again.

The Fires at Lake Charlevoix
Dan A. Cardoza

It was fire hot that summer.

Still, the boathouse wouldn't catch fire for years. It would have to wait. After all, the Charlevoix estate would be the first to burn to the ground. But, if anything, fire is very patient.

It was the beginning of August, 2006.

We'd enjoyed another magical day on the lake. Lake Charlevoix is pronounced (shaar·luh·voy). It's French Canadian. We boys referred to it simply as the lake.

We'd spent all day sailing through the heavy feathered late summer winds. Our lake is one of many in northern Michigan.

We'd navigated some distance away from the Campbell estate. We were pirates, after all, Joey, Jackson, and me, Roan Steel.

"'Arr, mate, grab the rope," Jackson Chandler, our rugged captain and Master Gunner shouted at Joey Campbell, our Boatswain. Jackson Chandler was the brawler among us, he demanded his gnarly pirate title.

"First Mate, give 'em som 'elp!" Jackson ordered. I never complained.

Discovery was in our blood.

We'd committed to remain best friends forever. But the winds of change were blowing, and the oceans of forever have no shores.

That last summer night we drank the beer Jackson stole at Quick Stop. Late at night we soaked in the moonlight along the shoreline of midnight, a long distance from Joey's large house. We fancied ourselves tobacco runners and liquor scalpers. We bellowed our lifted smoke, our toxic Sanskrit, in the direction of the stars.

During summers, we lived to jet-ski, snorkel, and catfish. We'd flirt with the older girls. They'd taught us a thing or two.

Joey's video games and his big screen T.V. kept us up late at night.

No matter what game we played, it was obvious luck had been one of Jackson's totems.

*****

Joey's father, Arthur Campbell, was sinfully rich. He'd inherited some, but in his business career, he'd turned money making into an art form. Arthur was a genius at planning. His business, Campbell International Logistics was headquartered in Chicago, with branches on the west coast.

Though Joey lived in the city limits of Charlevoix, his parents often commuted to Chicago for business. They'd wanted Joey, their only child, to live in the small Michigan community to experience a small town environment.

Since he was born, Joey's aunt, Jessica, had moved in to help looked after him. Aunt Jessica was Mrs. Campbell's sister. She'd been widowed in San Francisco several years before moving back home to Michigan.

It was a happy reunion. Jessica and Allison Campbell had been estranged for years.

While on the west coast, Jessica had worked as an accountant at Arthur's western operation in the Bay Area. She and Arthur spoke often, during the years the two sisters hadn't. It was Arthur who'd facilitated the sister's peace treaty. He'd agreed to the living arrangement.

Joey's birth was such a happy occasion. Jessica's relocation to Michigan and new living arrangement insured Joey would be well loved. Allison insisted that her sister Jessica live with the family in their spacious home on the shores of Lake Charlevoix. She could help raise Joey and watch over while his mother Allison visited their hometown in Chicago on occasion. It was a kind gesture, Jessica having recently lost a baby of her own.

Those in the know had said Jessica's baby had been the result of a love affair with a married man. Over the years, Jessica hovered over Joey as if he were her own.

Since Jackson seemed part of the family, Allison practically raised him too. Jackson was Rita's son. Rita Chandler is this hot single mother down the road who did waitress work on the side when she wasn't hooking or using drugs. Lovely Rita had been plagued with addictions for most of her adult life. Arthur Campbell would stop by now and then to help Rita with food, rent and utilities. He had a big heart. Jackson though attached to Arthur, always kept him at a safe distance, suspicious of his motives.

On a regular basis, Aunt Jessica would use the local Pellston Regional Airport to fly out to Chicago. It was back in Chicago, at the family mansion, where Allison and her sister Jessica would trade places, with Allison jetting back to Lake Charlevoix to watch over Joey.

The two sisters joked about how the whole thing was Joey having two mothers.

Yet, it wasn't a stretch to consider Allison Campbell as the lovely Cinderella. Then of course, we'd have to consider her bipolar sister, Jessica Womack, Jessica Womack as Anastasia and Drizella all wrapped up in one.

Needless to say, Joey never had a day without being truly loved. It had been the same with Jackson Chandler, well almost.

To Arthur and Jessica, sex was religion.

With Allison preoccupied back in Lake Charlevoix, during her visits, Jessica and Arthur Campbell performed the naughty in about every nook and cranny of the Campbell's Chicago mansion except the dirty laundry room. Typically, the clandestine engagement would last a few weeks, 3-4 times per year to be specific.

To Jessica, the arrangement wasn't much different than San Francisco.

After Allison and Jessica switched places, Allison cherished her time at Charlevoix estate. She never had the sexual appetite to keep up with her horny husband.

Years later, when I grew up, I thought it crafty the way Allison facilitated Arthur Campbell's sex addiction, how she must have been compliant in terms her sister and husband's tryst.

Joey didn't seem to mind all the parental shuffling. I doubt he gave two-shits. Maybe he'd figured things out, maybe not? Most likely, like Jackson and I, he was too preoccupied with growing the hell up.

*****

We'd been sailing. It was mid August. We'd just secured Arthur's 15-foot Dinghy. Jackson had insisted on demonstrating his new sailor knots.

After sailor knot school, Jackson and I raced uphill to the Campbell house, leaving Joey behind to clean up. Both Jackson and I needed to take a leak. I won the race.

I took my time in the guest bathroom. When I came out, Jackson was gone.

Through a crack in the door, I spied Jackson pursuing Arthur Campbell's desk drawers. Arthur's home office had been declared a sanctuary, designated off-limits to everyone, even the housekeeper.

Through a slit of light, I caught Jackson reading this sticky note he'd retrieved from Arthurs trash can.

"Nosy bastard," I shouted screamed on purpose.

Jackson jumped. After, he wadded up the note and slammed it back in the basket situated under Arthur's desk. Next thing you know he'd blown past me, crying mad.

"Fuck you," he shouted.

"Sorry, Jackson," I sheepishly quipped. Down deep I wasn't.

Next thing you know, I heard Jackson slamming the patio door shut.

I crept over to Arthur's desk. Having no shame, I dug into the trash for the note.

After untangling the yellow note, I read it. It said, '*Don't forget to pay her at the new monthly rate!*'

Once outside, I ran toward the boathouse. When I got closer, I could hear Jackson and Joey fighting. I opened the only door. Jackson had just smacked Joey to the ground.

After that, Jackson blew by me again. He raced off the property.

*****

For the next several days, Jackson avoided Joey and me. Something bad had pissed him off.

Then one day, while Joey was grounded and alone, we decided to clean up the boathouse. Out of nowhere, Jackson called Joey.

Joey put Jackson on speakerphone and signaled me to shut the hell up.

"Dude, so you are home?" Jackson's voice seemed abrupt and alien.

"Jesus, you're alive, Jackson? Joey though he was being funny.

"Fuck you, Joey. Of course, I'm alive. I'm coming over. I'll be there in about 30 minutes!"

The phone went dead.

Joey and I agreed to punk Jackson for being such a dick all week. So we hurriedly cleaned up the mess, except for this weathered oar that needed sanding and glazing. Joey placed the oar on his dad's workbench.

We threw the remaining crap: scrap lumber, a broken oar, and a few old life vests up into the boathouse loft.

Before Jackson arrived, I'd climbed into the loft using the attached boathouse ladder. I camouflaged myself well behind the pile of junk, anticipating Jackson's arrival. After Joey and Jackson got comfortable, my intent was to pop up and scream bloody murder, scaring the shit out of the moody Jackson.

Joey let Jackson in through the side door. The boathouse was windowless. Everything inside was dim and humid.

After a brief discussion, things got overheated between the two.

A fight ensued. Joey was knocked to the deck.

"Stop, Jackson. What did I do?" asked Joey.

In a stranger's voice, Jackson fumed, "Everything!"

It didn't take long. My friend Joey turned into a Salem Witch. He shrieked bloody murder after Jackson cracked his skull with the oar. Joey screamed as if he was being burned alive.

That's when I bent sideways into a fetal position. I heard Jackson stabbing Joey with a Philips screwdriver, the sticky thugs. My mind shut down after I'd counted twenty.

Silence!

Suddenly, Jackson tossed the bloody oar into the loft.

I could smell the blood and boy sweat on the old wooden oar. I could almost taste the rusty vapor of plasma. I puked into my mouth.

God, Joey's gurgling sounds, how could I ever forget?

Next I heard the side door slam.

I waited for the longest time.

Finally, once I'd gotten up the courage, I climbed down the ladder. I cried when I saw Joey lying on the deck with his face smashed in.

I ran out of the boathouse. I used the same route to escape as Jackson, uphill alongside the property line. Once on the road, I turned left toward home.

In a patch of woods not far from my house, I could see Jackson waiting. He waved for me to join him behind a patch of pine trees. He acted manic, looking side to side for anyone.

Not able to speak, I froze in front of him.

"Listen, numb nuts, carefully?" he said.

Jackson proceeded to cook up a lie. When he was done, he served it to me raw to memorize. If I didn't agree to it, he'd kill me too.

Adjunct fear took over my senses. I can say that survival is definitely primal. It will make you agree to anything to live another day.

I'd stick to his story, that we'd been a long ways away at our favorite fishing hole the three of us used to enjoy. I'd made my mind up, living with a lie was better than dying with the truth. Jackson's eyes were honest. They were black. He'd meant every word he'd said.

Jackson and I attended Joey's funeral. We kept to our story. We acted the part of grieving best friends.

A week later, we met with the detectives. There was no evidence. We were cleared.

*****

After Jackson and I grew up, we went in different directions.

After journalism school at Northwestern, I took a job with USA Today. I work at their headquarters now in McLean, Virginia.

I love what I do.

As far as Jackson, well, he couldn't afford to go to a four year college. His mother was broke, squandering all the money Arthur had given her. Instead, he'd completed mechanic school at North West Central, a local community college back home.

One late night I'd been looking online, bored. I'd been checking out photos of our Lake Charlevoix. There were wonderful summer cabins and rows and rows of boathouses.

Shortly after, I stumbled upon this article in the Charlevoix Courier. There had been a fire a few years back at the lake. I was shocked.

Barbed wire tangled my thoughts. I pulled myself closer to the monitor.

Arthur and Allison Campbell, and Allison's sister, Jessica, had all died in an arson fire. The Campbell house had burned to the ground. The article was dated 6/27/2015.

One of the photos showed the old boathouse in the background. It was the only structure left standing on the property.

This local detective, a guy named Charles Stetson, had been quoted, "It's only a matter of time until I catch the son of a bitch."

"Do you think Sam Elliot has a twin?" I asked my orange cat?

That night, I tossed and turned in my sleep, making fists in the sheets.

I woke Charley the cat when I shouted, "Jesus, you don't have to do this!"

*****

I'd gotten enough guts to make the phone call. It was in the middle of November, 2020.

"Hello, this is Detective Stetson. How can I help you?" The voice said.

Silence!

I'd gotten cold feet. *What is Jackson capable of doing?* I think to myself.

I froze in place on the phone.

"Hello? Shit-sakes, is somebody cranking my ass? Speak!" the grumpy detective demanded?

"No, oh, sorry, detective, there must have been a phone glitch. Got a minute?" I say.

"Son, did you just have a brain fart? I could hear your steady breathing. I'm a busy man. Make this quick!" says the annoyed detective.

"Ok, it's about the lake murders!"

Silence!

"Detective, are you there?"

"What the hell is this, some kind of hearing test? Of course, I'm here. I might be 62, but I have rabbit ears. Hell, I can hear carrots growing, dude. What can I help you with, son?"

I introduced myself, and gave him some context. I went into detail about how Joey had been murdered in the boathouse and who did it.

The detective knew my name, how I'd been cleared in Joey's case. My fingerprints, as well as most of the kids in the county, were all over the boatshed. The detective demanded we meet in person.

"I need to get some eyes on you, son," he says.

*****

Detective Stetson and I arranged to meet a week later at Sunnyside's. Sunnyside's is a local breakfast haunt in Boyne City. Boyne City is a few clicks of East Jordan, where Jackson lived. I entered the breakfast house. It was cringe worthy. Somehow Sam Elliot had squeezed his tall frame into a '50s dine in booth. The classic red vinyl curved around his square shoulders. He waved me over with his chin.

He'd been working over a husky hamburger.

I sat myself across from him.

"I'd shake your hands, kid, but as you can tell, I got a good wrestling match going on with a ½ pound burger. Have some fries!"

The detective used the worn elbow of his leather jacket to shove a dish of fries my way. The jacket's scrapes and scratches told me he was a hunter.

"Don't mind if I do. It's been a long day getting back out here." I say.

As I reach for the catsup, Detective Stetson shoves it toward me with his other elbow

I dig in, bad manners and all. Best fries I ever had.

"You got enough balls to wear a wire, son?" The detective asks.

"Excuse me," I say. "I guess so?"

"Where did you go to college, kid?"

I swallow hard, "Northwestern, sir."

"Sir's my dead daddy. Call me Stetson or detective."

185

"Ok," I say.

"Not bad, I went to Notre Dame. I see you moved away to Virginia?"

"I did." I say.

"I have a question, Roan, why didn't you take the lie detector test they offered you?"

I stare at Detective Stetson. Not knowing what to say?

"That's ok, son, you don't have to answer that. Loyalty and love, even fear, can mess up those snoopy ass electronic bastards. I don't blame you."

It was easy getting to know my imagined Sam Elliot. He was warm and engaging. Most of his poking fun at me felt good, like he was family. The detective was self-defacing when he needed to be. He bristled with intelligence, and showed feelings, alongside his tough guy persona.

"Roan, how long had Jessica shared salad-tossing duties with her sister, Allison?"

I almost blew a French fry out of my right nostril, hearing that.

"She'd moved out here from San Francisco, um, right after Joey was born, maybe in 2007?" I say.

"It was in 2006, son!" says the crafty detective.

"Ok, 2006. You want a medal detective?"

"Nope!" says Stetson. He wipes grease off his paws using one of several napkins and the back of his hand.

We talked a lot, we planned. I'd wear a wire and arrange a meeting with Jackson at the old boathouse. In the meantime, Detective Stetson, through subpoena, would look over every damned inch of the boathouse, especially the loft. I even told Detective Stetsen where he might find the bloody boat oar.

Detective Stetson said it was a long shot if we'd find Jackson and Joey's DNA together. But, that alone might trigger an arrest.

I had this hunch, a long shot then, in the back of my mind. The detective agreed. He'd order the crime lab to check the bloody oar if it was there for ancestral DNA markers.

A few days later, I contacted Jackson.

"I'm in town on assignment, Jackson. Would you like to meet up?"

"Sure! The Campbell's boathouse sounds good," he says.

After he agreed, his questions turned into arrows. I couldn't answer most of them.

Did he smell a rat?

*****

I waited for the longest time in the darkness of the boathouse. Darkness had set in. It was freezing cold inside the boathouse. The only access was through the side door.

I used my iPhone flashlight to look around.

Each passing minute filled my mind with, 'what if's.' I recall the smell: old fish guts, rat droppings, spider webs and what was left of a murder scene.

After Joey's death, the Campbell family had neglected the boathouse. It had turned into some sort of mausoleum. It was like the scary tragic space had been frozen in time. January was doing what January does best in northern Michigan, freezing the shit out of everything. The Dinghy's sails had rotted, tools had been stolen. Had Detective Stetson collected the needed evidence?

The large roll-up egress door of the boathouse had frozen in place, with at least 3 feet of snow piling up on the outside. Everything felt claustrophobic, with one way in and one way out. Suddenly the side door opened and shut. Was it Jackson? Whoever it was shined a flashlight in my eyes.

I flinched backwards, dropping my phone into the water next to the sailing Dinghy.

Jackson's eyes appeared fixed and evil. After I got back up, Jackson approached me.

He lunged forward and gave me a hug. The hug was awkward. It felt cold and distant.

He stepped back. I sensed he could tell I was wearing a wire.

"What's up?" he asks. "How have you been, Jackson?"

"Not much, I'm fine," he says.

"Great," I say.

"So why the meet up, you better tell me the truth, Roan?" insists

Jackson.

"Business, Jackson. U.S.A.-Today. Our paper will be doing a nature insert about the region in the spring. A colleague wants to write an article about the area's beautiful lakes. I said I'd come over here where I grew up and take some pictures for him."

"Really, Roan, that sounds sketchy. You can do better than that." says Roan. This time he barks out his words.

The detective had promised me that the sheriff's assault team would be on standby and listening and recording. And yet I felt isolated and abandoned. Were they really out there?

"I know what you're up to, Roan."

Jackson threw the beam of his flashlight up at the loft.

I wanted to run.

"I was here earlier this morning, Roan. The bloody oar is missing, the one I used to crack your little pal Joey's head open with."

For some crazy reason, I recalled what Detective Stetson had said. After he solved the two arson and murder cases, he'd purchase a tropical shirt and move to Costa Rica. That night, I wished I were in Costa Rica.

"My line of work in Northern Michigan is a young man's game, Roan." he'd said.

Hidden in place, outside, Detective Stetson fiddled with the hair trigger on his commando 44, just east of the boathouse in a clump of icy trees. He'd promised himself when he'd joined the force so long ago, that if he ever shot a man, he needed to put his fist through the hole in his chest. By god, his 44 would allow just that.

Little did I know, I'd grown on the grizzled detective. I'd learned he'd lost a son in Afghanistan. He'd grown on me too.

"I didn't touch the oar, Jackson. I just wanted to meet and catch up on everything," I say to Jackson.

I stepped backwards.

"Sure, liar!" he says.

That's when Jackson bum-rushed me. He rammed me onto the deck on my back.

Just as quick, Jackson grabbed the old can of watered down gasoline that had been left on the workbench. He unscrewed the cap. He began to splash gasoline everywhere.

After he'd emptied half the gas can, he quickly exited the boathouse, locking me in using the padlock outside.

Once out there, Jackson spattered the rest of the gas on everything flammable. He lit a match.

In an instant, the boathouse caught fire. He'd create an altar of flames for his crimes.

I held my breath and rolled into the icy water between the Dinghy and boathouse deck.

Outside, Detective Stetson and his assault team quickly tackled Jackson, placing him in handcuffs.

Fixing his hat in place, Detective Stetson walked as close as he could to the pyre. As the wind off the lake fed the hungry fire, it climbed higher and higher into the late night sky.

Detective Stetson paused.

He rubbed his sandpapered chin with his knuckles. Had he lost his new friend?

Just as quickly, the boathouse detonated from years of wood soaked motor oil and painting supplies. Stetson tripped backwards, fighting to suppress his emotions. Emotions, something he'd assumed he'd lost after his son's death.

Finding an old Adirondack chair some distance away from the blaze, Detective Stetson sat in the chair and slumped forward. He glanced to his right, over the frozen lake. There was nothing but red snow, winter and death.

That's when I shouted at him.

"Detective, please get off your lazy butt and grab me a blanket!"

Detective Stetson stood and turned to look at me. He fought his smile.

"What the hell, kid? I figured you'd get out somehow." he says. Stetson was lying.

"Getting soft, detective?" I chided.

I explained how Joey and I used to dive underwater from the

boathouse and swim to the neighbors. The Johnson boathouse was some 200 feet up shore.

"We were Navy Seals back then, detective. It was easy. We'd pull ourselves up in Mr. Johnson's boathouse, open the fridge and crack open a few beers before heading back."

"But how did you get out of Mr. Johnson's boathouse, son?"

"The older man never locked the sheds side door. Things were different back then."

Me and the detective laughed until our eyes got shiny and wet.

After I warmed up, Stetson made it a point to ask me to keep in touch.

"Listen son, I can't retire in Costa Rica, until Jackson Chandler is sent away for good. It might take a few years, but I'll get it done," he says.

"I'll be busy too," I say. "But, I'll make sure to check in, detective," I say.

I was almost certain the detective wouldn't be able to retire for a few years. Figuring out what had taken place and the why, would take some time to get a solid conviction. And, let's face it, when you have attorneys involved, they will stretch time like summer taffy.

But, I intended to speak with my old friend, Jackson.

*****

The world oscillates more than it circles.

I was upfront with Jackson Chandler, my old friend when we met after the fire.

The first time I visited him was at the county jail. I explained how I wanted to write a novel about his life. He said okay.

So we agreed to meet occasionally and communicate by phone and snail mail.

Life is strange. We remain friends to this day.

Over time, we both dug down deep where his feelings and motives had been buried.

"Roan, all I can tell you is that when I learned Arthur Campbell was my dad that day, and Joey was my half brother, I snapped. It broke me. Right then, I knew I had to end Joey's life."

"Wow, that's some heavy shit," I say.

"Dude, you were there that day. The day you caught me reading that note I'd gotten from the trash can in Arthur's office." Jackson furrows his brows.

"You mean the one Arthur wrote to remind himself to make his monthly payments?" I say.

"Yes, I'm not the brightest person, Roan, but I figured things out after I read that crumpled up note. Right then and there, I knew Arthur Campbell was my real father, not some ghost of a man named Chandler who supposedly rand away from Rita before I arrived. You see, Roan, Arthur had made monthly payments to my fake mother, Rita. Just imagine that Roan. Arthur hired her to raise me," he says. Tears well up in Jackson's eyes, he appears more boy than man in the visiting room.

"And so why did you kill the three in the fire, Jackson?"

"Don't you get it, Roan, Jessica was my real mother. She threw me away like trash. Maybe it was a conspiracy, which included Allison. When I started the fire at their home, I could care less who I burned alive. I was full of hate."

"How about me, Jackson? Why did you try and kill me?"

"Dude, I didn't want to get caught. You were going to be collateral damage."

It took the longest time for the DNA ancestral analysis in Detroit. The blood on the oar proved conclusively that Joey and Jackson were indeed half brothers.

That's something we all needed to know for sure.

I'll continue to visit Jackson. I'll know where to find him.

He's housed at the Oaks Correctional Facility in Manistee, Michigan.

I assisted Jackson and the public defender to arrange an Alfred Plea on Jackson's behalf. In exchange, Jackson owned up to all four murders and my attempted murder. His trade-off was a life sentence with the possibility of parole after 50 years, rather than 4 life sentences without the possibility of parole.

Jackson thanked me for what I'd done. I know how pathetic that sounds. He might die in prison. Things got wrapped up in less than a year with the plea.

*****

"Is that you, Roan?" Detective Stetson asks.

"No, it's Mick Jagger," I say. "Who in the hell does it sound like, detective?"

"Don't be an ass, Roan."

"I'm just trying to sound like you, detective."

We both laugh long and hard. Because of the Alfred Pleas, and no long drawn out trial, Detective Stetson got his early retirement.

Detective Stetson had phoned me from poolside. He was at a fancy resort in Costa Rica. He'd been looking for a small house.

He told me he was working on his third piña *colada* and was about to have an early dinner. We traded funny stories and pathetic jokes. He wished me luck with my novel.

"Keep killing it, Cody. Someday you're going to make a good fiction writer." We laugh, hard.

"Cody?" I ask, after this long silence. Did you call me Cody, detective?"

"Jesus, I'm so sorry about that, Roan. That was my son's name."

"No worries," I say, "And take it easy on the women and whiskey down there, dude —"

The detective interrupts, "Roan — got to go. Let's talk soon. There's a gorgeous woman with a red hot lobster coming my way."

We laugh.

Detective Stetson hangs up.

Forks in the Road

Alan J Wahnefried

The pickup veered off the road and crashed into a tree. Deputy Sheriff Karl Pedersen of the Alger County Sheriff's Department followed over a hundred yards behind. After the truck crashed, he turned on his cruiser's flashers.

It's only 8:30. A little early for drunks, he thought.

He pulled off on the shoulder and left the flashers going. He opened the truck's driver's side door and knew an ambulance was unnecessary. The driver needed a medical examiner, not a doctor. He called the dispatcher.

"I am west of Munising on M-28. I am on the scene of an auto accident. The driver is dead. Please inform the medical examiner. Also, dispatch whoever is the on-call detective. I will remain on-site," he said to the dispatcher.

The dispatcher acknowledged his request.

*****

Deputy Nils Gustafsen answered his phone. His week as Alger County's on-call detective was almost up. The call was from the dispatcher.

"There's an auto fatality on M-28 west of Munising. The medical examiner is on the way. Deputy Pedersen has requested your expertise," the dispatcher said.

"On the way," he responded.

He reached for his shoes and turned to his wife, Kirsikka. "There's a wreck on M-28. I hope there's not much to it. I'm looking forward to tomorrow," he said.

"I hope you're right — otherwise you could owe me big time."

Nils grabbed his pistol belt, jacket, and hat. He kissed her and headed out.

*****

Gustafson made it to the crash site in less than fifteen minutes. The medical examiner, Dr. Ilta Nikku, had arrived before him. Deputy Pedersen talked to the doctor. Gustafsen joined the conversation.

"Well, what have we got?" Nils asked.

Dr. Nikku answered first, "We have a Caucasian male about forty-five or fifty years old. Head trauma probably killed the driver. The airbag and seat belt malfunctioned. He smashed his head on the steering wheel. I'll know more after the autopsy."

Pedersen said, "When I first arrived, I thought it was just a drunk skidding off the road. Now I have my doubts. The road is dry. I see no skid marks. As the doctor mentioned, the airbag and seat belt malfunctioned. There was no smell of alcohol in the vehicle. The tires on the passenger side are soft and may be leaking. The vehicle could have been tampered with."

I was so hoping for a routine traffic problem, Nils thought.

Turning to Deputy Pedersen, he said, "Show me what you found, Karl."

The deputies walked to the driver's side of the pickup. Everything Nils saw matched Pedersen's description, and he photographed the inside of the cab before the deputies signaled to the doctor to take the body.

The officers walked to the passenger side of the truck. Nils bent down and pushed hard at the tire, and they were rewarded with the hiss of a slow leak. They walked back to the medical examiner's van where the doctor held the deceased's wallet.

Ilta looked up. "The deceased person's name was Edward Lombardi. He was forty-seven. He had a Munising mailing address, but it's outside the city." Nils made some quick notes, then looked at Pederson.

"Did you call for a flatbed?"

"I thought he'd be here by now," Pedersen responded, just before the crash site was illuminated by the lights of the recovery vehicle swinging around and parking up.

After storing the pickup in the secure compound of the Sheriff's Department yard, Nils got back into his car.

Now for the hard part —inform Lombardi's next of kin.

The address on Lombardi's license was a private road running off M-94 south of Munising.

*****

It was after nine when he eventually pulled up in front of the house. As he knocked on the front door he could see that the lights were already on behind the curtains. Moments later a woman, dressed in a robe and slippers, answered the door.

"Ma'am, pardon the interruption. I am Deputy Nils Gustafsen of the Sheriff's Department. Does a Mr. Edward Lombardi live here?" he asked in a calm voice.

"He does for a little while longer. What has the son-of-a-bitch done this time?" Her anger was obvious.

No way to sugar the pill. "Ma'am, he's dead."

The woman burst into tears, turned and gestured for Nils to follow her down the hallway and into the kitchen. Automatically she sat down at the table, and Nils sat across from her — waiting for her to compose herself. It took time.

When the sobs subsided, she asked: "What happened?"

"We think he lost control of his truck and veered off the road. We need to thoroughly examine the truck and get autopsy results to be sure," He waited for her to respond.

She wiped her eyes with the sleeve of her robe. "Where did it happen?"

"On M-28 heading east toward Munising,"

She looked at her hands on the table top. "I wonder how much he drank after our dinner group broke up...."

I don't want to push too hard, Nils thought. *I do need to get some more information. Best to let her talk.*

"Would you tell me about this dinner?" he asked.

"There were four of us at the casino. It's late September so Eddie's summer businesses are gearing back. We always celebrate the end of the summer by Eddie handing out bonuses."

Nils looked up from his note taking. "You said there were four of you?"

She nodded. "Yes. Eddie, me, and his business partners Matt Nurmi and Suvi Nikula. Our reservations were at six. Eddie stayed on after the three of us decided to leave. It must have been about eight. He was enjoying being surrounded by friends,"

"Thank you for that information. I know this must be difficult, ma'am," Nils responded. "But I take it you are Mrs. Lombardi?"

"No. Where are my manners? Eddie and I aren't married. My name is Marion Javi," She paused, then added: "Eddie and I went there in the truck, but I came back with Suvi in her car." Again the slight hesitation, then: "The reservation was early. Suvi and I have job commitments and wanted to get some sleep...." Her voice trailed off and she picked at the cuff of her bathrobe.

Nils didn't need more information immediately. He needed to read through the autopsy and crash site reports to help get a better picture. "Ma'am, I know you've had an awful shock, but we can talk more later." As he stood up to leave he asked, "Is there anyone I can call for you before I go?" He tried to make his voice sound sensitive.

"No, I...I'll be fine. Thank you." Marion tried for a smile, but didn't quite succeed.

Nils excused himself. "I am sorry for your loss, ma'am," he said as left.

Outside, in the car, he took several long, slow breaths, trying to clear his emotional turmoil before starting the engine and heading for home. The day at least was now over.

*****

Ramon Thickfoot's day was also over about the same time Nils headed home. Ramon was a busboy at the casino. Ramon wasn't the sharpest tool in the shed, and he knew it. His high school GPA was 2.1, thanks to his PE grades. People who knew him thought he was a good guy. His boss thought he was a hard worker. If Ramon had a flaw, it was he tended to fixate on things. Most of his fixations played out harmlessly. Tonight, one of Ramon's fixations played out maliciously.

Ramon's mother raised him by herself, and she'd never once talked about his father. Whenever Ramon asked, she'd always reply, "He's gone." Her answer left Ramon unsatisfied.

Ramon started working while he was in high school. The summer of his junior year, Ramon worked for Eddie Lombardi. He would always remember that time as it was the June when his mother had succumbed to breast cancer. Eddie had given Ramon three weeks off, with pay, and had even attended the funeral.

Afterwards, with an aunt and uncle, Ramon had gone through his mother's things. She didn't have much. One thing he found was a love letter she had kept at the back of her dressing table drawer. Going by the postmark, she'd received the letter before she'd started high school. The letter was puppy love on steroids, and was signed *Eddie*.

The letter caused Ramon to jump to an unwarranted conclusion.

Eddie Lombardi must be my biological father and he was being kind since he felt guilty.

Later that summer he'd shown Eddie the letter and asked if Eddie was his biological father. Ramon hoped for the best. Eddie read the letter in total surprise. Without meaning to do so, Eddie crushed Ramon.

Eddie tried to be sensitive, "I knew your mom in high school. We didn't date. It was a peck on the cheek at the prom if I ever kissed your mom. I'm sorry, Ramon. If you ever want to talk to me about anything, I will gladly talk to you. But I am not your dad."

Ramon mumbled something and left. Eddie thought the matter was closed but Ramon fixated on the idea that Eddie must be his dad.

Eddie lied to me. He will pay! Ramon thought.

Ramon waited, then made his move that Friday night. Earlier in the week he'd learned Eddie had made reservations for Friday night, and had traded shifts so he would pick up his shift after Eddie. He'd taken several forks from the casino and had bent them like the letter L. Then, when he'd arrived at the parking lot, he'd walked by Eddie's truck and acted like he had tripped, sliding a fork under each of the passenger's side tires. When Eddie backed out of slot, the forks would puncture the tires. A couple of flats would be a good start

How Eddie would connect two flat tires with Ramon, Ramon didn't know. He didn't care. He would get his revenge.

*****

Nils had planned to spend Saturday in Marquette. They wanted to attend an appraisal fair, and later they also hoped to hear a local band, *Mackinaw Headwinds*.

Kirsikka was in the shower and Nils was making coffee when Sheriff Wiklund called. Nils answered, dreading what could potentially happen to his plans.

"I understand we had a fatality last night," Wiklund began. "Who was killed? How is the investigation going?"

"Sir," Nils began. "The deceased was Edward Lombardi. He ran off the road, down an embankment and hit a tree. His vehicle is in our yard. It may be a simple case of someone having too much to drink. But, as the airbag did not deploy and two tires look like they may have been tampered with, I left a message with Jameison to have the vehicle inspected on Monday. I know the deceased had been drinking, both with dinner, and after, at the casino. I'll know more once I get to read the medical examiner's report."

"So, we're doing nothing until Monday?" Wiklund made the question sound like an accusation.

"Sir, the flat tires could have been caused by the potholes or debris on M-28. I didn't think you'd want to pay Jameison double time on scanty evidence," Nils responded quietly.

There was silence on the line, then Wiklund conceded, "The debris on the road is ridiculous so I guess your point is valid. Jump on it first thing Monday. Have a good weekend."

"Thank you, sir," Nils replied. Relieved, he hung up the phone as Kirsikka entered the kitchen. She wore an uncertain expression along with her bathrobe. In the past phone calls had usually meant disrupted plans.

Nils smiled reassuringly. "That was the Sheriff. He told me to have a good weekend and that the car crash will wait until Monday." He moved forward and put his arms around her waist. "Let's get ready to go."

A relieved smile crept over Kirsikka's face.

*****

A national TV program provided the model for the appraisal fair. The local TV station sponsored the Marquette version using local appraisers, and people could have multiple items appraised for the price of admission.

One of Kirsikka's aunts had died recently so she had inherited some jewelry and old coins. She was curious about their value, mainly for updating their insurance, and the appraisal fair seemed like a fun way to find out.

As it was, the Gustafsens spent most of their day in line. They talked to some nice people. Some people brought nice things. They also confirmed there is no accounting for taste. People came with items the Gustafsens would have used as firewood.

When their turn came, Nils and Kirsikka started with coin appraisals. As it turned out, the coin appraiser was Suvi Nikula. Kirsikka put the coins on the felt topped table and Suvi inspected them.

Ms. Nikula's name is familiar, Nils thought. *I know better than to mix police business with days like this. I've gotten in trouble before.*

He picked up Ms. Nikula's business card.

Several minutes passed, then Suvi smiled and looked up at Kirsikka. "You're a lucky woman. Your gold double eagles are in very fine condition with a value of about $2,000. The other three coins are probably worth less than five dollars combined."

As they walked away, Kirsikka asked Nils, "Why did you pick up her business card?"

"In case your aunt hid more coins," he replied with a smile as Kirsikka hummed her little 'happy tune.' As they moved around the fair Nils also picked up business cards at other booths to cover his tracks.

Kirsikka's jewelry turned out to be equally genuine — 14-carat gold with semi-precious stones — and she was even more happy they had been able to come to the event.

The rest of the day had been spent wandering through the farmer's market, and they had finished the day with dinner at a bar known for its fish and chips, and later the local band, *Mackinaw Headwinds,* played at the same venue. All in all, Nils had conceded as he had prepared for bed, they had managed to have a really good day.

*****

Nils' Monday began in the Sheriff's yard. Cal Jameison was waiting for him. Cal owned Jameison's Auto Service — a family business run with his dad and brothers. They maintained the Sheriff's Department's vehicles and were licensed to perform forensic analysis, and Cal and Nils had worked together before.

Cal asked, "What have you got for me today?"

"The pickup over there went off M-28 Friday night, killing the driver. The seat belt and airbags both failed. The two passenger-side tires were leaking and now appear flat. I need to know if someone tampered with the vehicle,"

"Let me get to work and I'll let you know what I find. I take it you want the report ASAP?" Cal said.

"Naturally."

While Cal worked, Nils went into the station and made phone calls. He wanted to find out more about what had happened at the dinner Friday night. He called Matt Nurmi. Nurmi picked up almost immediately.

"Sir, I am deputy sheriff Nils Gustafsen. I am investigating Edward Lombardi's death," Nils began.

"Been expecting your call. Marion phoned me late Friday night, and I spent most of the weekend with her. What can I do for you, deputy?"

"I'd like to talk to you about the meal the four of you had, plus anything you can share about Mr. Lombardi. What would be a good time and place to talk, sir?"

"I'm taking Marion to make arrangements at the funeral home shortly, then onto the church after that. Provided she feels up to lunch then we'll eat in town before we get to talk to Eddie's lawyer. So...could we say three this afternoon at Eddie's shop?"

Nils agreed to the time and place, concluded the call, then fished out Suvi Nikula's business card. Dialing the number he was surprised when a voice on the line answered, "Harbor Pharmacy."

"May I speak with Ms. Nikula, please?"

There was a pause as he heard the voice call out: "Suvi, you have a phone call."

Another short pause, a muffled "Thank you," then, "This is Suvi Nikula. How can I help you?"

"Ma'am, I am Deputy Nils Gustafsen of the Sheriff's Department. I am investigating the death of Edward Lombardi, and would like to talk to you about last Friday evening. When would be a good time?"

"Matt called and told me about Eddie's death. I don't know how I can help, but I take an early lunch break at 11:30. Could you come to the pharmacy? It's the one up on Lake Street, almost to City Park."

"I know the store. I'll be there at 11:30," Nils hung up and walked outside to the pickup as Cal was finishing up.

"What did you find?"

"Several things," Cal began. "Some vehicles turn off the seat belt buzzer if the buckle is in the socket, but not totally engaged. The battery wasn't dead. I tested the management system and found I didn't have to click the seatbelt to stop the buzzer. That's the reason the seatbelt failed at the crash."

He looked down at his notes for a moment, then, "The airbag also did not deploy. I don't see signs of tampering. I'll check all the sensors and also see if there are any manufacturer recalls outstanding when I get back to the office."

"You find anything else?"

"Someone punctured the tires deliberately," the mechanic began. He held out a bent piece of metal. "I dug this out of the front tire. It looks like a fork with three tines, so I know it wasn't anything natural." He held up the mangled remains for Nils to look at. "With the off-road tires, it's amazing it did anything. Eventually the leaking tires would have made the steering feel mushy."

"What about the rear tire?"

"There may be another fork under the tire, but I'll come back with a jack to raise the back end." He shook his head. "A vehicle with two flat tires is hard to control. I'll let you know what I find just before I file the formal report later today," Cal finished.

"Thanks, you've been a big help," Nils said before turning to leave.

As Nils headed into the station he had an uneasy thought: *I may be dealing with a murder.*

*****

Nils needed to report to the Sheriff, but he wanted to make a phone call first. He dialed the number of the casino and asked to speak to the manager.

"You want the casino manager? Hold for a minute please." Then, a few minutes later, Robert Bearheart came on the line.

"Sir, I am Deputy Sheriff Nils Gustafsen, and I'm calling because one of your Friday night customers died in a car accident shortly after leaving your establishment." Not waiting for Bearheart to answer, he carried on. "I'm not suggesting that any of your employees did anything wrong. I just need to review some of your security videos. Will that be okay with you? Or do I need to get a subpoena?"

"That's terrible news, deputy," Mr. Bearheart began. "We're always glad to cooperate with the police. You're going to have to be more specific about security videos though — we have dozens of cameras."

"Do we need to discuss this in person?" the deputy asked.

"That might be best. Who was the person who died?"

"His name was Edward Lombardi. I can be out to see you within the hour if that would be convenient?"

"Ask for me at the front desk when you come. I'll be expecting you," Bearheart replied.

*****

Nils swung by the Sheriff's office in the hope of talking to Wiklund. The Sheriff saw him coming and gestured Nils into his office.

"What news have you got?" Wiklund began.

"Lombardi may have been murdered. Jameison found someone had obviously tampered with the vehicle, so I am heading to the casino to arrange for the security tapes. I'll be out for the rest of the day, I have more interviews this afternoon, sir."

"Not good news. Does Lombardi's family know about the possibility

203

of it being a murder?"

"Lombardi doesn't seem to have living blood kin, but I've not said anything to his girlfriend yet. I'd rather wait until I know more, sir."

"Let's try not to make a bad situation worse than we must. Keep me posted. Did your wife enjoy Marquette on Saturday?" Wiklund concluded with a wink.

"Yes, she did, sir," *How on Earth did he know that?* Nils thought.

*****

After a back road drive he finally got to the casino at about 9:30, and asked for Mr. Bearheart at the front desk. After a few minutes a man came toward him from one of the back offices. He stood around 6ft 4, broad shouldered with a fullback's physique, like Grizzly Adams on steroids. He offered Nils his hand.

"Deputy Gustafsen? I'm Jerry Bearheart. How can I help you?" Bearheart's handshake was firm but not overbearing.

"Glad to meet you — is there somewhere we can talk privately, sir?" Nils responded.

Bearheart led Nils to his office. He offered the deputy a seat and a cup of coffee, both of which Nils accepted, and after a minute or so exchanging pleasantries, Bearheart got straight to the point.

"What can I do for you, deputy? You mentioned something about security video from the end of last week?" Bearheart asked, stirring his coffee.

"Sir, as I said on the phone, one of your customers died Friday night. We have evidence someone caused slow leaks in two tires. Plus, by the time he finally left here, the deceased may not have been sober. I was hoping your security footage may provide some insight."

"Friday and Saturday nights are as busy. We're going to need to narrow it down a bit more before we even go near the videos. Did the person's party have a reservation and under whose name?"

"I was told Edward Lombardi had a reservation in the main dining room at 6pm. Can you check your records and identify the table, sir?"

Bearheart picked up his phone and dialed a number. He paused as it rang a couple of times, then: "Cyd, did an Edward Lombardi have a reservation Friday night at six? Great. Can you call it up and I'll be with you in a few minutes." Bearheart turned to the deputy. "Cydnee Shownash co-ordinates most of the front of house stuff — she also doubles as our maître d' when things get busy over the weekends. She'll meet us at the entrance to the restaurant section."

A short walk later and a woman wearing black pants, a white shirt, and a bow tie in the dining room greeted the manager.

Bearheart smiled an amicable greeting: "Cyd, this is Deputy Nils Gustafsen. He is interested in the reservation I mentioned."

"If you gentlemen will follow me?" Shownash said as she walked toward a table set for four near the back of the dining room. "Mr. Lombardi requested this particular table. We call it table twelve."

Nils scanned the ceiling as Bearheart said: "Thanks Cyd."

She smiled and nodded, then left the two of them as Bearheart said to Nils: "Security should be able to identify the cameras that capture this table area." Then, cocking his head slightly to one side, asked: "Is there anything else, deputy?"

Nils looked around. He spied an arch at the back of the dining room. "Where does that lead?"

"To the bar and kitchen."

"May I take a look?"

"Certainly." Bearheart led the way.

The archway gave out to a neat, well stocked bar, and a server and buffet area for those who didn't mind and 'eat and run' style break.

Looking the area over, Nils asked, "Could I also get the video covering the bar and the serving area starting about 5:30? Some information suggests Mr. Lombardi was not completely sober, and I'd like to see if he was in the bar before the reservation,"

Bearheart shrugged. "I suppose that wouldn't be a problem. Do you know how late the party stayed?"

"I know the accident happened about 8:30. Could I get video through to 8:30?"

"I'll make the call and get security onto it. All our video is recorded and stored up on some fancy cloud server system —far safer than keeping them on site. I just need one of the techs to cut a copy of your timeline." Bearheart smiled. "Free of charge, naturally. I should be able make them available to you...say Tuesday? Wednesday at the latest?"

Nils considered: *I probably wouldn't have the autopsy until Wednesday. No point in asking about the parking lot, since I don't know where Eddie parked.*

"Wednesday would be fine." Nils took out his wallet and removed a business car. Please contact me at the station when you have the files, sir."

"Don't forget," Bearheart added. "Normal video encoding runs at around 24 frames per second. In places like the dining room, we record one frame a second, so it looks like you're flipping through a stack of still photos. The speed suits our purpose and saves on file size. We do use a much higher rate on the gaming floor, and far better image quality as well."

"Thanks. Could I request one other thing?" Gustafsen asked.

"Sure."

"Could I see one of your forks, sir?" Nils asked.

Bearheart shrugged. "Ms. Shownash, would you get a fork for the deputy, please?" Shownash retrieved a fork. The fork had three tines.

"Thank you, sir. I need to take a picture of the fork. We pulled what might be forks from Mr. Lombardi's tires. I want to see if those forks are similar to yours. Thank you, for your help," Nils replied. He snapped the picture. He shook hands with both men and headed back to Munising.

*****

Nils walked into Harbor Pharmacy at about 11:25, and asked for Suvi Nikula at the counter. The clerk called the pharmacist, and Nils was not too surprised when he recognized the pharmacist from the appraisal fair.

"Deputy Gustafsen? I'm Suvi Nikula. Didn't I see you on Saturday?"

"You have a good memory, ma'am," Nils responded. "I was at the fair with my wife. Is there somewhere private we can talk?"

Ms. Nikula told her clerk, "I'm going to take lunch. I'll be in the office if you need me." As she led Nils through to the back to her office, over her shoulder she said: "I hope you don't mind if I eat as we talk?"

"Not a problem, ma'am," Nils began. "I was surprised when you asked me to come here. Do you work here or own the business?"

She opened the door to a windowless box room sized office and indicated a chair to Nils.

Sitting at her desk she said, "I can understand your confusion. I own the pharmacy outright. Coins are just a sideline. I got into numismatics in college — U of M's Pharmacy School isn't cheap, and I still can use the extra money."

"OK. I understand you were also Eddie Lombardi's business partner, ma'am?" Nils asked.

"Eddie used the term loosely. We had a business arrangement, but we weren't officially partners."

"So how would you describe that arrangement then?"

"I'd better start at the beginning," Ms. Nikula said between bites. "I met Eddie at an appraisal fair like the one you attended Saturday. Your wife's double eagles are exceptional, by the way. Most people bring badly worn silver dollars and Indian head pennies. Eddie set the record when he produced five double eagles, grading as either fine or very fine condition. The coins were worth over $6,000. Eddie asked about having additional coins appraised. I handed him my card and told him to call. I did not expect to hear from him again."

After pausing for another bite of her sandwich, she chewed, swallowed and then continued. "Eddie called me the following week to arrange for an appraisal of over forty coins. I charge a fee based on the number of coins I appraise. Eddie said he had no problem with the fee, so we set a time to meet here in my office." Another pause, this time Nils thought it was to consider how she should carry on. Then:

"Eddie showed up with over forty coins — with 30 of them being double eagles. All the coins graded fine or very fine, and that alone made me more than a little suspicious. I asked how he's acquired so many coins, and he claimed he had a business cleaning out houses before they were eventually sold. He told me he'd found all sorts of stuff coins in hidden compartments in walls, or under floorboards — even behind the panels of a bath. A lot had also, so he said, been hidden in writing desks and the like. He claimed he'd been accumulating the coins for years. Either way, his stash of double eagles was worth about $60,000."

Suvi threw away her sandwich wrappings and wiped her mouth with a paper tissue from the desk.

"And did you report him to anyone?"

"Oh, Eddie was legal — he had contracts for every house clearance he'd done, and all had a Finders Keepers clause in them. If he found something then he could legally get to keep it."

Nils frowned a little. "So much for moral honesty."

Suvi smiled. "There's not much of that where money's concerned."

Nils nodded, and she carried on. "Eddie asked about the best way to sell the coins. No coin shop could manage that many because it would flood the market and depress the price. I suggested he should start an online coin exchange, but do it professionally. Control the number sold and keep the price up high. Eddie liked the idea and offered me a deal, based on me doing the appraisals, but taking my fee from the proceeds of the website business." She sat back in her chair. "What can I say? I took the deal, even though later I knew I should have bargained harder. I had no way of knowing how many coins Eddie sold, so I've been forever wondering if he was cheating me."

"Not a very good business foundation."

She shrugged. "At the dinner, Friday, Matt and I received checks from Eddie," she continued. "He always liked being dramatic. I got a nice meal and a check for $3,200. I left after dessert."

As Suvi paused to peel a mandarin orange, Nils asked: "How much alcohol was consumed at the dinner?"

"Most of us were driving, no one drank a lot." She paused to think it over. "From the appetizer to dessert, we were at the table for about two hours. We split two bottles of nice champagne, but I doubt if anyone was feeling anything. Just before we left, Eddie wanted to order a round of brandies to toast the end of the season. Matt, Marion, and I declined. Our glasses weren't empty, but Eddie had been putting it away a little and still ordered a brandy. We drank the toast, and just after that some of Eddie's friends came to the table, which the three of us took as our cue to leave." She looked over at Nils. "Anything else I can tell you?"

Nils thought for a minute. "I can't think of anything at the moment. I may be in touch if I have other questions. Thank you for your time, ma'am."

"You are welcome," Suvi replied as she finished her mandarin and ushered the deputy out of her office.

*****

Nils got a pasty at *Miner's Pasty Kitchen* for his lunch. While he ate, he checked his voicemail. Cal Jameison wanted him to come by the garage, but that was it. There were no other messages.

Cal was in the office when he arrived.

"I dug this out of the other tire," Cal said as he offered Nils another mangled fork.

The fork seemed to match the one from the casino, Nils thought. He signed Cal's receipt for both forks and put them in evidence bags.

"I also checked on the airbag," Jameison continued. "It was recalled two weeks ago. The owners may not have received notification yet. I guess it malfunctioned as expected. Everything we discussed will be in my report."

"Thanks, Cal," Nils said as he left for the Sheriff's Department.

He signed the forks into the evidence room at the Sheriff's Department and he was about to leave when he ran into Wiklund.

"Any progress?"

"I have more indications that Eddie Lombardi was murdered, sir. Though I have to admit I'm not totally convinced just yet. Cal Jameison dug two forks out of the vehicle's tires. The debris did not cause the flat, and yes, Lombardi did drink with his dinner, but from what I understand it wasn't excessively. I should have the casino's security videos on Wednesday." He smiled weakly. "I still need the autopsy report — if only for the alcohol levels. Plus I still have people to interview."

"Not what I wanted to hear — but that's what we get paid for." As

Wiklund turned and started to walk away, he added: "Keep me posted."

"I will, sir," Nils concluded.

*****

At 3pm Nils found the main entrance of Lombardi Woodworking locked. He knocked several times and after a few minutes there was the sound of locks being thrown, and a disheveled Matt Nurmi opened the door.

"Mr. Nurmi, we talked this morning. May I come in, sir?" Nils asked.

"Sorry. I forgot you were coming, deputy. I've had a rough couple of days. Please come in,"

Nurmi led Nils to a small office on the side of the shop, dropped behind a neat and tidy desk and offered Nils a seat.

"I have a pot of coffee brewing. Would you care for a cup?" Matt began. Gustafsen accepted. Nurmi left and returned with two mugs of coffee.

"I spent most of the weekend with Marion. She's taking Eddie's death hard," Nurmi said with a sigh.

"Had they been together long?"

"I introduced Marion to Eddie about four years ago. Eddie moved in with her over two years ago." He pursed his lips in thought. "Eddie talked about doing something big for Marion this week. He didn't say what though."

"Okay, well I'll try to be brief, sir. You were Eddie's business partner, right?"

"Eddie liked to throw that term around. I tried to get him to make me an official partner, but he just kept putting me off. I'm an employee. I get a base wage and some bonuses, and that's it." The resignation in his voice was obvious.

"OK. Can you please tell me about the dinner at the casino, on Friday?"

"It's September, so the summer tourist season is over. The dinner was to celebrate the end of a good season and for Eddie to pass out bonus checks. He gave Suvi and I checks, then Eddie and I ordered prime rib while the ladies had the fish or chicken. They also insisted we have tiramisu for dessert. I think we went through a couple of bottles of house champagne."

Nils took some coffee, then: "I already talked to Ms. Nikula about her business relationship with Eddie. Would you care to describe yours, please, sir?"

"I suppose so," Matt gulped coffee and continued. "Eddie's dad and grandpa were both cabinet makers. I started working for Eddie's dad straight out of high school. Eddie was a good cabinet maker too, but he was forever wanting more variety in his life. We make furniture during the winter, but during the summer, Eddie would always branch out into other things as well."

"Branch out? How?"

"He started by cleaning out houses when people moved," Matt said. "If someone's grandma dies and leaves a house full of junk, Eddie would clean it out for a fee. He had the homeowner sign a form stating everything in the home belonged to Eddie, but for a fee he would allow people to reclaim stuff. Eddie had high school kids do most of the heavy lifting. Me? I got paid the same if I was cutting wood or hauling junk. Most of the stuff we just took to the dump.

"Eddie had a good eye for furniture," Numri continued. "We brought some of the old furniture back here. Most of the furniture was just dirty. We cleaned it and polished it. Eddie looked for hidden compartments in the buffets or chests. Occasionally he would find some with stuff in them,"

"Is that where he found his coins?" Nils interrupted.

"Some of the coins. Some jewelry. Some stock certificates. Some embarrassing pictures. In addition to cleaning pieces of furniture, we'd re-glue loose joints and make other repairs. Eddie filed the forms to sell antiques and furniture in Wisconsin and Minnesota, and I was supposed to get a percentage of the furniture sales."

"Why didn't he sell the furniture in Michigan?" Nils expected a comment on Michigan's taxes.

"Initially, he did, but pretty quickly he decided he didn't want to risk the grief. We cleaned out a house for Tony Gearson. His aunt died and left behind a complete and utter mess. Eddie found a buffet in the house. After the buffet was cleaned and polished, it looked great. Eddie sold the buffet to an antique store on Lake Street. Tony saw it in the window and freaked out. Gearson stormed in here and accused Eddie of cheating him. Eddie reminded him of the clearance contract Tony'd signed. But Tony still tried to sue Eddie and got nowhere. After that, Eddie made sure the furniture went out of state."

Nurmi lit a cigarette and continued, "Eddie was an Instructor Dive Master. He started giving scuba lessons, but made a point of only working in the Lake. He said it made the school sound more exciting. He also sold gear, like dry suits, to his students. After the students got the basics down, Eddie took his students to wrecks outside the harbor. Most wrecks were ten-to-twenty-foot fiberglass cabin cruisers. The wrecks weren't historic. No one cared. Eddie took underwater videos. Everyone loved it."

"So Eddie was into salvage?"

"Most of the boats had been on the bottom for decades. Eddie had seen a video of people recovering stuff using airbags. He got the idea of raising the old outboard motors, and figured out how to make it work. Eddie hired high school kids to drive the boat for dive school. He paid them extra not to see anything. The motors went to the scrap yard. Eddie would claim he found the motors in the houses he cleaned."

"Was that legal?" Nils asked.

"Probably not. The motors probably belonged to some insurance company. Eddie didn't care. The way he figured, if the wreck had been on the lake bottom for twenty years, it was fair game."

Nurmi tapped his cigarette ash into a nearby ashtray and carried on. "Eddie did do legitimate underwater salvage as well. He took his videos to insurance agents, saying he would be prepared to investigate a claim for sunk boats and possibly raising parts. We got some business. Eddie was always thinking." Nurmi said with a proud smile. "I was getting a percentage of the salvage income."

Nils was perplexed. *It sounded like Lombardi had a conglomerate of sorts,* he thought. "Is there more?" he asked.

"Yes. One thing led to another. We were doing a legitimate salvage job. Eddie thought he saw the wreck of an old sailing ship. We took GPS readings and headed home. When Eddie checked the state records there was no known wreck anywhere near the GPS reading. We went back and explored the wreck. It was a fairly pristine 19th-century passenger and cargo ship. Eddie found a strong box in the captain's cabin and we salvaged brass navigation instruments in the wheelhouse and real silverware in the galley. We took the instruments and silver with us and returned later that week with gear to raise the strong box. Captains in the 19th century were entrepreneurs. They carried cash for buying and selling cargo. The strong box had over $500 in gold and silver coins. After we got the box safe, Eddie reported the wreck to the state and got a public pat on the back. Most summers, we found one or two wrecks. The wrecks gave Eddie most of his coins." Matt reported. "The navigation instruments and silverware went to the antique stores or auctions. You should be able to guess what Eddie did with the coins."

"Is there anything else?" Nils asked, hoping he had enough paper in his notebook.

"There's a shipwreck tour business in the harbor, so Eddie started a similar shipwreck tour out in the Lake. He thought it made his tour sound more thrilling, even though he'd stripped them before he included them in his tours."

"Anything more?" Nils's head was swimming.

"Almost done. Eddie dried out the strong boxes and converted them to toolboxes. He was careful to take the name of the ship off the chest. He had a waiting list for those tool chests."

"How well did you get along with Eddie?" Nils asked, changing the subject.

"Eddie was one of those persons people either loved or hated. We had a good time mostly. He wouldn't make me a partner, so I have no idea what's going to happen to this place now. The lawyers told me to keep the lights on until they settled the estate. I always wondered if he'd been shorting me on my percentages, but I cleared over $19,000 this year in bonuses. Yet…Sometimes, you know? It just didn't feel right," Matt said, stubbing out his cigarette.

"Have you completed the arrangements for Eddie's funeral?"

"As much as we can. The medical examiner won't release the body until the autopsy is complete. The services will be Friday at Sacred Heart Church. Not sure if it will be an open casket — you'll need to talk to Marion about the final arrangements but…could you wait until at least tomorrow? She has had a rough couple of days."

"I will respect Marion, sir. You mentioned Eddie's lawyers. Who are they?"

"He dealt with Lorentson and Rundquist. If Eddie had something else going, they'd probably know."

"Thank you for your time, Mr. Numri," Nils rose to leave and Numri showed him out.

Back in his car, Nils thought about the new light shed on Eddie. *Things just got more complicated. Is there a love triangle in the mix? How many people were upset by Eddie's dealings? Should I report Eddie for possible tax evasion or plundering shipwrecks? With the embarrassing pictures, did Eddie dabble in blackmail?* Nils shook his head, but it did nothing to help clarify anything.

Before he called it a day, he got on the phone and made an appointment to talk to Eddie's lawyers. Hopefully, his head would stop spinning before the morning.

*****

Tuesday morning found Nils still waiting for the medical examiner's report. Cal Jameison's report was in his email and said nothing Nils didn't know. That made the morning drag until 10am, and his appointment at Lorentson and Rundquist. He was surprised when both Rikkard Lorentson and Harald Rundquist greeted him with perfunctory smiles and limp handshakes before ushering him into an office with a comfortable conversation area. They offered the deputy a leather club chair and a cup of coffee. He accepted both.

After sipping his coffee, Nils began by asking, "Gentlemen, I am surprised both of you are meeting with me. I want to get some background on Edward Lombardi's business dealings —" he held up a hand to silence any possible protests "— I know what you can tell me is limited, though I will add that it looks more likely the death will be treated as suspicious."

Mr. Lorentson, taking the lead, replied, "You will need both of us to get an idea of Lombardi's business dealings and to help unravel the complexities. I am an attorney, and my partner is a CPA. I know our partnership may be unusual, but it makes sense in Munising. What do you want to know?"

Nils got out his notebook, "I know about Eddie's carpentry business, the house cleaning, scuba school, underwater tours, antiques, the recent coin enterprise, and" here Nils coughed, "His underwater salvage escapades. He was a busy guy. Was there anything else he dabbled in?"

Lorentson thought before replying, "You did not mention his furniture reproduction business."

"That's different from his antiques?"

"Eddie would restore antiques and sell them. He would inform the buyer he had repaired the piece. Eddie got some pieces he couldn't repair but contained solid wood or nice brasses. Eddie would make a new piece of furniture from several pieces of old furniture." He looked over to Rundquist. "Apparently they call that a marriage in the business." He turned back to Nils. "He had his grandfather's stash of antique hardware and tools and was apparently pretty adept at distressing the furniture to make it look old. How old do you think our coffee table is, deputy?" the lawyer asked.

"It looks like an antique to me, sir," the deputy replied.

Rundquist smiled. "It's five years old. We bought it from Eddie, though I have no idea as to how many other pieces contributed parts. We got it for a good price. Most of his reproductions got consigned to auctioneers in Wisconsin or Minnesota. The pieces sold as furniture, the age left to the buyer's imagination."

"Anything else?" Nils asked.

"That's the lot. I manage Eddie's taxes and payroll. My partner manages his legal affairs." Runquist answered.

"Isn't it a little unusual for a business Eddie's size to keep a lawyer on retainer, sir?"

"I suppose so. My retainer is not huge. I presume you talked to Mr. Nurmi. Did he mention Tony Gearson?" the lawyer responded.

"Yes, he did, sir."

"Let me finish the story. Gearson is a hothead. He came here breathing fire and damnation, claiming Eddie cheated him. I let him tell his tale. When he finished, I produced a copy of Eddie's cartage agreement. I asked Gearson if he had signed a form like my example. Gearson said he signed the form, so I told him he didn't have a case. Gearson made threats against Eddie and our business before he left. Gearson was the most extreme case, but other examples pop up on a semi-regular basis. Eddie paid me as a defensive move. I also advised him to discuss anything with me should he have an idea and wanted to know if it was legal," Lorentson rejoind. "Eddie sometimes had creative ideas which, if brought into reality, would have been, shall we say, of dubious legal standing?"

"OK. When will Eddie's will be read? Or can't you tell me?" the deputy asked.

"We are Mr. Lombardi's executors. We need the medical examiner's report before we can begin to settle the estate," the lawyer replied. "I can't comment on the disposition of Eddie's estate without a court order. I am sure you understand."

"Yes, I understand. Thank you for your time, gentlemen," Nils rose to leave, and the other two followed suit.

At the doorway, Rundquist said, "Always happy to help the police," then turned and shut the office door, leaving Nils alone in the corridor.

*****

Back at the Sheriff's Department, Nils checked his email, and found the medical examiner's preliminary report was waiting. The doctor classified Lombardi's death as a homicide. No surprise about the time or cause of death, because the drug and tox screen yielded a surprising amount of ketamine. The drug was something he hadn't dealt with before, so called the medical examiner's office and asked to speak to Dr. Nikku. The doctor came on the line after a few minutes.

"Dr. Nikku, this is Deputy Gustafsen. I just looked at your preliminary report on Edward Lombardi. I am puzzled by one of the drugs you listed. Ketamine?"

"It's part of a class of drugs that can be used for anesthesia — veterinarian mainly — but humans have discovered they can get off on it. It's also known as a date rape drug — a cheap alternative to flunitrazepam, aka Rohypnol. It odorless and tasteless, and is usually administered via a victim's food or drink."

"And the drug's effects?"

"It's a dissociative drug. It causes a distorted perception of sight and sound. It can also cause impaired motor function. Unconsciousness can result in a high dose. It's bad stuff." She sighed dispassionately. "My final report is going to classify Lombardi's death as murder."

"Okay, so is it usually a liquid or a powder?"

"It's usually tablets or a powder, but you could always use that to make a clear liquid suspension. Grinding tablets to powder is simple enough."

"Is the drug readily available?"

"Thank God, no. It's a controlled substance, but that's never stopped the dark web."

Nils thanked the doctor and hung up. He looked up, and Sheriff Wiklund was standing in front of him.

"Something new come to light?"

"Quite a lot, sir. I think we need to talk in your office."

*****

Wiklund closed the door to his office and moved behind his desk. Nils sat in a visitor's seat.

"Okay deputy, what have you found out?"

"Eddie Lombardi probably was murdered, sir. The preliminary medical examiner's toxicology report listed ketamine in his blood. The drug would have impeded motor functions. With two leaking tires, he didn't have a chance. I talked with two of his business associates and, well, they didn't completely trust Lombardi. His live-in girlfriend called him an SOB before I could tell her he was dead. The big question I now have is, how was the drug administered? Also, did the same person administer the drug and puncture the tires?"

"I never like this kind of case, even though it's seemingly becoming more commonplace. Still," Wiklund sighed, "It's all part of being a peace officer. So, what are your next steps?"

"First will be talking to Suvi Nikula. She's a pharmacist. The ME said ketamine is rare, so I want to know her take on how someone might obtain some. I should have the casino's security footage tomorrow, and I plan on talking to Marion Javi again. As the local paper comes out tomorrow, I'd be surprised if Eddie's death isn't on the front page. That could stir things up. "

Wiklund sighed heavily again, and as Nils left the office he wondered if the man ever had any optimism in him.

*****

True to Nils' assumption, Eddie Lombardi's death relegated pictures of the K of C fish fry off the front page of the *Munising Beacon* Wednesday morning, even though most people already knew about it.

Nils called the Harbor Pharmacy and asked to speak with Suvi Nikula. She came on the line after finishing with a customer.

"Ms. Nikula, this is Deputy Gustafsen. I need your expertise," Nils began.

"I'd be happy to help if I can," she replied.

"The medical examiner's report raises some questions I think could best be answered by a pharmacist," he replied.

"What kind of questions?" she asked.

"It relates to Eddie Lombardi, and the questions are sensitive. I want to discuss it in person. I don't think you'd want this discussion during lunch, ma'am."

"I don't know if I should be intrigued or scared. I have an afternoon shift pharmacist who starts at four. Would that work?" she asked.

"That would be fine. I'll be there at four. Thank you, ma'am," Nils said.

*****

Back at the Sheriff's Department, Nils checked his email. Dr. Nikku had sent her final report. She'd classified Eddie's death as a murder based on

218

the presence of ketamine in Lombardi's blood. She noted that although Lombardi had been given a low dose, higher concentrations uncommon in the case studies she had referenced. However, the dose was enough to have impaired his motor skills but not enough to render him unconscious.

Why a low dose? Nils wondered. *That makes little sense.*

Adding yet another question he was going to have to ask Ms. Nikula, he checked with the Sacred Heart Church and confirmed Lombardi's funeral would be Friday afternoon.

As he was getting ready to leave for his appointment with Ms. Nikula, his phone rang. Robert Bearheart was calling to say he had the security footage.

"They've put all the files onto one of those USB thumbdrives. Do you want me to get someone to courier it over, or do you want to collect it yourself?"

Nils wanted to check them out as soon as he could, but time was short, and he didn't know how long the interview with the pharmacist was likely to take.

"If you can store it in your overnight security safe, I'll come over tomorrow morning and collect it first thing."

He put the phone down, picked up his jacket, and headed out to Harbor Pharmacy.

*****

"Just a minute, deputy. I need to talk to Beatrice for another minute," Suvi called when she saw him standing at the counter. She spoke quietly with a woman in a white coat for a few minutes, then turned her attention back to him. The pair went to her office and sat down.

"What was so complicated we needed to talk in person?" she began.

"The medical examiner found ketamine in Eddie Lombardi's blood. I wanted to ..." Nils didn't get to finish his question.

"Ketamine? You know that's a controlled substance, right? Even if it weren't, I wouldn't have it in my store. That stuff has harmed so many women!" Suvi glared at Nils. "What makes you think I would have anything to do with the drug? Or Eddie's death for that matter?"

"I had no intention of suggesting you had anything to do with the drug or Eddie's death. Let me recount a little piece of history."

Suvi continued to glare but nodded her assent.

Nils began, "In the late 1940's somebody developed x-ray boxes for shoe stores. Kids could stick their toes in the machine, and their mom could see how much room was left in the shoe. Kids thought it was fun to see their toes wiggle. Later regulators figured out how much radiation the boxes emitted. The boxes got recalled in 1950 or 1951. My dad told me he had great fun watching his toes wiggle when he got shoes for kindergarten in 1954. The boxes got recalled, but that didn't mean everyone returned the boxes."

"Dr. Nikku told me the drug is controlled and rare — not in everyday use. I just want to confirm the information with a working pharmacist, just in case prescriptions were more common than the ME thinks. And as you have an interest in the investigation, I thought you'd be a good source of information."

Nils tried to smile. "Pax?" he concluded.

Suvi took a deep breath. "I guess I owe an apology. You didn't mean to hit one of my hot buttons," she began. "Ketamine has limited therapeutic uses. Most pharmacies I know of don't stock it and probably wouldn't order it. I can't remember the last prescription I saw for it. The hospital pharmacy might stock it."

"If the drug is controlled and despised, how could someone get it?"

The pharmacist thought for a moment. "I can think of several ways. A person could find a dealer at a rave, and ask if they had any Special K. The other would be to break into a veterinarian — or find one willing to sell them some." She was thoughtful for a moment, then added: "Or you could try mail order from Mexico."

"Thank you for the information, it's certainly been helpful." He leaned in a little closer. "Would you please keep our conversation confidential?"

"Of course," she replied, as she showed Nils out.

As Nils walked to his cruiser, he wondered:

How does any of that help? Why did she go off like that? I still must be missing puzzle pieces.

*****

Nils began his Thursday at the casino, but not on the gaming floor. Robert Bearheart had set up a viewer in a rarely used office.

"I've set up a display so you can watch the video here, deputy," Bearheart explained. "If you think you find evidence of a crime against Mr. Lombardi, take the USB drive with my blessing. But if you see nothing, I'd prefer to hold the videos here. I want to honor the privacy of all my customers."

"We can start there, sir," Gustafsen agreed.

After Bearheart showed Nils how to work the remote control, he poured Nils a large mug of coffee — putting it on a side table as Nils settled down to watch.

The speed of the stop motion video made it jerky, but Nils could follow the action easily enough. He slowed it down when he saw Eddie and Marion arriving and noted that the timestamp made their arrival as shortly before six. Next up in shot was Matt Nurmi. They ordered drinks and a plate of appetizers. Suvi arrived at the same time as the appetizers did. A bottle of champagne was ordered while the party studied menus and chit-chatting, munching on the appetizers. Orders placed, it wasn't long before a bus boy brought four house salads with cruets of dressing and cleared the appetizers.

The conversation continued throughout the meal. People stopped by the table, amicable hugs and handshakes were exchanged, but nothing untoward appeared to happen. A busboy brought the main courses and Nils could see him serve the plates without any problem. Desserts were ordered, delivered, and consumed, and eventually the waiter appeared with the check, to which Eddie then ordered his brandy. The waiter returned with the revised check and the brandy. The four drank the toast. The ladies and Matt left. Eddie paid for the meal and talked to his friends. At about 8:15pm according to the timestamp, Eddie left without finishing the brandy. His steps were unsteady.

If anyone at the table had slipped Eddie something, their talents are being wasted. They belong on the stage doing sleight of hand magic, Nils thought. Tapping the remote against his chin, Nils suddenly had a revelation.

The only thing unique to Eddie's meal was the brandy at the end.

Nils then queued up the video of the bar area, and noticed the wait staff placed drinks on their trays and headed for their customers. Nils fast-forwarded to Eddie's brandy order.

And there it was. The deputy noticed the waiter serving Eddie's party put the tray down and removed something from his coat pocket. The image quality wasn't fantastic, but over a series of stop motion shots Nils could see a powder of some kind had been dropped into the glass. The waiter swished the liquid before serving the drink.

Got you! Nils thought. *Now, who the Hell are you?*

Nils called the casino front desk

"Can you ask Mr. Bearheart to come to Room 6 please."

When he appeared, Nils rewound the video. "Please watch this service, sir," Gustafsen requested.

After the sequence finished, Bearheart commented, "That's not proper service. That looks very much like Tony Gearson."

"To me, it appears he dropped some powder into the brandy. Did you see the same thing, sir?" Nils asked.

"I did. But I've no way of knowing what the powder was."

Nils thought for a minute and then asked a question.

"Do you supply the wait staff's uniforms?"

"Yes, we do. We supply a locker room and require our employees to dress here. Why?"

"How often are the uniforms cleaned?" the deputy asked.

"Now I see where you're going. Let's go to my office, and I'll ask Cydnee.

*****

Back behind his desk, Bearheart called the assistant manager.

"When is the next time we are going to clean the afternoon shift's uniforms?"

"There's always one uniform in an employee's locker. We have extra uniforms in case of emergencies. Uniforms are collected Friday morning, and delivered back Friday evening, just before the shift change."

"Thanks Cyd." Then turning to Nils, he said, "They're due for collection tomorrow, so the one in Gearson's locker should be the one he wore last Friday."

There was a knock on the door, and Cydnee came in, nodding a greeting to Nils. "How can I help?"

"Ma'am, do the staff have lockable lockers, or are there separate facilities for valuables?

Cydnee turned back to Nils. "The locker rooms are partitioned into a vestibule and a changing area. Our employees have lockers in each area. In the vestibule, each employee has a locker containing their uniform, but it's not lockable. Staff are not to leave personal items in their uniform after their shift, because those lockers are unlocked. That way we can check the uniforms for spills and stains, and have easy access on a Friday morning. The lockers in the changing area the staff lock with their own locks, so their personal items are secure and safe. Does that help, deputy?"

"Thank you." Nils turned to Bearheart. "Could I ask you to swap out Gearson's uniform? The coat may contain residue of whatever the powder was."

Bearheart thought for a moment. "Okay, Cyd, can you personally change out the uniform in Gearson's locker and bring it here.

"Right away, sir" Cyndee said and left.

Bearheart sat back in his chair. "You're going to have some hoops to jump through before you can take the uniform, deputy. We're on Bay Mills tribal land. You'll need a warrant as a minimum. I am sure your sheriff knows what needs to be done. I'll contact the Tribal authorities."

"Once we have the clothing secure then I'll call Sheriff Wiklund."

Just then there was a knock on the door and Bearheart's personal assistant, Sharon Anang, poked her head into the room. "Sir, Ramon Thickfoot is outside. He's insisting he must talk to you and the deputy. He claims it's important."

Bearheart glanced at Nils. Nils shrugged, so Bearheart said, "Tell him to come in, Sharon."

Anang held the door open as both Cydnee — carrying Gearson's worn uniform wrapped in a spare plastic laundry bag — and Ramon Thickfoot stepped into the office.

Cydnee hung the jacket and trousers on the back of the door, then left, leaving Thickfoot standing in the middle of the room, facing the other two men.

It was obvious that Ramon had tied himself in emotional knots. He turned to the deputy. "Sheriff, I want to confess to killing Mr. Lombardi."

Just what I don't need, another wrinkle, Nils thought.

"Mr. Thickfoot, why do you think you killed Mr. Lombardi?" the deputy asked gently.

"I thought Mr. Lombardi had lied to me about being my father. I was mad. I bent forks and put them under his tires to get even. Now he's dead. I killed him," Ramon bleated.

Nils pondered his options. *That explains the forks. But they're not what killed Lombardi.*

"Mr. Thickfoot," Nils tried to sound reassuring. "I'm going to read you your rights, but that doesn't mean you're under arrest. It only means the Sheriff's Department will check what you say. I knew about the forks. The forks weren't the only factor in Mr. Lombardi's death. Just don't leave the county without contacting the Sheriff's Department, okay?"

Thickfoot nodded and Gustafsen read the Miranda warning.

Before Thickfoot left, Bearheart asked, "Are you going to be okay to work the rest of your shift?"

He smiled and nodded. "I'll be okay." He stopped halfway through the doorway, and turned to look at Bearheart. "Thank you for listening, sir." Then he left, closing the door behind him.

Nils ran a hand through his hair. "The forks only made Lombardi's vehicle hard to handle — they didn't kill him."

Bearheart grimaced a little. "Well, here's some more bad news — things just got a lot more complicated. As I said, we are on Bay Mills land. Mr. Thickfoot is Ojibwe, and he's under twenty-one..."

Half smiling, Nils just said "Wonderful," and hoped it sounded at least a little convincing. As he pulled out his cell phone, he added, "You call your people, and I'll call mine," then started in on his speed dial list.

By the time the two had finished making assorted arrangement and updating those who needed to be updated, it had turned 12:30.

Deputy Pederson appeared with a warrant and proper evidence bags, and Bearheart — ever watchful of adverse publicity — gave the deputies casino carry-out bags to help disguise their investigations.

The only upside was that both Nils and Pederson managed to take lunch in the coffee shop before they headed back to Munising. Pederson took the uniform to the Sheriff's Department to have it shipped to the State Police Crime Lab while Gustafsen called Marion Javi and arranged to go see her ASAP.

*****

Nils knocked on the door and waited for her to answer. *She's had a rough couple of days,* he thought.

"Won't you come in, deputy," she began. "Can I offer you anything?"

"No thank you, Ma'am. I just wanted to update you on our progress so far."

She looked emotionally drained, but led him into the living room. "Won't you sit down?" Nils obliged.

"We are pursuing several leads, ma'am, but we're pretty sure Mr. Lombardi was murdered." Nils noted that she didn't seem surprised, and he wondered if he was stating what was, to her, the obvious conclusion.

He carried on. "I want to talk to you about Eddie to be sure we don't miss anything."

She looked down at her hands, resting in her lap. "I had Eddie all wrong," she began with a sob. "I thought he was cheating on me. Friends told me they'd seen him with a blonde." She took a deep breath and continued. "I needed money to fix my car, and he wouldn't help. I was mad. Then on Monday I found out I was wrong. I got a call from Jamieson's asking when I could bring my car in for a service and repairs.

Eddie had paid for it in advance, including one of their rental cars. A friend, Julia Jokinen, called. She offered her condolences. She's a realtor, and she's blonde. Julia had been showing Eddie houses. Eddie was going to surprise me with a perfect house. She said it was a shame Eddie couldn't pull off the big thing he was planning. I had him all wrong." Tears came. Nils waited.

What can I ask after that? He tried to figure out.

When Marion calmed herself, Nils asked, "Can you think of anyone who would want to harm Eddie?"

"No, I can't. Matt might," she replied in a whisper.

"Thank you for your time, ma'am." Nils took out a business card and handed it to Marion. "If you think of anything, please call me, ma'am." Marion nodded and Nils let himself out.

*****

Nils was present at Eddie's well-attended funeral on Friday. Marion leaned on Matt's arm and kept it together.

Two weeks later, Lorentson and Rundquist distributed Eddie's trust. Suvi received seventy percent of the coin exchange and the related bank accounts. Marion received the other thirty percent. Matt got seventy percent of the woodworking business along with the business accounts, which were healthily in the black. Marion got Eddie's sizeable personal bank accounts and investments, his boat, an insurance claim on his truck, and his personal property.

When Marion eventually went through Eddie's things, she discovered a new engagement ring. That was when she realized what 'the big thing' was going to be. She cried for days.

*****

Unsurprisingly, Tony Gearson had not attended Eddie Lombardi's funeral. Tony had an exaggerated concept of his importance. He grew up believing he descended from nobility, but if he ever researched his family tree, he'd have known his ancestors cleaned the stables for a minor English count.

He hadn't set out to kill Eddie. But Eddie had cheated him. Tony just wanted to humiliate the man by having him do a face-plant into his mashed potatoes, and he'd decided to act when he saw Eddie make a reservation.

Originally he'd planned to use the ketamine to get even with a girl who hadn't shown him proper respect. Gearson had trouble finding a source for the drug. Before he had the drug, the woman had moved south of the Bridge. *She's not worth a three hour drive,* Gearson thought. Still, he figured, he would hang onto it — there was bound to be someone else who would piss him off enough for him to use it on them.

It had been hard to slip Eddie the drug, but Gearson prided himself on his wits.

It was a shame Lombardi didn't finish the brandy, Tony had thought as he cleared Table 12 and saw the remains of Eddie's final drink.

And then he'd become very nervous when he learned the deputy sheriffs showed up at the casino – talking to Bearheart and other staff.

But that had been over a month back, and everything had seemed to have died down.

I'm in the clear. I'm smarter than the police, he thought.

Then there had been an early morning knock on the door — and when he opened it he found Gustafsen and Pederson waiting on his porch.

As Pederson had turned him around and cuffed him, Gearson could hear Nils saying: "Anthony Gearson, I have a warrant for your arrest for the murder of Edward Lombardi…."

The State Police Crime Lab had taken weeks to find trace residue of ketamine in the pocket of Gearson's uniform coat. The crime lab turned up a quantity of ketamine powder in an envelope, covered in Tony's fingerprints. Come the finish, Tony had been left with no choice but to plead guilty to all charges.

*****

Ramon Thickfoot had been terrified about going to prison for what he'd done. He had no idea how many conversations had happened between the Sheriff, the County Prosecutor, and the Tribal authorities — nor how much Bearheart had supported him. However, they had all agreed

Ramon was at least guilty of the Willful Destruction of Property.

All parties had agreed that Ramon would receive a suspended sentence, under the tribe's supervision. It didn't hurt that Ramon's uncle had influence in the tribe. Ramon would be able to clear his record when he turned twenty-one.

Once the dust had settled, Ramon had found new positive fixations. He was promoted to waiter. He had to fixate on the casino's menu, keeping up with the catch of the day, weekly specials, and seasonal changes.

Ramon also fixated on Madeline Bearheart, Robert Bearheart's niece. They'd known each other quite a while. Suddenly, something sparked, and Ramon couldn't believe she could be interested in him. They were going to be married after the New Year. Ramon planned to fixate on Madeline for the rest of his life.

*****

Nils thought Kirsikka's aunt's jewelry made his wife look more beautiful than ever. When Nils had made a point of telling her, her smile got bigger. They were heading toward the casino — their anniversary was coming up, and Nils didn't want to tempt fate and get a call on that date, so they had decided to celebrate early with dinner at the casino and afterwards a show. Nils was happy he wouldn't have to deal with forks on the road tonight. He just hoped he'd use the right fork at dinner. Kirsikka still called him a barbarian at times. There were always challenges.

The Prospect

Sam Wiebe

Felipe Ramos, known alias Flip, 26, prospect for the East Van chapter of the Heavens Exiles Motorcycle Club, registered trademark, waited for the Rabbit to break off for a piss. The way the kid was downing rum and Cokes, ordering trays of Skittle shots, his bladder couldn't hold out. Flip leaned back from the merch table, in no rush.

He didn't know what the Rabbit owed, the exact dollar amount. Enough to keep clear of the Mountain Shadow Pub for over a month. Usually he was a fixture, the same as Flip. The Rabbit cranked out fake IDs. Hundred bucks for a guy, sixty for a female if she'd test it out with him, buy the first round. Then, being a gentleman, it was only right to buy one for *her*. Not a bad hustle for a bucktooth kid with a laminating printer.

Flip's wasn't much better. As a prospect he was here to waylay drunks en route to the ATM or the can. Set up at a folding table a safe distance from the waft of piss. The table was covered with support merch, snapbacks and hoodies with SUPPORT YOUR LOCAL VILLAINS, EAST VAN TOUGH, WE ❤ ONE PERCENTERS. Whatever dumb slogan Rigger Devlin thought up. Rigger the Exiles sergeant-at-arms, also Flip's sponsor.

Flip yawned, kept watch for the Rabbit. A college boy with white framed glasses staggered past, hand already on his fly. Look at those specs. No lenses in them, pure affectation. He stuck out a leg, blocking the narrow corridor and impeding White Glasses' route to the urinals.

"Shirts are twenty. Two for thirty-five. Hats fifteen or five with a shirt."

White Glasses had that college smirk, never been hit in his life. Looking down at Flip, who wore a hoodie *and* shirt at Rigger's insistence, the cheap fabric itchy and bunched around his shoulders.

"Oh. Cool. No thank you."

"Hat and shirt combo twenty-five."

White Glasses looked down at Flip's outstretched leg. Didn't say "Um, ex-*cuse* me?" but his expression did.

"Let me see your wallet."

The only moment Flip enjoyed was when they realized he wasn't like them. Felipe Ramos, graduate of Willingdon Youth Correctional and North Fraser Pre-Trial, record expunged but his crimes common knowledge. Body honed by the docks and the warehouse. Mood dampened by four a.m. wakeups and late nights slinging T-shirts. Asking nicely could I see your wallet.

White Glasses handed it over on reflex, the smirk leaving his face. College kids were smart. The corridor was the trick. No one was watching here. You didn't get a guy trying to impress a girl or kick up a fuss with the waitress. You bought a shirt and you pissed. Could piss all night long, now that Flip had your money.

He took out a twenty and shoved the wallet back atop a ONE PERCENT PROUD shirt. "Gave you a deal."

"Thank you," White Glasses said.

Flip turned his head away as the door marked GENTS swung open and shut. The table of fake IDs were having a great time. But the Rabbit was gone.

*****

He found the kid pissing outside, track pants down, pale ass broadcast to the Christmas lights of the house across the street. Whistling something catchy Flip couldn't place.

Turning, the Rabbit saw him, then *noticed* him. Panic. Eyes ranging around the lot, weighing his chances. Going for a grin instead.

"How you doing, Felipe?" The Rabbit everybody's friend.

"What do you owe?" Flip asked.

"Owe?" Putting on his best *who me?* dinner theater expression. "Oh, you mean for the—shit, sorry, man. Things've been crazy, my grandma…"

The wallet out, peeling off twenties and fifties. Probably what the table of girls had paid him. The Rabbit handed it over looking sheepish.

"Tell Rigger, there's any confusion, my grandma's cancer, I totally apologize."

Flip headed back inside, the Rabbit staying out to smoke a blunt and recover his cool. Probably telling himself what a good acting job he did. Crisis averted.

*****

No one had fucked with the merch table. Who would? Flip took his place and punched in Rigger's number. The one nice thing about the Mountain Shadow, the music wasn't so loud you couldn't hear yourself. He tried to think of what the song was the Rabbit had been whistling.

"How you doing, porkchop?" Rigger's pet name for him. For every Portuguese, Flip surmised.

"Guy with the teeth settled up."

"Showed his face, did he?"

"'Bout five o'clock." Time was Rigger's half-assed code for dollar amounts. The phones were burners—after showing Flip episodes of *The Wire*, the biker had insisted he buy three of the cheapest pay-as-you-go mobiles he could—but that didn't mean you spoke freely. Flip found it asinine, would have stayed off phones entirely it was up to him. But it wasn't.

"Great, bring it over," Rigger said.

"Now?"

"How many shirts you sold?"

"Four plus a lid."

"Slow night. Yeah, pack it in."

Flip drove to Rigger's place, a nice corner house on Adanac with a basement suite he rented out to students from mainland China. He'd sold six shirts and his cut of merch sales was thirty percent. Rigger expected a little skim.

He parked his Datsun in the alley behind Rigger's garage. The Exile was planning on turning the structure into a laneway home. Another three, four grand in rent. You owned a property in Vancouver, you owned a money printing press.

Rigger's Softail was under a dust sheet next to his day ride, a green Jag. When Flip had been struck, just out of Pre-Trial, he'd thought bikes would be a huge part of what they did. Silly him. A joke everyone was in on except the government. Sure, a full-patch member had to own a bike, and when called on, be able to ride. That way, instead of associating for criminal reasons, you were just a bunch of guys who liked motorcycles. A club rather than a conspiracy.

The motion light hit him as he crossed the yard to the back porch. Rigger and his current wife were in the hot tub, both naked, Mrs. Rigger's new tits not half bad. Flip handed over the money.

"Where's the rest?" Rigger looked at six hundred dollars like it was shit.

"What the Rabbit gave me plus the merch."

Once in a blue moon his sponsor would shake him down for extra. That usually didn't happen until tax season, or when the track opened. Flip got ready to hand over what he'd made tonight.

Rigger was pissed. "Thought you said you got all five grand?"

"The Rabbit owes you five K?"

"Why you think he's ducking me?"

Flip couldn't imagine a scenario where the Rabbit qualified for a five thousand dollar loan. Rigger with his million dollar house and his mint Jaguar, not to mention his wife's new silicone half floating in the tub, should know better.

"You know where the kid stays?"

Flip nodded.

Rigger stood, treating Flip to a view of a hornet's nest of grey pubic hair. 48, the Exiles logo on the belly and an East Van cross on his left arm. Ballbag shrinking in the January air. Rigger stuffed the money into the pouch of Flip's hoodie.

"Times make the man. Know what I'm saying? Your generation, Millennials, want the gravy without putting in the hours. My day, at your age, I was a step away from my patch."

"And walked to school uphill both ways," Flip said.

Mrs. Devlin giggled. Closer to Flip's age than her husband, she'd refilled and emptied her champagne glass while they'd been discussing the Rabbit's financial woes. She filled it again.

"Go get 'em, champ," Rigger said.

Flip nodded.

On his way out, Mrs. Rigger told him Happy New Year.

*****

The Rabbit had a black longhaired Persian that mewled in curiosity when Flip punched out the window. The cat curled around his leg and made friends. She hadn't been brushed maybe ever, her fur dragging on the dirty floor. Flip closed the blinds and turned on the oven's range light. He found a bag of Whiskas and filled a bowl for his new pal.

The Rabbit was your garden variety west coast male, messy but not a total slob. Poking through the cupboards, Flip found an ounce of coke, a half-smoked bag of BC Bud, an Altoids tin of roaches and shake. Rubbers and Ultraglide by the bedside. We live in hope. Passport and some silver coins, Franklin Mint shit in the little white squares, at the back of the bedroom closet.

The print shop was set up in the dining nook. Camera on a tripod with a blank background, fancy card printer with PROPERTY OF TRI-CITIES COLLEGE stamped on the feed tray. His boots crunched sand on the tile. Cat litter.

The box was overflowing, nuggets and clumps of piss. Flip changed the litter, locked the cat inside the washroom with the food. He turned off the range light. The Rabbit had a block of mismatched knives by the coffee maker. Flip selected one at random, took up a coffee mug. He sat at the table to wait for the Rabbit, wondering if life got better the higher up you moved in the organization, or was it just cat turds all the way to the top.

*****

His first time in trouble at school was for bringing a weapon into class. He was ten. One of his buddies had been bragging, my daddy fights fires, he's so brave. Flip just meant to shut the kid up, show him he wasn't the only one with a family. The knife had been his brother's. Timo was fifteen and already working in the Chop House with their dad, Timoteo Ramos, Senior. Holidays the whole family worked there. The turkey truck pulled up and the kids stood on the fender by the refrigerated cube and hand-bombed the birds to mom and dad, who stacked them in the back of the shop. Then the hams. The East Van Chop House was where you got your meat in the neighborhood.

Flip had brought Timo's knife and a whetstone to school for show and tell. His plan was to demonstrate how to put an edge on. He'd practiced the night before. His dad could hone a blade in seconds, dragging it over the back of a second blade he kept for that purpose. But every week Senior would haul out his whetstone and do the shop's blades properly, till each could fly through bone with no resistance.

Flip remembered his dad and the principal, discussing the 'weapon.' His dad explaining what the family did. A Ramos knows his way around a knife. I'm sure Felipe just meant to show it off. The principal probably bought his meat at Whole Foods, but finally came around, let Flip off with a warning.

In the school parking lot his father had clouted him hard enough his vision swam. Flip didn't care. He couldn't have loved the man more.

*****

The shop held its own when it only had the Safeway and the Italian Market to compete with. A lot of East Van Italians would give his dad their business, almost ashamed about it, but fresh was fresh. They ground sausage in-house, sold a few spices and staples as well.

Then the Overwaitea opened and suddenly the shop was caught in a price war between grocery chains. Geezers coming in asking why their black forest is ten cents more. His dad's stock answer: "'Cause I know the pig it came from".

Longer hours. A heart attack. His mom determined to keep the shop open. When their dad died, Timo dropped out to run the shop. His brother didn't seem to mind. "When're you gonna use any of that shit? Trigonometry? You triangulate anything this week?"

Flip wasn't allowed to drop out. He worked after school, sometimes into the night if there was a delivery in the morning. A real family enterprise, treading water.

*****

His second time in shit at school, all he did was fall asleep. The teacher had smacked him. Flip, at fifteen the same height as Mrs. Guest, had shot out of the too-small desk, took hold of the projector. Maybe he'd *thought* of throwing it at her, *considered* it, but instead he'd only toppled it over.

One month of detention. A mark on his record. An apology to Mrs. Guest and another one, teeth grinding, in front of the class. I will control myself. I'm not a beast. I want to be here.

Detention turned out to be the best part of his high school experience. An hour where he could just sit. Not feeding the grinder or jointing a side of beef. He could read, catch up on what he was supposed to be learning.

"Tell them we need you at the shop," his mom said. But he didn't.

His second week held after school, Elodie Martel joined him in detention. Pretty in a damaged way, Elodie smoked Gauloise Blues and spoke more Portuguese than Flip did. "Lotta Brazilians in Montreal," she'd said. Elodie spoke French at home, a little Spanish. She lived with her dad now in Strathcona, down the street from the Ramoses. She and Flip instantly became friends.

Elodie.

Sometimes he'd be over at the Martels', waiting for her to get ready. Elodie used to change stockings in front of him. Grinning as she did her toes, knowing she was giving him jerk-off fantasies for years.

One day she dragged him into her parents' room, filched a condom from the Donald Duck bowl on the dresser, and took his virginity. As casual about it, as comforting, as if they'd been joined their entire lives.

"Not a word," she'd said after. "Dad would fucking murder you."

Flip turned sixteen, in love, getting laid, and happy. That year was almost perfect. Even long nights at the Chop House couldn't dent him. And then within three months of his seventeenth birthday, his fine life was over.

*****

Timo had a second job at the Granville Club, waiting tables in a white coat and pants. He'd come back to the shop, pockets bulging with tip money. The Club members were all rich WASPS and Asians, generous and showing off. Some nights Flip's brother would bring home over a grand.

Timo was looking ragged, always blowing his nose. But he set the pace at the shop. Wire thin, handsome, he told Flip he'd put in a word at the Club when Flip turned 18. With the two of them making tips, hell, even if the shop's rent doubled, they'd be okay.

Flip remembered the morning. Alone in the shop when the cop came in. The officer was South Asian, wore a black turban with his uniform. Asked to speak with Mrs. Marta Ramos.

"Not here," Flip said, wondering if the school had reported him.

"I should probably speak with your mom," Officer Dhillon said. "Can you get hold of her? It's about her son."

Felipe has missed a shit-ton of class and the principal has decided to involve the authorities. He'd drop out, marry Elodie, he and Timo would run the shop. Get drunk together on weekends. All acceptable to him.

The cop hesitated and Flip knew it must be *something*.

"I guess he'd be your brother," Officer Dhillon said. "Timoteo, Junior, I'm very sorry, he's dead."

Timo had been shot at the bus stop on Pender coming home from his shift. A red Nissan pulled up, the person riding shotgun opened fire. One witness who could only say the windows of the car were tinted and the shooter had yelled something, couldn't make out the words.

Unsolved.

*****

In the weeks after he learned Timo was part of a different world. His brother had made the paper as "an alleged associate of a Lower Mainland trafficking ring." Flip barely understood what the news was talking about. He'd shown the paper to Elodie.

"They're saying he dealt," she told him, gently, no judgment attached. Then spelled it out even further. "That he sold drugs and shit."

"Like pot?"

"Probably coke."

He pictured Tony Montana, snorting a hillock of white powder in his mansion. Timo had nothing like that. His brother lived at home, made money from tips...

Like finding out the world had been lying to you. His brother dealt. Probably used, too. And still gave the money to their mom to pay the rent.

After a week he'd gone back to school, sat through condolences from kids he hated, teachers who thought he was a problem. I'm just so sorry, Felipe. If you need anything. Flip yeahed and looked at the ground and waited it out.

He found he was looking at the schoolyard with wiser eyes. Drugs got dealt here, too. The cops didn't care whether he lived or died. The Ramos kid's brother, keep an eye on him.

Dwayne Hood was a grade ahead and two years older, repeating senior year. He drove a nice Honda and hung out with a group of suburban kids. Tall and broad, an upright side of beef, nice shirt and nice Caesar haircut. Flip had mostly avoided him.

Rumors: Dwayne whipped a kid with a bike chain. Dwayne dealt pot in the parking lot. Dwayne kept a loaded gun in the Honda's glove box, he showed it to us one time. Dwayne's cousin was connected to the League of Nationz.

Flip started to understand. Timo had been dealing on League territory. The League had taken out Timo. His brother had died because somebody close to Dwayne Hood wanted that.

What saved him with the judge was that he'd gone to school empty-handed. If he'd brought a knife, even if he'd picked up a chair leg or a snapped section of ruler, that would have meant intent, in which case goodbye. Instead he walked up to Dwayne and his buddies, leaning on the bike rack, smoking. Dwayne making lazy circles with the bike chain, the translucent red plastic sheath whirring in the air.

Dwayne was smirking and called out something but Flip didn't hear it. He didn't rush at the older kid. You rushed, that meant you wanted to see if the kid would flinch. Flip didn't care if Dwyane flinched or not.

He walked up without knowing exactly what he'd do and saw the smirk and stepped into the red eye of the bike chain.

Dwayne stumbled back and slipped, Flip grabbing handfuls of Ralph Lauren, Dwayne's head striking the steel triangles of the bike rack. The chain had clipped Flip's ear, left a welt on his shoulder. In the retelling for the judge, that became Dwayne striking first. Another saving detail for his attorney to hold up.

He didn't know how to throw a proper punch but he had muscle from years working in the Chop House and had a hand on Dwayne's head and a thumb jabbing into Dwayne's nose as he punched the older kid, rocking the head with force again and again into the hard blue spokes. Dwayne screaming. The blood keeping the others off him at first.

He didn't realize he'd stopped. He was out of breath, arms tired and fist numb. Dwayne Hood was on the pavement, seizing up. Someone hit him from behind, in the spine, but Flip barely felt it.

He walked away quickly, across the rugby field, cutting down Napier Street to his home.

*****

Arrest, remand into custody, trial: a series of vignettes that meant nothing to him. His lawyer told him not to speak. The two mouthpieces conferred with the judge about his mental state, his grief, his intent towards Mr. Hood, without ever asking him. No reporters, either, since youth cases fell under a publication ban. When Flip *did* speak, the lawyer told him exactly how to phrase it.

Just saw red, Madam Justice. So sad about my brother. Never meant it. If I could take it back I would.

Flip went into Willingdon on August 3rd, 1999. He spent the turn of the millennium listening to a riot in the pod next to his. Flip served two thirds of his sentence and was paroled, and within a week of being out he'd run into Dwayne Hood *again*, or what was left of him.

Defendant upended Mr. Hood's wheelchair. Raised said chair over his head. Brought the chair in question down upon Mr. Hood several times.

Flip had to serve the last eight months as an adult, plus the charges tacked on for the second assault. Real prison time. Now he had something of a reputation. Now the Exiles were interested in him.

*****

Flip heard the scrape of the lock, the Rabbit coming home. The kid had struck out with his customers, had probably run out on the bill. The Rabbit threw the lights, tossed his jacket, still whistling that song. The hell was it? He called out for his cat, "Smo-kee, where you hiding, silly girl?" Clicking his tongue to call her.

The scrape of the knife on porcelain stopped him. An old trick. In lieu of a whetstone you can use the bottom of a coffee mug to freshen up the edge. Flip told the kid to take a seat.

"You're gonna kill me."

The Rabbit's underpowered brain ran through every mob film and *Sopranos* episode he'd ever seen. Not many judging from his shelves—more of a fantasy guy, *Buffy the Vampire Slayer*, one of the *Star Treks*, not the one with Shatner or the bald guy. A nerd.

"Not even gonna hurt you," Flip said.

"My cat?"

"Locked in the shitter. Take a seat."

Flip wiped the porcelain dust off the table, waiting for the Rabbit to accept he didn't have a choice. Scared shitless. The Rabbit sat.

As plain as he could, as patient as he could, Flip explained. "We need to come up with five grand." That was the best approach. Like the two of them were in it together.

"I don't have it."

He gestured at the apartment. "I'm aware."

"The five hundred…"

"Neither here nor there," Flip said. "What's your real name?"

The Rabbit told him.

"Okay, Jason. Your parents around?"

"Uh huh."

"Call 'em."

"They won't give me any more."

"Put it to them anyway."

"It's one o'clock."

Flip stuck him. The tip of the knife went into the chub under the Rabbit's arm a quarter inch. He didn't yell. They both watched the sleeve of the dress shirt bloom dark.

"You mentioned a grandma," Flip said.

The Rabbit nodded. "She really does have cancer."

"Does she have five grand?"

"I don't think so."

Another jab, this one above the nipple. The Rabbit shrieked before the steel touched him. A keen little steak knife, none of that serrated shit.

"Granny have a car?" Flip asked.

"Like a minivan."

"What make?"

"Honda Odyssey."

"New?"

"Twenty-fifteen I think?"

Now they were getting somewhere. "Borrow it."

Before the Rabbit voiced an objection, Flip feinted with the steak knife. A game he and Timo used to play. They'd nicked each other's hands and cheeks so many times. "You're gonna hurt yourself," their mom used to yell. Timo had said, the two of them giggling, "Sure, but I'll hurt him way more."

*****

The Odyssey drove like a box, good visibility when you weren't in reverse. Flip dropped the Rabbit at home, called Rigger Devlin to find out where to take the van. The Exiles had a garage on First and Clark, a warehouse nearby on Terminal. What did a 2015 Odyssey blue book for? Rigger would look it up and get back to him.

A Tom Jones disk in the CD player. "What's New, Pussycat?" A rosary hung off the rearview mirror. Flip tooled around in the general direction of False Creek.

He didn't plan to drive by her house, but found himself on a side street in Strathcona. Elodie Martel might not even live there anymore.

Everyone else he knew had left the city. Christmas lights were still up on the house but not lit, a gold JOYEUX NOËL hanging from the door knocker. Flip idled, burning up the old lady's gas.

A random particle, agitated and lacking bonds, the rest of the universe asleep.

Shoe Shoe Sh'Boogie
Jon Fain

Jesse Desmond spent the last Saturday afternoon in July drinking in his driveway. His parents' driveway technically, but they were off visiting cousins on his mother's side. It was the house he grew up in, with a bent basketball hoop in the turnaround. Where he'd been living again since his girlfriend Melissa kicked him out.

As he crushed a six-pack, Jesse half-assed cleaned out the inside of his car. His mother's technically, that she'd been letting him use. After he met with Leroy that night and got his cut, he'd take the red Sentra to one of those places that went whole hog—wash and wax, undercarriage too. Where the bums, druggies and guys on work release wave at the cars with white rags. Who you were supposed to tip but Jesse sure as hell wouldn't, because it was a Sentra, for fuck's sake. Or maybe he *would* give out some dollars. Having money for a change would give him options and not just for spiffing up his mother's crappy car.

At the Hawthorne Shoe warehouse, Jesse helped send inventory and equipment from the company's closed-down facilities throughout New England to South Carolina, where its headquarters and manufacturing had moved. Eighteen-wheelers would come in and drivers would drop off trailers. Jesse would unload them, and then after his boss Dick finished the paperwork and told him what was going where, he'd re-load stuff onto empty trailers new drivers brought, and they would head off down South.

When Jesse lifted up the trailer doors, he'd never know what he might find. It could be office furniture and office supplies, big boxes of mismatched shoes, or pallets stacked high with 4' x 4' leather pieces, raw material for shoes that had never been made. Two trucks came once and brought machines for making something called shoe lasts. The machines were over six feet tall and made up of mysterious levers, buttons, switches, shoe-shaped metal templates, and spray nozzles. Dick made Jesse use toothbrushes, and even wooden chopsticks he brought in from the local takeout spot, to try to get chunks of white plastic out of the workings before they were sent back out. It was a chunk of hours that sucked balls.

One hot afternoon, when he had raised all twelve of the loading dock doors to try and capture a cross-breeze, a tractor trailer came into the parking lot and backed up to the first open bay. Jesse couldn't unload until the driver checked in with Dick. This time, Leroy was the driver who came in with the paperwork.

He was a scrawny cock-of-the-walk, wearing peg-leg jeans, a Jack Daniels Old No 7 belt buckle, and a brand-matching black and white ball cap. When he got to where Jesse waited, Leroy danced out his right foot, brought it back, and then shot it back and forth like a joy boy doing a jig in an old movie. He had on red and black leather cowboy boots with thick heels that tap-tap-tapped the stained concrete floor.

"Hey there, Hot Shot! Gonna help me with that forking lift?"

Jesse was sick of drivers coming in and bossing him around. They were all prima donnas, never helping out with the unloading and loading. Thought they were special because they could kick a clutch and throw a gearshift around. He was sure this cardboard cowboy from the wild west of Pennsylvania was no different.

Another time after he'd dropped his load, met with Dick, and unlocked and rattled up the door of the trailer he'd brought in, Leroy nodded to a pair of large shrink-wrapped palettes.

"Know what those are, boyo?"

"Machines of some sort. More shoe shit."

"Wrong! Those there are your high-end Zayrocks copiers, the big boys, the cream of the dream. Picked them up in Lewiston. Place was deserted. Had to load them myself!"

The rest of it looked like more of the usual: office desks, chairs, and filing cabinets, as well as big, open-topped cardboard boxes filled with unsold shoes from various stores. Jesse always picked around to see if there was anything in his size.

"And lookee here."

Leroy held up the multi-colored, multi-paged paperwork.

"You see any mention of Zayrocks?"

Jesse didn't. No Xeroxes either.

"What I'm thinking? I go back and see Limp Dick again, right?"

Leroy took out a glossy magazine that he had in his back jeans pocket that he unfurled so Jesse could see, then rolled it up again.

"Let him *peruse*," he said. "While you my fine boyo…."

Jesse looked down at his left bicep where Leroy's yellowed fingers and bitten-down dirty nails had him in a hard squeeze. From the smell on his breath he had conversed at lunch with Jack or one of his amber cousins.

"You unload them… get rid of all that other shit… and *re*-load," said Leroy, nodding at the Zayrocks machines. "I'll take care of the rest."

"What's in it for me?" Jesse had the sense to say.

"That's my boyo!" Leroy said.

Using the forklift, Jesse picked up and took out of the truck anything on a palette, like the copiers, but there were odds and ends jammed into the spots in between—desk lamps, file cabinets, and at least two dozen of those metal things they use in shoe stores to measure your feet—so he had to get off and yank that shit out by hand.

He thought about what Leroy wanted. He figured what the hell, he could use some extra cash. Dick must have done plenty of perusing because Jesse had plenty of time to unload and… *re*-load.

*****

The Coronet Motel was part of a strip of motels, catering in the summer to budget-focused families wanting to go to the nearby beach, along with an all-year round clientele mix of couples, loners, kids with a case of beer, and truck drivers who could easily park their rigs in the motel's oversize lot. Leroy said he stayed there if he bunked in the area—even though it was filled with "fools and fuckers"— and it was where he wanted to meet.

Jesse had a take-out chicken finger and fries dinner with his parents, and drove over from the house, about a half hour away. The motel building was a faded yellow, with red doors and window trim. It had about two dozen rooms. The parking lot was mostly empty when Jesse arrived and he pulled into a spot in front, and walked into the motel office. Nobody was at the desk, but off to the right was a small bar.

A dark-haired muscular guy in a white T-shirt was behind the counter of the short four-stool set-up, talking to a woman sitting there. They both looked at Jesse as he came in.

"Bar's just for motel guests," the big-shouldered barman said. "You need a room?"

He looked familiar, but Jesse couldn't place him. The woman sitting at the bar had a tight white top too. She wore a lot of make-up, and might not have been as old as Jesse had thought.

"I'm meeting someone here… Leroy," Jesse said, realizing he didn't know his last name.

"Leroy!" the woman said. "What do you want with that old goat?"

Jesse took that as invitation enough and walked past her to the stool at the other end of the bar. The motel guy brought him a bottle of beer and Jesse took a big swallow. As Jesse lifted the bottle again someone came up from behind and roughly pulled his left arm back. Beer frothed out and went on the front of his shirt.

"The fuck…!"

Leroy let him go, slapped him on the back.

"Hey Hot Shot! You hittin' on my girl Marie here while I'm taking care of urgent business?"

"I ain't your *girl!*" the woman called. "I ain't *your* anything."

Jesse was pissed about his shirt. It was only beer, but it would stink. And his mother when she did his wash would want to come and talk to him about it. She was on him about drinking too much. Although not as bad as Melissa, who'd kicked him out for wrecking her car. Among other things.

"How'd it go?" he said to Leroy, wanting to get his money and get out of there.

"Go? You just got here! How 'bout another drink? Now that you've gone and spilled that one."

Jesse had been hoping for $500 as his share on the copiers. Those things had to be worth thousands. He knew he should have gotten clear on his cut.

"Calvin, give Mister Jesse here another one on me."

Leroy went down to stand next to Marie's stool. He began to joke about boner pills, made a show of taking out a small metal container that Jesse had seen him with before. At the Hawthorne building he'd seen Leroy take white ones and red ones, probably some sort of speed like he'd heard all truckers took. Or maybe a heart med. But what kind of loser talked about needing a boner pill with the girl he needed it for?

Whatever it was, Leroy popped one. Calvin lingered for a moment after bringing Jesse another beer.

"I know you from somewhere," he said, then walked away, went past where Leroy and the girl had started playing grab-ass, and into the motel office.

Jesse drank, and fell into his habit of stepping back when he was around people, mentally gearing down to be less engaged, drift deeper into his own thoughts.

All he wanted to do was get what was coming to him. He needed to get Leroy aside, go to his room or out to his truck.

Marie stood up off her stool—stumbling probably on purpose—Leroy right there with some full-fingered support. She had on a short purple skirt and that tight white top. It was pretty clear where this was going when Calvin came back from the office and slid a key with its numbered green plastic fob along the bar to where Leroy scooped it up.

"Lucky Number 7!" he said. "Let's go honey."

The two of them left the bar. Jesse looked at the parking lot through the window but didn't see them. Lucky Number 7 must have been down the motel in the other direction.

"We went to school together," Jesse said to Calvin, who was clearing the bar where Marie and Jesse had been drinking. "Same one, Passaconk."

It was the nickname for Passaconkaway, a regional high school, a combination of kids from three small Massachusetts towns that didn't have enough population for one of their own. Calvin Nesbit had been a two years ahead of him, maybe three. Melissa, Jesse's girlfriend, ex-girlfriend now, had gone there too. She was a year behind Jesse. She and Calvin were from one of the other towns, although in Calvin's case Jesse couldn't remember which one.

Calvin looked him over. "You were on the football team, right?"

"Yeah," said Jesse, even though he really hadn't been. Not after being on the freshman team, when he was the second smallest kid, and got his ass kicked every day in practice, and he never played in a real game. Then he'd gone out for basketball, but got cut, and baseball, when for all he played might as well have been. After that he didn't bother.

"How you know Leroy?" Calvin asked.

"I work in a warehouse... do all the work, Leroy's just a driver that comes in."

"He owe you money?"

Jesse tried to poker-face it.

"Yeah... good luck with that," Calvin said. "Hey. Want to see something?"

Jesse had finished his beer, wanted nothing more than another. Calvin left the bar and went into the motel office.

Jesse recalled in high school Calvin drove a blue pick-up with a rusted snow plow attached on front all year long. One day at the end of school Jesse was standing outside the main building, waiting for his mother to pick him up and take him to a dentist or doctor appointment or something, when Calvin's truck came barreling up the ramp that led from the parking lot. When the truck stopped before turning onto the road, Jesse saw not one, but two girls were in the front seat with him.

Calvin had waited for Jesse by a folding ladder that he had pulled down from the office ceiling, which led up to the motel's attic. Calvin climbed quickly. When he reached the top, he waved for Jesse to follow.

Jesse went up and when the hot air that had built in the summer heat hit his face he sneezed. He had to hunch down under the low eaves of the roof. He sneezed again.

"Keep it down!"

Jesse's eyes adjusted. He started to sweat. Calvin moved into deeper darkness on the bridge of plywood boards laid down the center. Jesse took a couple of tentative steps after him.

He heard mingled sounds: someone talking, maybe shouting, some mechanical noise, sort of like a blender, and what sounded like a TV.

Off the plank pathway, Calvin squatted on the beam over what had to be one of the rooms. He lifted a piece of loose insulation like it was a flap. Jesse got it then. Calvin had a way of spying down into the room where Leroy and Marie had gone. Lucky Number Seven.

Jesse walked back and down the ladder and into the much cooler air of the motel office. Calvin followed him a couple of minutes later, coming down the rickety ladder like it was staircase. He had dirt or dust across the front of his white shirt.

"They're just sitting and talking," he said. "All they need is a deck of cards. Guess you knew not to expect too much of a show from old Leroy."

Calvin couldn't have really wanted to watch Leroy's boney ass juking up and down on top of some girl, could he?

"Nah... you know... give a man his space."

It was looking like all he was going to get from Leroy for looking the other way on the copiers were a couple of beers, one of which he was wearing. The front of his shirt was still damp and he caught a faint whiff of what had been bitter-tasting hops.

"Hey...Calvin."

It wasn't just to change the subject away from Leroy and whatever he might be doing. Jesse was trying to become a guy who didn't miss out on an opportunity.

"Would you like to buy some toilet paper?" Jesse asked. "You know, for the motel?"

*****

Whenever trucks came in with pallets of unused shoe leather—swaths of tan, brown and dark brown pieces secured in stacks with thick twine or sometimes bright orange bungee cords—Jesse brought it all into back of the building. Even after it been cured or whatever was done to them it smelled like shit. When he realized nobody in the skeleton office crew working in the building could stand the odor and never went back there, Jesse started to set aside things from the truck loads, hiding it all under a blue tarp behind the pallets of stinky leather. Tools, shop towels, office supplies, shoes. Toilet paper. It was starting to add up, and had to be worth something.

Soon after the night at the Coronet, Jesse started moving the stuff out of the Hawthorne warehouse. He snuck out a first Sentra trunk load, but driving off after work that day wondered where he was going to put it all. He drove around for a while, ending up in the parking lot of the townhouse condo complex where he and Melissa had lived together. Where she still lived.

Her father had been paying for the place, no doubt still did. She was a Daddy's Girl. And she'd had the nerve to mock *him*—after she told him she didn't want him there—when he admitted he was going back to live with his parents.

What he was thinking was that while he didn't have a girlfriend anymore, he still had a key to the unit's separate storage area, in a many-doored garage-like building at the backside of the development's property, and which he and Melissa had barely used. There was plenty of space, and he was thinking he could slip some stuff in there, temporarily, until he could coordinate something with Calvin.

Jesse didn't recognize the cars that were in the two assigned spots in front of the townhouse when he drove past. Melissa had a Subaru—or did before Jesse wrecked it. So which one was hers? Probably not the dark blue pick-up truck, which looked brand new.

He kept driving, looped around the development parking lot again and stared at the two strange vehicles, and not knowing what it meant, left.

Later, during the dinner of store-made meat loaf, canned string beans and frozen mac and cheese with his parents, his father brought up for the third time Jesse looking into the Burger King management trainee program, because he had some college, and shouldn't waste it.

Jesse didn't bother to point out again that six weeks of classes before failing midterms wasn't much college. His mother told him she had bought him some new boxer briefs because all his had holes in the seat, and reminded Jesse to check in his father's closet for more work clothes and shoes if he needed any.

After the two of them had done their TV watching and gone up to bed—where Jesse's mom would rub in the latest pain relief ointment the latest doctor had given his father to try for his bum arm—Jesse came out of his room and got some big green trash bags out of the kitchen closet. He emptied the Sentra's trunk and put the filled bags into the garden shed in the back yard. He was the only one who went into it; his father had stopped doing any yard work two years ago, since his accident, and now since Jesse had moved back it was his responsibility. In the next few days, he got everything out of the shoe building he'd put aside.

It was a good thing he did. Drivers stopped coming in to the Hawthorne warehouse with full loads. Now they arrived empty but always left with something. One time two trucks came and Jesse had to load them with all the pallets of leather that had created his hiding place.

Jesse and his boss Dick became the last ones working there, as the rest of the employees finally got laid off. Jesse salvaged a desk and a chair that had belonged to the last guy. If Dick wasn't around, maybe off interviewing for a new job, Jesse went into the far back and played ball against the wall. He'd drawn a rectangular strike zone in black magic marker, and practiced his fastball, knuckler, and curve. Dick had told him that there was still a facility in Maine that was being shut down, but not how long he'd have his job, and Jesse was afraid to ask.

Another thing Jesse's father kept saying to him was, "There's no future in a dead-ass job in a dead-ass industry." If he was in one of his pissy moods, feeling sorry for himself because of what happened to him on his own job, he'd take it out on Jesse and his mom. As for her, she'd stopped asking him about his drawings. Both of them had stopped asking about him and Melissa getting back together. They'd started asking him to chip in on the chicken finger dinners.

One day, after he came back to the Hawthorne warehouse from

lunch, someone was driving a tractor trailer at the far end of the otherwise empty parking lot. Jesse parked and got out of his car and watched. Whoever was backing up was doing a shit job of it, weaving in a slow S and jack-knifing the rig and having to start over.

The truck, now driving forward and faster, swerved suddenly in the parking lot, and barreled toward the building's entrance where Jesse stood watching. It didn't look like it was going to stop. He ran up the stairs to the landing but the door was locked. He rattled the knob and kicked the door as the tractor trailer skidded to a stop than ten yards away with a piercing metallic scream, grinding gears, and a shudder.

The driver stepped down out of the cab. It was his boss, Dick. He wore a yellow short-sleeve dress shirt and a brown tie with small black diamonds, the bottom half of it tucked into the shirt. Short and bald except for a ring of gray hair around the back and sides of his head, he wore wire-rimmed glasses, and walked with his chest pushed out one way and his ass the other. He was more or less the same age as Jesse's father, but at least foot shorter.

"Hey, that's not so hard!" he said as he came toward the building. "Piece of cake!"

The red door on the passenger side of the truck opened and Leroy climbed down.

"You should have seen you scramble, boyo! Good thing Dick was stamping that brake with both feet!"

"Can't wait to get her out on the road!" Dick said.

He came up the stairs and Jesse moved aside so he could unlock the door. From the bottom of the two step staircase, Leroy pretended to wipe sweat off his brow with the back of his hand.

They followed Dick into the large staging area for the dozen truck bays. The forklift Jesse used sat parked in the center of the space, where it had been idle for the last week.

"Just give me time to call my wife, tell her I'll be home late," said Dick.

"Or never!" called Leroy, as Dick walked off.

Leroy came up to Jesse, grabbed his bicep. He did that a lot, and Jesse decided this would be the last time, jerked his arm out of the other man's grasp.

"I thought you were going to throw me something from the copiers."

"Throw you something?"

Leroy stepped back and crouched down, pantomimed being a quarterback with a ball in his hands. "Go deep!" he called, pointing and laughing. He danced around avoiding an invisible, would-be tackler, his cowboy boots clicking on the concrete.

Jesse went to the back to the desk and chair he'd salvaged, in the middle of a big empty space the size of an airplane hangar. He pulled out the top desk drawer and took out his ball, began bouncing it on the concrete floor. As Leroy came up, Jesse thought about whipping it at the other man's head.

"You know that safe back there?"

It sat alongside Dick's desk in the other giant room of the warehouse, next to a tan, four-drawer filing cabinet. It had been surrounded by boxes and covered by piles of papers and Jesse hadn't even known it was there until the other employees left and Jesse had to take down the cubicles and clean everything out of that area except for Dick's stuff. Like everything, he put it all on a truck to go somewhere else.

He hadn't thought much about what the safe might hold. Papers important to someone not him, probably. No way cash. Dick didn't need cash for anything, did he?

"What about it?" Jesse said.

"Little Dick's got a hankerin' to be out there ballin' the jack. Wants more lessons. And I want something more than a promised pint. Our boy Calvin's headed over. You help him get that thing out of here before we get back."

"You're joking, right?"

Leroy rubbed his finger along the right side of his nose. His pupils were like pinpricks and Jesse wondered what color pills he'd taken today.

"Now why would I do that?"

"There's no way Dick won't know—"

"Don't worry about Dick."

"He'll know I was involved."

"Oh, we've got a plan for that," said Leroy, reaching into the back pocket of his jeans.

He separated a bill from the folded stack he pulled out, and waved it at Jesse. Jesse thought he saw a ten but it was a less familiar hundred.

He took it from Leroy, just before Dick returned from his desk.

"Jesse… get a broom and give a good sweep around everywhere before you leave today, okay?"

It was about all Dick ever told him to do anymore. Jesse was probably going to be laid off any day now.

After Dick and Leroy left, Jesse half-assed around with the broom, and threw his ball against the wall, and sat down at his salvaged desk in the salvaged chair, and wondered if he should pull out the sketchpad and colored pencils he'd brought in and put in the top drawer. It was an old sketchpad and his drawings back then were all superhero stuff, characters in cowls and capes saving big-boobed damsels in distress. But he'd started to draw some new types of footwear for a couple of them, something beyond the simple boot. Shit with wings, jets, and flames.

After twenty minutes, he heard something.

"Hey!" Somebody called again from out near the loading bays.

Calvin came into the back room. When Jesse had asked him at the motel that night if he wanted some supplies, Calvin had seemed interested, and said he would be in touch. That had been over a month ago. He was dressed the same as he been that night, with a white tee shirt tight across his broad chest and upper arms, but his dark hair was cut shorter. It made his neck look even thicker.

"Where is it?"

Jesse had decided that Leroy had been kidding about taking the safe, but now here was Calvin. He thought there was no way, excited about his driving lesson as he might be, that Dick wasn't going to see the safe was missing, no way he wouldn't know who had taken it. Or at least helped. Was it worth the hundred dollars? And maybe more? But like before, he'd hadn't gotten clear about his cut.

All he had was that new declaration he was trying on for size, about not missing opportunities any more, and becoming someone moving his life forward. Not being the loser that Melissa had grown to believe he was. *Told* him he was.

And then there was the thing that maybe Calvin would get pissed if he didn't help. He wasn't quite sure what would happen after that.

Jesse walked over to the forklift, hopped on, turned the key, lifted the forks a little off the floor and a little back, and pointed where he was going. After he got there, Jesse waited as Calvin came up and squatted down and spun the dial on the safe.

He looked up. Jesse thought he was going to ask for the combination, as if Jesse knew it.

"This where you keep the toilet paper?"

"No... but yeah still got that stashed. You want it?"

Calvin didn't respond, stood up and fixed the metal forks of the lift so that they were flush against each other. He directed Jesse toward the safe, then helped by lifting it slightly off the ground as Jesse maneuvered to slip the forks under it. Jesse raised the safe up to Calvin's waist level as the other man balanced it. In tandem, they moved slowly off.

Calvin had backed his truck up to one of the loading bays, but he decided he didn't want the safe dropped from the forklift from that height, so they maneuvered over and out the side door where a ramp led down into the parking lot.

The blue pickup looked familiar. At first, Jesse thought it was because it was similar to what Calvin had driven in high school, only without the snow plow. Or maybe because he'd seen it at the motel.

But that wasn't it.

Jesse was pretty sure this was the truck he'd seen parked in front of Melissa's condo. The condo that used to be Jesse's too. Or at least where he'd once lived, with a girlfriend.

As Jesse drove forward with the lift, Calvin kept the safe balanced on the forks with one hand, and lowered the back gate of the pickup with the other. Jesse moved closer and dropped the forks. Calvin yelled at him when the safe fell off, and onto the truck bed with a bang.

As Jesse backed away, he saw Leroy's tractor trailer come back into the parking lot.

"Fuck!"

"It's just Leroy," Calvin said. "Chill."

"It's not just...." Jesse hoped it would be, that Leroy had driven Dick home, dropped him off with a quick kiss on the cheek, ending it like a lame date.

The rig made a slow, wide loop and pulled up near where Jesse sat on the forklift and Calvin leaned against the side of his truck. Dick had done better than before. Maybe Leroy was a good teacher.

He looked over and saw that Calvin hadn't even bothered to cover the safe with anything, no tarp, not even a piece of old cardboard.

Dick jumped down from the cab, leaving the engine running. He thought Calvin was somebody from Hawthorne Shoe, bringing some final something from somewhere.

"Is that another safe? From what facility?"

As Dick approached the pickup, Calvin stepped forward. Dick had taken off the tie he'd been wearing earlier, and the top button of his yellow shirt was open. Calvin grabbed the collar of the shirt with two hands, and shoved Dick backwards. The much shorter man's hands dropped and then Calvin jerked Dick back toward him. He slammed his head into Dick's face.

Dick made a sound and went limp, Calvin still holding him by the shirt.

"What the fuck!" Leroy shouted. He'd come down off his truck. "You fuckin' guys should have been gone already!"

He looked at Jesse, frozen on the forklift.

"That your car?"

"What... yeah."

"Give me your keys."

"What?"

"Give me those fuckin' keys!"

Jesse leaned back so he could get into his pants pocket, and tossed them to Leroy. The Sentra was parked on the other side of the pickup and Leroy went and opened its trunk. Then he took hold of Dick's legs, helped Calvin load the still-unconscious man into Jesse's car. Before he closed the trunk, Leroy went and picked Dick's glasses off the ground and tossed them in.

Jesse sat on the forklift as Leroy and Calvin moved closer to Calvin's pickup and talked. Jesse focused on the blue truck, trying to confirm by some calculation that this was the one he'd seen parked at Melissa's.

But he was having trouble concentrating.

Leroy came over to hand him his keys.

"Hey boyo. Wild shit, yeah? Our boy Calvin? Woo! Funny thing is… he was supposed to knock *you* out."

"What?" Jesse said.

"Yeah… give you the old black eye alibi," Leroy said, mimicking a punch to his own eye. "Park behind the swimming pool."

"What swimming pool?"

Leroy slapped him on the thigh. "Good one!"

He went and climbed up into the cab of his rig. Before he finished readjusting the driver's seat and mirrors, Calvin drove off in his maybe-familiar blue truck. Leroy gave Jesse a salute, then backed up and turned, and with a clattering of gears headed for the exit. Leaving the parking lot, he turned left, instead of right like Calvin.

Jesse brought the forklift back into the building. He got off and went around and shut off all the lights. He'd forgotten Dick, until he reached the part of the space where his desk and file cabinet were, and the safe wasn't. He turned off Dick's desk lamp. Jesse couldn't lock the main door because he didn't have a key, but there wasn't anything left to steal. Except for his sketchpad. And nothing in there but the old superhero stuff, and a few new drawings, Jesse's take on some crazy shoes.

Jesse started the Sentra. A red light on the dashboard came on, blinked out. It had come on when he'd started the car that morning, but like this time, it had gone off before he figured out what it meant. He drove out from the back of the Hawthorne warehouse and toward the Coronet Motel.

*****

Even though it was still summer technically, the motel's swimming pool was closed. Where its cover sagged in the middle, a large dark puddle had formed, and it partially reflected the yellow motel behind it. White bird feathers and streaks of bird shit were around the puddle, along with an empty sports drink bottle and red driveway reflector. A partly-deflated beach ball bobbed on the water, drifting and dancing with the wind.

Before Jesse had left the Hawthorne parking lot, Dick came to with a moan. As he threatened, kicked at the back seat, and finally fell silent, Jesse tried to imagine Leroy sitting in the passenger seat, holding a gun. Training a gun on him, like they say. Leroy probably had some sort of gun, he definitely had a gun, maybe stuffed in the top of one of those red and black cowboy boots. Maybe he had a hollowed-out heel on one of the boots that slid aside to reveal another gun. Derringer, those tiny guns.

The good thing, Jesse thought as he drove toward the Coronet, was that Dick didn't know where he was, in whose car. He'd been unconscious when Calvin and Leroy crammed him into the trunk. But Jesse's was the only car that had been there. He shouldn't have been so startled when Dick started calling him by name.

"Jesse you don't have to do this… we can drive to the police, you can't do this."

Dick must have been shifting his body and banged his head or something.

"Jesse! Pull over and let me out of here! You're in big trouble don't make it worse!"

Jesse kept quiet. As long as he didn't speak, it was possible that Dick wouldn't be able to say for certain it was him behind the wheel. Jesse's car, yes, but being driven by some mysterious unseen-by-Dick accomplice to Calvin. Some wheelman.

"I didn't have to keep you on for the last factory and stores to come in… you know that!"

During the drive and his boss's outbursts, Jesse wondered if Dick had kids. He didn't know much about him. Somebody else at Hawthorne had hired Jesse, through the temp agency he had signed up with, part of a crew to move everything from the adjacent office building that the shoe company also owned and was giving up, over to the warehouse. It was only supposed to be a two-day job, but then Dick, the manager of the last group of employees and in charge of the final liquidation, asked Jesse to stay on. He said Jesse was the only one of the bunch he could trust to get stuff done.

He hadn't been a bad boss, except when he made Jesse try to clean those shoe machines with chopsticks. Or when hundreds of spools of thread came in that he had Jesse sort by size and color before boxing them all to be sent out. Or that big barrel filled with something—no way it had been "old water," like Dick said— that he told Jesse to take outside with the forklift and drain out in a ditch at the end of the parking lot. And all the floor sweeping now that the building was empty—what was the fucking point of fucking that?

They arrived at the Coronet at the opposite side of the property than Jesse had before, this time south from the Hawthorne building in New Hampshire instead of from home, and as he came around a curve he almost drove past the entrance. There was a dumpster at this end of the building, flanked by tall, overgrown bushes, some of which were already turning fall colors.

Jesse drove along the front of the motel and past the few cars parked at some of the rooms. That the pool wasn't open probably kept the tourists away. Among other things.

He saw Calvin's truck, but not Calvin. He'd parked his pickup near a grove of trees at the back of the parking lot, next to a boat that looked like it had been sailing the deflated tires of the trailer it sat on for years. He had yanked the big black tarp that was still partially covering the boat over to the bed of his pickup to finally hide the safe.

Dick had gone silent, run dry of his attempted persuasions and outright threats, trying to figure out where he was maybe, now that they'd stopped. But if he started yelling again, somebody might hear him. Jesse parked behind the pool, but past the boat, away from the motel.

It had gotten cooler, the weather changing, a new wind bringing mist off the nearby ocean. There were no tractor trailers in the parking lot, no Leroy yet. So much for the brains of the operation, Jesse thought. His eyes began to water as he got of the car —it was change of temperature, not allergies like Melissa insisted, his father had the same curse—as he considered what to do next.

He started for the truck, looking for Calvin, but then turned around and went back to the Sentra. At the rear fender he bent down and spoke to Dick for the first time.

"Listen… Leroy and this… other guy… are really bad people. I won't tell you what they're doing to make sure I cooperate. I'm not proud… I put myself in a compromising position… but here we are. You're going to have to trust me. I'm your only hope to—"

"Leroy wouldn't have anything to do with this," said Dick. But he didn't sound sure.

"He's got a gun. Maybe two. Hang in there, and keep quiet," said Jesse. "I'm going to get us out of this."

When Jesse was little his family had an orange cat, a young stray that showed up, and when they took it to the vet to be checked out, they put it in a cardboard carrier and the cat chewed a hole in it in about two minutes, then jumped out and sat beside Jesse in the back seat. That cat was fucking cool.

He couldn't see Dick finding his way out of the trunk. And Jesse didn't give a shit about him. He had to figure out a way to protect himself.

Calvin wasn't around the truck and boat, or behind the motel building, where Jesse checked a narrow strip bordered by a fence that was filled with paint cans, ladders, loose scaffolding, two toilets, and trash bags filled with who knows what. He went back into the parking lot. Passing by the motel rooms, he saw some guests had left their bikes parked outside their red door, a pair of expensive, rich kid, fat-tired toys. The two of them together were probably worth more than the Sentra.

A guy was putting a dollar bill into a drinks vending machine by the motel's front entrance. Jesse ducked his head and put up his hand in front of his face when the man at the machine glanced over at him.

"Don't sign in as Bob Smith," the guy said, "that one's taken."

In the office, no one was behind the front desk, but the ladder to the attic was pulled down. Jesse went over and looked up into the darkness. He heard some glass clinking together, off to his right.

A large young woman with purple-dyed streaks in her otherwise dark hair stood behind the bar. She wore baggy blue denim coveralls over a red T-shirt from some bar in Key West. She was pouring the contents of one liquor bottle into another.

"Help you?"

"Calvin? I'm supposed to meet him here."

"Hi Jesse Desmond," she said. "I thought that was you. I didn't know you and that crazy brother of mine were friends."

"Oh yeah," said Jesse, recognizing her.

There were something like ten kids in the Nesbit family. She was in his grade. Maybe they'd had a class or two together. Maybe they'd just passed each other in the hall. Now she had ink along both sides of her neck, cross-hatched diamonds framing her broad face. Calvin had told him that his family owned the motel. And this was… Beth, maybe?

"Is the bar open?" he asked.

"It's five o'clock somewhere," Maybe-Beth said. "It's five o'clock here! I do believe I'll join you for old time's sake."

She brought shot glasses up from below the bar and poured from the bottle she'd been re-filling. Jesse took one and downed what was in it before she'd finished lifting hers in a toast.

He had gone past the line of being overwhelmed. Now he had started taking on water like that no doubt full-of-leaks boat out in the lot. Next to the stolen safe. A little ways from his boss in the trunk of his car.

Where was fucking Leroy?

"Like old home week around here," said Maybe-Beth. "Calvin's new honey's been around… went to Passaconk too. Forget her name. She was younger than us. Still is, I guess."

Maybe-Beth re-filled Jesse's shot glass.

"She's here now?"

"Who knows what goes on around here? I just come in for my Dad now and then to make sure Calvin's not skimming any more than he should. If she is here, she's probably down in his room."

"His room?"

"Number seven."

Jesse downed the second shot. "Lucky number seven?"

"Lucky? That's a stretch... in case you didn't notice, this place is a shithole."

Jesse didn't know if it had been her brother's truck in front of Melissa's condo. Or if she was tangled up in shithole sheets with him in Lucky Number Seven.

Jesse hadn't had hard liquor in seven months. Since before Melissa kicked him out, when he was trying to change for her, stopped for her, a pointless sacrifice, too late. He'd missed drinking like he used to. It brought gaps to his days and nights sometimes, but before he fell into them, it always made his thinking sharper. For a little while, anyway.

"I've got some supplies... he said up there." Jesse pointed at the attic ladder. "Would be a good place to put them. Can I check it out first to see if it's going to work?"

"You don't want to be carrying things up and down on that thing. And I was just up there, it's—"

"Light stuff... toilet paper mostly," said Jesse, moving toward the office. He thought about giving her some money for the drinks but all he had was the hundred from Leroy.

And where the fuck *was* Leroy?

Jesse climbed the ladder. It wasn't as hot in the attic as it had been the previous time, so his sneezing wasn't triggered. He stood and let his eyes adjust. He knew which direction Calvin had gone to spy on Leroy, but not how far. He walked carefully on the pieces of plywood laid down to make a floor.

Like the last time he had been up there, he heard noises from rooms below. Definitely a TV in one, playing a late afternoon game show; he could hear the clanging of winner's bells. He looked back at the light coming up through the hatch for the ladder.

Then he heard a woman's voice, her laughter.

Was it Melissa? He hadn't heard her laugh like that in a long time. The one that came at the end of things between them punctuated her mocking of him, not from any shared joy, nothing like the laugh from the room below.

He veered off from the center planks and walked out and balanced on a beam. He listened again but didn't hear anything. He took a few steps more, ducking his head under the slope of the low roof, and slipped off the beam. His right foot went through dirty ripped insulation, making a hole or finding an existing one and his foot blew through rotten wood.

He couldn't get his foot free. He twisted around but that made it worse.

Somebody grabbed hold of him. Started to pull him further down. The wood cracked around the hole as he got pulled down further, almost to his knee. Jesse shouted, kicked back and forth and got out of the grip but then the hand was back on his ankle and if it was Calvin— that beast was going to yank the shit out of him, bring him crashing into some shithole room.

Jesse had on a pair of his father's work shoes, almost brand-new, barely worn, and they were big on him. The next tug pulled the shoe off his heel, and then it was gone.

If Melissa was down there, directing the whole thing, Calvin under her spell, she knew how ticklish Jesse was, how he could never stand that—

He kicked and broke free from the grip. He yanked his lower leg and foot up and back through the hole. Jesse fell over, banging his hip against the beam he'd been standing on. He crawled out to the plank pathway, got upright and went for the escape hatch.

"What's going on up there!" Maybe-Beth shouted.

"Rats!" yelled Jesse, coming down the ladder front ways, like it was stairs. "Fucking rats!"

He hurried past her, out the motel office door, past the vending machine, into the parking lot. He stepped on a rock with his socked foot and with a shout started a hop, skip, and a hop.

Calvin, shirtless, came out of Lucky Number Seven. Jesse broke into a wide arc around him.

He had to get out of there. He didn't know how he ended up in such a shit-show.

Skip-hopping to his car, Jesse without looking knew Calvin was coming. He got in. When he turned the ignition key the red engine light that had come on each time he had started the car that day flashed and this time didn't go off.

The engine began sputtering. Smoke came rushing into the inside of the car. Jesse started to cough. He couldn't find the door handle. He slammed against the side, lifted the lever, and got it open. He fell out, scrambled up, stared.

Flames flickered up over the hood.

Calvin sprinted past. He grabbed the heavy black tarp covering his truck and the boat and began dragging it toward the Sentra with both hands up over his head and the tarp looked like a cape flowing behind him.

Jesse ran to the front office, thinking he had to call the fire department, the cops. But when he saw the two mountain bikes left out in front of somebody's room, he took the blue one. Maybe-Beth came out of the office and watched him go.

He pedaled away, trying to figure out the shifting of gears, trying to protect his sensitive sole. Picking up speed, he went in the direction of the beach, and the cool sea-spun air he rode into made him sneeze.

*****

After riding as fast as he could through the strip of cheap motels, soft-serve ice cream stands and seafood shacks, Jesse turned off before he reached the center of the beach community, kept to the back roads, and after it got dark, hid out throughout the night in various places. He ended up at an intersection in the shit-ass town that he'd never been able to escape. For many years, there'd been a misspelling of one of the neighboring towns on the directional sign planted there, that no one had bothered to fix. It was still wrong.

He'd stopped at a liquor store earlier. His town was dry. The misspelled town where Melissa had grown up is where everyone went. That's where he used the hundred from Leroy on a pint of Canadian Club, a small travel pack of tissues, and then the rest on scratch lottery tickets.

He walked the bike into the woods, bushwhacked to get away from the road, and found a place to hide under a large pine tree. He cracked the pint and began to drink whiskey. As he got drunker, he remembered he needed a black eye alibi. He took a couple of slow-motion practice runs, but kept missing his face.

The occasional late night traveler pulled up to the intersection. Most people stopped, but the later it got, some drivers didn't bother, just blew through the stop signs. More than one fool who did stop put their indicator on when they turned, even though there was nobody else around.

At one point he nodded off. He startled awake on the soft pine-needled ground as something scurried through the brush nearby.

Jesse abandoned the bike and started walking to his house. He took off his remaining shoe and threw it into the woods. He took off his socks and put them in his pockets and walked barefoot down the center of the road, as the trees on either side of him became more distinct with the approaching dawn. A dog in one house barked as he passed by, and the dog in the next house started in. He was still drunk enough to start a howl of his own. Otherwise it was quiet, except for the start-up songs of the morning birds.

When he reached his house, he went out back near the patio and turned on the garden hose, and after letting it run a bit, drank from its stream. Yellow light lifted off the horizon, visible through the trees. Jesse went across the yard to the shed.

He realized he didn't have his key, because it was with the one to the car.

But the door was unlocked and he closed it behind him. All the trash bags filled with what he'd taken from the Hawthorne warehouse were piled in the back corner. As soon as he saw the bags he began thinking about Dick. Depending on what happened, it might take them a while to identify the car. Although even if it had blown up, or burned completely, someone would be sharp enough to figure make and model. Then they'd have to check records. Hopefully not dental ones.

The shed was dark and it took him three tries to find the bag he was looking for, the first two he opened stuffed with toilet paper. Jesse reached around in the bag where he'd put a half dozen or so pairs of shoes and found some loafers. He put his socks back on, then the shoes. The right one was okay, the left one a little tight.

He sat in the shed, listened for sirens. All he heard was that the birds had stopped singing.

When Jesse came in the back door into the kitchen, the vent fan was going and the window over the sink was open for the morning sun and the breeze, but the smell of breakfast was still thick. His father got up early, as if he was still working. He'd shower and shave and come downstairs and sit at the kitchen table at 7 am and wait for his wife to bring him his first meal of the day. And he'd be there at 12 noon and 6 pm too.

His father looked him over from where he was sitting at the table as Jesse leaned against the kitchen counter. Jesse's mother was finishing up cutting sausage links into small, precise pieces.

"Hi, Jesse… were you outside watering?" she asked.

She must have heard him running the hose. His parents had seen him drunk before of course, but not in a while. And he was fine standing and didn't think he'd be puking on the kitchen floor this time. But his clothes for some reason looked like he had spent the night curled in a ball under a tree.

"That's not where he's been," his father said.

He pointed at Jesse's shoes, raising his good arm, the left.

"What's that all about?"

In the dark, Jesse had put on a mismatched pair. Both the same type of loafer, but one black, and one brown. No, make that one brown and one blue. No wonder Hawthorne Shoe went out of business. He'd only taken a pair of them because they were so stupid. What breed of clown wore blue shoes?

"Do you want breakfast?" his mother asked him. "The griddle's still hot."

The meat smelled good. His father with his food and his coffee and his newspaper and his vitamins and other pills took up the table in the breakfast nook, so Jesse sat on one of the stools at the center island. His mother rubbed his back as she passed behind him.

"Oh, it's all wet! You want to go shower and change?"

"I'm good," Jesse said. "Any of those chicken fingers left from the other night?"

"Chicken fingers? For breakfast? No, your father ate them."

Jesse's father made one of his sounds and went back to his newspaper. He moved it aside as his wife brought him his plate of eggs, sausage and toast. She went back to where she had an electric griddle that she'd had since Jesse was little. He liked his eggs scrambled.

"Hey Dad, remember when I used to play ball against the wall all the time, you got that piece of plywood and I drew in a batter and a strike zone, whatever happened to that? It's not in the—"

"I remember when you broke the living room window with one of your wild pitches," his father said, spreading jam, "and a few other stupid things like that I could mention."

Jesse remembered the window, although probably not all the stupid things he had done. Just the most recent. He wondered if they let you play ball against the wall in prison.

He looked at his father. Even in summer, he wore long sleeve shirts.

"More stupid than some guy so stupid he stuck his arm into a paper box machine?"

He'd never talked to his father like this before. Even when he'd been drunk, which right now he was and he wasn't.

"And got less of an insurance settlement because it was his own stupid fault?"

"Jesse!" his mother said.

His father poked his fork at the pieces of sausage she had cut up for him. He shook his head, then ate his breakfast, steadily, ignoring the paper, until he was done. He and Jesse's mother exchanged a look as he stood up.

When he had left the room, Jesse went over and sat down on the other side of the table in the nook from where his father had been. He felt like he might puke, empty stomach or not.

"Maybe just some toast and coffee, Mom," he said.

Jesse wondered whether he should say anything about the Sentra, since it was technically still in her name.

He figured she'd find out soon enough.

She brought him a mug, then cleared her husband's place setting. The steam off the hot coffee hit Jesse's face. His eyes watered, and he sniffed and rubbed his nose. He remembered the pack of tissues he'd bought at the liquor store. He found the scratch tickets in his pocket instead.

His mother came back with toast.

"Here," he said, holding up one of the lottery tickets.

She went to the cupboard where she kept her spare change jar, and fussed over which coin might be a lucky one. She sat down across the table from him and went to work. She took her time, being neat about it. Or stretching out the experience.

"What's this, Jesse... five dollars? I won five dollars!"

She slid it over to him. She'd stopped before she should have, so he took the quarter she'd been using and scraped off what she'd missed.

He discovered a different sort of disappointment than what he usually got from the stupid things. He slid the ticket back to her.

"What am I looking at?" his mother said.

"You didn't win five dollars," said Jesse. "It's five thousand."

It would buy a lot of chicken fingers. He sat in warm morning sunshine and buttered his toast.

Like a Brother
Mark James McDonough
1

The first person I saw when my Uber pulled up to Dolan's Funeral Home was Brendan Banks, Michael's best friend and partner in misdemeanors, an expert in telling it like it isn't. When it came to the local women, he had burnt those bridges and snorted the ashes. In another lifetime he'd be a reality star, just the right mix of awful and attractive to earn his own show. But that's not what happened, and so he tormented cops and bartenders alike and never ran out of money since there was always another purse to take it from. I hoped he wouldn't notice me. No such luck.

"Samantha, I'm so sorry. How are you? Let me know if you need anything. Anything at all. You still working at the book website? Here, do you want a butt? Oh, you don't smoke do you?"

There was a trick to responding to him. All you had to do is respond to one question and he'd forget the other three.

"No, I don't smoke. Thanks," I said.

"What's the matter?"

"Life and death."

I brushed past him because I knew he wasn't done talking. A sticky pen hung off the side of the visitor's book by a rope. I grabbed the disgusting thing and wrote my name in big, print letters. At least that way people would know that Michael's sister had stopped by. Our parents had died twenty years before and so that meant I was the only family he had left. When I joined the line full of half-remembered scratching post faces, I kept my head down hoping no one would recognize me. It wasn't until I was about to shake hands with the people beside the casket that I realized how bizarre it was that I wasn't one of

them.

Nothing excites people in that town more than a wake. Funerals are too early to draw much of a crowd. People like to wander into the building around four o'clock carrying iced coffees and energy drinks, wearing their red dress shirts, cheap sunglasses, and Jordans. Picture a sophomore semi-formal except everyone's an adult with unpaid bills and neglected children. Who were these people? They weren't family or loved ones or even comrades. I couldn't wait to get away from them.

An old babysitter, Mrs. Stinky, created a LinkedIn account just to let me know about the services. Mrs. Stinky, *Harbinger*, April 2023-Present. That wasn't her real name but that's what Michael and I had always called her. I'd have ignored her message and never went back except for the fact that I'd let the news slip during a quiet moment in the office. It's possible I started the journey so that my coworkers wouldn't think I was a monster.

"Wait, Sam...who died?"

"I didn't even realize you had a brother. I'm so sorry."

"Let us know if you need anything."

There was nothing they could have done to help. I just wish I had never told them in the first place. This detachment might seem cold and heartless, even cruel, but I had my reasons. Hopefully this next part will make you feel a little bit more comfortable. I cried when I knelt in front of his closed casket. Does that make you happy? I mean, I really let loose. My brother burned in a fire and his charred body was too gruesome to put on display and so I said goodbye to the last member of my family through a wooden box. I wanted to scream and tell everyone who I was, but after shaking the tears off of my cheeks I got up and left without further commotion. Unfortunately, another one of my brother's idiot friends followed me out. Dicky Shelley, The Baby Man, an imbecile that looked old and young at the same time, like an evil scientist had used a growth ray on an infant.

"Hey, Sam. I thought that was you. You good?"

"Yeah, I'll be fine. Listen, I gotta go, okay?"

"Okay, yeah. Hey, probably not the right time but I sent you a few

271

messages on Facebook. Just thought maybe we could get some coffee or something while you're home," said Dicky.

"I deleted my account, Dicky. I'm home for my brother's funeral not to take you on a date. Get a grip," I said.

I didn't feel bad for shutting him down so thoroughly, but still I couldn't stop thinking about the conversation on the way back to my AirBNB. I called a work friend from the "book website" (multinational technology and artificial intelligence company) to tell her about what had just happened. As I was explaining everything, she mentioned that I may have just temporarily deactivated my Facebook account instead of permanently deleting it. I opened my laptop back at the apartment to check and it turned out she was right. The messages from Dicky were there as expected, but it was something else that caught my eye and nearly hooked it out.

In the front and center of my feed there was a GoFundMe page to "support the family of Michael McQuillan". It had raised 50k of its 50k goal. The organizer was none other than Brendan Banks. I called back my coworker to rage-vent to her. She asked if I needed the money because she knew that I didn't. It wasn't about the money; it was about the principle. I wasn't going to let some rodent use my last name to get cash for drugs or whatever else he was after.

The problem was, Brendan Banks didn't bother showing up to the funeral the next day and not just because it was at 8AM. That shithead was on the lam and I was going to do whatever it took to find him, for better or worse (but probably worse).

2

I started my investigation after the funeral with the only person that I knew would answer my calls: The Baby Man, Dicky Shelley. We met at a pub called Shannon's. I didn't know who Shannon was but I wondered if they knew the bartender let a cat eat, shit, and sleep on the counter top. It was hard to keep Dicky on track; he kept talking about some job he got watching a vacant lot. I asked if he meant parking lot, and he didn't. His only responsibility was to watch an empty space. It was the perfect role for him really, and he was delighted to be so gainfully employed. If ignorance is bliss then he must have been the happiest son-of-a-bitch on earth.

"You know what they say, am I working hard or hardly..."

"Intelligible," I said.

"What?"

"Dicky, not sorry to interrupt. Do you know where Brendan is or not?"

"Oh yeah I gotta take a piss so I'll giv'm a call." He said it as if the only appropriate time to use the phone was when you were urinating. When he came back he told me that Brendan would meet the both of us at Dicky's apartment. I hadn't prepared for whatever it was I was going to do Brendan. Oh, well. I just had to suck it up and confront him. What was he going to do? Kill me?

Dicky's apartment looked like it was interior designed by a fourteen year old. Every picture on his wall was either a lion, a crown, a marijuana leaf or a lion wearing a crown smoking marijuana. Actually, I lied. Inexplicably, there was also a framed photo of Jesus Christ on his TV stand next to some remnants of blunt wraps, a bottle of lotion, and a pocket knife. If those walls could talk they'd have begged for mercy. Dicky turned on a TV that was perpetually set to play the same *Transformers* movie for eternity. Anyway, Brendan wasn't there and after a half hour I knew he was never coming.

"Dicky, you did all this so I'd come back to your apartment," I said. He was gripping a gallon of milk and there was some Kahlua on the table along with a couple of coffee mugs.

"Well, I don't know. Would it impress you if I did?"

"Impress me? There's gotta be something wrong with you. No offense. But, come on. I'm getting out of here," I said.

"Hold on a minute. I'm serious. Do you know one thing all my former girlfriends lacked?"

"A keen sense of smell?"

"No. Class! I want a girl like you." He stepped in front of the exit. I told him to fuck off but he wasn't having it.

"What if I take it out and you just look at it?"

"I'd rather stare directly into the sun," I said.

"I'm going to take it out," said Dicky.

"You better not…"

He took his hand off the milk and started fumbling with his belt. I calmly stood up and stepped towards him. I bent down, sliding my hand across the table. A smirk started to spread across his inchworm lips and then I slammed the gallon of milk off of his enormous head. I know what you're asking: Why didn't you grab the bottle of Kahlua? I thought the milk would be funnier. Anyway, he deflated like a lawn decoration after Halloween. I grabbed the knife and held it pointing down at him. "Jesus Christ, lady. Relax," he said. I brought the knife closer to his cock and told him I'd cut it if he didn't spill. He told me Brendan was either down south or in Aruba. I asked which.

"You think Brendan got a passport? He's probably at his aunt's in Florida. Don't bother asking where she lives 'cause I don't know."

I kept the knife and jetted out of the apartment. For the first two blocks I thought I was going to puke my skeleton out but an awful sweat came on instead and expelled something from my soul. By the third block I smelt like shit and felt amazing. If Brendan was actually at his aunt's house, he wouldn't be that hard to find. I checked his social media for any pictures with geotags from The Sunshine State and for an overtanned aunt on his friends list but came up with nothing. The odds that an older lady in Florida didn't have a Facebook were astronomical. I'd have to do the detective work the old fashioned way. Brendan had some type of half-sister, Nikki, that hung around the neighborhood. I figured she'd know the address. I was right about her knowing where he was. I was wrong for having gone to see her.

3

Nikki worked at a café and raked in tips with that beach ball ass of hers. Listen, I don't like objectifying women, but my tongue rolled out of my mouth like a cartoon wolf when I saw it. It wasn't just her caboose that was sturdy either, she was built like a mini-fridge and her cluttered tattoos were the stickers all over it.

"We ain't got one of those computer menus. You're going to have to use your words to order, hunny," said Nikki.

"Yes, I'm sorry. Can I just have a coffee to start?"

"Sure, but we may not have as many options as you're used to. We've got black or regular."

"I'm from around here actually. I'm Sam McQuillan, my brother…"

"Oh my God, sweetheart. I'm so sorry. Here, the coffee is on me. I was just kidding about the options. We even got the almond milk now, can you believe it? How do you usually take it?"

"From behind," I said.

"Oh! I like you!"

She patted my shoulder as I told her black. I had never had black coffee in my life but it felt like the right thing to say. She seemed overly interested in me and I couldn't tell if it was genuine curiosity or if she was sussing out how much I cared about her brother's scam.

"You married? You got a boyfriend?"

"Old maid."

"Don't say that! You're still young! There's plenty of fish in the sea," said Nikki.

"Yeah but I always seem to reel in an old boot," I said.

I wasn't interested in sharing more than I had to so I tried to pivot the conversation to warmer weather, then to Florida but she wasn't biting.

"You ever been?"

"Florida? Yeah, sure. You thinking of going down?"

"I am, but somewhere other than Orlando. My life is enough of a roller coaster. You got any recommendations?"

"You know I actually have an… nevermind."

"You actually have an…?"

"Sorry I'm so scatterbrained today I don't even know where I was going with that. Will you excuse me? I've gotta go check on something," said Nikki.

Dead end or maybe worse. She tucked her cell phone into her back pocket and as I was watching her reindeer ass sway back and forth to the kitchen, a bright idea hit me. I looked around and then casually pushed my salt shaker almost to the edge of the table. When she walked back by she knocked it off and shattered it. They say good things come to those who wait, maybe that's why I only found the bad. I reached over and grabbed her phone from her jeans. As she took the debris to the trash can I tried her home screen. Sweat started leaking from my brows again, more pungent than gasoline and possibly just as flammable. No pass code so I went straight to FindMyIphone and scrolled through the list of names. It was like a GPS for every ne'er do well in the state... and for one outside of it. Brendan Banks — Black Creek, North Carolina near a general store called *Ninja Spider Monkey*. I wouldn't forget a town or a store with names like those. I turned to put the phone on the ground next to where she had been kneeling but then...

"I've got that same cover! Wait I'll show ya..." She reached for the phone that wasn't there. "Wait a minute I..."

"Yeah, sorry. You dropped it when you were cleaning up," I said.

"But I just saw you scrolling through it," said Nikki.

"I was just checking the time really. Turns out I've got to go." I put a twenty on the table. "You can keep the change thanks for everything." When I stood up she moved so her nose was almost touching mine.

"Don't touch my fucking phone! I don't care who you are! If I wasn't on probation I'd slap the shit out of you," said Nikki.

I started walking away as fast as I could but she wasn't done yelling. She followed me out onto the street and shouted into the pizza shop next store. Her girlfriend was the delivery driver. A match made in purgatory. I tried to ignore everything and put some distance between us but I knew it wasn't good enough when I heard her gleefully chanting "She's not on probation! She's not on probation!" I looked over my shoulder and saw a lady scampering full speed at me like an alligator. My instinct was to run in a zig-zag formation but it didn't seem to be working so I stopped on a dime and tripped her. She skipped across the sidewalk like a stone finally coming to a stop when she hit a mailbox. I took off again and ran until I could hail a taxi. The cabbie asked why I was laughing so hard but all I could manage to say was what I had thought when she hit that mailbox. "Special delivery."

"Huh? Where to Miss?"

"*Cherchez l'homme.*"

"That French? Lady, I barely speak English," said the driver.

When I got back to my room I stuffed everything in my suitcase and looked for flights to North Carolina. There were none. In a bittersweet twist of fate a hurricane had swooped in and made air travel an impossibility. But, if things were as bad as they said they were, Brendan might have to hole up for the night. I decided to rent a car and see if I could catch up to him. It would be like trying to find a syringe in a haystack. No matter where he went he always stuck out. I just had to hope I wouldn't get pricked.

<h1 style="text-align:center">4</h1>

The crusty rental car smelled like ass but I didn't have time to haggle. I even paid for the insurance to save time arguing against it. With no real plan, I chugged another black coffee and hit the highway. The only thing I had to eat was a frozen-to-the-touch "gobbler" sandwich from the gas station. That wasn't exactly what I meant when I said I was going cold turkey. If the storm didn't fuck me up too much I'd be there in about twelve hours, but with no one to distract me, I was stuck inside my head for what seemed like a lot longer. My memory lane is full of roadside IEDs, yet I couldn't help but ramble down it. I could see Michael when he was seven years old opening a PS2 on Christmas. I could see him younger still, half asleep and sitting up on my father's shoulders on the way home from the St. Patrick's Day parade. I even remembered when they brought him home from the hospital and put him in my arms. *You're a big sister now. You have to look out for him.* I cried even harder than I did when I was in front of the casket. The horn of an eighteen wheeler snapped me out of it and turned my sadness to rage. I saw my eyes in the rear mirror, whirlpools of blood. I wouldn't let anyone take advantage of my name. Of our name.

Aside from stopping to use the bathroom at something called a Bojangles, I made the drive straight and ended up outside the Ninja Spider Monkey "general store" at just after midnight. I put quotes on that because as far as I could tell it was just a house but whatever it was, it was closed. I did a search for hotels in the area and drove fifteen minutes to a Days Inn. Yes, it was possible that Brendan was sleeping in his car somewhere or had risked driving through the rain as I had, but I knew he wouldn't be able to resist spending some of that 50K. My guess was that he got plastered with the locals and shacked up somewhere close. After checking for Massachusetts license plates in the parking lot and finding none, I ventured over to the Country Inn. As I pulled into the rain slicked parking lot, a car almost drove into my front bumper. Through thick, mucus rain, I could see Brendan scrolling through his phone from the light of his screen. He beeped, gave me the finger, and then sped past me finally revealing to me that there was a woman in his passenger seat. I caught sight of her long blonde hair flying upwards as the shitbox screeched out onto the main road. I counted to ten and then pursued, sure he hadn't seen my face but realizing it didn't matter either way.

We were the only two cars on the drenched backroads, one sewer rat chasing after the other. He would have realized he had a tail even if he was only half-paying attention. When he sped up I sped up and when he turned I turned and when his car finally came to a halt on the shoulder of the road and I swerved wildly in behind him. He took his time getting out, deliberating how far he was willing to go, and I only hoped that if he went far, he went all the way. I couldn't stand to be injured, I thought, *he better kill me.* When he opened his door, I mirrored him, and stood out in the storm. He raised his gun to fire and I know he would have if I hadn't involuntarily screamed his name. Brendan couldn't see me through the glare of the lights but he knew my voice like he had known Michael's. I didn't know much about guns back then but I could see it was big, a true extension of his hand, like a form of degenerate cybernetics. The blonde woman must have climbed over the clutch and exited through the driver's door because I saw her arms grab him and drag him back into the car before he could fire. I ran towards them and grasped at the door handle but couldn't find traction on the wet metal and slipped as they pulled away once more.

I picked the rubble from my hands and ran back to my car, trying to make up as much ground as I could. When I brought the machine through the flood I laughed as it half floated to a trident in the road. Right, left, or center, any choice would be wrong, but that's okay, all of my choices were. I chose left, the most evil option, drove until I found no one and then pulled over at an abandoned gas station. I never had a detailed plan exactly, but this was never part of my loose outline. There was nothing I could do and I likely would have given up altogether if not for Brendan calling me.

"I think we need to talk," he said. "How about tomorrow? Let cooler heads prevail," said Brendan.

"Where?"

"Jacksonville. 4'oclock. The Justice Pub," said Brendan.

"Poetic," I said.

"Huh?

"I'll be there."

5

It's every girl's dream to take a rental car powernap in the corner of the Myrtle Beach Piggly Wiggly parking lot. I got three hours of sleep and then finished the drive to Florida. There was still a lot of time to kill and I didn't feel like sightseeing so I checked into a room at the Hyatt Regency. With access to a comfortable bed, I of course couldn't get back to sleep. TV was no help, the news was even more depressing than my life. The first result in a Google of "things to do in Jacksonville" showed a recommendation for Kingsley Plantation and their '25 tabby slave cabins" and I closed the browser immediately and never searched again.

When it was approaching 3:30, I journeyed to The Justice Pub, embarrassed to be waiting outside of its doors before it opened. They must have assumed I was a genuine booze bag, a professional drinker. I did need something to even-out, so when it opened, I ordered a dirty martini stat. I was mellow by the time Brendan showed up. He sat down as if it was any of his other nights out at the bar and ordered the same as me and we watched the replay of a baseball game on the overhead screen.

"I know Mikey was your brother but he was my only real friend in the world. You might think I'm a monster, but this hasn't been easy for me either," said Brendan.

"You stole 50k from my family," I said.

"Do you need it?"

"That's not the point," I said.

"Maybe it is," he said, turning to look me in the eyes for the first time. I admit it had more of an effect on me than I had expected. The act might traditionally be one of truthfulness and respect but Brendan was inverting the whole process. His lapis irises looked like they had been under the heel of someone's boot, beautiful and crushed just like the rest of him, and he used them to get what he wanted. "I'm sorry about what happened, but you have a life," he continued. "I only had him and he only had me. You can argue all you want but believe me when I say Michael and I shared the same blood."

"Where were you when he died?"

"High at some girl's house. Ask the cops, they checked. I would do anything to change what happened but I can't," said Brendan.

"So, you'd just like me to forget this whole thing?"

"I don't want you to forget Mike. Just the other stuff. What do you think he would want in this situation?"

"He'd probably want you to keep the money, but that doesn't mean it's the right thing to do. Every decision that kid ever made was wrong," I said.

"Say, do you want to get out of here? I don't feel like being at a bar right now you know what I mean?"

"Is that the line you use on all the girls?"

"No, I usually ask them if they want to go do coke and then convince them to pay for it."

"And that blonde you were with? Just another person to buy you blow?"

"Don't worry about her. She doesn't even exist," said Brendan.

I told myself I'd find a way to punish him on the way back to my hotel room but realistically the only options were killing him or calling the police and I didn't want to do either. Forget the calm after the storm, it was dangerously hot when we sat in the backseat of the cab and hunting your dead brother's friend across the eastern seaboard can be exhausting. The buckle burnt my hand as I fastened it. Brendan left his undone and kept turning to look out the back window. I couldn't think of anything worth saying and he only said worthless things. He mainly aired his grievances about Florida prohibiting gambling apps. I could see a high-def image in my head of him driving to NOLA and back just to get his bets in. How quickly could you spend 50 thousand dollars that way? I'm not sure, but I know he'd break the world record.

When we reached the hotel, I led him into my room, still unsure of what I would do. He grabbed some drinks out of the minibar, something I'd never seen someone do in real life. I knocked the piccolo back like a seal swallowing a herring. Dicky's knife lay under my pillow where I left it and I slid my hand to grab it when Brendan was finishing his. The time had come to either get violent or to sleep with him. Before I had to decide, there was a loud knock on the door. Brendan said he'd get it and he made sure to put the chain lock on before opening it. The lock proved futile, as whoever it was had forced him to remove it slowly.

The blonde woman stepped into the room and before she even removed her wig and glasses it became horrifyingly apparent to me that it wasn't a woman at all. Even with the shenanigans, I could positively ID my own brother. The dirty martini and the mini-champagne shot up from my empty stomach and went all over the rug. I looked up and saw the same gun Brendan had been brandishing the night before, this time with a silencer attached.

"Samantha, it's me," said Michael.

"Obviously, you idiot," I said.

"Aren't you happy to see me?"

"Michael, you're confirmed dead, in disguise, and holding a live firearm. Even we've had happier reunions," I said.

"Mikey, this isn't fucking good man. Why'd you do this? You should have just stayed at my aunt's," said Brendan.

"What? While you go out and fuck my sister?"

"You know what would happen if you did this! You know what you'll have to do now," said Brendan.

"What will he have to do? I honestly don't care anymore. You two can have a nice life together," I said.

"We're not like in a relationship or nothing, it was just a scam for money and this is so people don't notice me," said Michael.

"I know that, dummy. I'm leaving now you'll never hear from me again," I said.

"Okay, that works. That works," said Michael.

"It doesn't work. Both of you know this," said Brendan, burying his head into his hands.

"And why's that?"

"Samantha, you're the smartest person I know. Don't act stupid," said Brendan.

"What are you saying? Why is this any business of mine anymore?"

"Because if Michael is here, that means someone else is inside of the casket."

It honestly hadn't dawned on me yet. I was too tired, too hungry, and too shocked to have come to that realization. I probably would have been on the flight home before I put two-and-two together. Michael pointed the gun at Brendan. I let the knife unfold and held it out in front of me.

"Mike, you know what you have to do," said Brendan.

"I don't give a shit about the guy in the casket. Honestly," I said. "I'm going back to California straight from here. You'll never see me. I promise."

I didn't expect much of a bang because of the suppressor but it wasn't like the movies. It sounded just like a gun.

The Usual Unusual Suspects

Ed Teja is a lifelong storyteller, as well as a martial artist, former Caribbean boat bum, blues musician, and magazine editor. His stories blend and crisscross crime and speculative fiction and the strange situations and people often come from his somewhat surreal life. For more information and news, go to www.edteja.com

John 'Jay' Andrew Connor has been writing and publishing under a menagerie of names and genres since the late 1970s — sometimes even professionally. He's worked at a variety of jobs, in a variety of locations, and has also published small press, and semi-pro magazines in the past. Sadly, even though he is now on full time medication, he's at it again.

So Long Ballentyne is the title of the as-yet incomplete second novel in the Harry Rhimes series — the first being *California Twist* (https://www.amazon.com/dp/1909498173 apparently on sale in the US, and https://www.amazon.co.uk/dp/1909498173 etc)

Ruth Morgan is based in Northern New South Wales, Australia. She has a love of storytelling involving the characters and outback country she knows and loves. Her preference is crime fiction with a twist, with her stories set in rural and regional Australia. The harsh landscape with its vast open spaces, floods, trees and isolation are essential elements in her stories, influencing how the tale unfolds, and how individuals react.
She is the 2020 winner of the *Great Clarendon House Writing Challenge* and has stories published on a variety of sites. Find out more at https://ruthmorgan.com.au.

Jesse Aaron served as a police officer in New York City and Connecticut for over five years and also worked in the field of private security/investigations. His first novel, *Shafer City Stories* is available on Amazon.com (https://www.amazon.com/Shafer-City-Stories-Tales-NYPD-Harlem/dp/1518853137/). Jesse's short story *The Leaky Faucet* was featured in *Crimeucopia – It's Always Raining in Noir City* and *The Gathering Puddle* in *Crimeucopia — One More Thing To Worry About.* Jesse has two more short stories on the way to publication and is currently at work on his upcoming serial killer thriller *Harlem Hipster Homicides*. Jesse's style is dark and gritty, and his stories focus on the underside of the police and private detective worlds. Jesse has a love of all things Noir, Science Fiction, and Fantasy.

Scotch Rutherford writes about dark corners between the bright lights. He is the author of the novella, *The Roach King of Paradise*, available in the collection: *L.A. Stories: Three Grindhouse Novellas*, as well as the screenplay adaptation, *The Roach King*, a 2023 Emerging Screenwriters Quarter-Finalist. Some of his short fiction has appeared in *Pulp Modern, Greasepaint & .45s, The EconoClash Review, Friday Flash Fiction, Pulp Metal Magazine, The Yard, Switchblade,* and *All Due Respect.* He lives in Los Angeles.

Billie Livingston is the author of four novels, a collection of short stories and a poetry collection. She has been the recipient of the Writer's Trust Award and been nominated for a National Magazine Award, the Journey Prize for fiction and the Scotiabank Giller Prize. Her story *Sitting on the Edge of Marlene* was adapted to a feature film. She has just completed her first crime thriller. You can read more at www.billielivingston.com

Robert Petyo is a Derringer award finalist whose most recent work has appeared in *Flash Bang Mysteries, The Black Beacon Book of Mystery, Asinine Assassins, Now There Was a Story, Whodunit, Mickey Finn 21st Century Noir,* and *Stonewall Detectives.* He has also appeared in the following *Crimeucopias — We're All Animals Under the Skin, Careless Love, Strictly Off The Record* and most recently in *Boomshakalaking!*

He writes primarily mysteries, but also SF, fantasy and horror and an occasional mainstream piece. He lives in Northeastern Pennsylvania, is happily married, and is recently retired from the Postal Service, which allows him more time to read and write. Unfortunately, there never seems to be enough time to read and write.

John Elliott has worked as a linotyper, pressman, bartender, social worker, biologist and teacher and survived life in desert, mountain and coastal environments. He has had play productions, notably about Federico Garcia Lorca, and has published fiction and poetry in *Acorn, Calliope, The Comstock Review, Southwestern American Literature, Poetry Quarterly, Borderlands: Texas Poetry Review, Tanka Journal, The Fourth River,* and three anthologies. The Daggett and Rochwal of his story are the main characters in a just completed novel.

M.E. Proctor was born in Brussels and lives in Texas. After all the years, she still struggles with the Imperial system. She's currently working on a contemporary PI series. Her short fiction has appeared in *Vautrin, Bristol Noir, Pulp Modern, Mystery Tribune, Reckon Review, Shotgun Honey,* and *Thriller Magazine* among others. She's a *Derringer* nominee. Her short story collection *Family and Other Ailments* (Wordwooze Publishing) is available in all the usual places. Website: www.shawmystery.com

William Kitcher's stories, plays, and comedy sketches (and one poem!) have been published, produced, and/or broadcast in Australia, Bosnia and Herzegovina, Canada, Czechia, England, Guernsey, Holland, India, Ireland, Nigeria, Singapore, South Africa, and the U.S. His stories have appeared in *Fiery Scribe Review, Ariel Chart, New Contrast, The Prague Review, Helix Literary Magazine, Eunoia Review, Shotgun Honey, Once Upon A Crocodile, Pigeon Review, Yellow Mama, Slippage Lit,* and many other journals. His novel, *Farewell And Goodbye, My Maltese Sleep,* will be published in 2023 by Close To The Bone Publishing.

Retrograde is **R.M. Linning**'s second published piece. His first is the horror story *The Book of Pleasures* which can be found in the *Ink Stains 14* anthology. He lives in the Okanagan Valley of British Columbia, Canada and writes fiction of all lengths and genres. Recently retired from his job as a molecular biologist / bioinformaticist he enjoys many interests including computer programming, watercolour painting, ancient history and gardening.

Annie Reed is a prolific, versatile, award-winning writer, who has written more short fiction than she can count. She's a frequent contributor to both *Pulphouse Fiction Magazine* and *Mystery, Crime and Mayhem*. Her stories have appeared in numerous annual year's best mystery volumes, including both year's best mystery volumes for 2023. Her latest novels include *Road of no Return* and *Gray Lady's Revenge*, co-written with Robert Jeschonek. A lifelong resident of Northern Nevada, Annie can be found on the web at: https://anniereed.wordpress.com/ and on Facebook at: https://www.facebook.com/annie.reed.142/.

Wil A. Emerson has been on the writing path for approximately 15 years. While not fresh out of college to write the Best Seller, she spent her early years as a Registered Nurse. Now on the fringe of being overlooked due to the inconvenient late start, she's successfully published in anthologies and has one novel under her belt. *Taking Rosie's Arm*, a Five Star, Thorndike publication, recounts the story of an elderly woman who befriends a troubled, but determined young girl. Writer, artist, traveler, cook: soup's on.

Wil's recent work is mainly mystery and women's fiction, and the first appearance her protagonist is in *Crimeucopia — Careless Love*, with her piece, *The Driver*. The unrelated *Unsolved Mystery* appears in *Crimeucopia — Strictly Off The Record*.

Also a struggling artist, her art can be viewed on her website. www.wilemerson.com

Dan Cardoza's most recent darkness has been featured in *BlazeVOX*, *Black Petals*, *Blood Moon Rising*, *Bull*, *Cleaver*, *Close to the Bone*, *Dark*

City Books, Dark Dossier, Dissections, Door=Jar, Dream Noir, Horror Sleaze Trash, The Horror Zine, Mystery Tribune, Suspense Magazine, Schlock, The Yard Crime Blog, Variant, and *The Five-2.*

Anthology appearances include: *Coffin Bell Two, Running Wild Press, Anthology of Stories, Vita Brevis Poetry, Pain & Renewal, Chilling Tales for Dark Nights, Audio Horror Anthology (13 stories).* He first *Crimeucopia* outing is in *Boomshakalaking! – Modern Crimes for Modern Times* with *Never Disclose What You Bury.*

Dan has been nominated for *Best of the Net* and *Best Micro-Fiction.*

Alan J Wahnefried at present resides in a suburb of Detroit, Michigan, with his charming and understanding wife. He is a graduate of the University of Michigan, and after a career in IT, he now considers himself to be either an experienced programmer or an old hacker. His writings have appeared in Nat1 LLC (Black Ink on a Blank Void), *As You Were: The Military Review* Vol. 16, *Round Table Literary Journal, Aphelion Magazine, Havok Publishing, From Beyond Press, Sci-Fi Shorts, 101words.org, commuterlit.com, halfhourtokill.com, CafeLit.uk.co.,* and *SuperFastStories.com.*

Sam Wiebe is the author of the *Wakeland* novels, one of the most authentic and acclaimed detective series in Canada. His work has won the *Crime Writers of Canada* award, the *Kobo Emerging Writers* prize, and a silver medal from the *Independent Publisher Book Awards,* along with being shortlisted for the Edgar, Hammett, Shamus, and City of Vancouver book prizes. His latest is *Ocean Drive.*

Jon Fain lives in Massachusetts and began publishing work in commercial and literary magazines in the 1980s, and later in some of the first online literary sites in the 2000s. Some of his more recent publications include short stories in *A Thin Slice of Anxiety* and *King Ludd's Rag;* flash fictions in *The Broadkill Review* and *Reservoir Road Literary Review;* and micro fictions in *Blink-Ink, The Woolf,* and *CLOVES Literary.* In 2023, stories of his will be in anthologies from

Running Wild Press and Three Ravens Publishing, and his chapbook *Pass the Panpharmacon! (Five Fictions of Delusion)* will be published by Greying Ghost Press.

Mark James McDonough is an avid motorcycle enthusiast. He doesn't own one or know how to ride them but he likes to sneak into people's driveways and sit on them.

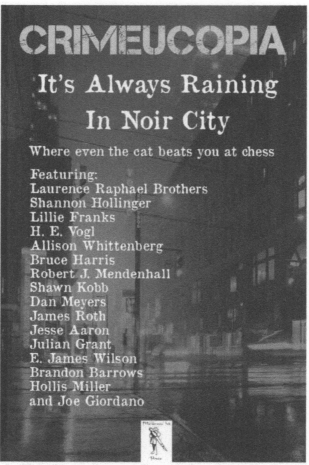

CRIMEUCOPIA

It's Always Raining
In Noir City

Where even the cat beats you at chess

Featuring:
Laurence Raphael Brothers
Shannon Hollinger
Lillie Franks
H. E. Vogl
Allison Whittenberg
Bruce Harris
Robert J. Mendenhall
Shawn Kobb
Dan Meyers
James Roth
Jesse Aaron
Julian Grant
E. James Wilson
Brandon Barrows
Hollis Miller
and Joe Giordano

Is the Noir Crime sub-genre always dark and downbeat? Is there a time when Bad has a change of conscience, flips sides and takes on the Good role?

Noir is almost always a dish served up raw and bloody - Fiction bleu if you will. So maybe this is a chance to see if Noir can be served sunny side up - with the aid of these fifteen short order authors.

All fifteen give us dark tales from the stormy side of life - which is probably why it's *always* raining in Noir City....

Paperback Edition ISBN: 9781909498341
eBook Edition ISBN: 9781909498358

CRIMEUCOPIA

WE'LL BE RIGHT BACK -
- AFTER THIS!

FEATURING:
JIM GUIGLI, GLEN BUSH, EDWARD LODI, CATE MOYLE,
JAY ANDREW CONNOR, BOB RITCHIE, MICHELE BAZAN REED,
EVE FISHER, MICHAEL WILEY, JOAN HALL HOVEY, J. T. SEATE,
AND MADELEINE MCDONALD

This is the first of several 'Free 4 All' collections that was supposed to be themeless. However, with the number of submissions that came in, it seems that this could be called an *Angels & Devils* collection, mixing PI & Police alongside tales from the Devil's dining table. Mind you, that's not to say that all the PIs & Police are on the side of the Angels....

Also this time around has not only seen a move to a larger paperback format size, but also in regard to the length of the fiction as well. Followers of the somewhat bent and twisted Crimeucopia path will know that although we don't deal with Flash fiction as a rule, it is a rule that we have sometimes broken. And let's face it, if you cannot break your own rules now and again, whose rules can you break?

Oh, wait, isn't breaking the rules the foundation of the crime fiction genre?

Oh dear....

CRIMEUCOPIA

One More Thing To Worry About

Featuring
Gerald Elias, Bob Ritchie, Michele Bazan Reed,
Terry Wijesuriya, Aran Myracle, Alexei J. Slater,
Nikki Knight, Issy Jinarmo, N. M. Cedeño,
Wendy Harrison, Andrew Darlington, Larry Lefkowitz,
Jesse Aaron, Madeleine McDonald, Joan Leotta,
H. E. Vogl, and Vinnie Hansen

New Crimeucopians *Aran Myracle, Alexei J. Slater, Gerald Elias, Terry Wijesuriya, Issy Jinarmo, Larry Lefkowitz,* and *Vinnie Hansen* smoothly rub literary shoulders with a fine collection of familiar Crimeucopia old hands: *Bob Ritchie, Michele Bazan Reed, Nikki Knight, N. M. Cedeño, Wendy Harrison, Andrew Darlington, Madeleine McDonald, Joan Leotta, H. E. Vogl* and *Jesse Aaron.*
All 17 tell tales that will make you realise there's always going to be One More Thing To Worry About....

With 16 vibrant authors, a wraparound paperback cover, and pages full of crime fiction in some of its many guises, what's not to like?
So if you enjoy tales spun by
Anthony Diesso, Brandon Barrows, E. James Wilson, James Roth,
Jesse Aaron, Jim Guigli, John M. Floyd, Kevin R. Tipple, Maddi Davidson,
Michael Grimala, Robert Petyo, Shannon Hollinger, Tom Sheehan,
Wil A. Emerson, Peter Trelay, and Philip Pak
then you'd better get
CRIMEUCOPIA - Strictly Off The record
by the sound of it!

As I best recall, it was one afternoon here at MIP Towers – must have been a touch after the start of tiffin, so around 4.35pm – when some smart young cove decided to politely call attention to himself by saying he had a proposal:

'Why can't we do an all-British Crimeucopia?'

And, bless my soul, after several pots of tea — Darjeeling (mid-season second flush, naturally) the general consensus was a resounding:

'Why not indeed?'

From there was born this anthology, containing, we hope, stories that, were you to cut them in half with a knife, they would flash you their Union Jacks without a moment's hesitation.

Rule Britannia - Britannia Waves The Rules

features fiction from Daniel Marshall Wood, Gerald Elias, S. E. Bailey, Alexander Frew, Kelly Lewis, Carew S. Bartley, Madeleine McDonald, Edward Lodi, Michaele Jordan, J. Aquino, David Rich, Kelly Zimmer, Sharon Richards, T. K. Howell, Maroula Blades, David William Johnson and Harris Coverley

The fiction ranges from general British cosy, through Harry Palmer and George Smiley territory, before going deep into very British Modern Noir. And as with all of these anthologies, we hope you'll find something that you immediately like, as well as something that takes you out of your comfort zone – and puts you into a completely new one. In other words, in the spirit of the Murderous Ink Press motto:

You never know what you like until you read it.

Milton Keynes UK
Ingram Content Group UK Ltd.
UKHW010654101123
432322UK00007B/446